DIRE STRAITS

BO BLACKMAN
BOOK ONE

HELEN HARPER

1

OF BLOOD AND BONDS

I sit in the driver's seat, sipping at my overly sweet – and now very cold – tea. It's been forty-seven minutes since Devlin O'Shea entered the house and I'm starting to get itchy. A few cars have driven up to the crossroads behind me before turning either left or right, but none so much as slowed down. Considering the neighbourhood, I'm not surprised at that. In fact, I know that if there were anyone around, they'd be startled to see a lone woman sitting here. This isn't the kind of street where anyone should spend time lingering, let alone someone on their own. I don't feel I have much choice, however.

I take my eyes off the peeling green paint on the door frame and scan ahead. There must be at least forty more houses in front of me before the road finishes in what I already know to be a dead end. If any of the buildings are occupied, their inhabitants are staying well out of sight. There's not even the barest twitch from any of the dirty curtains hiding the houses' interiors from sight. In front of each dwelling, there's a small patch of garden where the grass – if it can be called that – is either hopelessly overgrown to the point where you'd need a machete to cut a way through to reach the doors, or blackened and dying. There appears to be no pattern to whether the grass at each house is healthy or diseased, although the fact that the one O'Shea has disappeared into is fronted by deadened blades rather than a glory of jungle green seems to make sense. My attention drifts back to his building. There's nothing. No sign of life.

I sigh. I am tempted to fiddle with radio dial, if only to hear the buzz of static filling the empty space. O'Shea isn't a pure-bred triber. His hearing won't pick it up. But I have no way of knowing who – or what – else is inside that house with him and I dislike taking unnecessary risks. It's unlikely there's anyone else there … but still. I take another sip. Twelve more minutes to go.

A collection of dry, browned leaves skitter across the potholed road as the wind picks up ever so slightly. I flick a glance towards them, just in case, but there's nothing sinister. I'm getting too jumpy. I chew my lip and focus yet again on the house.

It's the very definition of nondescript. The red bricks were probably pretty once upon a time. Now, however, there are too many grubby stains from city pollution for them to look anything other than grimed and crumbling. There are a few tiles missing from the roof but the house is probably still water-tight. Except, that is, for the broken window on the first floor which looks as if someone has punched a hole through it. Whatever lies behind is dark and indistinguishable.

I check my watch again and feel my insides tighten. It's still not time. I loosen my fingers from the polystyrene cup and flex them, one by one. I shouldn't have accepted this job. Cheating spouses are easier than errant half-breed daemons. Then I amend that to quarter breed. O'Shea's grandmother was pure Agathos but the rest of the blood flowing through his godforsaken veins is bog-standard human. I should be thankful that he's not a quarter Kakos, I suppose. But then, if he were, I wouldn't be here right now.

Seven more minutes. I drain the last of the tea and toss the empty cup onto the floor of the passenger side along with the other rubbish. Then I grimace as I feel my bladder tighten. Damn it, now I need to pee.

I consider my options. I was instructed to wait a full hour before breaching the property and confronting O'Shea. If I entered now, it would probably take me at least five minutes to locate him – by which time, I reckon an actual hour will have passed. Or almost anyway. I decide it's good enough. I can still catch him in the act. I'm still hoping he's on his own.

I zip up my leather jacket to stave off the cold and carefully open the car door, trying to remain as quiet as possible. I probably shouldn't wear leather; it tends to have a mind of its own, groaning and creaking of its own accord whenever I make a move. Plus, its distinctive earthy smell can give away my presence in a heartbeat. But anything which has senses that are so attuned will know I'm coming from half a mile away and I like the fact that it makes me look kind of bad-ass. It's difficult to appear threatening when you're just over five feet tall so I'll take whatever help I can get. The jacket is far too large for me and, if it wasn't so elaborate in its embroidery and zips, it'd probably look ridiculous. I 'borrowed' it from an old boyfriend of mine called Zupper who I'd spent one sensuous, long summer with, zipping around on the back of his motorbike. He took off around Europe to find himself. I just took his jacket.

I step out, shooting a speculative look at the keys which are still in the ignition. I have a bad feeling about all of this and I'm starting to wonder if I need to be prepared for a quick getaway. To be fair, no one has come this far up the street while I've been here; I don't even think a single bird has flown overhead. And it's not as if my rusting heap of junk is particularly desirable to even the most desperate jacker. If I leave the keys where they are, I have a better chance of vamoosing out of here at warp speed should I need to. If someone appears from nowhere and nicks my car, however, I'll be pretty much screwed. Aside from the fact that then I'd have zero way to get out of this graveyard of a cul-de-sac, I simply don't have the cash to replace it and my insurance is virtually worthless.

I err on the side of caution and pocket the keys. I haven't had much time to research O'Shea but nothing I've learned points towards him being physically dangerous. Yes, he might have less friendly companions inside and, yes, the prickles on the back of my neck are far from comforting, but balancing an extra five-second fumble with the threat of ending up entirely car-less leaves me with no choice. I really should look into some proper alternatives for future encounters though. I silently add it to my ever-growing list of things to do.

I glance up and down the street. It's still deserted so I cross over quickly and jump the pathetic foot-high gate into the so-called garden, where I pause for a couple of heartbeats, cocking my ear for any sounds. Even though I'm barely a few metres from the front door, I still can't hear anything.

The grass looks worse close-up. It even smells of decay. In the far corner there's a one-eyed, blonde-haired doll, forlornly waiting for a long-since departed owner to return. Its sole iris stares at me emptily. I look away and move to the entrance, placing one cupped ear against it. I think perhaps I hear a dull thud from within, but I can't be sure.

The property has been sitting empty for the last eighteen months since its previous tenant ended up on the wrong side of the law so technically I'm not trespassing, but I still can't stop myself from checking the street again before I twist the knob and the door creaks open. Then I step over the mouldy envelopes with the tell-tale red of final demands peeking through their transparent windows and cross the threshold.

I pause for a moment, sucking in the stale air and listening carefully. I have no way of knowing which floor O'Shea is on, so I sidle against one wall and shuffle carefully along, making sure I avoid the centre of the corridor where the floorboards are more likely to creak. Although my aim is to confront him, I don't want to alert him to my presence before I'm ready. I unzip my upper pocket and pull out a small canister of pepper spray. In the unlikely event that he's armed and feeling twitchy, I'll be able to get the jump on him.

The door to the left is ajar, which makes my life easier, so I peek through the gap just to be sure. Even though I can't scan the entire room, my senses tell me that it's empty. I move forward towards the kitchen, wincing as my foot crunches down on something, and I freeze at the sound. Fortunately I seem to have got away with it as the silence continues. I gently lift my foot and look down, raising my eyebrows when I see the dull glint of a used syringe. Interesting. From the previous occupant's criminal history and my rushed research, I've learned that he was staunchly anti-drugs. So either he was an untidy diabetic or some vanished squatters took up residence temporarily after he left. Or there is something about O'Shea that Tam failed to tell me.

Pursing my lips, I kick the broken needle carefully towards the stairwell and out of my way. Now is not the time to start worrying about how I should have been better prepared before confronting O'Shea. I'm here. It's already too late. I edge up to the kitchen instead, pausing where the carpet curls up at the edges. The door is hanging off one rusty hinge and the odour coming from inside is so bad I can imagine someone has died inside and their rotting corpse is lying there in its own putrefying juices…

There's nothing more than a few bin bags filled to the brim with empty takeaway cartons and crumpled aluminium tins of lager. Upstairs then.

I back out, picking my way round to the front of the stairs, and peer upwards into the gloom. Annoyingly, the carpet on the stairs is gone, leaving scuffed bare boards which will make it harder for me to stay quiet. I step up, keeping on my toes to avoid making any more sound than I need to. I clutch the sticky banister and creep noiselessly upwards. When I reach the top, I stop for a moment and wipe my hand on my jeans. I'll need to scrub myself down with disinfectant as soon as I get home.

I'm about to ease open the first door when I hear what sounds like a gargle emanating from the room furthest away. Considering the state of this place, I doubt that O'Shea is taking time to worry about his dental hygiene. Then I hear a low moan. If I didn't already know better, I'd assume it came from something of the spectrally challenged variety of being. But this building is less than fifty years old and, smell in the kitchen aside, no records indicated that there has ever been a death on the premises. So it is something else. I bite down on the inside of my cheek and tiptoe forward.

The door is firmly closed. Bad for me. At least the two remaining rooms are also firmly barred, so I'm likely to hear anyone sneaking up from behind before they get too close. O'Shea has to be inside. I reach out for the steel door handle, drawing back with a hiss of breath when my skin touches it. It feels clammy and unpleasantly damp. Sniffing my fingers, I detect the faintest whiff of rose petals. Huh.

I pull the cuff of my jacket over my hand and try again, slowly pulling the handle down and opening the door, wincing at the sound. I give up the pretence of silence and kick it open the rest of the way. It bangs heavily against the wall, bouncing back towards me but I leap through, yanking out the papers from my inside pocket.

'Devlin O'Shea!' I deepen my voice and direct it at the dim shape in the centre of the room. 'You are hereby served.'

The shape doesn't move but there's another indistinct moan from its direction. I squint through the gloom. O'Shea may not be performing the illegal magic it has been suggested he would be, but there is still something very, very wrong here. I can smell vomit and urine and something else besides.

'O'Shea!' I shout again.

The figure droops. Skirting round it, I go to the windows and yank open the heavy curtains with one hand, keeping the pepper spray outstretched in front of me. Light floods in. I gape. Tied to a wooden chair, his face a bloody pulp, is one very badly beaten daemon. I realise that the other smell I couldn't identify is fear. He moans again. What in bejesus is going on here?

It's impossible for me to positively identify him as O'Shea; for all I know O'Shea's the perp who's attacked this guy. But I have to deal with what's in front of me, regardless of my almost overwhelming misgivings. The dark stain soaking the floor beneath the man indicates that he's losing a lot of blood. Staunching the flow is my priority.

I stuff the pepper spray canister into my pocket, ensuring it's still within easy reach but not about to fall out when I need it most, and immediately start searching the limp body for wounds. He starts gurgling again and I curse aloud. ABC, I tell myself sternly. Airway, breathing, circulation, in that order. I need to get him into the recovery position.

I realise that his hands are secured with an old-fashioned set of steel cuffs. I keep my own pair, passed down from my father for old times' sake, but I prefer using plastic ties these days, like most people. The fact that he's been tied to a chair with a cumbersome old set means something. Not that I have the time to muse about it right now. The cuffs are looped around the wooden bracket at the back so I lift my foot on to it and kick downwards. Thankfully the chair is as rickety as the rest of this godforsaken house and it snaps with one blow, allowing the daemon's arms to fall backwards. I extricate the hanging piece of wood and chuck it to one side, then yank him off the seat and onto the floor as quickly as I can, manoeuvring his body and neck to force his airway clear. He coughs weakly and my face is sprayed with a mist of blood droplets, letting me know I've been successful. Then I return to searching his inert form for the wound.

There are two: one piercing his side, just to the left of his upper rib cage, and one higher up at the base of his neck. Clearly it's the neck wound I should be most concerned about. Using the base of one hand, I press hard to try and slow down the pulse of blood that's pumping out. With my other hand, I dig out my phone and tap out 999 with my thumb. I lift it to my ear and, as it starts to ring, the daemon's eyes snap open, orange slitted pupils taking me in through a glaze of pain. Well, it's definitely O'Shea.

'999, what's your emergency?'

O'Shea shakes his head.

'I'm in a house on Wiltshore Avenue,' I say.

'No.'

'Number 23,' I continue. 'I need an ambulance immediately.'

He moans. 'No. Stop.'

'Is that Wiltshore Avenue in Belvedere or Trockston?' enquires the voice.

O'Shea reaches up and grabs my wrist. Given the state that he's in and the blood loss he's suffered, his grip is surprisingly strong. 'Tell them,' he rasps, 'and we're both dead.'

I stare down at him. Death threats are nothing new in my line of work; daemons, even quarter-daemons, bleeding out in front of me, are. His eyes implore me.

'If you don't get to a hospital in the next five minutes, then you're dead anyway,' I tell him.

I can hear the emergency responder repeating her question. The futility of the situation hits me. We're in Trockston, the worst end of Trockston, no less. No paramedic is going to rush to get here. They'd rather take their time so that whatever is going down has gone down by the time they arrive. Which means Devlin O'Shea won't make it.

'False alarm,' I mutter into the receiver and hang up.

O'Shea blinks gratefully at me.

'Don't,' I say, kneeling down and shoving him onto his side, then pulling out a pick so I can undo the cuffs and free his hands.

'Don't thank me. You're about twenty breaths away from rejoining your maker down in the depths.'

I'm surprised at the ease with which I manage to unpick the lock. The cuffs fall, one steel circle hanging loosely from his left wrist. He mumbles something into my ear.

'Nope,' I reply with as much forced cheeriness as I can muster, 'you'll need to speak up if you want me to hear you.'

O'Shea doesn't bother responding. I heave him onto my back in a piggyback and force his uncuffed hand up to his throat so he can continue to press on the wound. His weight drives my knees and shoulders downwards, but I do my best to ignore it and stagger to the door and on to the landing. I haul both myself and him down the stairs, this time thumping loudly with every step.

We're barely at the bottom when my watch beeps, indicating I should at this point be entering the property to find him, not leaving the property with him. And certainly not with him half dead. Those last seven minutes felt more like a bloody hour.

I nudge open the front door with my toe and edge out. The vacant one-eyed doll stares at me as I shuffle back through the garden with O'Shea's heavy body. I can feel his warm, sticky blood seeping underneath the collar of my jacket and connecting with my skin and I try to speed up. He can't have long.

Stepping over the garden fence is like scaling Mount Everest. I try to ignore that I'm about to collapse and instead run calculations in my head. Forty seconds to get him to the car. Another minute to get back to the crossroads. Praise the heavens that I don't already have to reverse and lose even more time. Then I can take the A road past Silverstein to Manorbridge hospital. Five minutes. Tops. I'll register him under a false name in case he was telling the truth about the dead part. It won't stop someone from finding him, but it'll stall them until I can speak to Tam and get a permanent guard stationed.

I try to reach into my pocket for my keys but his leg is in the way, so I'm forced to squeeze my fingers around to grasp them.

Yeah. I should have left them in the freaking ignition. I was stupid not to trust my instincts.

Gasping for breath, I lurch round to the passenger side and open the door. I throw in O'Shea's blood-soaked body, noting with satisfaction that he's still conscious and pressing tightly on his neck wound. I slam the door shut before dashing round to my seat and starting the car.

I move up the gears, accelerating down the empty street. Come on, come on. I turn left towards Manorbridge, then abruptly slam on the brakes as sirens scream their way into my consciousness. Part of me can't quite believe it. The emergency responder must have taken my half-baked, half-garbled and half-finished phone call seriously, sending ambulances in both directions. Relief floods through me and I glance behind to welcome the cavalry.

Except it's not an ambulance. I stare at the vehicle bearing down on us while O'Shea moans at my side. The familiar stripes of an armed response unit wink at me tauntingly as the tyres screech and it wheels round into Wiltshore Avenue. Trying to ignore the tremor in my hands, I very deliberately start the car moving again, away from the sirens.

I run over the phone call in my mind. I'm sure I said nothing more than the address and that I needed an ambulance. There was no reason to send goons with guns to check it out. And how in the hell had they arrived so quickly? I only hung up on the responder a few minutes ago; response times are never that fast. If I'd waited to enter the house until I was supposed to, O'Shea would have lost so much blood he'd probably be dead and I would be the sole witness to the crime. Or the prime suspect. I grip the steering wheel and swerve right.

'What in the hell have you gotten me into?' I say aloud to O'Shea, not expecting an answer.

His spooky orange eyes swivel in my direction and he opens his mouth.

'Don't speak,' I tell him curtly. 'Conserve your energy. You can give me answers later.' I'm damned if I'll let him croak on me before I find out exactly what is going on.

I press down on the accelerator, speeding up again, and make a snap decision. I don't know who this guy is and why the police – and someone else much more violent – are so interested in him, but my interest is piqued. The hospital is now out. There's only one place nearby where I can get him some proper medical help and avoid the suddenly undesirable eye of the law. I'd rather choke on my own tongue than go there but I'm out of other options. Shit in a hell basket.

2
FAMILY TIES

I IGNORE THE RED LIGHTS; RIGHT NOW I HAVE WORSE THINGS TO worry about than traffic violations. And it's not as if the roads round here are busy. I'd have been impressed with my speed if the situation weren't so dire. Even so, by the time we arrive outside the familiar terraced house, I can tell that O'Shea is beginning to fade. Blood is leaking from between his fingers where they continue to clutch at the gaping wound. Arse.

I stop the car and jump out, running up the path to the door. I bang on it loudly and try to open it, even though I know it will be barred. 'Open up!' I yell, crouching down to flip open the letterbox.

The door swings open noiselessly. A fat ginger tom cat is sitting in the hallway glaring at me.

I snarl. 'Where is he?'

The cat licks a paw before starting to wash its face.

'I don't have time for this. Where in hell is he?'

A man appears behind the animal. He has the kind of straight-backed posture a ballroom dancer would envy. He raises his eyebrows at me. 'Bo.'

'I need help. There's a...'

He interrupts. 'Obviously you need help. Otherwise you wouldn't be here. But this is not how we do things.'

I grit my teeth. This is one of the many reasons why I avoid this place like the plague. I step over the threshold, ignoring the cat and give the man a perfunctory kiss on the cheek.

'Grandfather. How lovely to see you again.'

He inclines his head. 'And you, my dear.'

'Now will you help me?'

His eyes drift down my torso and his upper lip wrinkles. 'You are covered in blood.' There is the faintest tinge of disgust in his voice.

'It's not mine.'

'I know that.' He sniffs. 'A triber. Agathos daemon, if I'm not mistaken.'

I sigh inwardly. Most people need to get up close and personal to recognise a triber. You can usually tell them by their eyes: Agathos daemons, even quarter breeds like O'Shea, possess pupils of different hues while vampires' pupils contain a telltale red dot. Both black and white witches don't have irises at all, whereas Kakos daemons …well, I'm not sure anyone has seen a Kakos's eyes and lived to tell the tale. Some people don't need to look into their eyes, however; they simply have an inbuilt intuition. It can be learned, much in the way that you can learn to tell the difference between the epicanthal folds of Chinese people versus Japanese people, or work out from two Caucasians which one is French and which one American. I can usually do so with tribers without getting into their face and peering at their eyes. My grandfather, unusually, can do it from fifty metres. He also enjoys making his talent known.

I try to keep the sarcasm out of my voice. 'Well done. But he's only a quarter Agathos and right now he's dying in my car.' I gesture outside. 'If you'd be so kind?'

He seems to be mulling it over. I curl my fingers into fists at my sides.

'Very well,' he agrees finally. 'But only because I don't need a corpse littering my front garden. I can do without the police asking unnecessary questions.'

I narrow my eyes at that comment. Right now it's a little too close to the bone. Fortunately he refrains from further discussion and I go back to the car, pulling open the passenger door. O'Shea falls against me, his head lolling. Cursing, I thrust my palm against his neck. I'm pretty sure I can still feel a pulse, although I'm amazed there's any blood left inside him.

I realise my grandfather still hasn't left his house. 'What are you waiting for?' I shout. 'He's dying. You said you'd help.'

He winces. 'Raising your voice is so vulgar. You should keep your tone more dulcet, it's more becoming for a lady. I said I would help the daemon and I will.'

'So freaking help!' Desperation is leaking from my every pore.

He gestures down at his clothes. 'This is Savile Row. I'm not about to sully it with arterial blood. Bring him inside and I'll save his life.' He purses his lips. 'For what it's worth.'

I watch open-mouthed, as he goes back inside. I swear the bloody cat is grinning at me mockingly. Then an ominous rattle comes from O'Shea's throat and I give in, hooking my hands under his armpits and dragging him up to the house while trying to staunch the wound at the same time. A snail's trail of blood leads from the open car door and up the perfectly paved path behind us. I huff with exertion, noting out of the corner of my eye that several curtains are being pushed aside as the neighbours look on. At least I know they won't be calling it in to the authorities. They wouldn't dare.

After what seems an age, I'm back at the door and trying to pull O'Shea inside the house. One of his shoes catches on the lip of the entrance and, even though I tug hard, it won't budge. Something taps my shoulder and I twist my head round. My grandfather has donned a plastic apron. He has kept his impeccable grey suit – complete with waistcoat, cravat and fob watch –

on underneath. I avoid rolling my eyes. Why he insists on wearing such clothes when he lives on a rundown housing estate in one of the less salubrious areas of London, I have no idea. I let him take O'Shea's upper body, and he produces a pressure bandage which he presses to the daemon's neck while I free his caught shoe and lift his feet. Together we manoeuvre him inside and onto the kitchen table.

My grandfather leans down to inspect the wound. 'He's almost gone,' he observes calmly. 'You've not given me much time.'

'There'd be a damn sight more time if you'd helped me get him inside.'

He clucks at my tone, elevating O'Shea's head and reaching for a steel instrument which is already glowing red at the tip. He lifts up the bandage and cleans away the worst of the blood, then presses the metal into the wound, cauterising it. There's a lengthy sizzle and the stench of cooking flesh fills the room. Bile rises in my throat.

I turn away and open a drawer, rummaging around until I find what I need. I crouch down next to O'Shea's neck and start cleaning the area with antiseptic while my grandfather cuts off his t-shirt to attend to the wound on his ribs. He hisses when he finds it, making me look up.

'Bloodguzzlers,' he states, by way of explanation.

I start. It doesn't make any sense for vampires to attack a daemon. 'Are you sure?'

I receive a withering look in return. Holding the palms of my hands up in surrender, I stand up. 'Is there a…?'

'Behind you.'

I turn round and spot the suture kit. Scooping it up, I eye my grandfather again. 'Is this…?'

'Catgut,' he grunts.

'Do you think you could let me finish just one sentence?'

'What's the point when I know what you're going to say?'

I pull out the pre-threaded needle and bend down to stitch up O'Shea's neck, counting to ten very slowly in my head.

'Have you spoken to your mother lately?' my grandfather asks.

I can't help snapping. 'You mean you don't know already?'

'There's no need to be impolite. This is small talk. It's what civilised people do.'

'And I suppose civilised people also spend their afternoons sewing up daemons as well,' I say under my breath.

He hears me. 'Only when their errant granddaughters arrive on their doorstep demanding that's what they do. It's been seven months since you were last here, Bo. The least you could do is pop round for afternoon tea from time to time.'

I stab the needle into O'Shea's flesh with a little too much vigour and he moans.

'I have to work. I told you.'

'You don't work every day.'

'When I don't work, I sleep.' He has a knack for making me feel both guilty and annoyed at exactly the same time.

'I can still put in a word with Thompson and Grant, you know.'

'So I can spend my days investigating insurance fraud? No thank you.'

There's a moment of silence. When I finally look up and meet his eyes, his hands are on his hips. He appears genuinely perplexed. 'You'd rather be saving daemons?'

I sigh. It would take more than the passing of a few laws to take away the old-school racism bred into my grandfather's psyche. 'He's Agathos,' I repeat, pointlessly. 'And only a quarter at that.'

'So you've said.' Something flashes in his eyes and I realise I'm about to get sucker-punched. 'You don't normally do this though, Bo. Save daemons, I mean. You normally hang around taking sleazy pictures of affairs or handing out summons. Does that make you feel fulfilled?'

'You've been keeping tabs on me.' I keep my voice flat. It's not a question.

'You're my only grandchild. Of course I'm keeping tabs on you! I'm concerned about the life you've chosen. You can do better than that seedy firm.'

'It's not seedy.' I'm lying. It's seedier than a prostitute's unwashed bed linen. I continue, 'And it's a meritorious corporate ladder. You start at the bottom and work your way up. I'm working my way up.' I finish my last stitch and tie the catgut into a granny knot. I stand up, drawing my shoulders back and looking my grandfather in the eye. 'This is what I want to do.'

He doesn't give way. He just remains where he is, staring back at me with a challenging look. Long seconds stretch out. Then O'Shea breaks the tension by moaning and coughing. He mutters something and twists on the table in a spasm of pain.

I bend down. 'What is it?'

He coughs again. I place my ear closer to his mouth, ignoring the distaste that crosses my grandfather's features.

'Thank.' There's a drawn-out pause as he sucks in air. 'You.' His pupils roll into his head and he lapses back into unconsciousness.

I straighten up and give my grandfather a triumphant look. He raises his eyebrows. 'So he's got manners. So what?'

I give up. I'm covered in blood, in dire need of a shower, and I have many, many questions which need answers. Dealing with my grandfather is not a priority. My bladder, however, still is.

'May I use your bathroom?' I ask primly.

He nods and gestures upwards. I walk out, taking care not to brush against anything and leave a bloodstained advertisement of my presence in my grandfather's immaculately kept house. I'd never hear the end of it if he came across a smudge of daemon blood on his flocked wallpaper.

In the bathroom, I finally relieve myself then lean over the small sink and wash off as much of the blood as I can. I'm not hugely successful; all I manage to do is smear it over my skin. I'm particularly pissed off that my jacket is covered in it. When I decide I can do no more until I get home and strip off, I rock back on my heels and stare at my reflection in the mirror. My skin is even paler than normal, and my hair is matted and untidy. I smooth it down but it appears that daemon blood is no better at keeping my unruly curls in place than expensive hair products, so I give up and head back to the kitchen. My grandfather is washing up at the sink. He turns round as I approach, no doubt assessing my remarkably unimproved appearance.

'Can I leave him here until nightfall?'

I'd rather not, but O'Shea needs to rest and I need to find out exactly what is going on. My grandfather may not appreciate his presence, but right now his unconscious body would be too much of an encumbrance, especially with the sodding police apparently after him.

His gaze remains on me. 'Is he dangerous?'

I look at O'Shea stretched out on the table, soaked in blood and in a semi-coma. Then I look at my grandfather. 'You're kidding me, right?'

He doesn't blink. 'He's going to come around. I would like to know if I need to take measures to guard against him.'

'I think you can hold your own,' I reply drily.

'Tell me why you tied him up.'

I'm momentarily confused. Then I realise the handcuffs are still attached to O'Shea's right wrist. 'Oh. That wasn't me. He was already cuffed when I found him.'

For the first time, my grandfather looks surprised. And worried.

I lean forward. 'What is it?'

'They're yours, Bo,' he says quietly. 'They're your cuffs. I was there when your father gave them to you. I'd recognise them anywhere.'

I'm taken aback. 'That's ridiculous. They're not mine – he was restrained with them before I arrived.'

Except I have to admit that my grandfather doesn't make mistakes like that. My eyes drop to the set of steel rings and I walk over and touch them. They're still smeared in blood. I think about how easily I picked the lock back at Wiltshore Avenue. I kneel down and examine them further. I wipe away some of the blood with my thumb and my stomach drops. There's a tiny zigzagged scratch along the side that's heart-rendingly familiar.

'Well, this is just getting better and better,' I murmur to myself. It appears that someone broke into my apartment and stole my handcuffs. Then they used them to tie up O'Shea and left him for dead, calling in armed police to arrive the moment I was supposed to enter the house. I'm being set up and I have no idea by whom or for what reason.

'What aren't you telling me, Bo?' My grandfather's voice is quiet.

I chew on my bottom lip. Whether it's O'Shea or me who is the focus of this utter bollocks of a situation, he has a right to know. As much as he's a pompous, crabby old son of a bitch, I can't keep him in the dark.

'It's possible I'm being targeted.' I keep my tone deliberately light.

There's no reaction from my grandfather but the length of time before he speaks again is telling. 'Not the daemon?'

I shrug. 'Maybe him too. At this point it's difficult to say.'

He nods thoughtfully. 'So what did you do?'

'Jesus! Why do you always think the worst of me? I've not done anything!'

'Bo, I was planning a quiet afternoon of Pimms and bridge. Now I need to batten down the hatches and worry about who might knock on my door. I deserve to know the truth.'

'I'm not lying.' I hold his eyes. 'If keeping him here is a problem, then just say so.'

'Why would having a half-dead quarter daemon on my kitchen table be a problem?' He runs a hand through his shock of white hair and takes a deep breath. 'He can stay for now.'

I exhale slowly. Thank God for that.

'So who is he?'

'His name is Devlin O'Shea. He's suspected of dabbling in black magic.'

'How black?'

I wave a dismissive hand in the air. 'More grey than black. I was told he's been selling a few glamour spells. Just your usual petty witchcraft, nothing to get anyone's knickers in a twist.'

'Was he selling to bloodguzzlers?'

I shake my head. 'Humans.' At least that's what I had been told anyway.

My grandfather sniffs. 'And you? How are you involved?'

'I was supposed to serve him with a summons to appear before the Agathos court. There was a bonus in it if I caught him in the act of dealing.' I look away for a moment. 'The thing is, the summons was only going to be activated at noon. I was to wait until then before approaching him. I may have been a little overly punctual.'

'You were early?'

I nod.

'Why?'

'I wanted to hurry home to catch the afternoon soaps. What does it matter?'

He growls at me. I don't care. I'm damned if I'm going to tell him that it was because I needed the loo.

'Have you been nosing into anything you shouldn't have?'

I take the question seriously, mulling over all my recent exploits. There's nothing that stands out. I've served a few other summons, but their recipients have accepted them with equanimity. And my other work has involved me staying out of sight on routine surveillance missions.

'I've been squeaky clean.' Just for the hell of it, I smirk humourlessly at the old man. 'Can you say the same?'

He snorts. I scratch at my neck. O'Shea's blood is congealing on my skin and starting to feel uncomfortable. I check my watch, focusing not on the panic which is swirling in my veins but on what I need to do next.

'I'll be back around nine,' I say. 'Can you hold the fort until then?'

He gives me a droll look. Say what you like about the old bastard, he's as tough as old nails. If the daemon's attackers are smart – or stupid – enough to come calling, they'll be in for a great surprise. I turn to leave but he grabs my arm. 'Be careful.' His tone is serious.

I nod, then walk out.

3

CLEAN AND CALL

MY CAR DOOR IS STILL HANGING OPEN. THE CAT, PRETENDING TO
be asleep on the pavement beside it, half-opens one green eye as I
approach. It lets out a tiny guttural meow and clambers to its
feet, stretching out its forelegs then padding off. I peer inside,
taking in the blood-soaked seat and sigh. I'd only just forked out
a wad to have it valeted the previous week. Slamming the door
shut, I walk round to the driver's side and get in. I'm tempted to
head straight for the office to face Tam and demand to know
exactly what is going on. I know that wouldn't be the smartest
move though, so instead I turn on the engine and shift into first
gear. This is one of those times when it pays to be friends with all
sorts of people.

As I drive, I pay close attention to the roads leading in the
direction of Wiltshore Avenue, just in case the police van shows
up again. There's no sign of it. I make a few u-turns, once pulling
into a service station and stopping for a minute with my eyes
fixed closely on my rear-view mirror. When I'm about as certain
as I can be that I'm not being followed, I drive across town. The
worst of the lunchtime traffic seems to be over, but I avoid the
busier streets. I have a lot to do if I'm to return to pick up O'Shea

at nine. I can't afford to waste time waiting in a grid-lock. Fortunately, it's not long after two when I pull up outside The Steam Team.

The pedestrians milling around on the street make me tense. At least they're only human and far enough away not to catch the scent or sight of blood. That's another good reason to wear black. I duck inside the shop, breathing in the clean scent of dry cleaning, and grin as I spot Rebecca behind the counter.

She raises her eyebrows. 'Bo. I'm surprised to see you here again this month. Haven't you already had your annual clean?'

'Ha ha. Just because I only come for dry cleaning once a month doesn't mean I don't know how to use a washing machine.'

'You forget I've seen the inside of your car.'

I grimace. Not recently she hasn't. She twigs that something is wrong and her expression grows serious. 'What's the problem?'

I point at my clothes. 'I need these cleaned. And I need to borrow something to wear in the meantime.'

Although her eyes light up with curiosity, she doesn't ask any more questions, filling me with gratitude. She just lifts up the counter and beckons me inside. As I pass by her, she draws back, evidently smelling O'Shea's blood.

'Whoa, okay. I guess you need a shower too.'

'Do you have one?'

She makes a face. 'Sort of.'

She leads me into a sparsely furnished back room. There are a few industrial shelving units with large bottles displaying complicated chemical names. In the corner there's a tap with a rubber hose and a rusting drain set into the floor next to it.

'Our power shower at its finest,' she announces.

'What's the temperature control like?'

She grins. 'Oh, you'll like it.'

I doubt that very much but beggars can't be choosers. I shoot her a smile of thanks. 'I appreciate it.'

Rebecca reaches out to squeeze my shoulder then obviously thinks better of it. She looks me over critically. 'We've got some unclaimed clothes that might fit you. I'm not sure they'll be to your taste though.'

I dread to think. 'I'll take whatever you can spare, Becks.'

She offers me another smile then leaves, closing the door carefully behind her. I eye the hose with trepidation before peeling off my jacket. The blood underneath is sticky and the underside of the leather has glued itself to my skin. When I'm finally free, I lay it gently on top of a nearby shelf and look at it sorrowfully before divesting myself of the rest of my clothes. I'm down to my underwear – which is far more functional than pretty – when Rebecca knocks on the door. I open it slightly, keeping my body behind it more because of the dark dried blood staining my skin than any modesty. She hands me a plastic bag and leaves me in peace. Hooking the bag onto a nail, I strip off my bra and knickers, twist on the tap and yelp at the forceful gush of water. It's icy cold and I spend several moments dancing in and out of its spray as I get used to the temperature. The water pressure is so strong that it feels as if my skin is peeling off alongside the dissolving blood. By the time I'm done, my body is red and raw – but at least I'm clean.

Rebecca has left a towel on top of the bag so I pull it out and vigorously rub myself dry. Then I peer inside to see just how bad the clothes are, and am pleasantly surprised as I shake out a floral mini dress. Just because I normally wear leather doesn't mean my hidden princess doesn't occasionally beg to be let out. The dress is decorated with sprigs of pink flowers and kicks out in a flare at the hem. I run my hands over my legs and sigh with relief that I shaved them recently enough to get away with the short skirt. I put my knickers back on but abandon my bra as it's damp with blood, then try to clamber into the dress. It gets stuck somewhere around my shoulders and I spend a few uncomfortable moments trying to yank it down without tearing the fabric. Eventually I realise there's a zip in the side which makes life a whole lot easier. I smooth it down and stare at myself critically. Not too shabby. I give myself a little Wonder Woman spin before flicking back my hair. Then I give up and get back to business.

I pull out the pepper spray and my phone from the jacket and stuff it, the towel, and the rest of my clothes into the bag and walk out to the front of the shop. When Rebecca catches sight of me, she starts to laugh. I scowl at her.

'Very fetching, Bo. I think the bow on the back is particularly attractive.'

I give her a twirl. 'Actually I rather like it.'

She just laughs harder. 'Yes, all you need is a bow in your hair and you can be Bo with a bow and a bow.'

I shake my fists at her. 'Is this the way I'm to be treated after all the help I've given you in the past?'

'No, you're right.' She wipes the tears from her eyes. 'You did a fabulous job helping me get rid of that gang of losers. It'd have been even better if you'd done it wearing that.'

'Well, at least they wouldn't see it coming this time.'

Last year Rebecca hired me, via Tam, to keep watch on The Steam Team after a series of break-ins. I camped out for a couple of nights and caught three teenagers sneaking in. As soon as they saw me, they high-tailed it. It took me forever to track them down. I was pretty fast at running, but I wasn't any match for teen boys amped up on drugs and the speed of youth. I still considered the venture a failure, even though I eventually managed to haul their arses into the local police station. Luckily Rebecca remained grateful. More than that, she'd become a friend. And as I'm learning, it's handy to have a mate who owns a dry cleaning service.

She finally sobers up and looks at me a seriously. 'You're in trouble?'

I bite my lip and nod.

'You look like what you really need is a stiff drink.'

I sigh. 'That'd be nice. Unfortunately I can't stay. I need to deal with,' I pause for a beat, 'other things.'

She nods in understanding. 'If there's anything else I can do…'

'Thanks, Becks.' I smile tightly and deposit the bag of clothes onto the counter in front of her. 'I really appreciate this. Can I pick these up tomorrow morning?'

'You mean you're not prepared to trade in your leather jacket for that dress?'

I tug at the bodice self-consciously. I like the dress but it's not really suitable attire for a private investigator. Not if I want to be taken seriously.

'Not just yet. Although maybe Tam will make it the new uniform when he sees me.' I try to keep my voice flippant, but my stomach remains a tight ball of tension.

'Yeah. I'd love to see what some of those hulking brutes you work with look like in a flowery dress.'

'With a bow at the back.'

She smiles, masking the worry in her face. 'Naturally.'

'I'll be back first thing in the morning.'

The door jangles, signalling the arrival of a new customer.

'Thank you! Come again!' Rebecca trills to me, in full shop-keeper mode.

I sweep a dramatic curtsey from behind the customer's back then make a hasty exit. As soon as I'm outside I turn on my phone. It flashes with three missed calls and all of them are from Tam. I suppose at least he's not working under the mistaken assumption that I am now in police custody. It doesn't really mean much though. If he's behind the plot to frame me for O'Shea's supposed murder, he'll already have the cops in his pocket and be aware that neither the daemon nor I were present at the house when they arrived.

I'm not prepared to speak to him over the phone. When I talk to him, I want to look into his eyes. Right now, he can wait. I've got other things to sort out.

I'm about to jab in the number I need when I reconsider. I gaze down at my phone for a moment then slap my forehead. I'm a prize idiot. If the police are looking for me, all they'll have to do is to track my phone signal. Until I'm completely sure about what is going on and who is on whose payroll, I'm not willing to hand myself in for questioning. I wouldn't trust the police; there are too many tales of corruption at all sorts of levels for some of them not to be true.

I glance back at The Steam Team. The police will already be able to follow me there. I'm tempted to go back inside and warn Rebecca but I decide against it. I know I can trust her and I'll only spook the customer who'll be more likely to remember me. No, better to ditch the phone now and pick up a burner instead. Without further ado, I drop it onto the pavement and crunch it under my heel. Then I turn my attention to the car and frown.

It may be a rusting heap of junk, but it's *my* rusting heap of junk. But now it's covered in blood and the longer I keep it, the more likely it is to become a liability. Its only saving grace is that it's too old to have an in-built GPS system which can be used against me. I could leave it here – after all, the phone will already have led the police to this location but I'm concerned about the blood. I don't need any more evidence tying me to O'Shea's attack than there is already.

I climb in and drive off. I know just the place to park. Right now, though, despite having a vague plan of action, I'm feeling less like Sam Spade and more like a fully paid-up member of the Keystone Cops. Hanging on to my phone is the sort of rookie error that's keeping me at the bottom of the heap at Tam's. If I'm going to get out of this unscathed, I need to be a hell of a lot smarter.

The lock up is less than fifteen minutes' drive away. I've been paying for it in cash under the counter for the last two years and for the last two years it's been lying empty. When I've been scrabbling around for money, I've often wondered whether keeping it is a stupid idea. Today, however, my pragmatism has won out. That doesn't quite make up for the phone error, but it helps. There's no record anywhere that I rent this place. And considering that the white witch landlord had his tongue cut out about a decade ago, I'm fairly certain he's not going to be blabbing to anyone. I root around in the glove box for the key which I eventually discover stuck to the yellowing service record by a chunk of gum – unchewed, I might add. I open the garage door, disturbing some small creature which scuttles off into the darkness, and drive in.

The lack of pockets in the dress is causing problems. I nip outside and look around, quickly finding a discarded plastic bag trapped against the door of another lock-up. Sending a grateful prayer up to the non-environmentally-friendly denizens of London, I pick it up and deposit my keys, pepper spray and wallet inside. Emblazoned on the outside are the words 'Funny Farm Meats: For All Your Butchery Need's'. I tsk at the misplaced apostrophe, then shut up the garage and walk away swinging the bag. Frankly, I've got bigger problems than poor punctuation.

Walking briskly, I hit the nearest row of shops in next to no time. As luck would have it, there's a kiosk selling cheap mobile phones, so I pass over an insulting amount of cash and buy three, then make sure I'm some distance away before I make the call I need. It's fortunate I've got a head for numbers and have memorised the phone number. I let it ring five times then hang up. I count to fifty in my head and repeat the call. It's not until the third try that someone actually answers.

'Yeah.'

'I need a place to stay.'

'Just you?'

'No. There'll be another.'

'Can I trust them?'

I don't hesitate. 'No.'

'14A Markmore Close. There's an upper-floor flat with views to the front and back. The key will be on the windowsill.'

I sense he's about to hang up so I screech into the phone. 'Wait!'

'What?'

'My flat. I think it's been compromised. I need it checked out.'

There's a pause. 'I can do it. Don't call back though. I'll come and find you.' The phone clicks off and I'm left listening to the dull mechanical burr.

I feel better now that I have somewhere to sleep and to take O'Shea. There are several hours until I need to pick him up; that means it's time to confront Tam.

4

BRUCE WILLIS

Now that I'm car-less, I'm forced to take public transport to get to Dire Straits. And yes, that really is the name. Tam is a hard-core eighties' music fan. I'm not convinced he thought the name through before christening his fledgling company but he weathers all the 'money for nothing' jokes with humour. I'm just thankful that the chicks aren't for free.

I'd be tempted to grab a taxi but keeping a low profile includes not accessing my bank account so I'm lumbered with only the cash I have on me. And there's not much of that. I'll need to be frugal.

As I sit on the train, I run through scenarios in my head. I'd been under the impression that Tam and I had a fairly solid working relationship, even if he didn't value me as much as I thought he should. Now I have to assume that he might be involved in setting me up. He was, after all, the one who sent me after O'Shea in the first place.

I've been working for Tam for the past two years. I'd initially had visions of spending six months with him before leaving to set up my own firm but it didn't take me long to realise that it was going to take a damn sight longer than half a year to learn this business. I had, on occasion, wondered if he deliberately kept me doing scut work because he knew I'd up sticks as soon as I felt confident enough. The thing is, I have a lot of respect for him and I doubt he's that petty or small-minded. I'm at the bottom of the ladder because I was the last one in and there are cavernous depths of detail and information involved in being a private investigator that I still don't know. But loitering on the bottom rung might make me the easiest person to target. Perhaps Tam needed to get rid of O'Shea for some reason and I'm merely a convenient tag to keep the police away from him.

I think about it some more. It could also be the connection to my grandfather that's initiated this move. Except that Tam has known about him from the start and the old man has been out of commission for years, so that theory doesn't really make any sense. I can't think of anything I've inadvertently done to piss Tam off this much. Sure, I've moaned a bit about being stuck with working over weaker tribers like O'Shea but it's only because acting like that's *de rigueur* in a firm like ours. The truth is I'm not experienced enough to trail fully-fledged vampires, daemons or faeries; I'm simply too human. And secretly I prefer focusing on the human side of things anyway. I find it hard to understand the motivation behind a lot of triber actions. Untangling whatever webs the humans have chosen to weave is far, far easier. The triber world may be more glamorous and exciting but I don't need it to get my kicks. The thought flashes through my mind that if I make it to the other side of this kerfuffle, I'm going to have some appropriately impressive triber experience to add to my CV. I may end up stuck with them whether I like it or not.

I return my focus to Tam, trying to remember if there was anything odd about the way he acted when he gave me this assignment on Monday. Nothing jumps out at me. It had all been same old, same old. Of course, it would also have been like that if he was attempting to pull the wool over my eyes and prevent me from suspecting anything untoward about the O'Shea set-up. I rub my eyes. I have to face facts: I have no evidence suggesting Tam is either guilty or innocent.

I'm careful when I disembark the train, getting off one stop before so I can take a circuitous route to the office. It's not paranoia if they really are after you – and I have to assume that they are. As a result, it's late in the afternoon by the time I'm staring at the pretentious, glass-fronted office block. I need to figure a way out to enter without anyone noticing, which is easier said than done. If Tam had located his business in an older building, I might have had an outdoor fire escape to climb up. As things stand, I have no way clambering up the side of the metal and glass of this one.

But all is not lost. When I started at Dire Straits, I made a point of getting to know all the janitorial staff. It doesn't take a genius to know where all the knowledge and power really lie. Unfortunately Tam knows this too and his extravagant tipping at each year end means that they are remarkably tight-lipped when I approach them for gossip. One thing I did learn, however, is the best place to go for a crafty cigarette. I even know which path to take to avoid the CCTV cameras. I don't smoke often but hanging out with the gaspers can lead to good tips.

I make sure there are no familiar faces or unfamiliar watchers hanging around, then I move across the road and round the back of the building. The emergency exit is clear, only a small tin bucket overflowing with tab ends indicating its other use. This is the part that gets tricky. I have no way of opening the heavy barred door from this side so I need to wait until someone opens it for me and get past without them noticing. I need to be very silent and very lucky. To avoid the rustle of the plastic bag in my hand, I jog over to the skip, which for some reason is always lurking here, and shove it in, covering it with a folded cardboard box. I keep the pepper spray on me, carefully tucking it into the folds of the bow at the back of my dress where it'll stay put, if not exactly hidden. Then I head back to the side of the door, moving the bucket an extra foot in front to give myself a bit of wiggle room, and I settle in to wait. At least it's summer and the air is warm.

I don't have to wait for long. I'm leaning against the wall, eyes half-closed, when I hear the tell-tale rattle of the inside bar being pushed. I quickly sidestep left to avoid the door hitting me as it opens, but keep myself pressed against the wall so that the secret smoker won't see me unless they actually turn around. The door swings open noiselessly and a man steps out, cigarette already dangling from his mouth. From this angle, I'm pretty sure it's one of the security guards. He cups his hands and lights up, not moving from the entrance. I curse inwardly and concentrate on not breathing too loudly. At least this location is fairly central, so there's a loud hum of traffic to mask any sounds that I make.

I watch his profile intently. He sucks hard on the cigarette, gazing off into the distance, but his feet still don't move away from the door so there's no way I can edge behind him and sneak inside. He smokes all the way down to the filter and, just as I'm sure he's going to do no more than ground the butt into the tarmac with his heel and head straight back inside, he walks forward to the bucket to drop it in. I swiftly tiptoe behind him and duck inside, bolting up the stairs before he comes back in. I can only think that he must have paused to move the bucket back to its original location because I'm already at the second floor, my heart pounding, when I hear the door clang shut. I grin to myself. There's nothing like a nicotine addict with OCD. Then I bound up to the tenth floor where Tam will be waiting.

The fire exit opens onto the main corridor of Tam's suite. I know from experience that at this time of day the other investigators will either be out on jobs or in the social room, regaling each other with inflated stories of their mornings' exploits. Equally, the receptionist will be far too concerned with her phone to pay attention to anything other than the front door. All this means that I only have to sneak past Arzo, Tam's PA, to get into his office. But Arzo is no push-over like the others and I want a chance to observe Tam before confronting him so, rather than heading directly to his sweeping corner office, I scoot into the ladies' restroom. It's time to put my *Die Hard* Bruce Willis' skills into action. I've always thought it would be possible, considering the entire building is finished with dropped ceilings, but I've never actually tried it before. There's no time like the present.

I hop into one of the cubicles but don't bother locking the door. I don't want someone to wander in and wonder why there's an empty toilet with a locked door. Women with full bladders are neither patient nor good-humoured. Carefully lowering the seat, I step up and onto the cistern then reach up and push aside one of the large ceiling tiles. The space above is dark and filled with pipes which will make it difficult to move around but I am determined.

I curve my fingers round the metal bracket and slowly pull myself upwards, unsure how much of my weight the structure will hold. It creaks and bends slightly but I decide I can make it, so I push my body further up, keeping away from the polystyrene panels where I'll be sure to fall through. There's not much space at the top, forcing me to bend my torso down and forwards to shimmy my hips through. It's a tight squeeze but once they're past, I wiggle forward so I can pull up my legs. The hardest part is edging backwards so I can replace the tile. Advancing through this space is difficult enough while lying flat on my belly; reversing without being able to see where I'm going is almost impossible. It takes me minutes to manage it and, by the time I'm where I need to be, I'm covered in sweat. Whoever once said that horses sweat, men perspire and women glow clearly hasn't met me.

I stare down for a moment at the empty restroom and wonder if I'm crazy for doing this. I'm sandwiched between a layer of polystyrene and snaking pipes while looking down on a toilet. From this vantage point, it's easy to spot where the cleaner has been lax and not bothered to reach round the edges of the bowl. I make a slight face and stiffen my resolve. Just like those weeks of built-up dirt, I'm not going to allow myself, my sanity or my freedom to be simply swept away. As ridiculous as this situation is, I need to find out where I stand with Tam. I push the tile back into its original position then begin my slow shuffle forward.

I barely manage a few feet before I feel the dress snag on something. Damn it. This is another reason I can't get away with looking pretty while attempting to work at the same time. I eventually untangle the material then tuck the rest of the fabric into my knickers to avoid it happening again. Bruce Willis didn't have that problem.

Although the straightest and most direct route towards Tam's office is diagonally across the space, I'm forced to go in a different direction as the pipes are blocking my way. I can only hope that's not the case once I get further along or this entire venture will be screwed. Inching forward in darkness, I stay as silent as possible. I have to strain to keep my weight balanced on the metal frames and not sag down onto the tiles. The pain of the exertion is attacking my core, as if I'm permanently holding myself in a plank position. At least I won't have to worry about going to the gym today. It seems like an eternity before I hear the ping of the lift and realise I've reached the reception area.

'Hi, doll-face,' drawls a deep voice that I immediately recognise as Boris, one of the other investigators.

His weak attempt at flirtation falls flat as Tansy, the receptionist, sighs. 'Why are you late?' She sounds bored to tears.

'Were you worried about me?'

The silence that greets his question pretty much provides an answer. I smirk and am about to continue quietly onwards when I freeze at his next question. His tone is overly casual, which makes it even worse.

'Is Bo back yet?'

'Not seen her.' There's an odd grating sound.

'Has she phoned in?'

The sound continues. I finally realise Tansy must be filing her nails. 'Nah,' she says. 'What's it to you?'

Every muscle in my body tenses as I wait to hear his answer. I'd always pegged him as large and dumb, nothing more than an annoyance, but now my mind is racing at the thought that he might have something to do with all of this.

'One of my contacts rang me on the way in asking about her. Says the pigs want to talk to her about something that went down this morning.'

I'm disappointed; I'd been hoping for more. Life would be a hell of a lot easier if I could pin the blame for this on Boring Boris and move on. I suppose the confirmation that the police are definitely after me is useful though. I don't wait to listen to more; instead I shuffle onwards, making sure I'm as quiet as death. Their voices were as clear as if they'd been standing next to me and the last thing I need is for them to realise there's something crawling around above them.

Fortunately the pipes twist right, allowing me to continue forward to Tam's office unhindered. Arzo worries me. He's a canny bastard. I'd swear he has traces of Kakos daemon blood running through his veins were it not for the fact that he's been with Tam for more than two decades. No Kakos daemon could spend that long in a human's company without giving into the temptation to eat their heart or drive them insane. Still, I'm fairly certain he's more triber than human and that I have no hope of being silent enough to pass over his head without him noticing. At least his desk is outside Tam's office and slightly to the left, so I reckon the pipes will give me just enough leeway to avoid him. The problem is that, thanks to the ceiling tiles, I can't see down to check; they are so well fitted that there are no cracks or gaps where I can peer down. I know the layout of the office – I've sodding worked there for two years after all – but up here in the ceiling, and with an ache developing through my body as I keep myself aloft, I'm becoming more and more disorientated.

I suck air in through my mouth and hold it for a few seconds, attempting to regain my equilibrium. When I finally exhale, I feel more centred. I side shuffle to my right, getting as close to the pipes as I can. It's just my rotten luck that the one closest to me is carrying hot water. A couple of times the bare skin of my legs lightly brushes it, scalding me. Each time I have to pause and bite the inside of my cheek until the pain subsides. It takes me at least ten minutes to reach the threshold of Tam's inner sanctum and ease myself over. I can hear the clacking of computer keys and the hum of distant traffic but little else. I grimace. I really need to find a way to see what he's doing.

At the edge of my small space, where I presume the large window looking out over the city is situated, there's a tiny chink of light. That might just be enough of a gap to look down from. It's at least eight feet away and, as I've already discovered, moving sideways for any distance is considerably harder than moving forwards. I decide that shifting my body around will cause too much noise so, painful centimetre by centimetre, I edge towards it. I'm about halfway there when there's a hard knock at the door and I curse inwardly. I'm not sure how much longer I can hold myself in this position.

I hear the door open.

'Boss?'

I roll my eyes. It's Boring Boris again. Now that I've discounted him from my list of suspects, listening to him is going to be of little help. Unless he has more details about what the police are saying about me, that is. Tam must have beckoned him in because the floor squeaks as if someone is moving forwards.

'I'm concerned about Bo.'

I'm both surprised and a little touched by this. A trace of guilt about my attitude towards the big man snakes up my spine – but I still really want to hear Tam's response.

'What is it?' His voice is gruff, but I can't detect any particular emotion in it.

'The police scanners are after her. There seems to have been some kind of incident at Wiltshore Avenue. You know she had that assignment there with the daemon? Now she's wanted for questioning.'

Silence. It draws out to an uncomfortable point where I feel my heart begin thrumming faster and faster. What is Tam going to say?

'I see.'

Damn it. Why does he always have to be so bloody non-committal?

'I could go out and talk to my contacts. Find out more.'

There's another long pause. Then Tam speaks again. 'You do that, Boris. Thank you.'

Tam's response tells me absolutely nothing. My hands, which are still gripping the criss-cross ceiling frame, tighten. I hear Boris murmur something about leaving straight away, then his footsteps squeak again on their way out. The door closes. If only I could see down to check Tam's expression. I'm about to start moving again when I hear him lift up his phone and jab in a number. It's only three digits so he's calling someone in the office.

'We have a problem.' I stiffen at his words. 'Get in here.'

Tears spring to my eyes and I almost choke. Despite my current precarious position spying on my employer, I hadn't really believed he was involved. Not deep down.

Shuffling more quickly now, I use the sound of the door opening to mask my own noise and make it over to the ceiling gap. I push myself hard against the wall; if I angle my head just right, I can see into the office. I force down every betrayed, angry and impossibly wounded emotion and blink away the tears. Then I look.

I hiss when I see Arzo's unmistakable heavyset shoulders. His head begins to tilt and my eyes widen in alarm. Then, just as I'm sure he's about to stare right at me, there's a high-pitched scream from somewhere behind him. It lasts barely a second before it's cut off, as if the screamer had just dropped dead. Arzo whirls around and I see Tam pulling open a drawer to scrabble for the illegal gun he keeps there.

It's already too late. I watch, horror struck, as something dark and very fast snaps into Arzo's midsection. He spins around then falls to his knees. Whatever attacked him launches itself at Tam. I register the attacker's broad shoulders and brown hair, tied back at the nape of his neck, before seeing his flashing fangs sink into Tam's throat and rip at it with one swift, vicious bite. He pulls away a chunk of bloody flesh. Tam clutches at his neck and gasps a loud, incomprehensible word before falling in slow motion onto the desk.

I raise my hand to punch through the flimsy tile and do whatever I can but then I see Arzo's large brown eyes staring at me. He shakes his head, mouthing at me. It takes a moment before I realise what he's trying to say.

No.

Helpless, I gaze down as the life drains out of his body and I try to make sense of what has just happened.

5

KNOWLEDGE

I stay squeezed in the dropped ceiling until I can no longer bear it. Even though my emotions are numb, every muscle in my body is screeching with pain by the time I yield and shove across the nearest tile so I can drop down into Tam's blood-spattered office. Any semblance of tears is gone as I take in the scene. The air reeks of dark smoke from the vampire who attacked Tam and Arzo. I try to avert my eyes from their fallen bodies and use my brain to assess what I witnessed and what I'm seeing now. But my gaze drifts to the sickeningly large chunk of flesh lying next to the wall and I swallow hard.

Something catches my peripheral vision and I spin round, shoulders braced and ready for an attack. When I realise it's Arzo's chest moving, I rush to his side. He's unconscious but definitely still alive – a miracle considering what has just happened. But I have no hope of dragging him out in the same way I did with O'Shea a few hours before. Arzo is too large and the whole building is too central for me not to be stopped in mid-stagger. His only chance is to receive immediate medical attention.

I glance back at Tam's desk and realise he's fallen across his phone. A dim flicker of logic settles in my brain. I'm in these offices every day so there will be traces of me everywhere for the police to pick up on, but allowing my fingerprints to smear their invisible way across Tam's corpse would be tantamount to suicide. I step away carefully, avoiding treading in any blood, and pick up the phone on Arzo's desk, trying to ignore the very visible shake in my hands.

'999, what's your emergency?' asks the cool, collected voice on the other end for the second time today.

I deepen my voice to avoid recognition. 'There's been a vampire attack at Dire Straits. Tenth floor of the Artisan Building on Fitch Street. One of the victims is still alive and requires immediate attention.'

'Can you give me your name and telephone number?'

I drop the phone on the desk, leaving the voice hanging, and prepare to leave, hardening my heart against Arzo's state to focus on my own precarious chances of survival. If I end up in a police cell because of this and what went down at Wiltshore Avenue, I'll never find out what is going on and I may end up as a puddle of blood on a floor. Common sense might suggest that I stay and answer any questions as honestly as I can, but my day has been anything but common. And the way things are going, I can't trust anyone but myself.

I'm forced to pass through the social area. It is a bloodbath and I stare open-mouthed at the chaos that's been left in the vampire's wake. At least five of my co-workers are sprawled across the floor. Everywhere I look all I see is red. It appears that the attack happened too quickly for any of them to defend themselves. I shake my head to clear the fog that's forming there and quickly move out. We're in the city centre. The police and ambulances will be here soon.

As I move through reception, Tansy's glazed eyes stare at me with the emptiness of the dead. Her nail file is still clutched in her hand. For some reason this detail is seared into my brain as I open the fire exit and run down the stairs to the ground floor.

There's not a soul in sight, not even a die-hard smoker is out taking a few hasty puffs, so I grab my plastic bag from the skip and leave, just as the sirens begin to scream.

This time I duck into the nearest underground station, keeping my head down to avoid the CCTV cameras. I receive several wide-eyed stares and for a moment I wonder if I'm drenched in blood. When I look down, however, I see that my borrowed dress is still tucked haphazardly into my knickers. I smooth it down, too shocked and numb to feel embarrassed, but I know that my presence here will be remembered. Bugger.

Once I'm safely on the train and rattling back to the outskirts of the city and my grandfather's house, I squeeze my eyes shut and press my hands against my thighs so hard that it hurts. Of course I was worried after what happened with O'Shea but I was still calm. Now all I feel is a suffocating panic. Nothing makes any sense. Not O'Shea being attacked and left for dead, not me being set up for his apparent murder, not the vicious genocide at Dire Straits. Why a vampire? It obviously wasn't just because they were hungry. There's enough fresh blood on tap for any bloodguzzler to drink their fill from a willing victim. It's a well-known fact that adrenaline and fear make even the sweetest blood taste sour, and vampires prefer to use the many human vampettes who are always lining up to be sucked. Besides, neither O'Shea nor any of my co-workers were tasted. Equally, this can't be about me; as much as I'd like to believe otherwise, in truth I am a nobody.

I think about Tam's betrayal. His reaction to Boris's worries about the police being after me proves he was involved in setting me up. Did he frame me at the behest of someone else who then turned the tables on him? I have no way of knowing. At least the brutality of the attack precludes me from being a suspect. No one would believe a five-foot-one human woman did that. Would they? And why did Arzo tell me to stay hidden instead of try to help?

The police could easily believe that I tried to kill O'Shea. My grandfather may have instinctively known the daemon's wounds were from a vampire but if I'd been found at the scene with his body tied to a chair with my handcuffs, it's likely the post mortem would be rushed and I'd be put away for the rest of my life. If things had happened the way the perp had planned though, there's no way I could be implicated in the office massacre. I wouldn't even have been there. Now I'm wondering whether, in hindsight, staying at Wiltshore and allowing myself to be arrested might have been the best course of action after all.

I want to scream in frustration and anguish. Instead, I open my eyes slowly and take a deep breath. This is not the time to panic. The train trundles into the station and I make my way back to my grandfather's house. Now, more than ever, I need O'Shea to be conscious long enough to answer my questions. I can feel myself teetering on the edge of sanity and I need something to pull me back.

When I arrive at the small cul-de-sac, my grandfather's door is open and he is standing at the threshold, watching my approach. I don't have time to deal with any of his usual theatrics and I'm too numb to care about pissing him off, so I reach up to kiss him on the cheek before he prompts me. He surprises me, however, and puts up a hand to stall my action. The fact that I recognise sadness in his normally steely eyes is disturbing.

'It's all over the news,' he says gruffly.

I feel a wash of fatigue. 'What are they saying?'

'That seven people at Dire Straits are dead. One is critical and in intensive care.' He gives me a hard look. 'They are looking for you to help them with their enquiries.'

I almost – but not quite – snort with laughter at the euphemism. 'They can't seriously believe I'm responsible.'

The cat pads out and snakes round my ankles. I half-leap out of my skin. It's never bloody done that before. Things must be even worse than I thought.

'I made a few discreet enquiries of my own. They don't.' I exhale loudly, but my grandfather continues. 'They do, however, think you are involved in some way. That maybe you're working with a new bloodguzzler Family or something.'

'That's stupid.'

'I said as much. No granddaughter of mine would be in league with those things.'

My mouth twists. 'No, it's stupid to think that there's a new Family. The other Families would never allow it. Besides, what would any of the vampires have to gain from all of this?'

His gaze is frank. 'Dire Straits must have done something to annoy them.'

'But we don't work for vampires,' I point out. 'They have their own in-house investigators.'

He speaks quietly. 'Maybe your firm was working against them.'

I mull this over. It seems implausible. We did look into vampires from time to time for some client or other but, as far as I know anyway, nothing Dire Straits has ever done would come close to deserving retaliation on this scale. In fact, I'd been under the impression the vampires allowed us a modicum of professional courtesy and would help us out from time to time if it served their interests. But then again, my own employer framing me for the murder of some two-bit, magic-dealing, half-breed daemon is equally implausible. Speaking of…

'What about O'Shea?'

'Who?'

My grandfather's confusion is faked. I roll my eyes at him. There's something about his attitude that's reassuring and makes me feel normal again. 'The daemon?'

'Oh. Him.'

I put my hands on my hips and give him a death stare. The trouble is that I'm just not as good at it as he is and he knows it. 'Is he awake?' I demand.

He shakes his head and gestures inside. Disappointed, I follow him into the small kitchen. O'Shea is still sprawled out on the kitchen table, his chest moving up and down regularly. I watch him for a few moments.

'He's involved in this,' I say eventually, as much to myself as to my grandfather.

'Yes. So what's your next move, Bo?'

Despite everything, I feel a flicker of pride. He may be an ornery bastard with an entrenched core of racism, but he believes I can sort this out on my own and without his help. If he thought otherwise, he wouldn't be asking me what I planned to do next. A thought strikes me: *unless he has no idea what to do now, of course.*

'I have a safe house,' I answer. 'I'll take him there.'

'Are you sure it's safe?'

'Yes.'

'And you're just going to wait until he wakes up?'

I bite my lip. 'I don't have any other choice.'

He regards me silently. I wonder what's going through that head of his. He had better not be gloating about the demise of my firm.

'I suppose you'll need some form of transportation,' he says finally.

I look at him hopefully. I had been counting on the old man realising I'd had to dump my car and that he needed to help me out with a vehicle if he wanted to get shot of O'Shea before nightfall.

He throws me a set of keys. 'It belongs to one of my neighbours. If you get a scratch on it, they won't be happy.'

'I'll look after it,' I promise. 'Thank you.' I really mean it.

He inclines his head. 'You take care now,' he says. Then he walks out of the kitchen. 'I like the dress,' he calls back. 'You should wear one more often.'

I sigh in exasperation and glance down at O'Shea's prone

body. 'He doesn't like it enough to help me get you out of here,' I say to him.

Unsurprisingly, the daemon doesn't answer. I shrug to myself, then bend and push his body up and over my shoulder in a fireman's lift. At least he'll be easier to carry now I don't have to worry about him bleeding out. My knees buckle for a moment but I manage to steady myself and stagger outside. There's a shiny car waiting in the driveway. I could swear it wasn't there when I arrived less than five minutes ago. Shaking my head at my grandfather's ability to get people to do exactly what he wants, I press down on the key and the car beeps loudly, signalling it's open. I heave O'Shea's weight onto the back seat, making sure his legs are inside before I slam the door shut. Then I get in and drive away.

WHEN I WAS fourteen years old and particularly precocious, I came home from aceing an arduous mathematics test and spent a considerable amount of time crowing about my accomplishment to my father. It didn't take him long to grow bored with my egotism and he told me in no uncertain terms that it hadn't been as difficult or as complex as I supposed.

'That's not true,' I sniffed back at him. 'It's one of the hardest tests there is. And one of the hardest subjects.' I had no way of knowing whether this was true but, to my teenage mind, I had to be right.

'The hardest test isn't something you sit in school, Bo,' he told me gently.

I completely misunderstood what he was driving at. 'Grandfather says university is for wimps. That even the exams you sit at Oxford are easy and that they're breeding a nation of incompetents.' I told you I was precocious. The memory of my snotty tone still makes me wince.

My father sighed heavily and patted me on my shoulder. 'There are other tests.'

'Like what?'

I remember the look he gave me: measured and calm, but still assessing how far he could go. Of course I know now that the hardest tests aren't even tests. They're how you cope when your life falls apart. When you bite your tongue and let your best friend cry on your shoulder because the loser she's been dating has dumped her. When the same loser comes on to you too strongly at a party the weekend after. When you're trying to decide between paying the rent or eating. When one of your parents dies. I think my father knew that I would snort with adolescent derision if he pointed this out to me, so he took a different tack.

'The Knowledge,' he said instead. 'That's the hardest test.'

'What's the Knowledge?'

'It's what all taxi drivers have to do before they're allowed to drive a black cab.'

I probably curled my lip. 'You mean a driving test.'

'No. I mean memorising 35,000 London streets so you always know the fastest way to get from point A to point B. It takes a minimum of two years to learn. Most people take five.'

He folded his arms and looked at me pointedly. I think I tossed my hair and wandered off in search of someone who would be more willing to listen to me boast about my accomplishments. But he had stirred my interest and the next day I stayed late after school to look up the Knowledge in the library. Imagine my surprise when I realised he was right.

Deciding then and there that I would become the youngest person to ever pass the Knowledge, regardless of the fact that I had no desire to become a taxi driver and was three years away from being allowed to drive, I took up the challenge. I studied every evening and spent weekends cycling around the city to challenge myself. Had my father known what a monster his comments would unleash, he probably would have been happy to sit there for hours to listen to my blow-by-blow account of algebra and fractions. I bored my friends to tears by forcing them to test me. I wouldn't say I ever got to the point where I knew thirty-five thousand streets, or where I'd even have come close to passing, but I did learn a hell of a lot.

My study of the Knowledge was cut short abruptly about six months later when I discovered that Dean, the most annoying boy at my school, had hair that curled invitingly around the sexy nape of his neck and a voice that made my toes curl up inside my trainers. Boys, I decided, were infinitely more interesting than the streets of London and I ended my quest almost as suddenly as I'd begun it. A lot of what I'd learned in that time never left me, though. At least now I know exactly where Markmore Close is without having to worry about maps or GPS. I'll never know boys – or rather men, now that I'm older – as easily as that.

EVEN DRIVING CAREFULLY to avoid any undue attention, it takes less than forty minutes to get to the safe house. The sky, which was already darkening by the time I reached my grandfather's, is now definitely advertising that it's night. It feels like it's been the longest day of my life and it's far from over yet.

I'm fortunate enough to pull up and park directly outside the block of flats. I'm even more fortunate that there's a tiny lift inside, so I hook O'Shea's dead weight of an arm round my neck and hoist him up by the waist. A fireman's lift would be easier but any curious residents might think he's spent the afternoon in the pub and had one too many if I haul him up this way instead. It's a struggle and seems to take forever, but finally I find the key exactly where I was told it would be and get him inside.

It's a small place; property is at a premium in this part of the city so I'm not surprised. At least it's clean and well kept. I flop

O'Shea's body down on the small bed which was probably advertised as a double – but only if you are sharing with a midget. It'll do, I suppose. I can crash on the sofa when I need to sleep.

I turn to leave when I suddenly think of something. The last thing I need is the daemon waking up and doing a runner. He's the best lead – the only lead – I've got right now and I'm not letting him slip through my fingers. I turn back, grab hold of the cuffs which are still dangling from his wrist and clip them onto the frame of the bed. It's not particularly sturdy but I figure he'll still be weak from blood loss when he wakes up and the cuffs will hold him. Then I head back down and move the car a few blocks away. Better safe than sorry.

By the time I get back to the flat, I am buzzing with nervous energy. It's probably just as well because I won't be able to sleep. I'm pretty sure that whenever I close my eyes from now on, I'll see flashbacks of dark smoky figures and splatters of blood.

I sit down on the sofa and stare at the wall. Then my head drops and I'm out for the count.

6

MARTINIS AND MISTAKES

I wake up with a start. A shaft of moonlight falls on my face and, for a moment, I'm completely disorientated, trying to work out where the hell I am. Then it all comes flooding back and I'm overwhelmed by all that has happened over the last twenty-four hours. The walls feel as if they're closing in on me and I can't breathe. I gulp in air and my heart thumps painfully against my ribcage. I lurch to my feet and half run to the small bathroom to splash cold water on my face, then I lean against the sink and stare at myself in the mirror until my heart rate slows down.

'Pull yourself together,' I mutter.

Padding into the bedroom, I check on O'Shea. He's in exactly the same position as when I left him, one arm raised slightly where it's cuffed, but his face looks more relaxed and his breathing is easier. There's even a tiny snore. It occurs me that he's very attractive, with chiselled cheekbones and flawless dark skin.

I bend down and check the wound on his neck. The stitches have done their job and it seems to be healing quickly. I guess that O'Shea has inherited the daemons' ability to regenerate,

50

along with his crazy orange eyes and model's good looks. I sit down on the edge of the bed and consider what to do next. I'm tempted to shake him awake and demand answers but I might have a better shot at getting them once he's recovered. I need to be patient.

I check my watch and see that I haven't slept for as long as I thought. It's only just gone midnight and this is the city that never sleeps. I don't feel tired any more and I need something to distract me until my patient – or prisoner, depending on which way you look at it – wakes up.

By now my dress is crumpled but I decide I can get away with it. I find the Funny Farm plastic bag and pull out my wallet, taking out some notes and stuffing them into the tight bodice. I should probably keep more back because I have no idea when I'm going to be able to get hold of more cash. But I think I deserve a drink.

It takes me less than five minutes to find a place. If there's one thing you can be sure of, it's that in Britain you're rarely far away from some place where you can drown your sorrows. There's a bouncer on the door, a burly type but still human, who gives me a discreet once over, taking in my now less than perfect appearance. I give him a small smile and he lets me in.

As soon as I'm inside, part of me wishes I'd not bothered. The club must have great sound-proofing because what was little more than a dull beat from the street is now a heart-thumping, ear-churning level of decibels. I'm tempted to leave and find somewhere quieter but I decide to stick with it. Perhaps the level of sound will stop me continually worrying. I need oblivion, if only for an hour or two, not more time to think.

I give the dance floor a wide berth and head for the bar, perching on an uncomfortable plastic stool. Despite – or maybe because of – the loud music, there aren't many other customers and I catch the bartender's attention quickly. I order three martinis and down them in quick succession, shuddering at the strength of the alcohol. When they don't immediately work, I order another three. At these prices, I'll need to drink quickly if I want to achieve the effect I'm after.

The bartender is still making my drinks when I become aware of someone by my side. I tense, ready to do whatever I can to keep myself safe, but it's just a guy. Not a vampire or a copper or anyone else wanting to do me harm. He's not even a triber, just a guy who's after a bit of fun to finish off his night. He's good-looking in a geeky sort of way, with horn-rimmed glasses and a well-tailored suit. His appearance suggests he's more prepared for a board meeting than a nightclub, despite the five o'clock shadow around his jaw. His hair is an attractive tortoiseshell colour, enhanced by the club's bouncing multi-coloured lights, and his eyes twinkle at me with promise.

'Hello,' he says.

The bartender lines up my next three drinks. I remove the cocktail stick from the first one and pull off the olive delicately with my teeth, chewing it and savouring its fresh salty taste. I give him a half-smile.

He gestures at the three glasses. 'You must be thirsty.'

In response, I pick one up and throw the contents down my throat. I'm tempted to lick my lips suggestively afterwards, but I manage to stop myself. This man is a sure thing and, even though I don't normally pick up strangers, I can't think of any better way to obliterate the newsreel that keeps running through my head.

I stay mute, although I reach over and slide the second martini along the bar to him. He raises his eyebrows slightly, takes it by the stem and sips.

'Having a bad day?' His voice is gentle, not probing.

For one awful moment, tears threaten. He reaches over and softly brushes my hand. At least it's not my leg. I manage – just – to recover my equilibrium. I take the third glass and sip it care-fully, raising my eyes to his. He looks at me and I look at him while, disturbingly, the beat of music changes to a much slower song. We remain like that, watching each other and sipping the martinis until both glasses are drained. Then I push myself off the stool and tuck a hand inside my bodice to grab the money, throwing the notes down onto the bar. If he's surprised at my lack of height, he doesn't comment on it; he simply takes my hand and we walk out.

I've been in the club for only thirty minutes but the rush of cold air once we are outside shocks me. I'm vaguely aware of the bouncer nodding to himself, impressed at how quickly I managed to find Mr Tortoiseshell. A faint curl of nausea rises up in my stomach but I push it down and take him by the hand, tugging him away from the bouncer's prying eyes. We round the corner onto a quieter street and he stops, turning to face me. His hands cup my face as he gazes at me. It feels oddly as if he's staring into my soul. He tilts up my chin and gently kisses my lips. But the last thing I want is gentle.

I twist round and push him against the wall, enjoying the sensation of his hard body next to mine. His eyes spark in desire. I yank the lapel of his suit, pull his face down to mine and kiss him fiercely. He gets with the programme and returns the kiss with equal force. Mr Tortoiseshell obviously enjoys being in control, despite his initial softness, because he pushes me around so this time it's my back against the wall. One hand reaches up to my hair and the other down to my bare thigh. I can feel his erection pressing into me. His fingers slide higher up my leg and all of a sudden I come to my senses.

As I jerk my head away and duck out from under his arms, he blinks in surprise. I look up at him and feel ashamed. My cheeks heat up. This isn't me.

'I'm sorry.' My voice sounds strange, almost disembodied. 'I can't do this.'

And before he can do or say anything else, I turn on my heel and run. Away from him and away from the club. If only it was this easy to run away from my real problems.

IT TAKES me a while to get back to the flat. I walk first to clear my head and I berate myself for being an idiot. I feel bad for Mr Tortoiseshell. I suppose he thought I was leading him on then stiffed him – so to speak – in the final moments. But even if I could have found the words, it was just too complicated to explain.

I'm right outside the door when all my senses tell me that something is wrong. I pause, straining my ears. The only reason I catch the sound is because O'Shea is clearly still in pain and can't stop himself gasping aloud. As I watch, the door knob slowly starts to turn. I smile humourlessly. He's obviously not realised I'm standing on the other side.

I edge slightly left and wait for the door to creak open. When it's about an inch ajar, I snap my foot up and out, kicking it backwards with as much force as I can muster. O'Shea yells in pain and I leap through, the base of my palm ready to smash into his nose to prevent him from attempting to go anywhere. I needn't have bothered. He might have extricated himself from the bed, but he'd achieved it by taking the cheap gilt headboard with him. When the door hits him, he staggers backwards and succeeds in getting the corner of the bed post snagged around a wooden chair. He yanks at it several times in desperation, clawing with his free hand, but it's stuck fast. I watch him, vaguely amused, then step forward. It's not until I reach his kicking feet that he finally looks up at me and his body relaxes. Just as I thought. It's damn hard to come across as a badass PI when you're wearing a short flowery dress.

I crouch down. 'Do you remember me?'

The corners of his mouth turn up. 'Darling, how could I not?'

He's flirting. Idiot. The slim file Tam provided me with before the debacle at Wiltshore Avenue told me one salient detail that O'Shea was now stupidly trying to conceal in a bid to charm me:

I was most definitely not his type. I give him an exasperated look and I see comprehension dawn in his eyes.

'Oh.' He gives me a half grin. 'You know I'm gay.'

'Indeed.'

I settle myself at his feet, cross my legs, rest my chin on my hands and look at him.

'Are you going to help me get out of this?' he asks, holding up his chained wrist. The headboard rattles.

I shake my head.

He blinks at me with his large orange eyes. 'You saved my life.' It's not a question.

'Yes.'

'So now you're going to keep me tied to a bed to have your kinky way with me?'

'We've already been through that.' I keep my voice calm. The five martinis I recently downed help with that. 'Though it's not too late for me to change my mind about the saving your life part.'

There's a flicker of doubt in his eyes, as if he's already decided that a little girl like me wouldn't have the stomach for it. He has no idea. After the last twenty-four hours, I'm prepared to do whatever it takes. Something in my manner finally makes him realise this because the doubt changes to fear. Good. I stretch my arm forward and lightly touch the wound on his torso. The fear grows.

'Tell me what you were doing at the house.'

He swallows. 'It's my childhood home. I was taking a trip down memory lane.'

I press my fingers down and he gasps. 'Okay, okay! There's no need to go all Guantanamo on me. Jeez.' He rolls his eyes as if I'm infringing on his human rights. Alright, I suppose I am. But I've got cause.

'Tell me what you were doing at the house,' I repeat. I know what Tam told me but I have no reason now to believe what he said.

O'Shea looks hangdog. Unfortunately for him, his sunset orange pupils remind me of my grandfather's evil cat rather than a cute puppy.

'Fine. It's no big deal. I was just selling an enhancement spell, that's all.'

'What kind of enhancement spell?'

He grins at me, although I can tell it's forced. 'You know…'

'No, O'Shea, I really don't.'

He gestures at his crotch. 'An *enhancement* spell.'

My cheeks colour. 'For virility or for size?'

'The bigger they are, darling, the harder they…'

I interrupt him. 'Okay. I get it. Why the secrecy? Why there?'

'It's not exactly legal.'

'Elaborate.'

'There are some,' he licks his lips, 'side effects.'

I dread to think. Still, I need to know so I gesture for him to continue. He shrugs. 'Well, you're the one who brought up virility. Unfortunately the spell renders the recipient impotent. I mean, obviously they can still get it up.' He laughs. 'That's rather the point. But in terms of being able to reproduce, well, the spell kind of takes that away.'

I don't entirely understand. 'But I'm sure there are lots of men who'd be more than willing than to undergo a magical vasectomy. No more worries about any little accidents…'

He frowns. 'It's not a vasectomy as such. Magic is unreliable and this spell in particular is base physical magic. You start messing with that and all sorts of things can happen. Virility is linked to testosterone. Testosterone is linked to behaviour.'

'So take away virility and you take away testosterone. Take that away and you're left with … what? Passive men?'

'Pretty much.'

'How can they,' I cough awkwardly, 'how can they get it up without testosterone?'

'The spell contains a marker to artificially increase libido,' he explains.

I nod like it makes sense. It doesn't. This is one of the reasons why my grandfather hates magic makers. Then again, my grandfather hates everyone.

'I still don't see why male passivity is a problem,' I say. 'In fact, I think it sounds like a damn good idea.'

'You're not the only woman to think that. The client I was meant to be meeting is female.'

I can see a certain twisted logic there. I think of the odd scent of rosewater when I opened the door on his tortured body. But even though I didn't see his face, I'm pretty certain that the vampire who attacked Tam and the others was male.

'Did your client show up?'

He shakes his head. 'Just that fucking bloodguzzler. He leached the spell, cuffed me to the chair and then tried to kill me.'

'Do you know who he was?'

'No.'

'Was the female client a vampire?'

'I never met her. But no, I don't think so.'

'If you've never met her, how did you set up the drop?'

'A private chatroom. People contact me directly through that.' He shrugs. 'I used to contact them the old-fashioned way and write codes in birthday cards, that kind of thing, but it became too much hassle. Everyone prefers the internet these days.' He sounds miffed, as if it's a personal affront.

I gently manoeuvre him back to the real topic of the conversation. 'What's her name? The client's?'

'I only ever knew her via her avatar, Lucy.'

Just like Mina's friend in the book *Dracula*, I realise. The one who enjoyed ensnaring men while human but who then turned vampire. Appropriate. 'Lucy could still be a man,' I point out.

'Nah. I know how women write. This was definitely a woman.'

I'm not sure I can trust him on this but I'm prepared to let it go for now. 'Why would anyone want you dead?'

'I don't know. I'm a good boy.' He blinks at me innocently.

'A good boy who deals in dodgy under-the-counter magic and who was almost drained of all his blood.'

He juts out his bottom lip. 'It must be the spell.'

'How long do the effects last?'

'Please. I'm a professional. They're permanent. Cast this baby and, believe me, you ain't having any more babies.'

I'm startled. 'You mean you don't just deal? You created the spell?'

'Of course. There's no other spell like it,' he says, but then his face falls. 'Yeah, they tried to kill me for the spell.'

Perhaps. But that doesn't explain why they – whoever 'they' are – also tried to set me up for his murder. Or why they succeeded in murdering pretty much everyone in my company. Or what would make Tam involved. It all seems so sordid and very, very petty.

I remember something Tam once said to me about sex and money. I'd only just joined Dire Straits and I'd expressed my frustration about the lack of variety in the assignments I was given. He laughed and said that in the end there was never any variation, that cases always boiled to either one or both of two things: sex and money. I certainly have the sex element here but that seems unimportant. From what O'Shea has told me, it seems as if this has more to do with power. And power equals money. I need to start with that and track down his original client.

'How much were you being paid?' I ask.

Before O'Shea can answer, a phone starts to ring. The pair of us jump. I get to my feet and look for the source of the sound, eventually discovering an old-fashioned Mickey Mouse phone to the side of the sofa.

'You don't know where your own phone is in your own flat?'

'It's not my damn flat,' I snap and lift the receiver.

'It's me.'

I'm relieved. 'Excellent timing.'

'Your flat's fine. It's being watched but it's not been obviously turned over.'

I nod. That makes sense. It would be far too suspicious if the prime suspect in a murder had her flat robbed on the same day. The theft of my handcuffs was clearly done surreptitiously. I really hate the idea of someone rooting around my things. I think of my underwear drawer and shudder.

'You have only three more nights at Markmore.'

'That's fine.' I'll either be in the morgue by then or I'll have sorted out an alternative of my own. 'There's something else I need you to do.'

'I've got homework.'

'It's four o'clock in the morning!'

'So?'

The vagaries of teenagers. 'This won't take long,' I say, hoping I sound persuasive.

There's a heavy sigh. 'Okay. What?'

'Find someone called Lucy.'

I pick the phone up, annoyed at the short cable as I try to stretch it across the room, and hold the receiver to O'Shea's ear.

'You're going to tell the person on the end of this phone how to access your private chatroom,' I tell him.

'Who's on the end of this phone?'

'Just tell them.'

7

HACKER

I FIRST MET ROGU3 THREE YEARS AGO, LONG BEFORE I'D HEARD OF Dire Straits. He was eleven years old then, making him fourteen now. I'm terrified of what he'll be like when he finally matures into an adult.

I was working as an insurance fraud investigator at the time for one of those large faceless companies whose bottom line is always about profit. It was a truly awful job and I hated every minute of it. They were often happy to pay out small amounts as they felt that gave them an 'honest face'. When it came to larger sums of money, however, it was an entirely different story.

The organisation dealt mainly in life insurance. The basic package covered accidental death, such as car crashes, as well as dying as a result of long-term (although never pre-existing) conditions. The premium package included a much wider range, such as death by triber. It also provided a payout in the event that your loved one was inadvertently transformed into a vampire. They called this 'implicit passing' – the bigwigs at the company loved their euphemisms. Customers signed up for the premium package in droves. At the time, I suspected it was down to some carefully planted articles in the media about helpless victims who were turned while out shopping or at the park with their kids. It was all nonsense, of course. Each of the vampire Families only recruits new members once or twice a decade, depending on their attrition rates. And there is never any shortage of volunteers or 'vampettes' as the human hangers-on are known. No Family would be so crass as to randomly turn someone who was doing nothing more than going about their daily business.

Cleverly, the premium policies were considered null and void if someone voluntarily turned themselves over to the bloodguzzlers. So say you were dying a long and drawn out death of cancer, and you happened to luck into a Family recruitment drive and were chosen to be turned, then your loved ones received nothing. If you chose to die quietly, they got a semi-generous payout. I understand why so many tried so hard to achieve the alternative. Few succeeded. With such a large pool to choose from, the Families can afford to be choosy. There are plenty of people lining up who aren't sick; they want to be vampires because of a spine-chilling blood lust or a desire for a longer life.

Where the insurance company's genius really paid off, however, was that once you were recruited into a Family, you disappeared. Contrary to popular myth, it's only new vampires who are vulnerable to the sun's glare. To protect them from daylight, and keep them away from the general public because they can't control their desire to drink blood, new recruits are often not seen for years after their transformation. Even when they're finally allowed to make contact with their loved ones, few choose to do so, preferring to remain immersed in the new life they've chosen for themselves. Vampires are notoriously loyal and the Families are tight-lipped about whether someone has been accepted or not. Part of that is down to their own politics, and not wanting rival Families to see what new blood, so to speak, is available. But I've heard that it's also because often recruits don't survive the initial turning process.

This is a dream come true for insurance. If no one can prove that you've been turned, then no one can prove that you haven't – so the insurers don't have to pay up. Of course this only works in the absence of a body but if, for example, you bumped into a Kakos daemon and were in possession of a premium policy, there would be no body left as evidence and no one would receive the money. The insurance company would send out a standard letter informing the real family that in all likelihood the victim voluntarily went vamp and no money would be paid out. All due regrets and blah blah blah.

There are other tribers besides Kakos daemons who are also impressively circumspect with the leftovers of their attacks. Considering that the vast majority are of the 'live and let live' variety, however, I had strong suspicions that the company paid some less savoury tribers (and probably humans too) to dispose of many corpses of people who died from natural causes. I could never prove it. They were – and indeed still are – far too clever to leave a trail. But when I worked there, there was an incredible number of people whose bodies were never recovered and whose policies were cancelled as a result.

It was my job to investigate cases where the bodies were missing. I was green, which is probably why I'd been recruited in the first place. The insurance company could put its hand on its heart and say their investigators had done the best job they could but had discovered no evidence to prove it hadn't been a voluntary vampire recruitment. It didn't help that there was a bonus for investigators who *didn't* find any evidence to disprove voluntary turning.

I didn't last long at the company. To be frank, almost any job would have been better than depriving normal, hard-working families of the insurance payouts they deserved. God knows, they already had enough to deal with once their loved one was dead without being screwed by the company. I've come across other insurers since that have been far more honourable. But the guys I worked for were bastards.

Things came to a head with Alice Goldman. She disappeared when she was seven and a half years old, snatched in broad daylight half a mile from her house. It was all over the news. For a time, people assumed it was a straightforward abduction and that sooner or later she'd be ransomed then released, or her mutilated body would be found in a ditch by some traumatised dogwalker. But her body was never discovered. About two weeks after her disappearance, her discarded clothes were found in a bin, soaked in as much blood as a seven year old can have. The blood was a match for hers.

After months of grieving, the Goldman family pulled themselves together and put in a claim. Unfortunately for me – but perhaps fortunately for them – I was the investigator. I was given strict instructions from on high to deal with the case as 'quickly and quietly' as possible. I knew what that meant: spend a day or two looking for evidence then, in its absence, put in a standard report stating it was possible she'd voluntarily applied to the vampires. Even if the Families' own laws didn't prevent them from recruiting anyone who was under twenty-one, little Alice Goldman's biggest concern was whether Barbie would find her lost shoe, not whether she'd live to be two or three hundred years old.

It was the straw that broke the camel's back. I was going to find evidence to prove she'd not gone to the vampires and shove it under the insurance bigwigs' noses then force them to pay that family what they deserved. Why I thought I'd succeed in finding out what happened to her when half the British police force couldn't, I have no idea. But I wasn't going to let the Goldmans get that standard fucking response letter.

I spent a day tramping around Alice's former neighbourhood and knocking on doors, trying to find anyone who knew anything useful. People were polite but they were exhausted. The police had covered the area and spoken to everyone more than once. So had the journalists. The residents had had enough. After several hours, I sat down on the edge of a pavement, utterly defeated.

My gloom was interrupted by a small high-pitched voice. 'Are you here for Alice?'

When I turned round, I saw a scruffy little boy holding a skateboard and looking down at me.

'Yes,' I answered.

'You won't find her.'

'I know.' To this day I don't know why I continued talking to him. I guess I just needed someone to be on my side, even if it was a kid. 'But I need to find something that'll prove she didn't give herself up to one of the Families.'

'The bloodguzzlers? That's stupid. Everyone knows they don't take kids.'

Yeah, I thought sadly, everyone *does* know that. But it doesn't matter.

'You're not police,' he said, assessing me.

'No. I work for an insurance company.'

He sat down beside me, carefully propping up his board. He kept touching it as we talked, as if he needed to check it was still there.

'They won't pay, will they?' he said, understanding more than I would have given him credit for.

'No. No, they won't.'

A group of kids on bikes passed us. A few of them yelled obscenities at my new companion. He ignored them. 'I can go speak to them if you want. Stop them from bothering you,' I said.

'Nah,' he said. 'They don't bother me. They're just a bunch of losers.'

I dug into my pockets, found a crumpled pack of chewing gum and held it out to him. 'Want one?'

He suddenly grinned at me. 'Sure.' He shoved the gum into his mouth and chewed furiously. 'I can help you.'

I'm not sure if it was because of his chewing or because I was surprised by his words, but I had to ask him to repeat what he'd said said.

'I can help you. I can get you the evidence you need.'

Of course I didn't believe him. But rather than hurt his feelings, I tried a different tack. 'Why would you do that?'

He shrugged. 'Cause you seem nice. And Alice was my friend. She came round sometimes when her mum was working.'

He stood up, picked up his skateboard and started to walk away. When he was several feet in front of me, he turned. 'Well, are you coming or not?'

I came. I'm sure it was highly inappropriate, following a child back to his house and going into his garage alone with him, but it turned out to be one of the best decisions I've ever made.

His garage didn't contain a car or a lawnmower or half-dried-up tins of paint like most people's. This kid's garage was covered wall to ceiling in flashing state-of-the-art computers. I stared, open-mouthed.

'I built most of this myself,' the boy said proudly, closing the heavy door and plunging us into near darkness. 'I started out with an old system of my dad's then went from there.'

This was a nice neighbourhood but it didn't seem like the kind of place where the inhabitants had this kind of money to throw around. I felt as though I'd inadvertently walked into the Batcave.

'How do you pay for all this?' I asked suspiciously. If all this stuff turned out to belong to his father who worked for some government division, then I could get myself into a lot of trouble just by seeing it.

He gave me a cheeky wink. 'I've got skills. And don't worry – my parents never come in here.'

I wasn't sure whether to feel reassured or nervous at that

comment. He pointed at a dusty chair well away from the gleaming screens.

'Sit there,' he instructed.

I did as I was told. He turned his back on me and began tapping furiously into one of several keyboards. He didn't even bother to sit down. All I could see on the screens were lines of undulating green code.

'How many Families are there?' he asked. 'I've got the Medicis, Montserrat, Stuart and Bancroft.'

For a moment, I was so taken aback I couldn't think. 'Er…' I stuttered. 'There are five.'

He snapped his fingers. 'Gully!' His hands flew over the keys and he started to mutter to himself. 'Damn. The Montserrat system is well defended.'

I blinked rapidly. 'Are you hacking into the Families' computers?'

'Yeah. Cool, huh? Those bloodguzzlers should learn a bit more about the modern age and protect themselves. The Stuart firewall is a piece of shit.'

' Don't swear,' I said automatically, realising I still didn't know his name, 'I'm not sure this a good idea. If they find out…'

'Relax, lady. I've covered my tracks.'

I bristled slightly at being called 'lady' by a kid. 'You shouldn't mess with the vampires,' I said sternly. 'Even though you're young, they'll still be pissed off when they find you.'

He spun on his heel and faced me, then reached behind without looking and pressed a single key, all the while grinning and sticking out his tongue. 'Too late!' he sang out.

'What? What do you mean too late?'

'The Families have each just emailed the police in order to help them with their enquiries. They've never recruited anyone under the age of twenty-one. They have nothing to do with the abduction of Alice Goldman. Anyone who suggests otherwise, even by implication, will meet their wrath.'

My jaw dropped.

His grin widened. 'I like that word *wrath*. I used it in a story in school last week. The teacher almost wet her knickers in delight.'

'The vampires don't involve themselves in human matters. They'd never contact the police.'

'Except they just did.'

In a corner of the garage, a small red light began to flash and an alarm sounded. I leapt up out of my chair, half expecting a crew of vampires to burst in. The kid just scowled. 'Mum and Dad are home. You'd better go.'

'Um…'

He threw me a tiny piece of card. It was shiny and gold with ROGU3 embossed on it. 'These are my details. Like I said, Alice was my friend so this is a freebie. If you need me again, though, and you're willing to pay, then I can help you out in the future.' He looked wistfully at the now-darkened computer screens. 'There's a lot of more up-to-date equipment I'd like to get.'

I stared down at the card then back at him.

'Rogu3?'

He looked at me as if as I had about three brain cells to rub together. 'It's not Rogu-three. It's Rogue. Now, I really have to go. They don't like it when I spend too much time in here.'

Feeling as if I'd just been sneered at by a teacher, I watched as he pulled up the garage door. He shoved me out, leaving me on his driveway, blinking against the sunshine and wondering whether I'd imagined the whole thing. Had I just entered some strange eleven-year-old's twilight zone? But Rogu3 was true to his word. Less than two hours later, I received a call from my boss telling me to stand down. They had, he informed me, received an unprecedented warning from all the Families and decided it would be safer to pay the Goldmans rather than risk angering the vampires.

I quit the firm a couple of days later, but continued to keep in touch with Rogu3. It would probably be easy to find out his real name – after all I know exactly where he lives – but somehow I feel that would be a betrayal. He's proven to be more than his weight in gold over the last few years, although he has a good enough grasp of just how much his services are worth. In fact, he's become one of the top-grade hackers in the country. I think it helps that he has very little ego. He's not interested in leaving his virtual calling card to let people know he's been in and out of their private lives. He just takes what he needs. And no, the vampires never did catch up with him.

That's why I contacted him about a safe house. I know he always has a ready list of places to doss down in for both his mates and his clients. They're usually temporary hidey-holes, where the real resident has gone off on holiday and left the place empty for a while. He has programmes which track flight and travel agency information. From there it's easy to hack into email accounts and find out whether the hapless holidaymakers have anyone looking after their place and where they keep their spare key. I've never had to use this particular service before and I'm certain that the bill I receive from him once all this is over will be hefty. It's worth it though. It'll be even more worth it if he can also track down the mysterious Lucy.

8

ROOM BY THE HOUR

Once O'Shea has finished speaking to Rogu3, he passes back the receiver. I lift it to my ear but the teenager has already hung up.

'What did he say? Can he do it?'

'He mentioned the words "park" and "walking",' the daemon said grumpily. 'And he said to tell you that this week's word is pettifoggery.'

I smile.

'What's that?' O'Shea asks. 'Some kind of code?'

'No,' I answer. 'He just likes words.'

He rattles the cuffs against the bed frame again. 'Now will you help me get out of this?'

I regard him for a moment. 'I suppose so. If you run off though, you should know that it's probably more than just the vampires that are after you.'

'What do you mean?'

I tell him about the armed police who arrived at the house on Wiltshore Avenue just as we were leaving. His face pales. 'That doesn't make any sense,' he babbles. 'Why would the Families involve the human cops?'

'I don't know, mate. But whatever you do next, you'd better keep your head down.' I find my lock pick and free him from the handcuffs. He springs up then winces; clearly his wounds and blood loss are affecting him more than he realises.

'Are you okay?' I enquire.

'Do you care?'

I consider his question. I have nothing against him, even if his near-death experience almost resulted in my incarceration. I'm not sure he's done anything yet to warrant my care, however.

'The fact that you have to think about the answer tells me what it'll be,' he gripes.

I shrug. What can I say?

He sniffs. 'Maybe I'll stick around here for a few days.'

'Really?'

'If you don't mind.'

I'm surprised, but he'll come in handy if I think of any more questions. 'No, I don't mind.'

He looks at me curiously. 'Why are you so invested in this?'

'I was going to be framed for your murder.'

For a second or two he doesn't respond then he says quietly, 'They were trying to put you away. But they were trying to kill me. Anything I can do to help, I will.'

This time I believe him. 'Then I've got a job for you while we wait for Rogu3 to get back.'

I toss him one of the burner phones. I don't want anyone to trace the landline to this flat, even if Rogu3 trusts it. Besides which, it wouldn't be fair to run up the owners' phone bill. It's expensive enough living in London without my temporary break-in adding to the bills. I glance down at the headboard that is now lying in the middle of the living-room floor. I'm going to have to fix that before I leave, too.

O'Shea waves the phone in the air. 'What do you want me to do with this?'

'A,' I pause and search for the right word, 'colleague of mine was recently taken into hospital. It's related to this. See if you can find which hospital and whether he's still alive or not.'

'There are hundreds of hospitals in London!'

'You'd better get a move on then. And O'Shea?'

'Yes?'

'Don't tell them your name.'

Irritation flickers in his eyes . 'I'm not an idiot.'

'Good. You're looking for a man called Arzo.'

'That's it? Arzo? Is that his first name or last name?'

I consider. 'Huh. I have no idea.'

'Great,' he mutters, 'just great.'

WHILE O'SHEA STARTS on the phone, I ponder my next move. The most useful information at this point would probably be which Family the attacks originated from. Not that I have any hope of penetrating any of the Families, but at least I could narrow my focus and find someone connected to them who could provide more leads. I could go back and scour Wiltshore Avenue and Tam's office but they'll be sealed-off crime scenes by now and I can't risk bumping into the police. The veil of secrecy surrounding all five Families is annoying.

I chew the inside of my cheek. I may not be able to work out which Family is involved but perhaps I can work out which ones aren't. None of this could happen without the sanction of a Family Head. From what little I know, the Heads keep their vampires on extraordinarily short leashes; any vampire who killed or attempted to kill a human without getting the okay first would sign their own death warrant. It would be suicide to march up to one of the Heads and ask whether they were involved but I know at exactly what times the attacks went down. O'Shea's had to be in the window between 9 and 9.50am, just before I entered the house. The office assault happened at about 3.20pm. Whoever carried out the attacks would have contacted their Head immediately afterwards to inform them of their respective failure and success. If the Heads happened to be out in public, then maybe someone noticed whether they received any calls or not. It's a long shot, but worth pursuing.

I check my watch. It's still early in the morning but I reckon today's papers will already have been delivered to the newsagents. It's of little consequence that the shops themselves won't be open yet.

I leave the flat, taking the time to check whether I'm being watched. I don't think it's likely; if anyone knew where I was, I'd probably already be in handcuffs or dead. Fortunately I can't see anyone lurking in the shadows, but I walk slowly and double back once to be sure. It seems, however, that I'm still in the clear.

I locate a newsagent's on the corner of the next street. It's small and grubby, with several handwritten cards posted in the window offering things like discreet massages (any time day or night!) and mixed-breed puppies. As I'd hoped, there's a range of freshly delivered newspapers in neatly tied piles in front of the shop.

I ignore the broadsheets and head for the tabloids. The front pages turn my stomach. Each one details the massacre at Dire Straits in lurid colour. One of them, even more nauseatingly, includes a terrible photo of me with the headline 'Is this a killer?'. That's really not good. I realise how foolish I was to go to that nightclub earlier; Mr Tortoiseshell is unlikely to forget my face. One glimpse of this paper and he'll be on the phone to some hack, selling his story. This entire area is compromised. So much for another three days at 14A Markmore Close.

With no one but myself to blame, I pull out my last crumpled five pound note from my bodice and throw it down onto the nearest pile of papers. I sigh heavily. At least it's still dark.

As soon as I get back to the flat, O'Shea glares at me. 'Where have you been?'

I don't bother answering; instead I start tidying up the debris around him. 'We need to leave.'

'What? Why?'

I pick up the corner of the bed frame and release it from the chair leg. 'Help me put this back.'

He glances at me scornfully but he does as I say. The pair of us take it back to the bedroom and slot it back into place.

'Have you found Arzo yet?'

'No.'

'Has Rogu3 called back?'

'No.'

Damn it. I didn't think it would take him this long. 'Lucy' must have covered her tracks well. I debate whether to call him myself and decide against it. It's more important to get away from Markmore Close while the streets are still quiet.

I hand O'Shea the pile of newspapers. He stares down at the first headline. 'Wow. Did you see what happened to this firm?' He scans the story. 'It's a bunch of private dicks who've been slaughtered.' There's an element of awe in his voice that makes me want to punch him in the face. 'Damn silly name for a company if you ask me.'

'I saw it,' I say shortly.

'You're a PI, aren't you? Did you know these guys?'

I don't respond but something in my face must have given me away because his eyes widen. 'Oh.'

'This whole thing is about more than just you and me, O'Shea.'

He takes several rapid breaths. 'It was just a fucking enhancement spell,' he whispers.

I pick up my plastic bag and give the flat one last sweep, trying hard not to snap at him that clearly it's a hell of a lot more than just an enhancement spell.

'Let's go,' I mutter.

He grabs my arm on the way out. 'I'm sorry. I've caused you a lot of problems and I still don't even know your name.'

'It's Bo.' I have to look away from the sympathy in his face.

'I'm sorry, Bo,' he says quietly.

'Yeah,' I sigh, 'me too.'

WE WALK QUICKLY to the car. There's still no sign of anyone following, although a few early risers drive past us. 'Where are we going to go?' he asks.

'I've got a lock-up garage. It's safe.'

His nose wrinkles. 'A garage?'

'Do you have any better ideas?' I snap.

He roots around in his back pocket, pulls out a wallet and grins when he looks inside. He waves a shiny credit card in my face. 'Yes, I do.'

I roll my eyes. 'I thought you said you weren't an idiot. We can't use a credit card, it'll lead the police straight to us.'

'Duh, it's not my card.' He points to the name on it: Robert Thomson.

'Who is Robert Thomson?'

He shrugs.

'O'Shea?' I say, warningly.

'I found it.'

'You found it.'

'Right before I went to Wiltshore. It might not have been reported yet.'

'That's ridiculous! Of course, it'll have been reported. We can't use it. I can't believe you just nicked somebody's bloody credit card! Is that even your wallet?'

He looks hurt. 'Yes. And I only took it from someone who won't be needing it. The chances of it being reported are miniscule.'

My suspicion deepens. 'Explain.'

He glances out the window. 'Sometimes I help out a mate who works at a morgue.'

'Jesus! You robbed a dead guy?'

'Like I said, he won't be needing it.'

I feel disgusted. I can't believe I'm driving around the London streets with vampires and police chasing me in the company of a petty thief who steals from corpses. 'Even if it's not been reported, we can't just waltz into a hotel and hand it over.'

'Why not?'

'Look at the third newspaper,' I say tersely.

He flicks through, stopping when he sees my face. He whistles. 'That's a crap photo of you.'

'You are such a wanker. The point is, I'm likely to be recognised. And you're covered in dried blood.'

'I know.' He sounds cheery. 'But I also know a place to go. Turn left here.'

I give him my death stare. Unfortunately it doesn't affect him any more than it affects my grandfather.

'I mean it, Bo, trust me. It's my life on the line too, you know.'

I indicate and turn in the direction he's pointing. I have a feeling I'm going to regret this. After about fifteen minutes, when O'Shea tells me to pull up at the curb and I see the neon sign, I realise my feeling was right.

'A love hotel?'

'It's perfect,' he grins.

'O'Shea, if this is somewhere you often come…'

'It's not. In fact, I've never been here. I've just heard about it from a few friends.'

I'm not quite sure what's harder to believe: that he has friends or that I'm sitting in a car about to go into a love hotel with him.

'There'll be a front desk. We'll still have to register.'

He shakes head. 'Didn't I tell you to trust me?'

He gets out of the car. I have no choice but to follow him,

keeping my head down when we enter the lobby – although 'lobby' would be a flattering term for the tiny space at the hotel's entrance. It's lit with a buzzing fluorescent strip light and smells strongly of disinfectant. I dread to think what odour is being covered up. O'Shea's right though: there's no reception and no receptionist, just what looks like a vending machine.

'Ta da!' he trills. 'You've got to love the Japanese for giving us this concept. To avoid embarrassment, all you need to do is swipe your card.' He takes the unfortunate Mr Thomson's credit card and puts in the machine. 'And then you simply choose your room. Would you like the water bed or the S&M theme room?'

I look at him. He nods. 'You're quite right. I've had enough of handcuffs recently too.'

He jabs in his selection and there's a clunking sound as a key drops into the slot below. He scoops it out and offers it to me. I shake my head; I'm not touching that thing. I've got enough problems as it is without getting a communicable disease. He shrugs and pockets it.

'Well, Bo, let's see what delights room 302 has in store for us.'

God. I really want to punch him.

THE ROOM'S not as bad as I imagined it would be. The sheets on water bed smell clean and freshly laundered. It'll do, I suppose. It's better than sitting in the damp lock-up.

O'Shea sits down and takes out the phone I'd given him. 'Only 999 hospitals to go!'

I ignore him and spread out the newspapers, flicking past the front pages to avoid seeing those horrific pictures again. These papers are little more than gossip rags; if the Heads of the Families were out and about yesterday, I'm betting it'll be reported.

I get lucky in the very first newspaper. It seems the Bancroft Head spent all day in a very exclusive spa. Back, crack and sack, I wonder, before remembering the Bancroft Head is not a Lord – she's a Lady. I pull open the drawer of a small side table. This might be a seedy love hotel, but it's still got a Gideon bible in case you want a little spiritual as well as physical enlightenment. I rip out a blank page from the back and scribble down the spa's details. When I look up, I realise O'Shea has stopped speaking into the phone and is staring at me, aghast.

'What?'

'You're going to hell,' he whispers.

'You're kidding me. You'll steal from a dead man and deal in dodgy magic, but I'm the bad one for taking out a blank page from a bible?'

His expression doesn't change. Jeez. Daemons. I go back to scanning the newspaper. When I reach the classified ads, I throw it onto the floor and pull over the next one. This has the spa story as well as a more serious article about a breakfast meeting between Gully and Stuart. The journalist was speculating whether they were considering joining forces to rid themselves of the other Families. That theory is ridiculous but the fact that two of them were together at the same time and in the same place – and just when I was entering Wiltshore Avenue – is going to make my life a damn sight easier. God bless those vampires for ostentatiously sitting in the middle of Hyde Park at a fully decked-out table. And god bless the nosy tourist who captured the entire thing on film and uploaded it to YouTube. If only I still had my smartphone, I could watch it right now.

I'm just finishing skimming through all the papers when there's a crow of delight from O'Shea. He grins at me and gives a thumbs up. Excellent: he must have found Arzo. It finally feels as if we're getting somewhere. There are still no answers, but at least there are places to go to ask some questions.

'Brighton Hospital,' he says. 'I didn't think I was ever going to find him with that one name but it turns out I'm even more charming than I'd realised.'

I try not to look too exasperated.

'He's out of surgery,' he continues, 'and doing well. Visiting hours are from nine am.'

I'm shocked that Arzo is on the mend. I'd have sworn his swarthy cheeks were pressed up against death's door. 'Good work,' I say to O'Shea.

He pats himself on the shoulder. 'I know.'

I check my watch. The sky outside has lightened but it's still only seven am. The Steam Team will be open again in another hour. If I'm to venture outside though, I need some kind of disguise.

My eyes settle on the cream pillow case. It's not perfect but it'll do. I pull at the seams of the case, ripping it apart until it is one long strip of material. I pile my hair on top of my head and wind the fabric around it. I look at my reflection in the wall-to-wall ceiling mirror. It looks a bit weird, but it'll do at a push until I can get hold of something better. Judging by the expression on O'Shea's face, it's not the most attractive look in the world but I'm hardly trying to garner any admirers right now.

'You need to stay here until I can get you some clean clothes,' I say.

He seems relieved. To be fair, he was almost killed yesterday and he probably still needs rest and recuperation. In fact, I'd quite like to hunker down and hide away from the world too. But more than that, I want to find the bastard who's setting me up and who destroyed my firm. I raise a hand to O'Shea in brief farewell and return to the big, scary world.

It's considerably busier on the streets now. Fortunately, most people are in a rush to get to work and either half-asleep or too downtrodden to pay me attention. Equally helpfully, Londoners have this habit of avoiding looking strangers in the eye so they can pretend nobody else exists. Some days it annoys me; today it could save my life. I walk briskly to the car and nobody gives me a second glance, then I drive to The Steam Team.

I arrive early, parking round the back. I'm more nervous than I'd like to admit. The remnants of my smashed smartphone are probably still on the pavement in front of Rebecca's dry cleaners. It would be stupid to imagine that the police haven't already been around to check the premises and it's possible they're still keeping them under surveillance. At least I know that there's a back door.

I hurry down a small alleyway, then clamber over the stone wall at the end, jumping into the scrap of back garden that belongs to the shop. Whoever attacked O'Shea must have done this back at Wiltshore Avenue to avoid me catching sight of them. I smile grimly. I need to be better at sneaking around than they were.

I quickly pick the lock on the back door and let myself inside to wait for Becks. I'm relieved to spot my leather jacket and the rest of my clothes hanging up on one of the doors. As much as I like the dress, it's impractical and, given all the crawling around and sweating I've been doing, it's rather smelly. I nip into the room where I showered before and quickly change. It's a gamble putting on the same clothes I was wearing yesterday morning but I decide it's exactly what my pursuers – be they of the human or triber variety – won't expect.

In the back room where the unclaimed clothes are kept, I find a spare suit that looks like it'll fit O'Shea, and a flowery hat that was probably worn by some over-bearing mother-in-law at a wedding. It's an incongruous look with the dark leather, but it's a step up from the pillow case and I decide it makes me look like some kind of funky art student. I'm just adjusting it when I hear Rebecca come in.

'I don't know why you're here again,' she says.

I freeze. Shit. Someone is with her. 'As I told you, I've not seen Bo Blackman for at least a month.'

'And as I told you, I find that difficult to believe.'

It's a deep male voice. There's an edge to it that suggests it's more than just human. Which means he's probably a vampire. I keep very still and try not to breathe. Vampire is much worse than police.

'I don't want to hurt Ms Blackman.'

Lie.

'I just want to ask her a few questions.'

Utter horseshit.

'Well, if I see her I'll tell her you're looking for her. What's your name again?' I have to give it to Becks, she's remarkably unruffled. I silently applaud her control. But if this is the same vampire who's responsible for the other attacks, then she could be in a lot of danger. I tense, ready to spring out if need be. Not that I have any chance of facing off against a vampire, but maybe the sight of me will distract him.

'Ursus.'

I blink. Sounds like arse. Quite fitting, really.

'Here's my card. She can call me on that number day or night.'

The door jangles, signalling his departure. I hear Becks exhale in relief. I stay where I am, waiting for her to come round to the back to find me. Arse probably still has eyes on the front of the shop. I'm tempted to leave her in peace; she'll be safer if I leave without seeing her, but I need to see that card. I need to know which Family that vampire is from.

As soon as she rounds the corner and sees me, she shrieks, then clutches her chest and gasps.

'Bloody HELL, Bo, you just about gave me a heart attack!'

'I'm sorry.' I give her a moment to recover. 'I won't stay. It's not safe for you if I'm here. I just need to see the card that vampire left.'

She looks surprised, then passes it over. 'I was going to chuck it in the bin with the others.'

'What others?'

She looks grim. 'Wait here.'

While Rebecca disappears into her office, I check the card. It's a deep midnight blue, signifying the Montserrat Family. I'm feeling pleased with myself until she emerges holding several other cards. I flip through each one, my horror growing. Red: Medici. Black: Stuart. Silver: Gully. White: Bancroft. Every single freaking vampire Family has been here looking for me.

'Do you want these too?' She holds out several more cards. 'They're from the police.'

'No, I…' I stutter and end up just shaking my head.

'I saw what happened at Dire Straits, Bo. What the hell is going on?'

'I'm damned if I know.'

'You know if there's anything I can do…'

I know,' I say softly. 'You've already done enough, Becks. I'll stay away for the near future. Don't worry about me. I've got a plan.'

She looks at me sceptically. She knows me too well. I wish I really did have a plan though.

9

DOCTORS AND NURSES

By the time I leave The Steam Team and start driving towards Brighton Hospital, the London traffic is in full swing and it's not long before I hit full gridlock. I feel the frustration building up inside me. The driver in front seems more concerned with checking her make-up in the mirror than paying attention to the lights, whilst on my right there's a kid who not only looks too young to be driving, but also has some kind of godawful rap music blaring out at maximum volume.

Telling myself there's nothing I can possibly do to make the traffic move any faster, I grab the burner phone. I'll have to discard it after these calls; it's probably almost out of credit anyway. Ignoring all the laws about mobile phone use while driving – not that you could call moving at two miles an hour driving – I ring the ridiculously exclusive spa where the Bancroft Family Head spent her day. My call is answered within three rings.

'Good morning, Spa de Loti, Angelique speaking,' the receptionist trills. 'How may I help you?'

I adapt my accent to the way I speak when I want to needle my grandfather. 'Good morning, Angelique. This is Midnight calling from the Bancroft estate.' I know Midnight is a silly name, but I also know a human will accept it as a vampire *nom de plume* more readily than, say, Trudy or Jane.

There's the slightest intake of breath, then Angelique speaks again. 'I'll transfer you to our Spa Director.'

'Oh, goodness, Angelique, there's no need for that.' Repeatedly using someone's name helps them to connect to you; the more often I say 'Angelique', the more likely she is to trust me. 'It's not a serious matter. It's simply that La Bancroft enjoyed her day so much yesterday, I've been requested to make a note of her treatments so she can repeat the experience.'

'Oh, yes, okay, I'll get that information for you. It's the same treatment she has every Wednesday though. I don't think there was anything different this week. Shall I email it all across anyway?'

'There's no need for that,' I respond smoothly. 'It'll be more helpful if you could just tell me now.' I hope that the Spa De Loti receptionist is unnerved enough to be speaking to a vampire to not question my request.

'Uh, certainly, yes. Please hold the line.'

New Age muzak fills my ear. I hold the phone away for a moment, but that just makes the rap music from the next car seem louder. I have visions of Angelique wearing a white mock doctor's outfit, double checking with the Bancroft Family on another line and then telling me in a suddenly rediscovered Cockney accent to piss off. She's not that suspicious, however.

'Ms Midnight? The treatments were our acid burn exfoliate body scrub, smouldering hot stone massage and sensory deprivation tub.'

'I see. Angelique, can you confirm for me when the deprivation tub began and ended? I've heard it's so amazing that it feels like five minutes when it's actually an hour. I'd like to have the definitive answer for Ms Bancroft.'

'It started at two o'clock and finished at four. It's rather a long period of time but I guess you guys are used to be in small enclosed spaces like coffins.'

Oops, Angelique, I think to myself, you forgot yourself for a second there. 'We don't sleep in coffins,' I say, in my chilliest tones.

'Oh, goodness, I'm so sorry, I didn't mean to offend you! I'm sorry, I didn't…'

'That will be all.' I hang up on the poor girl who is still apologising.

The lights turn green and a slow trickle of cars seeps through. I drive forward, making it to the front of the queue just as they flick red again. Tapping my fingers impatiently on the steering wheel, I consider the information I've been given. Aside from the fact that Spa De Loti has some seriously disturbing sounding treatments – acid burn exfoliate, anyone? – I feel like I can cross Bancroft off my list for the incident at Tam's office.

The Families all have immunity from human prosecution. They don't stop randomly killing people because they're worried they'll end up in prison: they stop themselves because it's bad PR. I can't believe that the Head responsible for the worst bloodguzzler attack in years would be out of contact while it was going down. Then I think of the fact that every single Family dropped in to see Rebecca. Perhaps they've banded together, put aside their usual animosity and are all in it together.

No. They may have an uneasy truce but they've been at each other's throats for the last three hundred years. A stupid enhancement spell from a dodgy daemon isn't going to change that. I move the Bancroft Family to the bottom of my list of suspects. I have to trust my gut on this.

Once I'm past Marble Arch, the traffic eases and I put my foot down. I swing into the Brighton Hospital car park a little after ten o'clock. I balk at the displayed parking charges – how can a hospital expect people to pay that much? I'm down to my last few coins and they won't even cover half an hour. I'm tempted to drive around and find somewhere cheaper but the traffic has annoyed me and I'm going to have to return this car sooner or later. Where would be safer to leave it than here? I feel a little guilty about racking up hefty charges for the owner. I promise myself that I'll pay it back as soon as I can access my bank account safely again.

I stroll nonchalantly into the hospital's main entrance, going by the maxim that if you look as if you know where you're going, no one will stop you. It works. The ICU ward is on the third floor so I stick on a bright, confident smile and murmur good morning to several startled people. There's not a flicker of recognition on anyone's face, so the silly hat must be doing its job. I go into the lift and press the button for the fourth floor – paediatrics.

When the lift opens I ignore the main desk and turn right, hoping I'll find the doctor's lounge. I'm in luck. There's a nurse inside sipping a cup of coffee. She barely glances at me so I mutter a brief greeting and make a hasty exit. I walk to the end of the corridor, glancing into the rooms until I find what I'm looking for.

By the fifth room, where the occupant is hooked up to a beeping machine, I've got what I need. I look around then duck inside.

The person in the bed is a young boy, about eight years old. His face is pale and his eyes are closed. I smooth back a lock of hair from his forehead and check the chart at the foot of his bed. Cycling accident with internal haemorrhaging. Poor kid.

The beeping is from his heart monitor. It's not connected to anything other than the boy himself so removing it will do no damage. I fiddle with the back of it until I find the cable then I yank it out. It continues to beep for a few moments before falling silent. I check the boy is okay, while the alarm at the main desk begins to sound, then I dash out of the room and nip into the next one to avoid being spotted.

A small girl is sitting up in bed and clutching a teddy bear. She gives me a solemn look. 'You're not a doctor.'

I smile at her. 'I'm a special doctor.'

She juts her bottom lip out in an expression that's remarkably similar to O'Shea's. 'No, you're not.'

'I am. I'm a secret doctor. I only help people in dire straits.'

She frowns. 'What's dire straits?'

'When you're in lots of trouble.'

She tightens her grip on the teddy. 'I'm not in dire straits. I'm in remish.' She screws up her face to concentrate on getting the word out, 'Remission'.

'Oh! Then I'm in entirely the wrong room. Don't tell anyone I was here. They'll think I made a mistake.'

'But you did make a mistake.'

She has me there. 'Yes, you're right. I did. But I'll get into trouble if anyone finds out.'

''Kay then.' She looks at me shyly. 'I like your hat.'

Bugger. 'Then it's yours!' I pull it off my head and carefully place it on hers.

A huge smile spreads across face, making its loss suddenly worthwhile. 'Thank you.'

'You're welcome.' I place my finger to my lips and leave.

I only have a few seconds. I head back to the lounge and find a discarded white coat on the back of the door. I pull it on, glad it's large enough to fit over my jacket, then pull out several disposable surgical masks from a box on the coffee table and stuff them into the pocket. I duck out, just as the coffee-drinking nurse returns. I keep my head down, tie on one of the masks and take the lift back down to the third floor.

There's a different atmosphere here. Everyone speaks in hushed tones, as if by talking normally they might disturb the unconscious patients. I pray that Arzo isn't one of the unconscious ones.

The ward is bisected by a long corridor. I'll give myself away if I have to check every single room. Fortunately I spot a group of doctors clustered by the nurses' station. Students. Perfect.

I join them, hanging around at the back. A few turn round and give me odd looks but no one says anything. I nod at them as if I'm equally engaged in the serious business of learning medicine. I hope they're about to start their rounds and not just finishing them.

I'm in luck. An older looking woman approaches holding a clipboard. 'Come on then,' she says briskly and turns on her heel.

As one, we trot after her. She steers us into the first room, halting by a patient who is using breathing apparatus and is surrounded by an array of machines.

'Admitted three days ago after collapsing from chest pains,' she states, 'later diagnosed as a myocardial infarction. Subsequent exploratory surgery revealed the disruption of an atherosclerotic plaque in an epicardial coronary artery. The biotelemetry indicates returning function, however he still has ventricular tachycardia.'

It's just as well I'm wearing the surgical mask because my jaw drops. I've not been this baffled by the English language since the last time I ventured into Starbucks.

'You.'

I realise with horror that she's pointing at me. 'What next steps should the trauma team take to ensure recovery?'

Oh shit, oh shit, oh shit. My mind races, alighting on a re-run of *ER* which I saw recently. 'Er, pulmonary embolism.'

'What about it?' Her eyes bore into me.

'We should be careful of it,' I say, feeling and sounding like a total idiot. Going by the expression on her face, she feels exactly the same. I'm dismissed with a disgusted wave of her hand and she directs her question to someone else. I stick my head down and look at my feet. There must be an easier way to sneak into a hospital room.

At least I was so rubbish at answering her first question that she doesn't ask me anything else. We shuffle from bed to bed and room to room, discussing a range of patients who all seem to be at death's door. Between the clinical hospital smell, the endless trail of misery and the emotionless Q&A, I feel like my soul is being sucked away. I had been nervous about seeing Arzo again but, by the time our little group comes across him, I'm so relieved I have to stop myself from leaping on him to give him a great big kiss.

Despite the fact there are eleven of us in the group, his eyes immediately fall on me. His expression doesn't change but I get the feeling he's been waiting for me to arrive. I praise the gods that he's conscious and alert. He doesn't actually seem that sick.

'Um, doctor?' One of the students puts up a nervous hand. 'Why is this patient in ICU?'

She chuckles. I'm surprised by the sudden show of humour. 'He presented yesterday with severe trauma after an attack. As you can see he is recovering swiftly, however, and is about to be transferred to another ward.'

The students are murmuring to each other. If he were a triber, he wouldn't be in this ward; he wouldn't even be in this wing. But his bright-eyed awareness and rapid recovery time are causing a bit of anxiety. I'm feeling somewhat anxious myself. I'm convinced there's something odd going on here. After all, I could have sworn he was bloody well dead yesterday.

I hover behind when the group leaves, hoping they won't notice my absence. I close the door quietly and turn to face him.

'Hey darlin'.'

I give him a half smile. 'Hey Arzo.' I don't have time to beat around the bush. 'Did Tam try to have me framed for murder?'

'What? No grapes or flowers?'

I pull off the mask and glare at him. 'Answer the sodding question.'

There's a spark of answering anger in his face. 'Tam's dead.'

'I know. I was there.'

'Hiding in the ceiling like a goddamn rat.'

I guess we're past the 'hey darling' stage now. 'I had good reason.' I lean forward. 'Whether Tam's dead or not doesn't answer my question.'

'You've worked at Dire Straits for two years, Bo. Why would he do something like that?'

'You tell me.'

'Tam wouldn't do that.'

'Then how do you explain the fact that the target I was supposed to serve with a summons yesterday was about to bleed out? And about thirty seconds after I was supposed to enter the property the freaking police showed up? And not just the normal police either – these guys had guns! Since when do armed police make house calls at a place like Wiltshore Avenue?' My voice is getting higher and I can feel myself shaking. But I don't care. I need some answers.

'If Tam was trying to set you up, why was he attacked a couple of hours later?'

'How in the hell do I know? Maybe they were pissed off that it didn't work so they came after him instead.'

'What do you mean "it didn't work"? All I know is you had a summons for the Agathos court against some half-breed called O'Shee.'

'O'Shea,' I correct, suspicious of his pleas of ignorance.

'I don't know what happened to you yesterday, Bo. Talk me through it.'

I circle his bed like a caged cat. 'Put your hands where I can see them first.'

He looks at me, exasperated, but does as I ask, placing them on top of the sheet. 'I'm in ICU, Bo. I'm hardly in a position to attack you.'

'You look pretty damn healthy to me.'

'Check my chart,' he says quietly.

I retrieve his chart and scan it. My face pales.

'That vampire severed my spinal cord.'

I stare at him.

'I'm never going to walk again.'

I swallow hard. 'I'm sorry,' I whisper. 'But that doesn't mean you didn't betray me.'

'There was no betrayal, Bo. Not from me and not from Tam.'

I sit on a chair by the bed. 'So talk to me, Arzo. Tell me what happened and how it went down.'

A muscle jerks in his cheek. 'All I know is that we received a request from a barrister over at the Agathos court. It was nothing out of the ordinary. They just needed someone to deliver a summons to a daemon dealing in under-the-counter magic. We've had hundreds of cases like it. You know that.'

'What's the lawyer's name?'

'Something French. D'Argneau, perhaps.'

'Has he used us before?'

'Once or twice.'

I'm not going to give him an inch. 'Was it once or was it twice?'

He gives an odd, humourless laugh. 'You know, when Tam hired you I had a lot of misgivings. Now I'm starting to under-stand what he saw in you.'

I don't blink. Arzo sighs. 'It was twice. Both were summons. I think Boris took them.'

'Why didn't Boris take this one?'

He shrugs. 'He was on another case.'

My body tenses in anticipation of my next question. 'I need to know this, Arzo. Did this lawyer ask specifically for me?'

'No.' His gaze is frank and honest.

'Why did Tam assign me?'

'Because your name was at the top of the fucking list, that's all. You were the next person due out.'

I absorb this information. As far as I can tell, he's speaking the truth.

'So why was Dire Straits attacked?'

'I don't know,' he says helplessly. 'I have no goddamn idea.'

'It has to be connected to O'Shea. It's too much of a coincidence not to be. Which Family was the vampire from? From where I was hiding, I could only see his head.'

'There was nothing. No colours or badges that I saw.'

I give him a hard look. 'Are you sure?'

He nods.

'It's possible that all the Families are involved.' I tell him about the different cards that have been left with Rebecca. Oddly, he doesn't seem too surprised. In fact, he shifts somewhat uncomfortably.

'Ah,' he says, 'yes, they're all taking an interest.'

I'm immediately on my guard. After all, he's been in hospital for the better part of the last day. 'How do you know?'

A shadow falls across the bed and a deep voice interrupts us. 'Because I told him.'

I look up and immediately recognise the Montserrat Family Head.

10

THE OFFER

It takes me less than three seconds to leap to my feet, pick up the chair and lift it in the air. I fling it with all my might at the vampire but he neatly sidesteps, moving faster than I'd have thought possible, and the chair splinters against the opposite wall.

'You work with some interesting people, Arzo,' the vampire comments in oddly accented English.

I growl and back away. There's a window to my left but we're on the third floor. Even if I could open it and jump out, it's unlikely that I'd escape without breaking several limbs. The vampire is blocking the only other exit. Flight is out; I'm going to have to fight.

I fumble inside my jacket to pull out the pepper spray which I returned to its usual pocket before leaving The Steam Team. Due to the stupid doctor's coat I'm still wearing, it's hard to extricate although I finally manage it.

'Bo,' Arzo begins.

'Shut up,' I hiss. I can't believe I fell for his freaking lies.

'It's not what you think, Bo,' he continues.

I ignore him and keep my eyes trained on the vampire. He's

larger in person than he looks in the photos. His frame fits the entire doorway although it's clear there's not an ounce of fat on his body – if vampires can get fat, that is. No, this guy's all muscle. He's wearing a well-tailored suit in the Montserrat colour of midnight blue, but it defines the strength in his body rather than disguising it. Trust me to get on the wrong side of the one Family Head who's capable of doing his own dirty work. It'll be a miracle if I get out of this alive.

He inclines his head. His hair is dark and close-cropped. He's not the bloodguzzler who attacked Dire Straits but that doesn't mean it wasn't one of his minions. In fact, it's looking increasingly likely. No wonder Arzo survived when everyone else was slaughtered – he must be working for them. I bet he's pissed off about having to spend the rest of his life in a wheelchair as a result. I wonder for a moment if that was part of the plan to make his own story more believable. It's a hell of a sacrifice if it's true.

'I've met your grandfather a few times, Ms Blackman. He's an' – the vampire licks his lips for a moment, displaying white, even teeth – 'interesting person.' At least he's keeping his fangs hidden.

'He'll be an even more interesting person to know when he discovers you've murdered me,' I snarl.

He looks surprised then smiles. 'Oh, I'm not here to hurt you.'

'Bo,' interrupts Arzo, 'listen to him. He's telling the truth.'

'I thought I told you to shut up.'

The vampire raises his eyebrows at Arzo. 'She's feisty.'

I grip the pepper spray. Maybe if I can get a small dose in his eyes, then leap over the bed and kick him in the side to get out of the door…

'Ms Blackman,' he holds his palms up towards me, 'please put that silly spray down.'

I raise it an inch higher. If I'm going down, it's not without a fight.

'It's not going to help you.' The tone is his voice is slightly patronising. It's amazing how often people speak to me like that because of my height. Normally it doesn't bother me; right now I feel intensely annoyed.

'Just tell me one thing, Arzo,' I say, deciding to piss off the vampire by ignoring him. 'How long have you been working for the fucking bloodguzzlers?'

'I don't work for them, Bo,' Arzo begins.

Before he can finish, I take advantage of the fact that the looming vampire flicks his eyes towards Arzo and press down on the canister, letting loose a jet of stinging spray. Then I bounce up, using one toe on the edge of the hospital bed to launch up and over. I'm not even back on the ground when I realise my attempt is futile. The spray hasn't affected Montserrat and, even though I attempt to kick out and connect with his ribs to knock him to the side, he grabs me by the waist. Pulling me down, he twists my body round until he's holding me against him but facing Arzo.

'Dumb move,' he whispers in my ear. He smells of dark masculine spice.

I draw my elbow back to ram it into his stomach but his arm tightens until I can't move. In fact, I can barely breathe.

Arzo looks exasperated. 'You're good, Bo, but you're not that good.'

'It was worth a try,' I mutter.

'As I was saying,' he says, 'I don't work for the vampires.'

'That's not what it looks like from here.'

'I work *with* the vampires,' he continues.

I sneer. 'Nobody works with the vampires, Arzo. They stick to their own. You're fooling yourself if you think otherwise.'

Montserrat chuckles. 'Oh, but he is our own, Ms Blackman.'

I stop trying to resist his hold. 'He's no bloodguzzler.'

'No,' says Arzo. 'I'm Sanguine.'

I frown at him. That was Rogu3's word of the week a couple of years ago so I know exactly what it means. 'Optimistic and buoyant in the face of adversity?' I ask sarcastically.

'He was recruited,' says Montserrat. 'But it didn't take.'

'What in hell do you mean?'

Arzo sighs. 'What do you know about the Families' recruitment?'

I try to shrug but my movement is limited thanks to my captor. 'Every ten years or so they recruit enough new members to keep their numbers steady at around five hundred. The process is kept secret but not everyone makes it. That's it, that's all I know.'

'In order to turn you,' Montserrat says silkily into my ear, 'I would inject you with blood from of one of our higher-order vampires. It takes a full moon cycle to change completely.'

'So? So what?'

'Your body only accepts the change when you drink.'

'When I guzzle blood, you mean.'

His grip tightens until it's painful. 'We don't like the term bloodguzzler, Ms Blackman. And as I was saying, you need to drink blood to fully turn. It's a show of strength to last the full term. Most only hold out a couple of days but some make it right up to the end.'

'And some,' Arzo adds, 'never drink.'

I look at him. 'You were turned? But you didn't drink blood?'

He nods.

'So are you a vampire or not?'

'I'm not. I'm Sanguine. I have traces of vampire blood in my system so I heal quickly and I'm stronger than most.' He glances up at Montserrat. 'I'm also loyal to my Family. But I'm still human.'

'Are you sure about that?'

'The Families aren't evil, Bo.'

'Try telling Tam that.'

'He wasn't a sanctioned hit,' Montserrat says.

'Bullshit. No vampire makes a move unless the Head says so. Even I know that.'

'That used to be the case. But there have been several unexplained deaths and disappearances across all five Families. And in each case, we've tracked their movements. They've all met with the daemon.'

'O'Shea?'

'Yes.'

'So you ordered someone to take him down and sent me to take the fall?'

'We don't want him dead, Ms Blackman. We want to talk to him. We had nothing to do with what happened to him.'

'It was a vampire. There and at Dire Straits.'

'We know. That's why we need to find the culprits and deal with them before this becomes a bloodbath.'

'It's already a bloodbath,' I retort. 'Besides, I don't know where O'Shea is. I've not seen him since yesterday.'

Montserrat finally releases me. I spin round and take several steps backwards. He watches me with cool, dark eyes.

'You're not a very good liar.'

I'm a damn good liar. I scowl at him.

'We have O'Shea.' He folds his arms across his chest. 'I'm not sure your employer would be pleased to know that your target is also your lover.'

I stare at him blankly.

'Water bed?' His eyes dance.

I feel sick to my stomach. 'My employer's dead.' I look into his eyes. 'Is O'Shea?'

'I told you. We only want to talk to him.'

If O'Shea refuses to answer their questions, I can only imagine what the consequences will be. Montserrat must sense what I'm thinking because he adds quickly, 'We're not going to hurt him. We're not monsters.'

I snort.

'You've proven yourself resourceful, Ms Blackman. You got this far and you're still alive. You're also out of options.'

'No, I'm not,' I'm betting he doesn't know about Rogu3.

'The police are after you because of the daemon. And you don't even have him any more. It's just a matter of time before one of the other Families catches up with you and drains you of every drop of blood in your system.'

I sense there's something else he wants to say so I wait.

'I'll recruit you.'

Whatever I'm expecting, it isn't that. 'It's not even recruiting season. And I don't want to be a damn vampire.'

He takes a step towards me. I hold my ground. 'The recent deaths allow me to set a precedent and open up the ranks early. I can include you on the list.'

'Why?'

'I need someone with investigative skills who can find out what is going on with my vampires.' There's a note of frustration in his voice that *his* vampires might be turning traitor but I can't shake the feeling that none of this fits.

I jerk my head at Arzo. 'Use him.'

'He's already known. You're not.'

'I don't want to be a vampire,' I repeat.

'Just don't drink,' Arzo interjects. 'Hold out for next full moon and you'll remain human.'

I throw him a look. From what he's already intimated, that might be easier said than done.

'It's hard, Bo,' he says softly. 'It's not impossible.'

'No.' My response is flat.

'You'll be protected from the police.'

'I can protect myself.'

'The other Families want to talk to you. They know you're involved. I doubt they'll be as reasonable as I'm being,' Montserrat says

'Except I'm not involved,' I point out. 'I was just in the wrong place at the wrong time.'

'Involved by default.' He looks at me seriously. 'Do this and you'll find out who set you up. Who killed your boss and your friends.'

'I don't need to be a fucking vampire to do that.'

'Yes, Ms Blackman, you do. You'll gain access to everyone who might have something to do with this. You already know it was a vampire. Sign up and you'll find out which one.'

'I won't do it. Every Family wants to talk to me. That means the mastermind behind all this knows I was at Wiltshore and that I worked for Dire Straits. Let's face it,' I scoff, 'my picture's been all over the news. As I soon as I show up as a newly-minted vampire recruit, I'll be mincemeat.'

His eyes gleam. 'But that's where the genius of this lies. You can be so angry that your life has been taken away from you that you'll do anything to screw up the Families.'

'I *am* angry that my life has been taken away.'

'So do something about it,' he challenges.

'No.'

'Bo, take a day or two to think about it,' Arzo says. 'It's not the new moon until Saturday. You've got time.'

I stare at them both defiantly. 'I'm not going to change my mind.'

Montserrat remains impassive although Arzo visibly sags.

'Are you going to let me leave?' I ask. 'Or are you going to kill me because I won't accept your desirable offer?'

A muscle throbs in the vampire's cheek. For a moment, I'm genuinely not sure what he's going to do then he steps aside and gestures to the door. 'You're free to go.'

'Bo, don't do this. Don't walk away,' pleads Arzo.

I straighten the lapels of my doctor's coat and start to walk out. I'm almost at the door when Montserrat catches my arm. I stop and look at him. His face is inches from mine. He reaches into his suit pocket and pulls out a card. It's midnight blue, like his suit.

'I've already got one of those,' I say, thinking about the ones Rebecca gave me earlier.

'This is a direct line.' He holds it up. 'In case you change your mind.'

I look at the card then at him. 'I'm not going to change my mind.'

'Take it anyway.'

I sigh and, for the sake of getting out alive, I take it.

'I'll see you around, Ms Blackman.'

I give him an evil look. 'Not if I see you first.' And without a backward glance at Arzo, I stalk out.

11

THE TAIL

It's not until I'm back in the car park, with the surgical mask firmly in place, that I finally allow myself to relax. In fact, I stagger round the side of the hospital out of sight from any curious eyes and double over. Nausea surges through me and I yank up the mask to be sick but nothing comes up. Becoming a member of one of the Families is obviously not the most appealing prospect.

When I finally straighten up, I think about what just happened. I'm still not convinced that Tam wasn't involved in framing me but I'm prepared to acknowledge that Arzo is innocent. As innocent as someone in league with the vampires can be. No wonder he survived the attack at Dire Straits. Being Sanguine clearly offers a lot in terms of physical strength. I can't believe I'd not heard of them before. It also occurs to me there are hundreds, perhaps thousands, of people out there who would be thrilled to be given a direct pass like this into the Montserrat Family.

I smile slightly at the thought of what my grandfather would say were he to find out I'd joined forces with the vampires, then I get with the programme. I feel bad about O'Shea and I hope they don't kill him. He may have his faults but I don't think he's a bad sort. I don't care about him enough to stage a rescue, however. He's on his own – much like I feel now.

I could walk away. Whatever is going on, the Families are going to deal with it. I could give myself up to the police and let the cards fall where they may. But I still find it hard to believe any vampire would turn on their Family Head, regardless of what Montserrat has told me. Equally, there's the burning need for revenge for all that's happened. I also like the idea of solving this case and getting one over on the vampires. And I still have two leads: O'Shea's mysterious client Lucy, and now the lawyer, D'Argneau. I ain't giving up just yet.

I have one burner phone left. I'm tempted to call Rogu3 to find out what he's discovered but he'll be in school now and won't thank me for interrupting. He may be a hacker but he takes his education seriously. That leaves the lawyer.

With nothing more to go on than his name, I need to do some research. I'm fairly certain there's a public library less than twenty minutes away so, ignoring the car, I jog off to find it, shoving the doctor's coat into a nearby bin as I go. I keep the surgical mask on. Maybe I can get away with looking like someone who's trying to avoid picking up a seasonal cold.

It works. Even though I pass a police station with my own badly-posed photo staring out at me, no one bats an eyelid. How on earth do the police catch anyone when the public walk around in their own little worlds, never registering the people around them? Good for me; bad for the world.

It doesn't take long to get to the library. It's an old building, its grimy bricks testifying to years of pollution, but it has a certain elegance. I slow to a walk as I reach the front entrance and pass under an impressive colonnade. There's a warm and welcoming atmosphere inside. Brightly coloured posters tell of forthcoming readings and new books. A young guy pushing a loaded trolley smiles at me. I ask him where the computers are and he directs me towards a sunny area at the back of the building.

As it's still early, most of the computers are free. There's a tired looking woman at one of the desks scanning through job advertisements, and someone who looks like a student writing an assignment. Other than that, I've got the space to myself. I pull up a chair and start typing.

Thanks to the fact that D'Argneau is an unusual name, it doesn't take long to find what I'm looking for. There are only two barristers with that surname and one deals only with the human family courts. I click on the second one and am taken immediately to D'Argneau & Associates. That's interesting. He's not just a lawyer – he leads his own firm, and a large one by the looks of it. It seems strange that he wouldn't use his own investigative facilities or that he'd waste his time dealing in what initially appeared to be such a small matter.

I scan through the different pages on the site until I find the bouncily titled 'Our Team'. When the photos and biographies appear, however, I'm absolutely floored. I stare at D'Argneau's picture, trying to make sense of it. There's no doubt – same horn-rimmed glasses, same snappy suit and same hair. The lawyer D'Argneau is none other than Mr Tortoiseshell whom I almost shagged in the middle of the street. I try to ignore the return of rising nausea.

I clench and unclench my fists, reading his history. He graduated from Cambridge, opening D'Argneau & Associates when he was only twenty-five years old. Since then the practice has gone from strength to strength. He's worked with both triber and human clients, although there's no mention of any of the Families. There's nothing about his personal life. I search some more, hoping that the less corporate websites will offer more information. All I find are news articles about different cases he's fought. He seems to have a high success rate. Many of them involve the Agathos court; one includes a high-profile case that I remember reading about. Something to do with a daemon deciding to launch an attack on Buckingham Palace, of all places. The daemon was banged up for five years, although he's likely to be freed sooner than that. The legal community seemed to be of the opinion that D'Argneau did a sterling job of defending him and, were he to have had any other lawyer, he'd be in prison for a good deal longer.

I make a note of the firm's address, quelling the tremble in my hand and trying to remain unemotional. It's pretty fucking difficult. They have swanky offices smack bang in the centre of the city. D'Argneau is clearly doing very well for himself, although not so well that he doesn't feel the need to hang around lousy nightclubs in the middle of the night. Unless that's part of the plan – whatever it may be.

I move to YouTube to find the video of Gully and Stuart's public meeting. I'm not about to take Montserrat's word that the Family Heads are not involved. The library's internet isn't particularly fast and the video takes a long time to buffer. I lean back in my chair and glance around. The student is fast asleep, his head buried in his arms, while the jobseeker is looking more optimistic, tapping enthusiastically at her keyboard. Another person is sitting in front of the computer next to her. I casually crane my neck around and freeze. It's a woman whom I've definitely seen before: she was the driver putting on her make-up in the car in front of me when I was on my way to the hospital. I realise she couldn't have been doing her lippy at all – she was observing me.

Ice-cold fear hits my stomach. I thought I'd done a good job checking for tails. Clearly I'm getting sloppy. This is a screw-up which could cost me dearly.

Trying not to appear obvious, I swivel back to my screen and clear the history. Someone like Rogu3 could easily find out which sites I visited and what I searched for; I'm banking on the fact that few people are as skilled as him. Once I'm satisfied I've done the best job I can concealing my tracks, I head for the restroom.

As soon as I enter, I realise I've made a mistake. It's a tiny room with only one stall and the window is too small to squeeze through. I glance at the ceiling for old times' sake but, even if I could clamber up inside it, it would be a stupid idea. I wouldn't get anywhere fast and I'd end up stuck inside this building with someone who may very well want my head on a bloody platter. However, my follower is unlikely to know there's no way out so I take my time, hovering at the sink.

I'm correct in my assumption. After a few minutes, the restroom door opens and she enters. I give her the brief meaningless smile of a stranger and turn on the tap. Now she's up close, I can tell she's entirely human. She doesn't seem like a copper so I have to assume she's either working officially for one of the Families, which would be odd given her humanity, or she's with Montserrat's theoretically rogue bloodguzzlers. At least she doesn't smell of rosewater.

My plan is to confront her and find out who she is and what's going on but, as she heads into the stall to maintain her cover of having a pee, I register the tell-tale bulge at her back in the mirror's reflection. I'm not about to take any chances with anyone who has a gun. There are smarter ways to play this.

I make sure the tap is on full blast so the gushing water will cover the sound of the opening door, then I quickly duck out and head for the library exit. As soon as I'm outside, I race across the road, dodging a couple of irritated drivers, then crouch down behind a parked vehicle opposite. If I stick my head up far enough, I have a clear line of sight towards the library doors. It takes her less than twenty seconds to appear and she's less circumspect now, glancing up and down the street to work out where I've gone. I watch her, taking note of her panicked expression then, when she decides to turn right and head for the busy pedestrian precinct, I follow.

I'm aware that I'm in a precarious position. She has no idea which direction I've gone in so she keeps twisting her head around to look for me. I have to veer in between people to stay hidden from her view. Once I dash into a shop when she stops in her tracks and turns towards me. I maintain a good distance from her but my situation is far from ideal. Any good tracker will never be alone; there could be a team which can switch places with her and avoid detection. I'm on my own although, as far as I can tell, so is she. I can't help wondering if she's O'Shea's online Lucy.

We continue like this for some time. There's something about her twitchy attitude that confuses me. The fact she's carrying a gun suggests she's a professional. We're not in the United States of America, after all. It's not easy to get hold of a weapon in this country, even in London, unless you're connected. She's not particularly well versed in the art of tailing though and that makes me think she's more amateur than she should be.

Eventually she seems to give up on me and stops in the middle of the street. I watch her from behind a bus shelter while she stares dejectedly at her feet. Then she turns round, makes her way down the steps to the Underground, and the darkness quickly swallows her up.

I dash back across the street, narrowly avoiding being run over by a courier cyclist who has other things on his mind, and jog down after her. If she's getting on a train, I'll lose her.

I hop over the turnstile, ignoring the shocked gasp from the commuters around me, and sprint forward. My heart sinks as I register two separate platforms: one for trains heading north and one for the southbound. I have a fifty-fifty shot of getting it right. I choose north and run down the next set of stairs. As soon as I hit the platform, I realise I've made the wrong decision. She's standing across the tracks and her mouth opens wide as she spots me. I'm expecting her to pull out her gun and shoot.

Instead, she continues to stare as a train trundles noisily into view, stopping on her side. I remain where I am. I have no hope of getting round to the southern platform in time to catch the same train. My view of her is blocked. Either she's now scared that I've turned the tables on her and she's going to get on the train and get as far away from me as she can, or she's running back up the stairs in my direction. I have the feeling she's not out to kill me unless she can possibly help it. If she were, she had the perfect opportunity in the library bathroom. It doesn't mean she won't threaten me with her gun, though.

It takes an age for the train to leave. I keep one eye on it and the other on the staircase leading down to where I'm standing. When the train finally departs, I'm surprised. She's still on the opposite platform, staring at me.

'What do you want?' I shout, trying to sound threatening.

The few other people around me turn and gape. I ignore them. Even from this distance, I can tell she's shaking.

'I need to find Devlin,' she calls back across the tracks.

It takes me a moment to realise who she means. With O'Shea already in Montserrat custody, I can rule out that she's working for them.

'What do you want him for?'

'They'll kill me if I can't find him.'

'Who? Who will kill you?'

'The vampires,' she answers. There's a hiss of shock combined with rubbernecker delight from the waiting passengers.

'Which ones?' I try not to sound as desperate as I feel.

She shakes her head, aware of our growing audience.

'Stay there,' I yell. 'I'm coming over.' I glance at the people bouncing their eyes between me and her as if they're at a championship tennis game. 'Performance theatre,' I mutter to them, before running to the other platform.

She's still there when I reach the other side. I walk slowly towards her. I don't know who she is or how she's involved in any of this but she's obviously more spooked than I am. A train comes in, ridding the northern platform of our audience. When I reach her, I stop a few feet away and hold up my palms to indicate that I'm unarmed.'

'Are you Lucy?' I ask.

She looks startled and more than a little afraid. I nod, satisfied. That's one mystery solved at least. It turns out I didn't require Rogu3's services after all.

'Where's Devlin?' she asks, not acknowledging my question.

'The Montserrat Family have got him,' I tell her. I can give her that much information.

It doesn't appease her fears. 'What? No, no, no, no, no, that's bad.'

I take a step towards her and she flinches. 'Why, Lucy? Why is it bad?'

'They needed the spell. If he tells anyone about it…' Her voice drifts off and she wrings her hands.

O'Shea's little enhancement project. I wonder why it's so important though right now I'm less concerned with motive than perpetrator. 'Who are they?'

'They made me contact him. They wanted the spell,' she babbles. 'They needed it.'

I'm getting impatient; this much I already know. 'Who are they?' I repeat.

'I don't know!' she yells. 'They're all involved with the Families though. Every single one of them.'

I watch her carefully. She seems to be telling the truth. That means Montserrat was too but it doesn't make me feel any more warm and fuzzy towards him.

'No vampire has ever done that, Lucy. They obey the Head. It's part of who they are.'

'They are obeying their Head,' she moans.

I curse. 'Which one? Is it Montserrat?'

'No, you don't get it.'

'What? What don't I get?'

'There's a new Family. A new Head. They're obeying her.'

My eyes narrow. It actually makes sense. The vampires' innate desire to follow the leader would still hold. None of the existing Heads would normally risk the fragile peace between the Families by stealing each other's members. A new Head, however, might not feel the same sense of responsibility. I wonder if Montserrat realises this. He has to, otherwise he'd never believe that there were traitors. I don't know why he wouldn't tell me though.

'Who's the new Head?' I keep my voice quiet and steady.

She opens her mouth but whatever she says is swallowed in the roar of an oncoming train.

'Pardon?'

Out of nowhere, there's a flash of movement that comes from behind me and launches itself towards her. I spring forward but it's already too late. Her body is shoved directly into the path of the train. It happens so fast that I can do little more than stare aghast as her blood spatters across the platform and hits me in the face while she is dragged along the tracks. I'm dimly aware of screams and yells from the other people on the train and the platform.

I look up and the vampire grins at me. He's blond so obviously not Tam's murderer. Not that that is going to help Lucy – or whoever she was. He lunges towards me and I instinctively put up my hands to protect myself. There are several shouts from behind me. The vampire pulls back and gives me another grin that chills me to my core. 'Another time,' he hisses, before vaulting onto to the roof of the stationary train and disappearing down the other side.

I've not even lowered my hands when someone from behind grabs my wrists and yanks them behind my back. In one swift, practised motion a plastic tie secures my hands.

My captor leans in towards me. 'You're under arrest for murder.'

Bugger.

12

THE CELL

I'M HAULED AWAY UNCEREMONIOUSLY WHILE AN IMPOSSIBLY YOUNG looking copper reads me my rights. I'm about to protest my innocence when I think better about opening my big mouth in case I blab something I shouldn't. As we pass the gaping commuters and the train with Lucy's gruesome remains clinging to its front, I try to avert my eyes but I can't stop myself from looking. I wish I hadn't.

Ten minutes later, I'm shoved into a small beige room complete with CCTV camera, what is obviously a two-way mirror mounted on one wall, and a small desk and chairs. The door is slammed shut and I'm left on my own. I kick the nearest chair and swear loudly. In the mirror I can see high points of colour on my cheeks. My hair is a dark, unruly mess of curls. I look like a mad woman. The sort of mad woman who would be capable of pushing someone under a train. I grit my teeth, use my foot to return the chair to a standing position and sit down. I'm not going to get anywhere if I lose my cool.

It's not long before I'm joined by two plainclothes police offi-cers. The first one has a lined face, reflecting the many injustices in the world. He glances at me warily as he enters. His partner, a younger woman, smiles. Ladies and gentlemen, I give you every cliché of police work in the book, I think sardonically, from good cop, bad cop to old partner versus new copper. I just manage to avoid rolling my eyes.

They sit down across from me.

'Hello, Bo,' says the woman. 'I'm Sergeant Nicholls and this is Inspector Foxworthy. Do you know why you're here?'

I keep my mouth resolutely shut.

Foxworthy opens a manila folder, placing a series of photos in front of me. There's a shot of the façade of the Wiltshore Avenue hellhole, followed by several of the interior. Then there are technicolour displays of the room where O'Shea almost pegged it: the blood-spattered walls, the half-destroyed chair, a set of footprints.

'Where did you bury his body?'

I'm surprised and a little alarmed that they believe O'Shea is dead.

'Bo,' Nicholls coos, 'we know Devlin O'Shea is no longer with us.'

'And we know you killed him,' interrupts Foxworthy. Nicholls shoots him an annoyed look; clearly these two have their routine down to a perfect art form.

'What we don't know,' she continues, 'is where his body is or why you did it. He was a lowlife, Bo, we know that.' She ticks off her fingers. 'Dealing in black magic, stealing, ripping off innocent people. He was scum. Let's face it, the planet is better off without him.'

All I can think is that I really hope he's still alive. If Montserrat has killed him and disposed of his body then I'm well and truly up shit creek without a paddle.

Foxworthy leans in. 'Is that why you murdered him, Ms Blackman?' He draws out the 'Mizz' until it sounds like an insult.

'We wouldn't blame you if you did,' adds Nicholls, trying to appeal to my better nature. 'His family will want to know where he is. They'll still want to give him a decent burial. Most of them are human, Bo. Even if he was a bastard, they still care for him.'

I'm interested in her line of questioning. Is she suggesting that his daemon relations don't care for him? Or is she assuming that I killed him because he was a daemon and I'm a racist bitch?

Foxworthy changes tack abruptly. 'Who was the woman you threw off the tracks?'

I stare at him. There must have been upwards of a dozen witnesses to the vampire, not to mention the footage from the security cameras.

'You look surprised, Ms Blackman.'

I forget my promise to myself to stay quiet. 'It was a freaking vampire!'

I receive a scornful look in return. 'Why would a bloodguzzler kill someone by shoving them under a train? That would be a waste of good blood, don't you think?' He folds his arms. 'Besides, we can't prosecute vampires. But we can prosecute you.'

It'd take less than two minutes of their time to find proof that I had nothing to do with Lucy's murder. They obviously know this and they don't care. Or they're using the fact of her death to lure me into telling them about O'Shea. I gnaw at my lip. There's more than enough evidence to prove I didn't kill either Lucy or O'Shea. I wonder if they care.

'Don't you have anything to say?'

'Come on, Bo,' Nicholls urges, 'just tell us what's going on.'

I could call my grandfather and get him to send someone round but I have a better idea. 'I'd like a lawyer,' I announce.

Something flickers in Nicholls' expression although Foxworthy remains impassive. 'We can appoint someone for you,' he says.

I shake my head. 'No. I have a lawyer.'

'Who?'

'D'Argneau,' I say calmly. 'Harry D'Argneau.'

I'm left cooling my heels while they make the call. I honestly have no idea whether D'Argneau will actually show or not. I rest my forehead on the table and close my eyes. Lucy's horrified expression as she flies in midair into the path of the train replays itself in my head over and over again. Several times I have to force down rising bile. At some point Nicholls re-enters and leaves me a glass of water. I chug it down then continue to wait.

With no clock in the room, and my watch removed with my other few personal possessions when I entered the station, I have no way of knowing what time it is when the door eventually re-opens. I look up and see D'Argneau striding in. I'd forgotten how good looking he is. He pauses for a moment, his eyes widening infinitesimally in what can only be an unfaked reaction to my presence. Then he quickly recovers and takes the chair vacated by Inspector Foxworthy.

'You're Bo Blackman?' he asks.

I nod.

'I once met your…'

'Grandfather. Yeah, whatever,' I grunt.

He takes out a notepad. 'So, you're being investigated on the count of two separate murders. That of Devlin O'Shea, an Agathos daemon, and an as-yet unnamed human woman.'

I think of Rogu3. He's probably discovered her true identity by now. There's no way I'm going to tell D'Argneau about him, though. At the moment, even though I'm the one cuffed and being held in a police station, he's one of my prime suspects. I don't care that he's not a vampire, there's no way he's not involved.

'Lucy,' I say. 'All I know is that she called herself Lucy. Check the surveillance cameras. She was pushed onto the tracks by a vampire.'

The lawyer raises his eyebrows then scribbles something. 'I'll do that. How do you,' he coughs, 'sorry, how *did* you know her?'

'She was following me.'

'And the cameras will also attest to this.'

Ah. Not exactly. 'She was following me then I turned the tables and starting following her instead.'

His eyebrows knit together. 'I see.'

It's clear he doesn't. 'Look,' I sigh, 'check the cameras from the station and talk to the witnesses. I had nothing to do with her death.'

'And the daemon?'

'He's not dead.' I watch him carefully for his reaction.

D'Argneau looks at me. I look back at him unwaveringly. I do hope Montserrat isn't making a liar out of me.

'Where is he?'

I shrug. 'Tied up.' Most probably.

'Okay. Is he likely to present himself at any point?'

'Well, that's difficult to say.' My ear itches so I lift up one shoulder and rub it awkwardly. 'You see, he's still rather worried about losing his life. The firm I work for…'

'Dire Straits,' he interrupts. 'The one in the news.'

'Yes. And I'd like to point out I'm no more responsible for what happened there than for anything else.' I direct this comment at the two-way mirror. Lawyer–client conversations are meant to be confidential but right now I don't trust anything. 'They tasked me with serving O'Shea with a summons. I found him half dead.' I smile humourlessly. 'The summons came from a barrister seconded to the Agathos court.'

D'Argneau's pen stops. I meet his eyes and we stare at each other. The silence chokes the tiny room.

'I have nothing to do with this, Ms Blackman.'

I press my lips together.

'Are you setting me up?' he asks quietly.

'I'm the one being framed here, D'Argneau. You hired me to serve the summons on O'Shea.'

'I hired Dire Straits. I'd never even heard of you.'

I ignore him. 'And then you suddenly show up in the middle of the night at the same club I decide to have a drink in.'

His face tightens with anger. 'Let's get one thing clear, Ms Blackman. I was already at that club when you walked in. I didn't follow you. You followed me.'

'Where else was I going to go at that time of night?'

He leans in towards me, his voice lowering. 'Is that what the little show was out on the street? Were you trying to get hold of my DNA?'

'Are you fucking kidding me?' I sound screechy, but I don't care. 'I'm the one in handcuffs here! I'm the one about to be charged with murder! And I'm the one who walked away from you after the club!'

His eyes flash. 'Maybe that's because you'd already got what you wanted. A few strands of my hair perhaps? Or some saliva?'

I make a face. 'Ewww! You think I sucked your spit and kept it in my mouth for a later date? Get real, buster.'

'I don't care what family connections you've got,' he snarls, 'you won't get away with this.'

Nothing is going the way I expect. I try to calm down. 'D'Argneau, look at me. I'm not getting away with anything. But I've not *done* anything.'

He pushes back his hair and stands up. 'Whatever game you've got going on here, it's not going to wash.'

'Wait! D'Argneau!'

He doesn't stop. Instead he just walks out of the little room, the door banging behind him. My shoulders sink and I stare at the empty chair. Either that was an Oscar-winning performance or the lawyer is telling the truth. I mull over the idea that it was merely a coincidence we bumped into each other. It's just so incredibly unlikely.

'Your barrister doesn't want you,' states Foxworthy, strolling into the room.

I glare at him. 'Charge me,' I growl, 'or let me go.'

He smirks, making a deliberate show of checking his watch. 'We've got forty-one hours to question you before we need to make that decision, Ms Blackman. There's no rush.' He pulls my arm, forcing me to my feet. 'How about a little break from all this?' There's a nasty gleam in his eye, the first real emotion I've seen from him. It sends a ripple of uneasiness through me.

'I can keep going,' I say. 'I'll answer your questions.'

'Like I said,' he smiles, 'there's plenty of time for that.'

I'M LED INTO A CELL. There's already another occupant, an older man with no irises in his eyes and an instantly recognisable tattoo on his cheek. Just when I thought things couldn't get any worse.

'Foxworthy, let me out of these damned restraints!' I call desperately.

'You're here as a result of a double murder. You may have been involved in the slaughter of several of your work colleagues. That makes you a potential serial killer and far too dangerous to be allowed to go unfettered, Ms Blackman.' The emphasis he puts on my surname is unmistakable. The black witch in the corner straightens, interested.

'Blackman?'

I back away, warily. 'Look, honour among thieves, right? We're both in this cell together.'

'Any relation to Arbuthnot Blackman?'

I try to feign ignorance. 'Er, who?'

It doesn't work. The witch opens his mouth and runs a red tongue over his lips. Then he takes a step towards me. His hands, I notice, are uncuffed.

'Okay,' I say, 'let's not be hasty here. Yes, I'm related to Arbuthnot Blackman. But I think he's as much of a bastard as you do.'

The witch takes another step. The cell is tiny and my back is literally against the wall. I glance up at the ceiling and note the camera mounted there. Much good it's going to do me. Not for the first time, I curse my grandfather.

The witch launches himself at me. Despite my best efforts to protect myself, his fist flies into my face and I see a flash of blinding light and feel an explosion of pain as he breaks my nose. Threads of pain travel outwards across my cheekbones and up through my eyeballs. I lash out instinctively with my foot, catching him in the stomach. He staggers back, groaning, then he's on me again.

He knocks me down hard onto the floor and I narrowly avoid hitting my head on the steel corner of the bed. I roll underneath it. The last thing I need is to come on too strong and do the witch some serious damage. If I do, it'll no doubt be added to the list of grievances against me. He shakes the bed and it rattles hard against the floor, but fortunately it's screwed tightly into place. He bends down. I spit out blood and push myself further back but he grabs my ankle to pull me out. I kick against his grip but it's no use. With my hands behind my back, I can't fight against him and I'm dragged out, inch by inch. His other hand swoops down and encircles my throat, then he thrusts me up against the wall. He's not trying to kill me; he's having far too much fun for that.

I flail against him. I've just about had enough of this. My knee jerks upwards, connecting with his groin. He snarls in pain.

'Having fun?'

The pair of us twist round. Both Foxworthy and Nicholls are standing in the doorway, watching us.

'Enjoying the show?' I say, as the witch finally releases his grip. My voice is weak. I put a hand up to my face and it comes away covered in my own blood.

'There's someone to see you,' Foxworthy says, moving aside.

For a moment I think he's addressing the witch, then I realise he's referring to me. I wonder if my grandfather has been informed.

Foxworthy offers me an old, greying towel. I'm tempted to throw it back in his face but I need something to wipe off the blood. The centre of my face feels as if it's been smacked with a sledgehammer. I follow him and Nicholls out of the cell and I'm expecting to be led back into the same interview room but, instead, I end up out at the front of the station. Standing there are Montserrat and a very pale Devlin O'Shea.

'The daemon's alive,' says Nicholls cheerfully. 'And we've reviewed the footage from the station. It appears it wasn't you who threw Charity Weathers under a train.'

I realise that Charity Weathers must be the unfortunate Lucy.

'However, Ms Blackman, we would like to question you further regarding your role in the Dire Straits massacre. So don't do anything stupid like leave the country.'

Without looking at Montserrat, I tighten my core muscles and take a deep breath. 'Actually, you're no longer in a position to do that,' I say.

'Why not?' Foxcroft enquires coolly.

'I'm about to be recruited into the Family Montserrat.'

As soon as the words leave my mouth, an ache rises in the centre of my chest. Out of the corner of my eye, I see O'Shea looking shocked and Montserrat smiling with a little dimple displayed in one cheek. He takes my arm and together we walk out into the cool night. I resist the urge to look back and smirk.

13

THE CAR

MONTSERRAT DOESN'T SAY ANYTHING UNTIL WE'RE IN THE BACK OF his extraordinarily large limousine and driving away from the police station. I hope we're driving very, very far away.

'I'm glad you've decided to help us.'

I pull the towel away from my face. 'I'm not helping you,' I snarl. 'I'm helping me.'

He shrugs elegantly. 'Regardless.'

I flick a glance at O'Shea, then back to the vampire. 'Thanks for coming to get me,' I mutter. 'And for not killing him.'

Montserrat opens a small compartment to reveal an array of neatly stacked drinks. I point to the whisky and he pours me a generous shot.

'I told you, Ms Blackman,' he says, handing me the drink, 'we're not monsters.'

I take a sip, wincing as it burns down my throat. The monsters part remains to be seen although I wisely refrain from saying so.

After Foxworthy's interrogation, I decide I hate the moniker Ms Blackman. 'Call me Bo,' I tell the vampire.

He smiles. 'In that case you may call me Michael.'

'Michael?'

'Yes. Like Michael Douglas.'

More like Michael Corleone, I think. I dab carefully at my nose. 'Okay then.'

'May I check your face?' he asks politely.

I draw back for a moment and he laughs. 'I've been around too long for your blood to tempt me, Bo. I think I can manage to restrain myself.'

I realise my reaction was stupid and I turn to face him. He cups my face in his hands and frowns. 'Did the police do this to you?'

'No. There was a black witch. He recognised my name.'

'Ah, I see.'

Does he indeed? I try to sniff and end up wincing with pain. He takes the towel and is about to wipe my face with it when he grimaces and tosses it away. He pulls out a handkerchief from his top pocket and carefully wipes away the worst of the blood. I try not to stare. I'm not sure I've ever seen anyone other than my grandfather use a linen handkerchief before.

His touch is surprisingly gentle. It's making me feel a little uncomfortable so I focus on O'Shea as a distraction. 'Are you alright?' I ask him.

He nods. 'They've treated me well.'

Well, he would say that given his captor is sitting right next to him. O'Shea's next words belie that thought, however. 'Perhaps, *Michael*, when you're done cleaning up her face, you can touch up mine.' He pouts and, despite myself, I start to giggle.

'I take it you two didn't share the water bed then,' Montserrat says.

'I'm sure it's still available.' I look at them from under my lashes and grin.

Montserrat rolls his eyes but O'Shea returns my smile.

'How's Arzo?' I ask.

The vampire tuts. 'You need to stop talking. I can't get all this blood off when you keep moving. And Arzo's fine.' He grimaces. 'At least as fine as a paraplegic can be.'

'Why can't his vampire blood heal that?'

'I told you to be quiet,' he says, wetting a corner of the handkerchief with his tongue and brushing it across my mouth. 'Arzo is Sanguine. His blood helps him to heal more quickly but it won't work miracles.'

I open my mouth to ask another question, but Montserrat scowls at me and I subside into silence.

'Let me guess,' he says drily, 'you want to know more about the Sanguine?'

I blink in acknowledgement, while his fingers trace the tender flesh around my nose.

'It's an odd phenomenon. The Sanguine aren't exactly secret but we don't go around broadcasting their existence. To be fair, there have never been enough of them to warrant making a big deal out of it. Most people who come to us to be recruited want to be vampires. I'm not going to tell you Arzo's story, that's up to him. Suffice it to say, the path to becoming Sanguine isn't easy. It's only fair that you know that.'

'How many of these Sanguine are there?' asks O'Shea.

Montserrat doesn't answer immediately. I narrow my eyes and his hands leave my face. 'You'll probably need to get that set before you turn, or you may be stuck with a crooked nose.'

Right now I don't give a damn about my nose. 'How many?' I say, repeating the daemon's question.

'As I said, most people want to be vampire.'

'Montserrat…'

'I told you to call me Michael.' He rubs his chin with his thumb. 'There are three,' he says finally. His voice is quiet.

I swallow. 'Three? You mean in London?'

'No, Bo. In the world.'

For a moment, kaleidoscopic pinpricks of light dance in front of my eyes. I squeeze them shut. 'Why so few?' I ask. 'I mean, I get that most people don't want to be Sanguine. But…'

'There are others,' he answers, 'who wish to take the Sanguine path. And in the 1940s, there were experiments to create more. But to become Sanguine you have to resist the pull of blood. You have to avoid drinking. The temptation is high.'

I open my eyes and look at him. He meets my gaze.

'As I told you in the hospital, it's considered a show of strength to last as long as possible before tasting blood. It's not been proven but it's believed that the longer you last, the more powerful a vampire you eventually become.'

'How long did you last?'

'Twenty-two days. Most, however, don't make it beyond day three.'

Jesus. I'd understood from Arzo it was going to be difficult. I hadn't reckoned on it being virtually impossible.

'We need you, Bo. We need someone to infiltrate the new recruits and find out what is going on. I understand how much I'm asking of you, though. You can still change your mind.'

I think about the events of the last two days. It would be smart to walk away from all this and hide under a stone somewhere until everything blows over. I have no idea how far I can trust Montserrat, even though I sense that everything he's told me so far is the truth.

With this in mind, I go for a full-frontal attack. 'When were you planning to tell me about the new Family?'

For the first time, he appears nonplussed. 'What?'

'The new Family,' I repeat. 'The ones who wanted O'Shea's spell.'

He is obviously baffled. 'There is no new Family. What are you talking about?'

I tell him about Lucy – or rather Charity Weathers – and what she told me before her life ended so abruptly. He leans back in his seat, his face shuttered as he absorbs the information.

'I assumed it was a few malcontents. I mean, it's serious. We've never had a situation like this before and I wouldn't be involving you if it wasn't something that required fresh eyes and a different way of thinking. But a new Family? There's not been a new Family since Mary Queen of Scots was executed.'

'The Stuarts?'

He nods.

'Let's say someone did want to start a new Family,' I say. 'How would they fit in with the current set up?'

'It simply wouldn't work.' His dark eyes are troubled.

'Why not?'

'It's difficult for outsiders to understand, but there's a considerable amount of rivalry between the Familes. The ties and alliances shift depending on the issue at hand. However, because there are five of us, it works.'

'Explain.'

He frowns. 'It'll be easier to give you an example. The last time we all met, it was because the government wanted to send in monitors. There's growing unease amongst the humans about the way we keep the Families' actions and motives secret. The Head of the Stuarts and I wanted to agree. Openness will provide better understanding. The population will be less wary of us and we'll open more trade doors as a result.'

'But the others disagreed?'

'Medici and Bancroft. They argued that how we conduct ourselves is none of the humans' business. They were also concerned that it would create problems between the Families themselves. With everything above board and openly advertised, we'd each have a better gauge of the state of the other Families and, if we so chose, be in a position to undermine each other.'

I imagine that 'undermine' in the vampire world means a bit more than merely giving out a few playground taunts. Although I agree with Montserrat's position, I can see that there are potential problems.

'And Gully?'

'They listened to both sides and ultimately went with the Medicis and the Bancrofts.'

I nod my head thoughtfully. 'Without an odd number of Families, disagreements will rarely be solved.'

'Indeed.'

'Except,' I add, trying to glean as much information as I can from him, 'why should I care? If there's a new Family and it means you're all at loggerheads, what does it matter to humans?'

'The power afforded by being vampire is heady. And the power granted to the Families as a result of their combined strength is almost incomprehensible. It's the reason we cap our own numbers at five hundred.' He takes my hand and gently squeezes. An odd tingle runs up my arm. 'Imagine a new Family with no allegiances and no desire to follow any of the rules that have been in place for hundreds of years.'

'Vampires could over-run daemons,' whispers O'Shea, realisation dawning.

'And humans,' says Montserrat grimly. 'And without checks in place to prevent unwarranted attacks…'

'The results could be catastrophic,' I finish. I ponder the very real danger this new Family might pose. 'But what if it's not like that? What if these vampires just want a new Family and will abide by the laws you already have?'

'Then why are they being so secretive? Why not be open about creating a new Family? Breaking the ties of loyalty that already exist in each Family is proof that they won't toe the line.'

I'm tempted to point out that perhaps he should be doing more to encourage that loyalty and to stop errant Family members from leaving but I reckon he's probably worked that out by now.

'They've already shown that they're remarkably keen to kill people,' muses O'Shea, rubbing at the remains of the wound on his neck.

'Why would this new Family want your spell?' I ask him.

'I have no idea. Maybe they're kind of horny?'

'It has to be to do with the passivity side effects. Maybe it's how they're getting so many previously loyal vampires to join them.' I glance at Montserrat. 'How many do you know who are involved?'

'I'll give you the files later, if you decide to join us that is. But there have been at least half a dozen confirmed deaths and several more disappearances in Montserrat. The other Families have given similar numbers, although they may be lying.'

'And they all met with you?' I ask O'Shea.

He nods.

'You didn't think there was anything odd about having so many vampires interested in your spell?'

He looks slightly embarrassed. 'I was making a lot of money. How was I to know what it was really about?'

I exhale in irritation, then pull my knees up to my chest and hug them tightly. My nose is still throbbing, although the hurt is somewhat diminished after Montserrat's ministrations. I gaze out of the window at the passing streets. It must have rained recently because there are puddles reflecting the street lights as we zip by. Most of the shops are closed now but, from time to time, I see an off-license or take-away restaurant which remains open. I gulp down the remainder of the whisky. Imagining a world where the vampires don't self-limit their own power is terrifying.

'Stop the car,' I say suddenly.

'Bo…'

I growl, 'I said stop the goddamn car.'

For a moment, Montserrat doesn't respond, then he taps on the window separating us from the driver and slides it open, muttering something into the front seat. The car glides to a halt.

'I wish you'd take a bit more time,' he begins.

'Wait here,' I say, opening the door and stepping out. Then I duck my head back in. 'Do you have any loose change?'

He looks confused but digs into his pocket and hands over a few coins.

'Thanks.' I slam the door shut and jog over to a payphone. I grab the receiver, dropping in the coins as I dial. Rogu3 picks up straightaway.

'Hello?' His voice is cautious.

'It's me,' I say.

'Where the fuck have you been, Bo? I've been trying to track you for hours! I got you to the police station near Piccadilly, but then you were released...'

'I'm fine. Honest.' And then, more because it's automatic than for any other reason, 'Don't swear.'

'Where are you? What's going on?'

I lick my lips. 'Let's just say the investigation is taking a new turn.'

'Fine, well thanks for keeping me in the loop.' He says it sarcastically and I can tell he's hurt that I've not been in touch.

'I'm sorry, Rogu3, but it's better for you if you don't know too much.'

He sniffs. 'I know a lot about your Lucy character. Her real name is Charity Weathers. She works as a dental nurse out of some surgery in Brixton. Looks like she's got a real habit for ice.'

I bite my lip. Being a drug addict would make her an easy target. All these bloody vamps would have to do is promise her some ice – or withhold it from her – and she'd be theirs to command. Poor bitch.

'Can you tell who else she's been in contact with?'

'You mean other than your daemon buddy? Nah. She kept a pretty low online presence. No Facebook or Twitter or anything like that.' He snorts. 'You can tell by the way she writes online. All properly punctuated and with Standard English spelling. Not so much as a single emoticon.'

I remember what O'Shea said about being sure she was a woman because of her writing style. Not just a woman, but a woman who had no need for the internet. I wonder how she got herself wrapped up with the vampires in the first place. Via some scabby dealer, no doubt.

'Thanks, Rogu3. That's really useful.' I don't bother telling him I already know her name – I don't want to hurt his feelings. 'Look,' I continue, 'I'm going black for a while so I won't be in touch. I might not ever be in touch again.' I cross my fingers against this thought.

'What?' he screeches. 'Why?'

I smile into the phone. 'I didn't know you cared.'

'We're not best buds or anything, but I thought we had an understanding.'

'We do. That's why I've got one last job for you. There's no rush because, like I said, I don't know if I'll be in touch again but...'

'I get it, I get it. What do you need?'

I give him Harry D'Argneau's details. As honest as the barrister seems in person, he's still a lead. I'm tempted to ask Rogu3 to hack into the Montserrat intranet for me as well. But for all his posturing, he's still just a kid; the vampires are too big and too damn scary and I need him to stay safe.

'I'll make sure you get paid, no matter what.'

'I don't need the money,' he says grumpily. 'For what it's worth, Bo, take care of yourself.'

I'm touched. 'Thanks. Right back at you, kiddo.'

I hang up before I get too emotional. Then I take a deep breath and call the next number.

'Arbuthnot Blackman.'

'Hey, grandfather,' I say softly.

'Bo! Where are you? I was told you were arrested.'

I don't want to get into that now. 'I'm going away,' I tell him. 'I might not be back.'

He's immediately suspicious. 'Where?'

I think about all those families I investigated when I was working for the insurance company and how desperate they were to know what had really happened to their loved ones. I take the plunge and tell the truth. 'I'm being recruited.'

The silence stretches out for so long that I'm starting to wonder if he's still there.

'Grandfather?'

His voice is strained. 'Why?'

'It's just something I have to do. I'm going to try to come back though.'

'You mean Sanguine.'

I'm surprised. 'You've heard of them?'

'Please.' He sighs. 'Very few people make it that far, you know. We tried with someone once. Sent them into the Bancroft fold. Never heard from them again.'

'There are always exceptions,' I say, attempting to keep my tone light.

'If anyone can be an exception, you can. I've always been proud of you, you know.'

I'm taken aback by the softness in his voice. 'Uh, thanks.'

'Is there another way? Is there something I can do to help?'

'No. I need to do this on my own. Don't try to…' I swallow. 'Don't try to send anyone after me or anything like that. I'll either make it or I won't. Either way, this is best course of action.'

'Then I trust your judgment. But don't trust the guzzlers, Bo. There's more to them than you realise.'

I wonder if I've gotten the old man wrong all these years. The last thing I'd been expecting was his implicit blessing. 'Thank you,' I say again. 'There is one thing I need you to do, though.'

'Name it.'

I give him Rogu3's bank details. 'I'll pay you back, one way or another. There's money in my account which I can…'

'I'll sort it out. Can't have the hoi polloi going destitute because a Blackman hasn't paid their bills, can we? Bo, have you told your mother about this vampire business?'

'I don't know where she is.'

'Gallivanting somewhere, no doubt. When she gets in touch, I'll let her know.'

'Tell her I love her.' My voice shakes. 'I love you too.' Blood is thicker than water after all.

'Goodbye, Bo.' He hangs up.

I stand there for a moment, still holding the receiver. Then I replace it and walk back to the limousine. The driver gets out this time and opens the door for me. I smile at him briefly and get in.

'I have a phone,' Montserrat says stiffly.

'Just because I'm going to work for you doesn't mean I trust you. It was a private call.'

Something flashes in his eyes but it's gone before I can work out what it means. 'You made two calls.'

'They were both private,' I say shortly. He can mind his own damn business. Allowing myself to be recruited into the Montserrat Family doesn't mean I'm going to be their property.

A muscle throbs in Montserrat's cheek. He taps the driver's window and the car glides off. 'You're going to stay?'

'Yes. I'm also going to be Sanguine. I can stick out a month of bloodlust,' I say, with far more confidence than I feel.

He merely nods and we lapse into an uncomfortable silence.

14

FEAR

I'M EXPECTING US TO HEAD STRAIGHT FOR THE MONTSERRAT headquarters on the edge of Hyde Park but, instead of going in that direction, the car turns left and we pull up outside an old building. It's a majestic piece of architecture, built out of sandstone; it looks as if it's been here for hundreds of years.

'Nice place,' I comment.

'Recruitment doesn't start until tomorrow so you can stay here. It'll be safe.'

'And where is here, exactly?'

'My apartment,' Montserrat answers shortly.

O'Shea clambers out and whistles. 'I like a man with style.'

'If you want to stay alive,' Montserrat tells the daemon, 'then you'll stay here and out of sight.'

O'Shea purses his lips. 'Do you have satellite TV?' Montserrat looks at him. 'Okay, okay. I'll stay here and hide away. It's nice of you to be so concerned for my safety.'

I smile involuntarily and Montserrat glares at me. 'You can stay here tonight too.'

'Great. Thanks,' I mutter.

There's no doorman at the front but the security is still

impressive. Montserrat enters by pressing his thumb to an electronic sensor. 'If you leave, you won't be able to get back in,' he warns.

O'Shea and I nod dutifully. The door clicks open and we wander into the grand lobby. It's a darn sight better than the last place I stayed at.

Montserrat leads us to the lift. The walls are mirrored and I wince at my reflection. There are dark bruises under my eyes and my nose is an interesting shade of purple. I touch it gingerly and hiss with pain. Both of them look at me.

'It hurts, alright?'

'So don't touch it,' Montserrat says. He turns away while I stick my tongue out childishly at him. Unfortunately, he catches me in the mirror.

'You're not going to get away with that when you're recruited.'

'I didn't ask to join your Family,' I point out.

'You've agreed now.'

I sigh. I suppose I have. Never one to let a moment pass, however, I say, 'I can still back out.'

'Yes. You can.' Then, without warning, he leaps towards me.

Alarmed, I lash out with my fists, but he reaches for my nose and, with one swift movement, jerks it hard to the side. There's a loud cracking sound and I scream.

He inspects his handiwork. 'There,' he says. 'That's better.'

I slap him. O'Shea stares at us with wide eyes.

'Um, Bo?'

'Yeah?'

'Maybe don't piss off the bloodsucking powerhouse.'

I shoot the daemon a nasty look. 'He started it.'

Montserrat smirks. It's just as well the lift stops at that moment or I might not be responsible for my actions. My nose is smarting like hell but I stride past the vampire as if I've never felt better and gaze around.

'Wow,' O'Shea says. 'This is a serious pad.'

He's right. Montserrat's place is as sharp as his suits. The floor is wooden, a burnished amber that warms the room, and is covered in expensive looking rugs. A vast sofa faces a fireplace and there's a modern kitchen towards the back. The wall to my left is covered from floor to ceiling with books; to the right, great bay windows look out over the London skyline.

'It'll do.' I hope I don't sound over-awed. I'm still pissed off with him for the nose thing.

'Not as nice as the love hotel?' Montserrat asks.

'How did you know we were there?'

He puts on a mock accent. 'Vee have vays.'

I stare at him. The vampire Head has a sense of humour. Who knew?

He smiles. 'Come on. I'll show you the bedroom. The daemon can sleep on the sofa for tonight. I'll take the floor.'

He opens a huge wooden door and I gape. The bed is king size and then some. It's covered in black satin sheets and looks like it's been designed for the set of a porn movie. I guess Montserrat is currently single.

'I think the bed is big enough for both us,' I say, grinning. 'I won't bite if you don't.' As soon as the words are out of my mouth, I realise they sound like an invitation and I start to blush. Montserrat doesn't seem to notice.

'Whatever you're comfortable with.' He points to another door to the left. 'The bathroom's in there if you want to clean up. I can get you a clean t-shirt or something to wear.'

Feeling awkward now, I mumble thank you. He stands in front of me and gazes down, his dark eyes glinting. 'Thank you, Bo. I know what you're giving up by doing this. I won't forget it.'

'I'm not giving up anything,' I answer. And it's the truth. 'I no longer have a job. I've got a bunch of traitor vampires out for my blood. And it's only until the full moon. I'll be Sanguine.'

His eyes fill with unexpected warmth. 'Good.'

We both remain standing like that until O'Shea calls out from the main room. 'Do you have any snacks?'

Montserrat shakes himself. 'I'll get you that t-shirt.'

'Cheers.' I walk into the bathroom and take a very deep breath.

MONTSERRAT COMES to bed far later than me. I'm not sure what he's doing, whether he's telling O'Shea where he can find the cornflakes and how to work the remote control, or he's off doing some mysterious 'Head of Bloodguzzling Family' work. Hell, for all I know, he has a willing victim tied up in a cupboard somewhere and he was off for a snack. Regardless, when he finally clambers in to the far side of the huge bed, I'm still wide awake. I don't pretend to be asleep; he's a vampire, after all, I'm sure he'd know if I were faking it. But I'm not in the mood for night-time chit-chat and my glib remark about not minding sharing a bed with him now seems rash. I don't turn around but I sense him keeping a fair distance away and doing his best not to disturb me. I lie there, listening to his steady breathing, and gaze across the room.

I'm worried about whether I'm making the right choice. I think part of me had hoped that my grandfather would put his foot down and refuse to let me to take this step. Of course, I'd have ranted and railed and gone ahead regardless. Except … despite being a grown woman, sometimes a tiny part of me hankers for the simplicity of being a child again and having big decisions taken out of my hands. With only three Sanguines in the entire bloody world, my chances of making it through the moon's cycle are miniscule. That's not to mention the dangers of trying to turn vampire in the first place, and the fact that the group of traitorous bloodguzzlers may want to continue their efforts to slit my throat rather than welcome me into the fold.

Whatever does happen when I turn tomorrow, I'm going to have to tread carefully.

I flip onto my back, annoyed with myself for still being awake. This is probably the last time I'll have the opportunity for safe, uninterrupted sleep. Montserrat doesn't stir. I glance over at him, registering his bare skin and taut, clearly delineated muscles. The dark twisting shape of a tattoo is etched across his upper back and curves round his arms, although the light is too dim to work out what it actually is.

Something in me tenses. It's not that I expected him to be wearing stripy pyjamas but he looks as if he's completely naked. It's difficult to tell because the satin sheet is pulled up to his waist. Without thinking, I turn fully in his direction to check. Maybe it's *de rigeur* for vampires to sleep in the buff. Despite my snarky comments to Angelique about not sleeping in coffins, I actually have no idea how vampires sleep. Or eat. Or do anything. I smile grimly to myself. I suppose I'm about to find out.

Curiosity gets the better of me so very, very carefully, I tug at the sheet. It falls half an inch, displaying well-toned dimples on either side of his spine. I'm convinced now that he's naked. The man has no sense of propriety. Apparently neither do I because I tug the sheet down a little bit more.

'Bo.'

My hearts leaps in my chest. Oops.

'What are you doing?'

I can't think of any answer that makes sense. 'I can't sleep,' I mutter eventually, sitting up.

He turns over, resting his head on one elbow. Despite the darkness, I can make out the wicked dance in his eyes as if he is perfectly aware of what I was trying to do. I look down and see that the tattoo travels all the way from his tanned back to his broad chest. I realise it's an intricately drawn set of wings that wraps around his skin from his shoulder blades to his collar bone, the lower edges just millimetres away from his dark nipples.

'I can help you with that,' he murmurs.

I feel tense and suspicious. 'What do you mean?'

He rubs the stubble around his jawline. 'I can help you sleep.'

A tiny, terrified part of me wonders if he means permanently. 'Oh?' I squeak.

He sits up, swings his legs over the side of the bed and stands up. He's wearing white drawstring trousers. Oh well.

He grins, as if he knows what I'm thinking. 'Wait here.'

He pads out of the bedroom. Avoiding thinking about how I just made myself look a total idiot, I also get up. Instead of following him, I walk to the window and draw back the heavy curtains to stare out at the night. I can't see the moon from here, which is just as well because it would only remind me of what is to come. There are, however, several visible stars. I stay where I am, even when I hear Montserrat return. I can't help wondering if this will be the last time I look out on the night sky with human eyes.

He comes up next to me, his bare footsteps as light as a cat's, and hands me a mug. I stare at it stupidly.

'It's hot cocoa,' he tells me.

He'll be offering me a pair of fluffy slippers and a dressing gown next. I take the mug and sip it cautiously. It scalds the inside of my mouth but it tastes good.

'Thanks.'

He watches me with hooded eyes. 'I stayed up all night,' he says, suddenly.

I'm confused. 'What...?'

'The night before I turned. I stayed up all night.'

'I'm afraid,' I whisper.

'I know.'

I'm grateful he doesn't waste time offering platitudes. It's enough to know that he understands how I feel. I drain the mug.

'Go to sleep,' he says softly.

'I'll try.' I head back to my side of the bed and lie down. Moments later I'm fast asleep.

IT'S EARLY when I wake up. The sunlight streaming in from the open curtains has a bright new quality – the sort you only get shortly after dawn. I turn over but Montserrat's not there, although there's a dent in the pillow where his head was. Butterflies dance in my stomach. I have no idea what the day will bring but I know that it will change my life irrevocably. I stay where I am for a moment, thinking about Charity Weathers and Tam and Tansy and everyone else from Dire Straits. I think about how different things might be if O'Shea had died in that grubby room. And then I get out of bed, splash water on my face and get dressed before carefully making the bed and erasing any evidence of my presence. Bring. It. On.

Unfortunately, when I go to the living room, my determination is already starting to desert me. I find O'Shea sprawled across the sofa, his arms stretched behind his head. He springs up. 'Hey!' His voice is far too bright and breezy. 'How are you feeling? Ready to join the triber clans?'

I give him a dirty look but he just shrugs amiably. 'At least you'll be busy. I have to stay holed up here.'

I'm tempted to tell him he's damn lucky to be alive but I manage to bite my tongue. 'Where's Montserrat?'

'Michael? He's gone already. Said to tell you not to worry about breakfast, it'll be provided later. There'll be a car to pick you up in about a couple of hours and take you to the headquarters.'

'Okay.' I sit down heavily down on the sofa. O'Shea sits next to me.

I need something to take my mind off my impending doom.

'Do you have records I can look at for the vampires who came to get the spell?' I ask.

'Are you nuts? Keeping records is a sure fire way to get caught.'

'Well, how many clients were there?'

'At least sixty.'

Christ. 'Do you know any of their names?'

O'Shea shakes his head.

'Distinguishing features? Especially for the Montserrat ones?'

'Mate, all vampires look the same to me.'

I struggle to see how this is true. I try a different tack. 'Why do you think they tried to kill you? I mean, if sixty of them used the spell, why not keep going? Or why not kill you after they took it the first time?'

'Copyright.'

'Huh?'

'I copyrighted it. I don't want some other dealer stealing my shit and making money from it that should be mine, so I placed a copyright on it.'

I frown. 'What does that mean exactly?'

'That each spell only has a one-time use. You can't buy it, then pass it round all your friends for free. If they want it, they have to purchase their own. I'm a businessman.' He rubs his fingers together. 'It's all about profit.'

'Look where that profit got you,' I mutter. 'What changed?'

'What do you mean?'

'You said they leached the spell from you before trying to kill you. If it's copyrighted, as you say, then how could they use it?'

'They must have found a way around it.' He doesn't appear particularly upset. 'People usually do eventually.'

It sounds remarkably similar to what Rogu3 does. He told me once that companies keep putting in place bigger and better fire-walls and security systems to beat the hackers, but they are only temporary measures because sooner or later the hackers always find a way round them. I wonder if there's an endpoint – a time when people will stop this cycle of security and slash. Probably not.

TWO HOURS LATER, I'm still feeling anxious and wondering whether I'm doing the right thing when my musings are interrupted by the doorbell. The butterflies in my stomach go into overdrive.

'That'll be your chauffeur,' O'Shea says cheerily.

I stand up but my legs shake, so I sit back down abruptly. The daemon pulls me upright and grabs the lapels of my jacket. 'You'll be fine. You'll find the killers, solve the mystery and get to the end of the full moon cycle as a newly fledged and wholly powerful Sanguine. Go you!'

I don't want to be a wholly powerful Sanguine though. I'm perfectly happy being a weakass human in a leather jacket.

O'Shea gives me a push towards the door. 'Off you go.'

For a moment, I dig my heels into Montserrat's perfectly varnished floor. I have to force myself to walk forward. I now realise where the phrase 'rooted to the spot in terror' comes from. I swallow hard. This is the fate I've chosen. I need to deal with it.

LESS THAN TWENTY MINUTES LATER, I'm deposited by the taciturn driver at the front of the imposing Montserrat headquarters. If you were to look up 'vampire lair' in a visual dictionary, the building in front of me would probably be what you'd see. It may be situated on the edge of a busy thoroughfare and right next to the bustle of Hyde Park, but there's an odd atmosphere of silence around it, as if it's in a bubble. The masonry is old; I have no idea how long the Montserrat Family have been holed up here although I've heard tales about how they still hold a grudge against the human royal family for opening up the park to the public. Considering that happened back in 1637, I guess they've been there for a bloody long time. Chillingly, if you turn and look back at the park, the old site of the Tyburn gallows is perfectly visible. The last person to have been executed there might have been way back in the eighteenth century but it still gives me the willies.

I stare up at the grey stone walls and the turrets and gargoyles. I've passed this building many times before and never given it more than a cursory glance. Now, as I'm about to enter, I find myself looking at it with entirely new eyes.

Unusually for this time of year in London, there's not a single cloud in the sky. The sun beams down at me mockingly. I have to admit that as I step over the threshold, I'm kind of hoping some burly bloodguzzler will clamp their hand on my shoulder and throw me out because there's been a mistake and I'm not supposed to be here after all. My luck, such as it has been over the last few days, doesn't change.

The interior is bright and airy, quite the opposite of what I expected. Standing to my left is a fully tuxedoed butler, holding out a silver tray with glasses of brown liquid. I take one and sniff it suspiciously but it seems to be nothing more than sherry. As tempted as I am to partake of a little Dutch courage, I don't drink it. I want to keep my senses fully alert. Besides, who knows what the vampires have dropped in to the alcohol?

A trim female vampire holding a clipboard glances at me from the crowd in the centre of the hall. The people surrounding her all appear to be human. I'm surprised at how many of the new recruits have brought family members to see them off, as if they were going on a European cruise rather than giving up their lives to the vampires. A couple of the family members are upset: there is one older woman in particular whose muffled sobs provide an uncomfortable backdrop to the smiling faces of the majority. I'm with the sober. The logical part of me recognises that the vampires offer security and inhuman longevity and health. It's the inhuman part that bothers me. I don't have anything against tribers – far from it. I'm just happy with who I am now. I wonder if my feelings will be different this time tomorrow. I sincerely hope not.

Still holding the sherry glass, I push my way carefully through to Clipboard Lady and give her my name. She smiles at me, but it's far more functional and perfunctory than welcoming or reassuring. I sense a coldness in her that seems to be directed entirely at me.

'Ms Blackman,' she says. 'Welcome to Family Montserrat.'

For some reason I think of the soundtrack to *The Sound of Music*. I can't quite imagine Michael Montserrat in lederhosen, though.

'Thank you,' I murmur, hoping I have quelled the fear in my voice enough to avoid raising suspicion.

'You may say your last goodbyes now. The opening ceremony will begin in about fifteen minutes.'

I have no one to say goodbye to. I spare my mother a brief thought but I know that, unlike my grandfather, she feels her job as a parent was done and dusted the day I reached eighteen. There are no bad feelings between us and she wasn't a bad mother. Merely … busy with other things, I suppose. It would be different if my father were still alive. I hope he'd have understood what I am doing.

I make my way through a set of mahogany doors and into what looks like a hotel conference room. Apart from the vials of glistening red blood sitting on the silver platter at the front, that is. There's only one other person in here – a silver-haired man who is sitting near the vials and staring at them. I can't work out whether the expression on his face is resignation or anticipation.

I'd like to head for the safety of the back row but I'm here for one specific reason. The other recruits will probably be too new to be involved in what is really going on but that doesn't mean they won't be targeted at some point. I need to get each one to take me into their confidence. The last thing I want is to have a dozen new BFFs – actually, no, scratch that: the last thing I want is to be turned into a vampire. But if I'm going down this route, I'm going to make it worth everyone's while. I draw back my shoulders, take a deep breath and smile. Not too broadly – any recruit would feel a bit scared and nervous – but hopefully enough to put the man at his ease.

I sit next to him. He twitches slightly as if he's trying to pull away.

'This is surreal, isn't it?' I offer as an opening gambit.

His head jerks but he stays quiet. I stick my hand out. 'Bo Blackman,' I say. 'By the look on your face, I think we're both feeling the same right about now.'

For a moment, I think he's going to ignore me but eventually he grasps my hand and shakes it. His palm is dry and his grip is strong, contradicting what I assumed was terror on his part.

'Peter,' he answers. 'Peter Allen.' He raises his eyes to mine. 'And how are you feeling then?'

'Excited. Nervous.' I swallow. 'Scared.' At least I don't need to fake those last two emotions.

He looks down at his lap. I realise with a jolt that he's holding a crucifix, twisting it over and over in his fingers. It seems baffling that a devout Christian would want to give themselves over to the vampires. Back in the sixties, there was a long drawn-out publicity campaign to persuade the public at large that vampires did indeed have souls and that they were not an affront to God, no matter which version of God you believed in. I remember watching one of those nostalgic television programmes a year or so ago – you know, the type that's dirt cheap to make, pulls in an audience by the million and includes Z-list celebrity pundits commenting on a countdown of the best moments of … whatever. One of the clips which made it into the top ten was of a bloodguzzler being doused in a vat of holy water, grinning and smiling into the camera the entire time. As I recall, this particular clip wasn't included as proof that vampires aren't harmed by religion (and therefore are not considered evil in the eyes of God) but more because at the same moment the vampire volunteer's head went under, a seagull decided to dive bomb the outdoor bath constructed specially for the event.

Despite the success of the campaign across middle England, many humans still rail against the vampires' existence. They point to sections of the Bible like that one from Leviticus: 'If any one of the house of Israel or of the strangers who sojourn among them eats any blood, I will set my face against that person who eats blood and will cut him off from among his people.' They conveniently choose to forget other parts which don't fit with current beliefs. Pointing out that the Bible also says stubborn children should be stoned doesn't lessen their antipathy to the bloodguzzlers. It's easy to pick and choose quotes to suit your purpose. Regardless, the majority of churchgoers avoid the vampires whenever they can.

Peter notices my reaction to his cross. He tries to laugh, although the result is more of a choke than a guffaw. 'Silly, isn't it?' he says. 'I guess I am feeling scared and nervous, just like you. I need something to cling to.'

I'm curious. 'Is it helping?'

'The cross?'

I nod.

'No, I think it's actually making me feel worse. What if…?' his voice trails off.

Impulsively I reach over and squeeze his hand. 'You're no longer considered clean in God's eyes? We're probably all thinking that, even those of us who aren't sure if we have faith in a higher power.'

'Why are you here?' he asks.

I'm prepared for this. O'Shea and I spent time discussing various scenarios to explain why I've decided to join the vampires and then choosing the most plausible – and the one likely to garner me the most 'friends' as a result. For this plan to work, I need the traitors to believe I'm prepared to turn on the Family and help destroy it from the inside. I also need the other new recruits to trust me in case they are approached themselves. I'm not in a position to lie too blatantly either – I've been in the news too much lately to pretend to be someone I'm not.

I give a heavy sigh. For a moment I think I've been too melodramatic but Peter squeezes my hand as if to reassure me. 'Joining any of the Families wasn't something I considered until a few days ago,' I admit. Lies are always more believable when they're woven with half-truths. 'I had a good life. I mean, I was lonely, but I had a good life.'

'Lonely?'

'My father passed away several years ago and my mother is always away. I have a grandfather who I see from time to time but he's,' I pause, as if searching for the right word, 'difficult.' I let Peter read into that what he will. 'And I have no significant other to speak of. I always wanted children,' I add sadly.

'But you're young! There's plenty of time to meet someone.'

I nod. 'Well, I had met someone. I was in love with my boss.' Sorry, Tam, I tell him silently. It's for a good cause.

A knowing look flashes across Peter's face. 'Is he married?' he asks gently.

'Divorced. I thought there was a chance that one day…' I sigh again. 'Except now he's dead. A vampire killed him and all my colleagues.'

He looks shocked. I hope I've hit the right balance between bitterness and pain.

'Why would you join a Family when a Family killed the man you loved?'

'I need to understand why. Maybe by becoming a recruit, I'll discover how he incurred their wrath. And…' I look down and awkwardly tug at my hair.

'Yes?' prompts Peter.

'I've heard that vampires don't experience emotions the same way that we do.' According to my grandfather this theory is rubbish but it serves my purpose, so I continue. 'This could be a good way to shut off the pain. It also means the police won't come after me any more.' I glance up at him. 'They think I'm responsible for killing Tam. My boss.'

'You?'

I try not to be irritated by Peter's incredulity. 'I know! It's ridiculous to think that I could do such a thing!'

He moves his hand up my arm and gently turns me towards him. 'That's terrible. Simply terrible.'

I sniff and sneak a look at his eyes from under my lashes. Peter Allen does indeed appear to be swallowing my story whole.

'If you can't beat 'em, join 'em,' he murmurs.

I try not to smile. Score one for the daemon, then. I'd suggested to O'Shea that I say that myself. He told me the words would be too pat but it was a good strategy to imply them. I have to give him credit for being more cunning than I'd thought. No wonder he got away with his dodgy dealings until now.

'How about you?' I ask, deciding the time is right to encourage my fellow recruit to take part in everyone's favourite pastime – talking about themselves. Now that I've delivered my own story, I can focus on everyone else. With any luck, Peter will turn out to be a bit of a gossip and I won't need to repeat my tale to every new recruit.

He withdraws, however, and his face clouds over. 'I'd rather not talk about it.'

I wait a few beats. It's amazing how often people will say they'd 'rather not talk about it' and then open up. Apparently, Peter is the exception to the rule. He stays mum.

'I understand,' I murmur, cursing inwardly. 'We all have our secrets.'

He smiles gratefully. I wonder if his reticence has anything to do with the crucifix that he is still clutching tightly. Before I can say anything else, however, the relative silence of the small auditorium is interrupted.

'OM smegging G!'

I wince. The 'I'm too lazy to use actual words' voice belongs to a bouffant bottle-blonde. She's done up to the nines: high heels, tight black dress, sparkling jewels and long scarlet fingernails. So much for it being difficult to gain admission into the Families. Maybe Michael Montserrat is wanting a little relief from his darker Family members.

The blonde is followed by several others. Peter goes back to staring at the floor but I reckon a little curiosity about the other recruits won't be out of place so I stare openly at them all. By the time everyone is inside, I've counted an unlucky baker's dozen. I'm not particularly superstitious, but I can't help thinking it isn't a coincidence that our little band numbers thirteen.

There is a young girl in a wheelchair; no prizes for guessing her motives for being here. I spot a couple of older men including, I note, a retired politician who has often been on the front pages for all the wrong reasons. I seem to remember there were allegations of fraud. It surprises me that he's here; I guess he was innocent after all. The others are a mish-mash of the nondescript and the showy: bespectacled nerds, beefed-up athletes and strait-laced suits.

Someone once said not to judge a book by its cover. Whoever it was clearly never worked as a private investigator. How people look can give an observer information about who they really are. Attention to detail is vital. It's something I'm not particularly skilled at, but I'm training myself to get better. For example, the youngish man in a suit who sits diagonally behind me may look dapper but his cheap, scuffed shoes and ever-so-faint twitch in his upper eyelid suggest an entirely different story. I'm interested in one woman whose hair suggests downtrodden housewife but whose clothes are more rebellious teenager. Anyone sporting contrasts in their appearance usually reflects those same contrasts in their personality. According to Tam, anyway. I make a mental note to talk to her as soon as I can.

I realise that the loud blonde is assessing me in much the same way as I am examining everyone else. She lifts an eyebrow in my direction when she sees me watching her, and raises a tanned hand to her perfectly coiffed hair. I register the watch on her wrist: a Timex. It doesn't match her clothes and make-up or the way she holds herself. Perhaps I'll speak to her soon, too.

By my side, Peter mutters something. I turn back to him just as the door closes with a deafening finality. My stomach drops unexpectedly at the sound. I see a vampire looping a twisted red rope around the handle, effectively locking us in. I understand it's symbolic rather than a real barrier, but it's clear that everyone in the room feels the same. The turning is about to begin.

15

BLOODY POWERPOINT

I suppose I'd been assuming it would be Michael Montserrat himself. Instead, the door behind the table of vials opens and a large male vampire strides in. As soon as he begins to speak, I recognise his voice: it's Ursus, the one who came after me at The Steam Team. He doesn't waste time smiling.

'Good morning. The Family Montserrat is pleased to welcome you into our midst.' He gazes around at all of us expectantly as if waiting for a reply. When there is none, he continues. 'Before the turning takes place, there are some matters that need to be addressed. I understand that you are all nervous and keen to start as soon as possible.' His mouth widens as if he's going through the motions of smiling but not quite managing it. 'However, it is vital you fully understand what is about to happen.'

He gestures to some invisible force and a projector screen drops down. A part of me squirms. Death by PowerPoint.

As soon as the screen clicks into place, an image appears of the Montserrat logo. It's a twisting, almost Celtic, design and no doubt familiar to everyone in the room. I think it's supposed to suggest eternity and strength; it's unfortunate that these days it looks more like a tattoo you can get in any high street shop. In fact, I'm fairly certain I've seen it for sale as a temporary skin transfer. But I suppose that pretending to be a vampire for a day is easier than actually becoming one.

Ursus clicks on a handheld device and the next slide appears, filled with dense, tightly packed writing which he reads aloud. Despite the style of his delivery, I am rapt.

'You are the lucky few,' he intones. 'Thousands apply to join us and few are accepted. It is not an easy road to take. From the moment you accept the Montserrat blood into your veins, you are beholden to us. Loyalty is non-negotiable and we do not tolerate anything other than obedience.' Given the current circumstances, that's obviously not as true as he'd like us to believe. 'You will leave your human lives behind. Many of you will never see your biological families again. Some of you may not survive the turning process.'

Out of the corner of my eye, I see one of the more serious looking recruits raise a nervous hand. 'How likely is it that we won't make it?'

Ursus moves onto the next slide. Clearly this question has been anticipated. 'Between eight and fourteen percent of new recruits do not make the turn. The reason why is unknown. We have studied our intakes for many years and there is no pattern. However, expect that at least one of you will not see what tomorrow brings.'

There's a sudden nervous shifting. People start eyeing each other up. Who will be the statistical death? Several turn to the girl in the wheelchair with knowing glances. I feel my insides tighten. Ursus's words remind me that I could well be making the worst decision of my life. I think of the alternative: of running away and hiding so I can be tracked down and killed by the rogue vampires while their buddies take over the world. It doesn't make me feel a whole lot better.

The next slide appears. 'There are numerous myths you need to be aware of,' Ursus continues. 'To begin with, vampires are not immortal.' I already know this and I'm sure the rest of the recruits do too. Everyone, however, leans forward slightly. 'Your lives will be lengthened to an expectancy of around three hundred years. You will not be invincible, although you will be freed from the majority of illness that strikes other species. Accidental death and,' he pauses, 'death by design do still occur occasionally. Predators remain.'

Another hand goes up. 'What about sunlight?'

'You will be vulnerable to the sun's glare between the first twenty to sixty months from the date of your turning. Everyone is different. After that, while you will not enjoy beach holidays, you will be able to venture outside without feeling too uncomfortable. Holy water and crucifixes will not hurt you. By becoming one of us, you are neither relinquishing your soul nor your faith.' Next to me, Peter sits a little straighter. 'A stake through the heart will pretty much finish you off, as will fire or beheading. And for the first year, you will find your body remains as weak as a human's.' Ursus attempts another smile. It still doesn't work. 'However, the concept of threshold boundaries holds true – unless the property is a business or uninhabited.'

I'd often wondered about that. It's reassuring to know that a vampire cannot just break into your house and drink from you.

'By joining our Family, you are subject to our laws. Let me stress that murder is *verboten*. You will drink blood but you will not drain, and for the first few years you will only drink from pre-assigned volunteers.' I repress a shudder at the thought the many vampettes exposing their jugulars for our delectation. 'There are, of course, other crimes. If you are found guilty of any crime, the response is usually immediate execution.'

'So you can be killed even if you just steal something?' someone blurts out.

Ursus turns cold eyes on the speaker. 'Are you planning to steal something?'

'I... I...' she stutters. 'No, of course not but...'

'Well, then, what's the problem?' He carries on as if she's not spoken. 'Until your solar weakness is diminished, you will remain here. We will train you and help you find your new path in life, whatever that may be. Once you leave here, you will be required to attend meetings and fulfil duties as determined by the senior members of the Family. You will also pay a monthly tithe. Contact with other Families is not forbidden but we do require you to inform us of any exchanges that occur, no matter how innocuous. These are issues that we will explain in more detail before you venture back into the real world.'

Clipboard Lady appears and hands Ursus a bundle of papers. He holds it up. 'Here are the contracts. You will sign in your own blood then, when you feel ready, collect a vial and exit through this door.' He points to the one behind him. 'The Montserrat blood will be injected directly into your system, after which it will take up to three days for the turning process to complete. You may experience some discomfort during this time.'

I push breath out through the gap in my teeth. Whenever a doctor tells you there will be some 'discomfort', it usually means there will be considerable pain. With seventy-two hours to turn, I dread to think what it will really be like.

'You may still change your mind. We simply ask that you remain in this room and sign a binding non-disclosure agreement about what you have experienced thus far.'

I force myself not to look at the roped door. The distrustful human part of me finds it hard to believe that we can simply leave after all of this.

Ursus turns to go but there's one more person with a question. It's the blonde.

'So when do we meet Michael?' she asks.

The vampire doesn't bother to turn around. 'You will address him as my Lord.' He disappears out the door along with Clipboard Lady without answering the question.

Once he's gone we sit in silence for several moments. Then

someone stands up and walks over to where Ursus left the contracts. It's one of the muscle-bound recruits. He twists his neck round and flashes us all a confident smile. I dislike him already. Everyone watches him, holding their breath. He picks up a small silver knife, polished so skilfully that I could probably do my make-up in its reflection, and pricks his index finger. A bead of blood appears. He flips through to the contract's final page without bothering to read the words and presses the tip of his finger down. Nothing happens – no thunderclap or applause. He scoops up a vial, takes the contract and follows the vampires.

As soon as he disappears, it's like a spell is broken. People move to the table, forming an orderly queue. Even in a situation like this, the British sense of propriety is in place and there's no jostling or shoving for position. I watch as, one by one, they follow the protocol then disappear out the door. A few people grimace in pain when they prick their fingers and the blonde lets out a small squeal. I notice that everyone else has the sense to take the time to read the pages first. Despite this, it's not long until the only people left are Peter and I and the girl in the wheelchair.

'I'm scared,' she whispers.

I give her a quick smile. 'Me too,' I admit.

Peter just wrings his hands.

'What's your name?' I ask.

'Nicky.' She takes a deep breath then wheels herself up to the table. I'm tempted to ask if she needs any help but she may find that insulting, so I wait instead. She has no problems reaching the contract and the blade.

'I hope don't catch any nasty disease off this,' she jokes half-heartedly. Her hand shakes visibly as she cuts. She, like Mr Muscles, doesn't read the contract before adding her blood to the final page. I put his lack of care down to machismo; I wonder what her reason is.

She struggles with the door, so I jump up and open it. She gives me a grateful smile, then she's gone.

I look at Peter. 'Are you okay?'

He licks his lips nervously. His gaze flicks between me and the remaining two vials, then back to the door through which we entered.

'I'm not sure.'

'You can change your mind. It's not too late.'

'Do you think the non-disclosure agreement really works?'

I know what he's asking. 'I'm pretty sure that they won't kill you if you change your mind.' I hope I'm right.

He stands up. 'No,' he says finally. 'I'm going to do this.' He signs and then I'm left alone.

The silence in the room is oppressive. I look at the table and away again. I'm not usually an indecisive person but signing my life away is a whole different kettle of fish to the sort of decisions I normally make. Deep down, I know what I'm going to do; my fate was sealed the second I walked out of that police station with Montserrat. But I want to feel as if I really am in charge of my own fate. I realise that reading the contract isn't going to make any difference so, like Nicky and the gym fiend, I flip to the last page. There's a dotted line and nothing more.

I pick up the knife. It's surprisingly heavy for such a small thing. It's also remarkably clean considering it has already sliced the fingers of twelve people. I take a deep breath. I'm glad I waited to the end so that I'm doing this without an audience. I touch the knife tip to my finger and watch the bright red blood well up. Then I press down and sign, sealing my fate. I take the one remaining vial and am about to open the door when my gaze falls on Peter's crucifix. It's lying forlornly on his empty chair. I scoop it up then shove it in my pocket, just in case.

It's time to go.

I FIND myself in a small ante-room with several doors. Clipboard Lady raises her eyebrows at me and points to the right. I follow her directions and walk through. There, waiting, is Michael Montserrat. Unfortunately he's fully dressed this time, although the well-tailored suit does nothing to hide his toned physique.

'I wasn't sure if you were going to go through with it,' he says, his dark eyes boring into me.

I shrug. 'I wasn't in a rush, my Lord. I thought I'd take my time.'

He scowls. 'You don't have to call me that.'

'I'm going to be a good girl and do as I'm told.'

He laughs. 'Really?'

I grin. If you make people think you're toeing the line and following the rules, it's amazing what you can get away with. 'Of course,' I tell him.

He obviously doubts me but lets it go for now. I hand him the vial and roll up my sleeve. 'Let's get this over with.'

He takes it but, rather than pulling out a syringe as I'd expected, he places the blood to the side. 'We're going to do this the old-fashioned way, Bo. You'll have a better chance of beating the bloodlust and becoming Sanguine that way.'

My mouth dries. 'Uh, the old-fashioned way?'

'I'm sure you've seen *Nosferatu*.'

'You're going to *bite* me?' My voice is high-pitched and squeaky.

He looks amused. 'Yes. And then you're going to drink a pint of my finest.' He unbuttons the cuff of his left sleeve and rolls it up, exposing his tanned forearm.

I back away, my fingers scrabbling for the doorknob. 'No! I can't drink. If I drink I won't become Sanguine,' I protest.

He smiles at me genially although I can't help likening him to a cat gazing at the mouse it's about to pounce on. 'Human blood, Bo,' he says softly. 'You can't drink human blood. Mine is vampire through and through. It won't provide you with sustenance after you've turned but you will need it to complete the process. It's the same as injecting.'

'Why doesn't everyone turn this way then?'

Montserrat looks momentarily pained. 'This isn't always the easiest process. It's very intimate. It can create feelings of possession in the vampire doing the turning.'

I don't like the sound of this at all. 'And the turnee?'

'Sometimes they feel obligated towards their sire and can become overly attached to them.' He takes a step towards me and holds out his hand. 'But as I'm the Family Head, you're going to do what I say regardless. Remember you just said that you're going to do as you're told.'

I stare at his outstretched hand. 'If it's all the same to you, I think I'll pass.'

He shrugs. 'It's up to you. But if you really mean to avoid drinking blood so you can become Sanguine, this is your best shot. The injection, which is made up of mixed blood from all the senior Family members, hits your bloodstream so directly and quickly that it can be almost impossible to fight the feelings that come afterwards.'

'That's even if I survive this,' I grunt.

'Somehow I think you're too stubborn to allow yourself not to make it through the turn. But,' his face remains impassive, 'ultimately it is your choice. If you'd rather have the jab, I can have someone come in here to administer it properly.'

My legs feel like jelly. Neither option is particularly desirable. The last thing I want is to feel 'overly attached' to him. But if I can sweat through the lunar month and become Sanguine...

'Fine,' I say. 'Lets it do it your way.'

Montserrat inclines his head towards me. 'As you wish.' He extends his hand a little further. When I don't move, exasperation fills his voice. 'Bo, you're going to need to come a bit closer.'

Shakily, I step forward. He smiles down at me. 'You really are very short,' he comments.

I scowl. 'So?'

'So nothing.' His tone is mild. 'If I can stoop down to kiss you, then I can certainly make it to your throat.'

'Kiss?' I half shriek.

'I just meant that I can still do this, Bo. Nothing else.' His eyes gleam. 'Although I *will* bite even if you don't.'

My entire spine is rigid with wariness, despite his amused reference to my faux-pas in his bedroom. So much for thinking that he'd not registered what I'd said.

He sighs. 'It'll go easier if you turn around.' When I don't immediately respond, he reaches out and brushes his thumb across my cheek. I flinch. 'You can trust me.'

'Said the spider to the fly,' I mutter. However, I turn around so my back is to him.

I feel him step towards me until his entire body is warm against mine. He bends down until his breath is hot against the flushed skin of my neck. I feel his fingers gently pull away my hair and I stiffen involuntarily.

'Relax,' he whispers softly in my ear. Then his teeth graze my throat.

His tongue darts out and licks and I stop breathing. I can sense him shifting his weight behind me, one hand remaining at my head, fingers entwined in my hair to keep it back, and his other resting lightly on my hip. I feel more nervous than I've ever felt in my life.

'Last chance to change your mind,' he says.

'I can't,' I begin, 'I've already signed...'

I gasp as there's a sharp nip of pain. His teeth sink into my flesh and I'm dimly aware of a rippling shudder running through his body behind me before a warm glow starts in my throat and begins to spread down my veins as he sucks. I lean against him, closing my eyes, while his fingers tighten their grip. My heart is thudding so loudly in my ears that I'm amazed Montserrat's not deafened by it. There's pain, but it's not unpleasant and I can feel my toes tightening in an almost enjoyable response. I moan lightly.

His hand leaves my hip and moves upwards across my ribcage until it rests just under my breasts and pulls me tighter against him. Sparking pinpricks of light dance across my shuttered lids and I involuntarily reach behind and grab his body, my hands now gripping his hips. He makes an odd sound, almost like a purr and I can feel his fangs pushing deeper into my throat. My breath quickens.

Abruptly, and without warning, his mouth leaves my skin although his hard body remains in place. He removes his hand from my hair, letting it drop back into place, then shifts his arm upwards. He's breathing as hard as I am.

'Open your eyes, Bo.'

I do as he instructs. His exposed arm is now in front of my face and there's a single trickle of blood travelling down his nut-brown skin from a small wound in his wrist.

'You need to drink,' he says, moving his wrist towards my hungry mouth.

Weakness attacks my legs and I'm sure I'd fall if he weren't holding me. I clutch his arm and pull it closer, then begin to suck. Salty blood fills my mouth and my gag reflex automatically kicks in. I choke but he murmurs something in my ear and I relax and swallow the hot sticky liquid, mouthful after mouthful.

Just when I think I can't take any more, he pulls his arm away and twists my body round. I look up into his dark, glittering eyes. His face is flushed red and he is staring at me. Then I'm overcome by a wave of dizziness and everything fades to black.

16

TRUTH AND LIES

When I finally come to, I'm lying on a single bed in a tiny room. I try to sit up but the effort is too much. Nausea fills my stomach and I'm covered in sweat. At least I'm alone. I twist onto my side, panting with effort. There's a small wooden table next to me with a jug and an empty glass.

My mouth is painfully dry and my lips are cracked and sore. Just how long have I been here? I reach for the jug but it's just out of my grasp. Bugger – I'm going to have to sit up after all. I curl my fingers round the mattress and pull my feet up, take a deep breath and push myself up onto my elbows. The room spins.

Gritting my teeth, I force myself upwards until I'm almost sitting. I turn my head too sharply and my stomach lurches in response. I breathe in through my mouth, until I manage to regain a little equilibrium. I'm still wearing the clothes I arrived in, although my leather jacket is missing. My arms are bare and covered in goosebumps. I rub them up and down and try to reach the jug again.

I misjudge the distance and fall onto the cold tiled floor. I grimace in pain, cursing my stupidity. The effort to get back up seems too great so I lie there, cold, shaking and very much in need of a drink.

The door to the room opens. From the angle I'm lying at, all I can see is a pair of shoes so shiny that I can see my reflection in them. There's a loud tut, then arms reach down and pull me back onto the bed. I hear the sound of liquid being poured and a glass is placed in my hands. I raise it gingerly to my lips, sniffing first. Fortunately it is just water. I sip it carefully then look up. My benefactor is Ursus. He's standing there, watching me with his arms crossed.

'So,' he says, 'you made it then.'

'I'm a vampire?' I croak, with equal measures of dismay and relief.

He laughs humourlessly. 'Not yet. For that you need to drink.' He gestures down at the cup in my hand. 'And I don't mean water.'

'Blood.'

He nods. 'Would you like some now?'

Hell no. I shake my head then wish I hadn't as the room starts to spin again. Ursus raises his eyebrows but doesn't say anything.

'Did everyone make it?' I ask.

He shakes his head. 'We lost three.' For a second, his impassive mask wavers. I realise he's angry about it and he goes up in my estimation. I feel a flicker of sorrow at the deaths but I quash it. Whoever they were, they knew what they were getting them-selves in to. But I can't help hoping that nervy Peter Allen wasn't one of them.

Ursus points to the door. 'When you feel ready, you'll find a shower room two doors to the right. There is clean clothing. Let me know if you change your mind about the blood.'

'Thanks, Ursus.'

He stares at me and I kick myself mentally. I know his name from overhearing him at The Steam Team; he has never intro-duced himself to any of us. He must know who I am and be wondering how I went from running from the vampires to joining them. I'm too shaky to think of any good answers right now, so I'm grateful that he does nothing more than purse his lips before opening the door.

I watch him go. Clearly, he is unaware of my real reasons for being here. I'm glad. It seems obvious that there are traitors at the heart of the Montserrat Family. It's good that Michael doesn't trust anyone; that will make my job easier if any of the culprits turn out to be men he thought he was close to.

I touch my neck where Michael drank but there's nothing there – not even a scab. It throbs under my fingers when I press down, although I can't be sure whether that's a real sensation or I'm imagining it. I suppose my new healing powers will prevent any awkward questions about why I have a fresh wound when I was meant to be injected. To test my theory about healing, I reach up with both hands and prod at my nose. It doesn't hurt. Maybe there are benefits to being a vampire after all.

I stand up when I feel strong enough. I wobble slightly but maintain my balance. I feel grubby; a hot shower is definitely in order to make me feel more human again. So to speak. I slowly edge my way towards the door. The exertion is draining and seems to take an age but I finally reach the shower room.

It's a large communal area with cubicles lining either side. On one wall there are hooks, each one holding a midnight-blue jumpsuit. I count ten in total, meaning that, with three already dead and gone, none of my fellow recruits have yet emerged from their own private hell of turning.

When I lean forward, I see names printed on small labels above each hook. Both Nicky's and Peter's names are there and I exhale in relief that they are among the survivors. Without knowing anyone else's name, it's difficult to tell who else has made it. I'm fairly certain that two of the men and one woman are the unlucky ones though. Three seems a high number considering Ursus's statistics. I wonder if more people would have backed out had they known in advance how many would die.

I pull off the jumpsuit under my own name and frown. It's certainly not an outfit I'd have chosen for myself but I suppose it'll have to do. I take it and my tired body into the nearest shower and strip off. There's already a towel hanging on the back of the door.

The water is hot, scalding my skin. I grab the bar of soap and scrub myself from head to toe before washing my hair. Then I simply stand immobile under the torrent of water for a long time.

When I finally emerge from the cubicle, another shower is running. I'm curious to see who else has made it so I check the names on the hooks. The missing jumpsuit belongs to someone called Matt. If he spends as long in the shower as I did, I'll be waiting for quite some time to see who he is, so I decide to leave him to it.

As I step into the corridor, I jump in surprise. Clipboard Lady is standing there. She points to a basket on the floor; I'm sure it wasn't there when I went into the shower room.

'You can leave your old clothes in there,' she tells me.

I hug my clothes to my chest. I don't want to give them up. Right now, they're all I have to remind me of who I really am. Her eyes narrow, however, and I know I can't appear too eager to hang on to my old life so I drop them in.

'You've been fast.'

I stare at her, not sure what she means. She explains, 'Turning. You've recovered in record time. I think only Lord Montserrat himself managed to wake up more quickly.'

It's probably because I went through the turning process by being bitten rather than injected but I can't help feeling a flicker of pride.

'I'm not the only one,' I tell her. 'Someone called Matt is in there too.'

She nods. 'Yes. He's been fast too.'

I wait for her to pass further comment but she doesn't say anything, instead just points down the hall. Rather than following her directions, I get to work.

'I didn't catch your name,' I say.

She appraises me coolly. 'Ria.'

I smile at her. 'It's good to meet you. I'm Bo.'

'I know who you are.' She doesn't return my smile. 'Why are you here?'

I try to ignore the flash of panic and keep my amiable expression firmly in place. 'Why does anyone become a vampire? Long life, ready-made family, lots of perks. It's win-win.'

She leans towards me. 'Lord Montserrat put me in one of the teams that looked for you after the daemon was attacked. You looked like someone who was trying to avoid having anything to do with us.'

'I thought you were trying to kill me.'

'Who says we weren't?' Her voice is low; there's definitely a veiled threat in it.

'I was being framed for the daemon.' I deliberately don't say whether O'Shea is dead or alive; I have no way of knowing what information Michael Montserrat has disseminated to his followers. 'Everyone I worked with was slaughtered.'

'By a vampire. And yet you choose to become a vampire yourself.'

I stare her down. 'I realised that if I was going to survive, I needed to join you. Not fight you. Michael, I mean Lord Montserrat, assured me that the Montserrat Family had nothing to do with any of that. The boss I loved is dead. I've got no one else.' I shrug. 'I had no reason left not to join.'

Her pupils narrow to slits. 'Revenge is a good reason.'

I have to tread very carefully. 'Oh, I'm angry,' I say, with conviction. 'But revenge is a tricky thing. Without knowing for sure who is ultimately,' I stress this last word, '*responsible*, revenge becomes meaningless. I hope that by joining the power of the Montserrat Family, I can prevent other innocents from being hurt.'

I pray that my answer is ambiguous enough for the traitors to believe I'd be willing to join their side. Theoretically, if they believe I can be persuaded into thinking that Michael Montserrat and the Montserrat clan are responsible for destroying my life, then I might be approached. It's a long shot but if the traitors are desperate enough it may just work. I'll need to ensure that if I come face to face with Michael in a public setting, I show enough dislike of him to be believed. Considering what he told me about the side effects of my turning, I'm hoping that's not going to be too difficult.

Ria glares at me. 'You think you can stop innocents from being hurt? What do you think the rest of us have been doing?'

I've clearly hit a nerve. I'm not surprised. If she's got no part in the new Family, then she'll feel threatened by the idea that vampires are going around willy-nilly and killing whoever gets in their way. I don't get a chance to respond, however, as the shower room door opens and we both turn round.

Matt is the muscle-bound man who stepped up first to the table. He appears surprised and not particularly pleased to see me. 'You recovered first?'

I try not to grin at the incredulity in his voice. I need to ingratiate myself with everyone, not piss them off, so I shrug and look baffled. 'Yeah, I don't know how that happened. I feel like shit though. Maybe I should have slept for a bit longer.'

He seems slightly mollified and flexes his muscles. It must be some kind of unconscious reaction. 'I feel fine,' he informs me.

'I wish I was that lucky.' Ria is looking at me suspiciously so I smile at her. 'I've got nothing to hide. I just want to fit in and make a new life for myself.'

She makes a noncommittal noise but I feel that I've pacified her – for now. I drop my head just a touch to appear subordinate to the pair of them and leave them to it. Keeping this front up is going to be bloody hard.

A FEW HOURS LATER, there are four of us. Matt and I spend the first hour sitting on comfortable sofas, shooting the breeze. Well, to be more accurate, he talks and I listen. He is full of bravado and wastes no time in telling me that he is going to 'shake things up in the vampire world'. He asserts that he'll be able to hold off drinking blood until the final day of the lunar month. I wish I shared his optimism.

We are joined by Nell, the woman who was so affronted by the idea that she might be summarily executed for stealing and, surprise, surprise, a now upright and walking Nicky. Her steps as she enters the room are shaky, but she gives us a tremulous smile and refuses to sit down. Half an hour later she is still standing, an expression of wonder on her face every time she glances down at her legs. I feel happy for her.

The door opens again and Ria comes in. She's carrying a tray of crystal goblets filled with what looks like blood. I swallow hard, my eyes tracking her every movement as she places the tray down in front of us.

'You are all welcome to partake,' she says, gesturing to the glasses.

No one moves. A tiny, knowing smile curves at the edges of her mouth. 'In that case, Lord Montserrat is ready for you.'

'What about the others?' Nell asks.

'They're not ready yet. I imagine they will join you tomorrow.' She eyes us all. 'Turning is harder for some than others. Remember, the process is not fully complete until you take your first drink.'

We all know she's not referring to water. She walks out, holding open the door, so we trail after her. Matt is in the lead, then Nell, Nicky and me. We go back down the corridor, past the bedrooms and out to a vast sweeping staircase that even Scarlett O'Hara would be proud of. There's a huge ornate mirror at the top. Matt stops and glances at his reflection.

'I can still see myself!' he exclaims. He touches his hair then, satisfied that it's looking good, opens his mouth and examines his teeth.

Ria rolls her eyes and I grin at her. We share an amused glance before she remembers that she's supposed to be suspicious of me. 'We wouldn't always look this good if we didn't have reflections,' she says, brusquely.

I realise she's not boasting, merely telling the truth. And she's right. I don't think I've ever seen a vampire who's not perfectly turned out. My thoughts turn involuntarily to Michael and his elegant suit. Then I force him out of my mind. I run my tongue over my teeth and turn back to Ria. 'Our fangs…'

'Will start growing after your first drink.'

Matt continues to admire his reflection. 'Mine are going to be huge.'

Nell nudges me. 'You know what they say – big fangs, small…' Matt frowns at her in the mirror '…feet,' she finishes.

I smirk.

We follow Ria down the staircase and into an atrium. I realise with a jolt that it's night time. Stars twinkle at us from far above the glass roof.

'It's dark,' Nicky whispers.

Ria hears her. 'Until you develop immunity to the sun, you will remain fully nocturnal. It's safer that way.'

'Why have this at all then?' asks Nell. 'Wouldn't it better to avoid sunlight altogether?'

A familiar voice speaks. It's Michael. 'You'll find that when you get used to the sun's rays, you will crave them and seek them out whenever they are not too strong to hurt you. And we're not taking any chances as you are all so new; these glass panes are specially treated to filter out any ultra-violet light.'

We all gape at him. He's a well-known figure and it's clear that he's immediately recognised. His gaze flicks briefly to me and my stomach squirms while Matt rushes forward and takes his hand, starting to pump it enthusiastically.

'It's an honour, sir. My Lord.'

'You're Matthew Baldwick. Your military experience will serve us well.'

Matt beams proudly. I should have guessed from his bearing that he was ex-army.

Michael turns to the rest of us. 'Nell Singer.'

She flushes. I watch her, interested. I wonder whether she'll still be able to blush once she's a fully-fledged vampire. Then I remember the red tinge on Michael's skin after I drank from him. I guess she will.

'Nicola Temerlaine.' Compassion lights his eyes as he looks at her. I file it away for future reference.

Nicky grins, her cheeks dimpling and making her look even younger than she probably is. He looks at me, although this time his face remains bland.

'Bo Blackman.'

I dip into a curtsey. 'My Lord.' Although my words are respectful, I inject them with the faintest hint of disdain. I hope he understands why. Something flashes across his eyes, but otherwise he doesn't react.

'From now on, you will no longer use those surnames. You are part of the Family Montserrat and will be addressed as such.' He smiles. 'Although you will lose your name, you will gain much, much more.'

I try not to cringe. All I hope to gain is the status of Sanguine and the names of the traitors who've ruined my life.

'We were told we were going to be trained, my Lord,' Matt interjects eagerly. 'When does that happen? What do we learn?'

'That will begin tomorrow,' Michael responds smoothly, 'once your companions have also recovered. Your schedule is light for the first month until the transition period is complete. For now, I suggest you explore the house and the grounds.'

'We can go outside?' exclaims Nicky.

He smiles. 'Only the garden. But, yes, some fresh air will probably do you good. You may also enter any room, apart from those tied at the handle with a red ribbon.'

I raise my eyebrows. It's like the dorm of an American university.

'We are a close-knit Family,' he adds, 'but personal privacy is still important.' He looks at me as he says this. I try hard not to look away.

Michael draws Ria to the side. A frisson of emotion runs through me as I watch his head bend towards hers and I realise that what I'm feeling is jealousy. Bugger it – my turning really has produced the side effects he promised.

'Come on,' I mutter to the others, 'they're obviously busy. Let's explore.'

Matt snorts. 'I'm going off on my own. The last thing I need to listen to right now is a bunch of chicks talking.' He walks off.

I gaze after his retreating back. I'll need to do some more ego-stroking to get him to trust me. No matter; there'll be plenty of time to work on that later.

'Ladies?' I say, glancing at the other two.

They both grin.

'Let's do it,' Nell says, taking my arm in hers.

Nicky darts round to my other side and does the same. 'Yes,' she says, her eyes shining. 'Let's.'

BOTH NELL and Nicky's excitement buzzes until I feel almost the same as them. Almost. We wander around the enormous house, gawping at the artwork, stained glass and intricately carved mahogany woodwork. We're careful to avoid the rooms with red ribbons tied around the doors, though I wonder how long it will be before I'm sneaking into those closed-off areas on my real quest. Still, I can feel a bond forming between us; we may have been thrown together by chance, but there's a strong sense of kinship as we explore together.

We venture down one long hallway, the walls of which are covered in portraits. I recognise several of the Montserrat Family Heads from years past. It's apparent that the gender imbalance which affects the human corporate world is alive and kicking in the vampire world too. Apart from the Bancroft Family the other Heads are male and it appears there's never been a female Montserrat Head.

When we reach the end of the corridor, we come to Michael's portrait. The artist has done a fine job of capturing his enigmatic dark eyes and strong jawline. There's just the faintest suggestion of the dimple in his cheek. I look at it, trying to ignore the light shiver that runs deliciously down my spine.

Nell comes up to my side. 'He's good-looking, isn't he?'

I turn away, embarrassed to be caught admiring his likeness. 'If you like that sort of thing.'

'Damn, I do,' Nell says. 'I doubt he'd be interested in little old me, though.'

I force myself to smile. 'Never say never.'

'Guys! Over here!' Nicky calls out.

I breathe a silent sigh of relief at her intervention. 'What is it?'

'The garden.' Her chest is moving rapidly up and down. 'It's been a long time since I've walked anywhere outside.'

Sympathy fills me. 'What happened?'

'I was very young so I'm not entirely sure. I remember some things. My mother screaming. My father...' her voice trails off.

'You were attacked?'

'Yes.' She straightens her shoulders and stares out at the dark trees and bushes. 'That part of my life is over now. I have a new family now.'

I squeeze her arm. 'And new legs.'

She grins at me. 'Then I'd damn well better make use of them, hadn't I?' She opens the door and steps outside, with both Nell and me following close behind.

I suck in the fresh night air. It feels good to be outside. It reminds me that I'm not dead. I'm not a vampire – not quite and not yet. I watch Nicky dancing forward and smile. Perhaps there's hope for us all.

We follow the twisting paths. I can't help marvelling at the size of the garden; considering we're in central London, this is quite some space. It's very well kept; patently there's a Montserrat gardener or two in the mix. The three of us stop and breathe in the heady smell from a rosebush in full bloom.

'I love roses.' Nicky sighs, sinking down cross-legged.

Nell joins her, stroking one of the petals. 'Beauty and danger all at the same time,' she agrees. 'You've got to admire nature.'

'Yup. Every rose has its thorn.'

Nell and I glance at each other and burst into song. Nicky looks baffled. 'What did I say?'

'It's an old rock song,' Nell laughs. 'You're probably too young to know it.'

'I'll have to find it and listen to it.' Suddenly she looks worried. 'Do you think vampires listen to music?'

'They must, surely.'

'I dunno. For some reason I imagine them all sitting around listening to piano concertos.'

We giggle like a bunch of school girls.

'I still can't believe it's true,' Nell says. 'That I've been recruited. I hoped I would be, but you hear such stories. I thought all the recruits would be like Matt.'

'There must be a reason why you were selected,' I say.

'I'm an artist,' she replies, although an inexplicable shadow crosses her eyes. 'Not a scientist or a soldier or anything useful at all.'

I feel an absurd sense of warmth towards the Montserrat Family for recognising art as meritorious. 'Art feeds our souls,' I tell her. 'I guess even vampires appreciate that.'

'What about you, Bo?'

I have to tell the truth here. 'I'm a private investigator.' I pick at the grass. 'I've only been doing it for a couple of years and I'm not particularly good. Maybe with a bit of direction from the Montserrat investigators, I can get better.'

'I'm sure you're better than you think,' Nicky says loyally. 'Otherwise they wouldn't have recruited you.'

They recruited me because I have too much invested in this whole mess, I think, not because I'm particularly skilled at my job. Aloud I ask, 'And you?'

'I fix things. Clocks, music boxes, toys, that kind of thing. I'm not much good with modern things, but if it's old-fashioned and has been around for a few decades then I'm a dab hand.'

'I guess we're all going to serve a purpose,' I say slowly. I think about the vampires who were killed because they went to see O'Shea. Perhaps their purpose in serving the Montserrat Family would be a good place to start. I lean back, knotting my hands behind my head, and gaze up at the sliver of moon. I have limited time to do all this and I'm itching to get started.

'I'm pretty exhausted,' I tell the others. 'I might head in and get some kip.'

'You were the first of us to turn, Bo. You've been up for longer.'

'Either that or I'm getting old,' I joke, then stand up and dust off my jumpsuit. 'I'll see you two tomorrow.'

They grin at me and wave. Feeling like I've achieved something, even if it's only getting a couple of the other new recruits to trust me, I head back inside, hoping I don't get lost along the way. Navigating the streets of London seems easier than finding my way around the vast maze of the Montserrat house.

I get lucky and find the staircase we descended with Ria. I go up, thinking I'll catch an hour's sleep before looking for Michael to give me some useful intelligence on the Montserrat vampires. I pause, however, at the door to the small living room area where we'd congregated and push it open. The four crystal goblets still stand where Ria left them. One is empty.

I pick it up. There's not a single drop of blood left in it, not even at the very bottom. Matt's self-control clearly isn't as good as he thought it was. I place it carefully back down and pick up another one by the stem, raising it up to my nose. I'd have thought that after all the blood I've been subjected to recently, the smell would make me retch. But the vampire is taking root inside me because my stomach actually grumbles. I return the glass hastily to the tray and leave.

17

SHOWERS AND HEELS

AS SOON AS I GET BACK TO MY ROOM, I KNOW THAT SOMETHING IS different. I can't tell whether it's a smell in the air or just a spooky sixth sense that I've now gained from the turning, but I know that things are not the way I left them. It doesn't take long to work out what. Underneath the pillow there's a laptop. Since I'm fairly certain that even in my weakened state I'd have noticed if I'd been sleeping on its hard shell, I assume that Michael left it very recently.

I open it up, waiting for it to whirr into action. The cursor blinks at me and I'm asked for a password. I lean back, frowning. Whoever left it, whether it was Michael or someone else, expected that I would know what to put in. I think for a minute, then type *sanguine*. Satisfyingly, the computer immediately accepts it and I'm through to the main desktop.

'Take that, computer,' I tell it, with just the slightest tinge of gloating.

There's almost nothing there, not even wifi access so that I can sneak a look at what's happening in the world. All that I can see is a folder marked Personnel and a desktop picture of O'Shea grinning out at me. I roll my eyes at the virtual daemon and click on the folder.

Scanning through the contents, it's clear that Michael Montserrat has come good. There are 497 names, accounting for all the members of the Montserrat Family, and one section marked with an X which I take to be those vampires who are no longer with us. I scroll down and, although I don't recognise most of the names, I can't stop myself from halting at Michael's to open his file. It reveals a single sentence.

Naughty, naughty, Bo. I don't think you'll find your traitor here. M x

I smile. Clearly, I'm just too predictable. I close down his file and move on, deciding to start with the people I've already met. It's easier to think about those I know than those I don't. I find Ria's name and open up the file.

Ria, who was originally known as Maria Temple, has been with the Montserrat Family for almost forty years. She was recruited back in the seventies after suffering a horrific car crash. I feel a brief shiver as I read that she'd been drink driving. What was not widely revealed at the time was that she was the then Prime Minister's secretary. I think of her clipboard and brisk efficiency. Yeah, it fits. She had a son who was told she had passed away and who, by all accounts, is now close to retirement himself. She seems to have risen through the Montserrat ranks remarkably quickly but I can't find anything to suggest that she would be involved in all this. Lucy – or Charity, as I keep reminding myself to think of her – made it very clear that this new Family Head was female. It fits with what I know of O'Shea's enhancement spell as it only works on males. However, despite her apparent wariness towards me, I can't find any shred of evidence or a gut feeling that points towards Ria. I create a new folder and mark it 'Unlikely' before dropping in her file.

I pull out all of the other files pertaining to Montserrat's female vampires and place them in a separate folder too. Other than Nicky and Nell, I've not met any other female vampires, so at this point I have nothing more to go on than the hard facts detailed by the Montserrat record keepers. There are fewer than two hundred and I wonder why fewer women than men choose to turn bloodguzzler. I'll have to ask Michael next time I get the chance.

I pick a new file at random and start reading. Alison Jones, recruited in 1892, lives off site in the Lake District. Goodness only knows what use she is there. She apparently killed her husband after years of domestic abuse. I try another: Ursula Hauptman, 1921, works for a famous celebrity publicist. She was a suffragette who used arson to draw attention to her cause. Good grief. Linda Tomkinson, 1753, journalist. Back in her day, she worked as a back-street abortionist and many of her patients died as a result of her ministrations. I shudder. An inordinate number of these vampires seem to have done bad things in their former lives. I guess the human race has more capacity for, if not black evil, then at least several shades of grey. After skimming through eighteen files, I massage my temples. Even if I knew what I was looking for, I doubt whether I'll find it.

I give up on the women and switch to the X files. The ache in my shoulders and the persistent throb in my forehead stop me smiling at the name. I open the most recent additions; these have to be related to O'Shea and his spell, which means they have to be linked somehow to the mysterious killer queen.

Five of the vampires are missing, presumed but not confirmed dead. Either that or they're holed up somewhere plotting against the other Families. The other eight have been discovered. The first few bodies were mutilated to avoid identification but the Montserrat labs are top-notch and it didn't take the boffins long to find out who they really were – even the first two, who were virtually cremated. Whoever was involved in their deaths must have realised this, because the more recent ones have simply been dumped at random locations around the city. No one has, as yet, discovered a pattern to the drops. All of the victims were male and several showed signs of increased libido in the weeks before their deaths. I smile grimly to myself. O'Shea's spell. But did they take it voluntarily or was it forced upon them?

I think that Michael must have been remarkably restrained in his dealings with the daemon to allow the deaths of several of his flock to go unpunished. Whether O'Shea intended it or not, it's his spell that links them together. I'm no forensic investigator but I'd love to be able to pull apart his enhancement potion to find out how it really works.

My thoughts are interrupted by a loud thump. I hastily return the laptop to its hiding place and go out to investigate. On the floor, in a tangled pile of limbs, are Peter Allen and the blonde.

'Smegging Jesus,' she hisses, 'get off me!'

He mutters something from underneath her, which I think is an admonition about taking the Lord's name in vain. It's difficult to be sure.

I'm tempted to reach down and help them extricate themselves but it's far more entertaining to watch. The zipper of the blonde's jumpsuit seems to be caught up in Peter's clothes. He's not yet changed so he must be on his way to the shower room. They roll around, banging against the walls, and several other doors open. I realise from the number of heads peering out that most of my fellow recruits have now turned. Like Peter, they look drawn and tired. The blonde, irritatingly, appears fresh faced and well rested. I'm amused to note that instead of the standard issue slip-on shoes, she's still wearing her stilettos. She digs one into Peter's calf and he yells.

Ursus appears from nowhere. He growls at all of us – the curious onlookers as well as Blondie and Peter. Something in his manner terrifies me, so I crouch down and help the flailing pair to separate. As soon as they're free, they leap up. Peter looks embarrassed.

'What in hell is going on?'

'He wasn't watching where he was going!'

'If you'd not been lurking around the corridor,' Peter grunts, with more vehemence than I'd have thought he was capable of, 'then I wouldn't have banged into you.'

Ursus snarls, 'Beth, you're supposed to be on the tour. Why are you still here?'

I watch her carefully. Yes, Beth, why *are* you still here? Peter's words suggest she was hanging around outside my door.

'I'm tired,' she sniffs, 'I was going back to bed.'

She doesn't look in the slightest bit tired. There's definitely something going on – and that means it's time for me to put on my best friend-making face.

'You too?' I exclaim. 'My head hurts, my muscles ache and all I want to do is sleep.'

She turns to me with a look that's more wary than grateful. After staring at me for a long moment, she finally mutters, 'See? I'm not the only one who's feeling crap after this turning nonsense.'

Ursus's eyebrows shoot up. 'Turning nonsense? You volunteered.'

I'm hoping to hear her response, but he launches into a tirade about her shoes. I let him continue while Beth does her best to stand up to him about her choice of footwear and sidle over to Peter instead. 'How are you doing?' I whisper.

'Okay.' He gives me a wan look, raising one hand to his neck then suddenly dropping it again.

'I'm glad you made it,' I tell him, and I mean it. I rather like the quiet man.

His mouth turns up at the edges but it's a forced smile.

'What actually happened?'

He shrugs. 'I wasn't looking where I was going. But she,' he jerks his head at Beth, 'couldn't have been moving or I'd have noticed her. She must have just been standing here.'

Right outside my door, I think. Stilettoed Beth is definitely my new pet project. I interrupt Ursus's lambasting. 'I think Beth's shoes are lovely,' I say. 'Who cares what we wear?'

'It's not about what you wear,' he growls, 'it's about doing what you're damned well told.'

'Come on, Ursus,' I coax. 'A pair of shoes is hardly going to bring the Montserrat Family crashing down upon our heads.'

A shadow crosses his face and he opens his mouth to say something but thinks better of it. I take Beth's arm and smile. I can feel her tense under my touch but she doesn't pull away.

'Fine,' he snaps eventually. 'But the whole lot of you need to get to bed. You've got a long night ahead of you tomorrow.' There's a threat in his tone. I continue to smile. Smiley, happy Bo, that's me.

Ursus turns on his heel and stalks off.

'Thank you,' Beth says once he's gone. 'I appreciate the help.'

'Hey, it's all in the name of female solidarity, right?' I hope I'm striking the right note. It doesn't make sense for a recruit to be the new Family Head but I'm more and more certain that blonde Beth is involved somehow. I spot Nicky's face peeking out from behind her door, her dark eyes a striking contrast to her pale skin. I give her a reassuring grin.

'We should do what he says and get some rest,' I tell them all. 'This turning stuff is bloody hard.'

'Speaking of blood,' Beth murmurs giving me an arch glance, 'have you drunk yet?'

I scan her face. It's obvious that I've not, so I'm curious why she's asked the question.

'No, not yet. I want to hold out a few more days. I've heard that the longer you last without drinking, the more powerful you eventually become.' I pat my stomach. 'I can cope with a few hunger pangs.' As if in immediate response, my tummy growls and I flinch slightly. I can't tell whether Beth is displeased or not at my comment.

'Well, thanks again, Bo,' she says, and glides off down the corridor to her room. I watch her go. She just made the same mistake that I did with Ursus: I hadn't told her my name.

I smile at Nicky and Peter, say goodnight, then slip back into my room. I take the jug and glass off the bedside table, place them on the floor and move the table to the door. It's not particularly heavy and won't stop someone who is trying to get in. One hard kick of a stiletto and it'll open, but it'll give me enough warning if I'm asleep. Then I pull out the laptop again and search for Beth's file.

I AWAKE up all at once, like a cat. Considering I used to doze in bed for hours, I'm not sure I like this vampire side effect. I sit up and glance at my makeshift barrier. It remains firmly in place; no one has tried to get in while I've been asleep. Satisfied, I put the table back in its original position and go for a quick shower. Unfortunately for me, Matt is standing, stark naked, in the middle of the room.

He gives me a slow lazy smile. I try to quash my shudder of disgust but don't quite manage it. I'd have thought he'd be a bit shame-faced after giving into the bloodlust so quickly. Clearly, he's not ashamed at all.

'I was hoping for Beth,' he drawls, 'but you'll do.' He points to the nearest shower cubicle. 'Let's get clean.'

My eyes travel down his body and I register that he's fully erect. I give him and his penis a pointed stare.

'It'll take more than that to interest me,' I tell him with a sniff. Determined not to let him think I'm intimidated, I push past him into another cubicle. It's not until I'm under the hot scalding spray of water that a thought suddenly occurs to me and I yelp in alarm. I twist round and wrench open the shower door, leaping out.

'Matt!'

The shower is running in the cubicle he'd gestured me towards. I thump on the door. 'Matt!'

He doesn't answer. Shit. I step back and lash out with my right foot, attempting to kick it in. With my bare feet slick from soap and water, I do little damage. I slam my shoulder against the door instead. It doesn't budge. Cursing, I jump up and curl my fingers around the top edge of the door. There's about a foot gap between it and the ceiling so I pull myself up and peer over. As soon as I see Matt, his jumpsuit wrapped tightly round his neck at one end and to the shower head at the other, I climb over to join him. His lips are blue and his eyes are bulging, tell-tale shots of red blasting through the whites of his eyes as he suffocates.

I grab his waist and try to haul his body upwards to take his weight. He's bloody heavy, however, and he keeps slipping down. I start yelling and kicking the door behind me, making as much of a racket as I can without dropping him. I hear someone's voice on the other side as they try to open the shower door. They have more success than me and it springs open, catching my back and making me fall down and drop Matt's body.

'Smeg.'

Beth pushes me out of the way and grabs hold of him. Even without her heels, she's considerably taller than me so she has more success at holding him up. She still struggles, though, and it won't be long before he falls again.

I leap up, my hands and arms on opposite sides of the cubicle walls, and shimmy upwards. I reach over for the jumpsuit noose but no matter what I do, I can't undo it: Matt's body is stretching the knot too tightly.

I bring my legs up and over Beth's body and squeeze round Matt's hanging form. Then I jump with as much force as I can muster onto the shower head. I slam my weight down onto the metal several times until I feel it breaking away from the tiled wall. I pull and pull until I'm falling backwards onto Matt's inert body.

Beth scrabbles out from underneath him and rips into the jumpsuit with her fingernails, loosening its hold around his neck. Without saying anything, she moves to his face and tilts his neck back while I crouch by chest and begin to pump.

'Dah, dah, dah, dah, staying alive, staying alive,' I sing to give myself the rhythm we need to start his heart again. As soon as I finish my final 'alive', Beth pinches his nose and breathes into his mouth.

We do it again. 'Dah, dah, dah, dah, staying alive, staying alive.'

She breathes and I start pumping again. It's not until the fifth time that he finally chokes and his chest moves of its own volition. I lean back, exhausted, and stare at Beth and then at Matt.

'Interesting technique,' she says.

I shrug. 'As long as it works.'

She glances down at Matt's face. 'It doesn't seem right that he could die like this. He's meant to be a smegging vampire.'

'A newly fledged vampire.'

I look up and see Michael watching us, a grim expression on his face. He gestures at someone behind him and two vampires appear. 'Take him to the infirmary immediately,' he instructs.

Beth stands up. Water is still gushing from the hole in the tiled wall where I yanked out the shower head, and she's soaked from head to toe. At least she's still wearing her jumpsuit, I think, suddenly abashed. I'm not usually particularly modest but crouching naked on the slippery tiles in front of them is making me feel vulnerable. Michael hands me the towel that was probably meant for Matt.

'You've only just been turned. For the first six months at least, it's easy to find ways to die if you want to kill yourself,' he says.

I take the towel and wrap it round myself. I meet his eyes for a moment; we both know this is no botched suicide attempt.

'I don't understand why he'd want to do that.' Beth is apparently oblivious to our shared look.

'He drank last night,' I inform her. 'I think he wanted to hold out for longer. Maybe he felt like he'd failed.'

Beth's expression is sceptical but my mind is whirring. Although I found little in her file to suggest she is with the traitors, I'm still convinced she's wrapped up in all this. It doesn't make sense that she'd help me save Matt's life if that's the case, though. And the blood that Matt drank – it had been sitting unguarded in the social area for at least two hours. Anyone could have dropped O'Shea's spell into the goblets, and whoever drank would be affected. I wonder what the side effects are on women. I need to talk to O'Shea again.

Troubled, I turn back to Michael. 'Will he be alright?'

'I don't know.' His voice contains a note of barely controlled rage. If he finds out who's responsible for this, they will wish they'd never been born. 'You two should get yourselves cleaned up,' he says tersely. 'Your training is due to begin in an hour or so.'

I can't believe that everything's going to carry on as normal but I have no idea what the alternative could be, so I nod stiffly. Michael glances at Beth before looking at me for a long drawn-out moment. Then he turns and leaves.

18

LOVE AND BLOOD

When we gather later, the mood is subdued. The news about Matt obviously whipped round the other recruits like wildfire. I note that Nicky's hands are shaking. I take special care to downplay my part.

'I heard something like choking,' I tell them. 'Something just didn't feel right. Thank goodness Beth was there or he'd probably have died.'

Beth gives me an odd look but remains quiet. When Ursus enters, he doesn't have the simmering rage that was evident in Michael, but his body is tense and his words are curt. 'What happened to Matthew is regrettable,' he says, 'but we cannot let it interfere with your own turning. Whatever his reasons for wanting to kill himself, I am sure we'll find them out when he regains consciousness. For now, you need to focus on your own progress. We have made a counsellor available. You may speak to him later about this appalling turn of events or about your own concerns regarding the change.'

I'm surprised that vampires use therapy – it seems a very modern phenomenon. I suspect that if I start talking about the trauma I've experienced over the last few days, I'll end up a bawling, shaking mess.

'Bo, your appointment is already scheduled for 3am.'

'I don't need counselling,' I protest.

'Regardless, you will take it.' His tone brooks no argument.

My chest tightens. It is an almost impossible situation. I won't be able to trust the counsellor so I'll have to skirt around the important stuff as well as trying to appear to open up. Yet another thing to worry about.

Ursus turns on the projector and another PowerPoint presentation beams up, uninspiringly entitled 'Rules and Regulations'. Despite our anxiety about Matt, there's a collective groan. We settle in for a long session.

By the time we break for coffee and muffins – because it turns out vampires do eat real food – I've realised there's an element of genius in Ursus's monotonous lecture. It provides information we need to know and is delivered in such a boring manner that we have no choice but to calm down and stop fretting. More goblets of blood are produced, along with typical teatime fare, although I note that Ria hovers over them as if afraid to let them out of her sight. I bet they won't be sitting unattended in any empty rooms from now on. I speculate whether she knows the truth about what's going on, or whether she's merely been told to stay with the blood without being given a reason.

One of the other recruits, an amiable man wearing glasses who has told me that his back acne has miraculously cleared up since he woke from his turning, eyes the goblets then makes a move towards them. Even though the others are engaged in conversation, everyone glances towards him and watches, some more surreptitiously than others.

He murmurs something to Ria and she hands him a glass, her face expressionless. He stares down at it, takes a deep breath and raises it to his lips. He gingerly takes a sip and his eyes widen. In about three seconds flat, he drains the whole thing. His eyes close in ecstasy although nothing else happens. I'm not quite sure what I was expecting. He certainly doesn't immediately sprout long white fangs and there's no clap of thunder.

My hands are trembling so I shove them into the pockets of my jumpsuit and turn away. As I do, I see Ursus looking at me. 'It's time,' he says.

I nod, just as I see another one of our little group venture cautiously over to the blood. It's been less than two days; there are still twenty-seven more to go. Unhappily, I follow the large vampire out.

He leads me towards the back of the mansion. We pass the corridor I discovered yesterday with Nicky and Nell, although this time I avoid pausing to check Michael's portrait. I'm taken to a large office, complete with Victorian fireplace, vast mahogany desk and comfortable leather-backed chairs. Ursus backs out, closing the door behind him.

I'm expecting to see a friendly counsellor. Instead Arzo is by the window, gazing out from his wheelchair.

'Are you my therapist?' I ask him drily.

He turns, deftly spinning one wheel as if he's been practising all his life, and looks me over, scanning every inch of my body as if to check I'm still in one piece. 'In a manner of speaking.'

'I kind of thought you'd be prettier.'

He snorts. 'So did I. How's it going, Bo?'

I lift my eyes to his. 'Pretty bloody awful. You?'

'You don't want to know the trouble I've had with my bladder.'

'Yeah, you're right about that.' I give him a half-smile. Pity for his situation is not going to be appreciated.

'I heard about the recruit who tried to hang himself.'

'Hmm,' I murmur noncommittally, 'right after he tried to shag me.'

'It was definitely the spell then?'

I shrug. 'What else could it be?'

Arzo runs his hand through his hair. 'There's never been anything like this before. It's crazy.'

I sit down in one of the leather chairs. 'Did Michael tell you about the theory that there's a new Family Head trying to usurp everyone else?'

'Michael?' Suddenly I feel embarrassed. Arzo must register my discomfort because he dismisses it with a wave of his hand and answers my question. 'Yes,' he says grimly, 'he told me.'

'It's got to be a woman. I smelled rosewater at Wiltshore Avenue just before I found O'Shea. And the fact that his spell targets men means it makes sense that a female, who'll be immune to its effects, is orchestrating all this.' A thought begins to form but it's cloudy; before I can fully grasp it it's gone and Arzo is speaking again.

'There's no evidence that it's contagious.'

'No, but it somehow makes sense. And Lucy, I mean Charity Weathers, told me it was a woman.'

'You mean the human who was shoved under the train?'

I nod. 'I would have been too, if the police hadn't showed up.'

There's a glimmer of anger in his eyes. 'I heard about that.'

I shrug. Foxworthy and Nicholls' actions seem like they happened an eternity ago. Besides, what was I going to do about it? I tell him about Beth and how it's possible she's involved.

He frowns. 'And yet you say she helped you save this Matthew character?'

'It could be a double bluff. You know, gain everyone's trust, make it look like she's the good guy. Maybe she knew I was on to her and this was the only way she could think of to make me believe otherwise.' At Arzo's look, I give a short laugh. 'Yeah, I know. It seems unlikely to me, too. But there's something about her that I don't trust.'

'So what's next?'

'I'm going to continue getting everyone to like me. Especially Beth.'

He starts to chuckle. Affronted, I glare at him. 'What?'

'You probably don't need to try very hard.'

'What do you mean?'

'People generally like you, Bo. I've never seen you try very hard yet everyone who meets you wants to be your friend.'

'That's not true.'

'Yes, it is. Give me an example of someone you know who doesn't like you.'

I think about my grandfather. I'm sure he loves me; like is another matter. But I don't think he likes anyone apart from that damn cat so I don't suppose he really counts.

'Boris,' I say finally. 'He despised me.'

'Is that the best you can do?'

'Michael Montserrat. I tried to attack him.'

'Under duress,' Arzo replies mildly. 'Besides, I think Lord Montserrat likes you very much.'

I have nothing to say to that so I change the subject. There is something else I need to know. 'Arzo, how hard is this going to be?'

He knows I don't mean finding the creepy new vampire Head. 'Harder than anything you've experienced before.'

'Well, gee, don't sugar coat it,' I try to joke. It falls flat.

His expression is serious. 'How do you feel so far?'

'Tired. I've got a headache that doesn't want to go away. And,' I lick my lips, 'earlier when someone else drank, my hands started to shake.'

'That'll get worse, Bo. Have you ever seen a heroin addict trying to kick the habit?'

'Only on TV.'

'Then you have no idea how rough it's going to get. Night sweats, hallucinations, your body screaming in pain…'

'You failed to mention all this before, you know.'

'Would it have made a difference?'

I think about it. Probably not. 'Why did *you* do it?'

He's silent.

'Why did you choose not to drink?'

'I understood the question. I've just never really told anyone about it before.'

'Not even Tam?'

He laughs slightly and shakes his head. 'No, not even Tam.' He sighs. 'There was a girl. Dahlia. The most beautiful person I'd ever seen. We met in the National Gallery of all places.'

I try not to look surprised. I find it hard to imagine Arzo wandering around looking at paintings.

'Yes, Bo,' he continues gently, 'I do have a cultured side. I've even been known to read poetry from time to time. Anyway, I bumped into Dahlia in front of Jane Austen's portrait. She was a huge fan of *Pride and Prejudice.*' His face twists. 'I think she was looking for a Mr Darcy.'

I stay quiet. This is obviously a difficult story for Arzo to tell and I don't want to interrupt with an inane question that'll make him clam up.

'We went on several dates. I knew within five minutes of meeting her that I was in love. Spending the rest of my life by her side was all I wanted.' Pain crosses his face and he looks away. 'Then she disappeared. There was no trace of her. She didn't answer her phone. I couldn't track her through it because this was in the days before mobile phones. Her family didn't know where she was and she didn't show up to work.' He lapses into silence again.

I watch him for several moments. When it's clear he's not going to speak I ask, 'You thought she'd been recruited?'

He nods. 'My best friend told me she'd suggested it was what she was going to do. One day, when I'd been working, she'd taken him to look at this very house. So, because I would follow her to the ends of the earth, I persuaded Lord Montserrat to recruit me too.'

'Michael?'

He nods.

'Out of season?'

Arzo smiles faintly. 'I can be very persuasive. And they had the space. For some reason, that was a particularly bad year for recruits surviving the turning process.'

Horrified, I stare at him. 'Was Dahlia one of those who didn't make it?'

'No.' He laughs humourlessly. 'No, she wasn't. She was back out in the real world, eloping to Gretna Green with my so-called friend.'

'Oh, bloody hell, Arzo. I'm so sorry.' I reach over to take his hand but he draws back. Pity is a bitch.

'Of course, I didn't know that at the time. I just thought I'd made a terrible mistake by turning because she wasn't here after all. I didn't drink. It was hell but I damned well didn't drink. I was going back to get her. Except when I made it to the full moon and became Sanguine instead of vampire and went back out, I found them together.' His mouth twists. 'Blissfully happy.'

There's nothing I can say that's going to make him feel any better. This is a whole load of hurt that he's obviously been carrying around for a long time. 'I can't believe he didn't tell you,' I murmur.

'My friend?'

'No. Bloody Michael Montserrat. I can't believe he didn't tell you she wasn't here.'

'It's vampire policy, Bo. You know that. It's a pledge of silence.'

'He could have made a sodding exception. He didn't have to recruit you.'

'He needed an investigator.' Arzo sighs. 'It suited his purposes. No matter what else happens, Lord Montserrat is all about the Family.'

I feel guilty for making this about me but I can't help feeling conned. 'And now he's got two.' At Arzo's confused look, I explain. 'Two investigators.'

Comprehension flickers across his face, combined with sympathy. 'He has more than us working for him these days. And he didn't frame you for O'Shea, Bo. Nor did he have anything to do with the attack at Dire Straits.' Arzo's voice drops. 'I helped persuade you as well.'

I look away. No one actually makes me do anything I don't really want to do – my grandfather will attest to that. But Arzo isn't lying when he says he joined in with Montserrat to persuade me. But what's done is done. I still feel a prickle of betrayal but there's not much I can do about it now.

'I'm sorry about what happened to you, Arzo. I really am,' I say. Not just with Dahlia but with the Dire Straits' attack too. I look him in the eyes. 'I just don't want to be a vampire.'

'It's less than a calendar month, Bo. You might be likeable but you're stubborn as a goddamn mule. You'll make it.'

I wish I had his optimism. I return to the matter in hand. 'I need a phone and internet access, Arzo. It's too suspicious for me to talk to Montserrat on his own so can you tell him to get them for me? I've got the personnel files but I'm sure he and half the freaking bloodguzzlers in this place have gone through them over and over again. I've got leads on the outside I need to follow, as well as what's going on in here.' And I don't want to speak to Montserrat himself because I'm pissed off with him after hearing Arzo's revelations.

My old colleague nods in agreement. 'I'll let him know.'

I stand up to go. 'Is there anything that'll help me beat the cravings?'

His face is curiously bland. 'I found masturbation helped.'

I blink, nonplussed. 'Er … okay.'

He grins. 'You'll be fine.'

I wrap my arms round my body and hug myself. 'Mmm.'

19

BETRAYAL

The following nights pass very slowly. I continue with project Be Nice to Everyone In Case They Tell You They Are Part Of A New Vampire Conspiracy. I've brought Beth into our little girlie fold since Matt's 'suicide attempt' and she, Nell, Nicky and I often spend our precious free time together. Keep your friends close and all that. It doesn't really get me anywhere, though. I just feel more and more tired and Beth rarely seems to open up.

The day after my request for a phone and the internet, I receive a terse note in Montserrat's now-familiar script. It informs me that I can tell him who to contact and what leads I want to follow outside the Family and he will see to them. As I'm not about to give Rogu3 up to anyone, no matter who they are, and I don't want to subject the potentially innocent D'Argneau to a vampire-induced interrogation, I scribble a message back asking him to find out exactly how O'Shea's spell breaks down and how women are affected by it. I expect another message in return, implying that if that's all I have to go on then I'm a fairly useless private investigator. Oddly, however, I hear nothing.

I'm fairly certain I didn't imagine the teasing, light-hearted turn our relationship had taken so the current silence between us troubles me. I still feel annoyed on Arzo's behalf and, as the hours and days pass, that emotion grows. I've scarcely seen Michael except when he's swept by on his way to goodness knows where, and that encourages the antipathy. This is his sodding Family – what is he doing exactly to keep it intact and safe? There's not even any information about what's happening with Matt, although I assume he's still alive or we'd have heard otherwise. I try to catch Montserrat's eye when he passes by, indicating that I need to talk to him, but he either doesn't notice or ignores me.

The lack of action disturbs me so, by the third night when I'm confident that the others are tied up in a debate over Edgar Allen Poe and why he saw fit to hide his vampiric self from the world when his writing made it so patently obvious, I try to be more proactive. At least Tam would approve. All this skulking around and ingratiating myself is getting me nowhere.

On the pretext that I need some study notes, I head back to the recruits' bedrooms. Matt's door is wide open and the room is clearly unoccupied; his bed has been stripped of its sheets. The sight makes me shiver. I guess they're not expecting him to return any time soon. I go past my own room then down to Beth's. Like most of us, old human habits die hard and her door is firmly closed. Theoretically, there's no reason for it; none of us have any personal possessions or things to hide. We're all one big happy Family. Of course, I've got Montserrat's laptop – much good it's doing me – but neither Beth nor anyone else should have any contraband. I'm keeping my fingers crossed that's not actually true.

I pause outside, one ear cocked just in case one of the others has decided to follow me. When I'm positive there's nothing but silence, I twist the doorknob. The door creaks slightly and I wince at the sound. I nudge it open and peer inside.

Her room is identical to mine in size and layout. Beth is apparently a bit of a slob. A discarded jumpsuit lies crumpled at the foot of the bed and her sheets are twisted. Not that I'm a neat freak or anything – the state of my car attests to that – but I've never been able to leave my room in the morning unless my bed is made up. I guess everyone has their little foibles.

I make a mental snapshot of what the room looks like. Normally I'd use a camera to avoid making silly mistakes when I carry out a search but I don't have that option any more. Once I'm satisfied that I have memorised the details, I start with the bed. There's nothing under the pillow or inside the pillowcase; the mess of sheets hides nothing more than the off-putting smell of stale sweat and body odour. It's good to know that Beth's sleep is being disturbed in the same way as mine: I'm waking up several times a night covered in clammy sweat while the pit of my stomach whispers to me that it needs just one tiny drop of blood to settle it down.

I lift up her mattress. There's nothing there. The walls are bare and, other than some clean underwear shoved into the drawer in the bedside table and the standard-issue recruit shoes that she refuses to wear, I can't see anything suspicious. I pick up her jumpsuit and pat it down, then stick my hand into each pocket. Again I come up empty. Either Beth is cleverer than most blondes get credit for or there's simply nothing here.

I'm just about to edge my way back out again when my gaze falls on the jug next to the bed. It's exactly the same as mine. I glance inside, swirling the dregs of the water that remains at the bottom. It's just water. Disappointed, I put it down, making sure it's in exactly the same position. That's when I realise that something feels wrong.

I pick the jug up again and inspect the base. As soon as I register the slim white packet stuck underneath, I stop breathing. I sniff it and can detect no trace of anything peculiar. But if there is nothing peculiar about it, then Beth wouldn't have hidden it. I'm desperate to peel it off and check its contents. Whatever is inside has got to be tiny. I poke it and feel a grainy substance, almost like sand.

I debate my options. I could take it to Montserrat as proof of Beth's underhandedness. Surely this is some physical version of O'Shea's spell. She has to be in league with the traitors. The trouble is, if I take it away she'll know that I'm on to her and I'll scare her off. Or whoever gave it to her in the first place. Right now, without any lab work, it's not much proof of anything – but if I leave it where it is and she uses it to hurt someone else…

I return the jug to its original place. At least I have a better idea about where to focus my efforts and I'm glad that my instincts about her were right, regardless of the way she helped me 'save' Matt. It's impossible that she's the mastermind; she's not even a full vampire yet. But I'd bet all my meagre savings that she is wrapped up in all this. I need to act fast and find Michael.

I double check the room to make sure nothing appears disturbed, then leave. I'm barely three feet away from her door when she suddenly appears.

'You didn't find what you needed then, Bo?'

I freeze. Damn. Yes, I did find what I needed and now I'm bloody scared about what you're going to do, I think.

'Your notes?' she prompts.

The relief is overwhelming. 'Er, my handwriting is so messy, I can barely decipher what I've written,' I stammer. 'I decided to leave them.'

Beth laughs, although I sense an edge to the sound. She leans her head to one side and regards me steadily. I try to read her expression and fail.

I try a different tactic. 'Actually, the truth is that I got distracted,' I admit. 'I passed Matt's empty room and it completely threw me. It's as if he's never going to return and everyone's already accepted it.'

Her eyes narrow. 'Yes,' she agrees, 'it's smegging unnerving.'

Not as unnerving as finding the physical form of O'Shea's spell hidden under your water jug.

'Do you think he's dead?' I ask.

She shrugs and looks uncomfortable. 'I don't know. He was alive the last time either of us saw him. As recruits, we're not exactly in the loop. Did you talk about him much to the counsellor?'

I suddenly see a way out. 'No,' I say slowly, 'I didn't. It was too soon, I guess. But maybe I should talk about it some more. All I can think about is the way his eyes…' I let my voice drift off. I don't need to fake the horror in my tone at the way Matt looked hanging from that showerhead.

She nods her head. 'I think she's free now actually. Alan came out from talking to her while you were gone.'

'I'll do that.' I hadn't realised there was a real counsellor hovering around and that it wasn't just a ruse so I could meet with Arzo. I try not to feel too hurt that I was never offered the option to speak to someone. Maybe Michael or Arzo were too afraid I'd end up blabbing.

I force a smile in Beth's direction then walk past her, trying not to pick up speed and start running. I begin to panic about her room. Was the jumpsuit crumpled into the same shape as when I entered? I curse. I need to find sodding Michael and talk to him as soon as I can, whether he's trying to avoid me or not.

I jog quickly down the stairs, just in time to see the man himself stalking past. He's surrounded by a group of vampires, most of whom now look familiar. Unlike my fellow recruits, however, they've all resisted my efforts to become their friend. I guess it doesn't matter whether you're human or vampire, newbies the world over are treated with the same distance and suspicion.

When Michael catches sight of me, his face shutters and he looks away quickly. What in the hell is his problem? I decide I've had enough. Vampire propriety be damned; I need to speak to him.

'My Lord!' I call.

Several of his hangers-on look in my direction. Bloody Michael Montserrat ignores me and carries on. I persist.

'Lord Montserrat!' I pick up speed, landing with a heavy thump at the foot of the staircase and trotting up to the group. When he continues to ignore me, I skirt round them and block his path so he has to stop. I ignore the other vampires' affronted expressions. 'Lord Montserrat, it's imperative that I talk to you.'

A tiny line creases his smooth forehead. 'Who are you?' he asks.

'Bo,' I say, keeping up the pretence. 'We met a few days ago. I'm one of the new recruits.'

'Ah, yes. What can I do for you, Bo?' His voice is controlled but I sense a lot of deeper emotion – and none of it very positive – rippling under the surface.

'I wish to make a complaint.'

The vampire directly behind him, an impeccably coiffed woman, steps forward. 'Then you need to take it up with the programme director. Lord Montserrat doesn't have time.'

Montserrat lifts his right hand and the woman stills. I try not to gloat. 'No, it's fine, Suzanne. I can spare a few minutes.' Despite his mild expression, a cloud of darkness rolls across his eyes. 'I will meet you in my office in half an hour,' he tells me. 'I trust you can find the way?'

I bob my head and mutter a thank you. Then I think of my grandfather and follow it with a curtsey. Montserrat eyes me as if he's not sure whether I'm taking the piss or being serious. Before he can call me on it, I move to the side and let him and his entourage pass by.

Forty minutes later, I'm still cooling my heels outside his office. Irritation is gradually developing into full-blown anger. Just as I'm about to go looking for him, he shows up. He's alone this time but his face remains a mask. I know why I'm annoyed with him, but I have no idea why he's being so standoffish with me. He opens the door and steps aside to let me go in first. The back of my neck prickles and I wonder if I'm about to feel a knife slamming into my shoulder blades. No attack comes though. I sit down in one of the chairs opposite the large desk and wait for him to settle himself.

'So what is it, Bo?'

I stare at him disbelievingly. 'You're kidding me, right?'

He rewards me with a blank expression. I stand up, kicking away the chair and glare at him, my hands on my hips. 'What's the point in going to all the trouble of getting yourself a spy if you're going to ignore me? I've been trying to get your attention for days! You seem to have forgotten that I even exist! I gave up my life for this shit!' My voice is high pitched and perilously close to a scream. I don't care.

He leans back and regards me mildly; if I'm a spitting, hissing cat, then he's an impassive lion idly watching one of his pride go berserk.

'Have you found anything out?' he enquires.

I fold my arms. 'Yes, I bloody well have. Beth has got some strange powder hidden under the jug in her room. It's obviously contraband and probably a physical version of O'Shea's stupid spell. You need to get hold of her straightaway and find out exactly what is going on and who she's answering to.'

He's annoyingly unfazed by my revelation. 'Which one's Beth?'

'Blonde. High heels.'

'Ah.' A quick grin flashes across his face, making me even more irate. 'We'll check it out,' he tells me. 'You can go now.'

'I'm not going anywhere. I asked for a phone and internet access days ago. I need them to continue investigating.' I hold out my hand as if I'm expecting him to magically drop a mobile into it. I know it's ridiculous but I'm beyond caring. His apathy is making me so angry I can't even see straight.

He shrugs. 'I'll see what I can do.'

'Why do I get the impression you won't bother?' I demand. 'What exactly is going on here?'

'You tell me, Bo,' he says. 'What *is* going on?'

'What do you mean?'

'I trust Arzo implicitly,' he says. 'And when he suggested that you would have a better chance of infiltrating whatever group is forming, I agreed because of that trust.'

The knowledge that my recruitment was Arzo's idea stings but I try not to let it show. 'So?'

'Matthew regained consciousness.'

'He is alive, then?'

Montserrat doesn't blink. 'Does that bother you?'

I'm beyond confused. 'I tried to save his life, remember?'

'Yes, that was convenient, wasn't it?'

I don't like his tone. 'What exactly are you implying?'

'Matthew said one word before lapsing back into a coma. Bo.'

'What was the word?'

'I just told you.'

'Eh?' I rub my forehead and comprehension dawns. 'Bo. He said Bo?'

Montserrat doesn't reply.

'So now you think that it was me who gave him the spell? It was in the blood he drank! It had to be.'

'There aren't many people who had access to that blood.'

'It was left unattended in the recruits' social room. Anyone could have got to it.'

'Were you alone in that room at any point?'

I gape at him. I was, of course, but to believe that I had anything to do with it is crazy.

Montserrat continues. 'O'Shea never saw his attacker. Then you magically showed up right afterwards. You were present at the massacre at Dire Straits and yet you didn't intervene.'

'Because Arzo told me not to!'

'Arzo was half dead. How could he have told you anything?'

'His eyes…' my voice falters. This is ridiculous. 'I saved O'Shea.'

'You're barely five foot. How could you save a thirteen-stone daemon?'

I shake my head. 'You're nuts. I had a good life. Why would I mess with it?'

'Bo, even the police think you're involved. I was blinded by Arzo's faith in you. I won't make that mistake again.'

'Michael, this is all circumstantial…'

His face closes. 'You will address me as Lord Montserrat. And you're right. So far this is all circumstantial. But I won't tolerate anyone threatening my Family. The second I find a shred of evidence,' he smiles at me grimly, 'and, believe me, Bo, I will find that evidence, then you will feel the might of Montserrat justice.'

'Beth…' I begin.

He silences me with a wave of his hand and picks up the phone on his desk. 'Ursus, I've had a complaint that one of the recruits is hiding some illicit material. Beth, I think her name is.' He listens for a moment. 'Yes. Apparently it's underneath her water jug. Can you check it out for me?'

He hangs up and raises his eyebrows. I sit back down, shoving my hands underneath my legs to avoid curling them into tight fists.

'I'm not involved in this. I have no motive. You're jumping to conclusions based on one word from a semi-conscious guy. I was the last person he saw before he tried to hang himself. That's probably why he said my name.'

Montserrat doesn't respond. I lapse into silence. Beth's little white envelope is the best thing I have to prove my innocence right now. I'm going to have Lord bloody Montserrat begging at my feet for forgiveness in about two minutes' time.

It takes less than that for the telephone to ring. Montserrat answers it. 'Yes.' I watch him smugly. He is going to be so damn sorry. 'I see. You're sure?' He listens for another moment then replaces the receiver. 'There's nothing there.'

'What? They didn't look hard enough then! It's right underneath the jug. It was there less than an hour ago. Have them look again.'

A muscle throbs in his cheek. 'You can go now, Bo.'

'I had nothing to do with this!'

His gaze is implacable. I feel numb, as if I've wandered into some bizarre episode of *The Twilight Zone*. 'If you're so sure I'm involved in this, why are you waiting?' I ask him quietly. 'Why not execute me and be done with it?'

'I owe it to Arzo to find the proof first. And losing another recruit at this stage without the evidence of your betrayal will merely unnerve the others.'

'So what am I supposed to do?'

His eyes are hard. 'Pray.'

20

VODKA

I FEEL EMPTY INSIDE AND MORE ALONE THAN EVER. I'VE GIVEN UP everything and now I'm trapped in the Montserrat House with vampire blood running through my veins and not a single friend. Beth could be about to unleash hell upon every single Montserrat vampire any minute now and there's nothing I can do about it.

To add to my woes, I seem to be suffering from permanent nausea, although whether it's from my growing bloodlust or despair at my situation, I have no idea. I'm incredulous that Michael Montserrat believes I'm involved. Time is ticking away on the real mastermind's invisible deadline and he's wasting his days thinking I'm one of the culprits. Jeez, maybe he even thinks I'm the one who started it all, who wants to create a new Family. Considering how little I want to be part of the bloodguzzler world, how could he entertain such a thought?

The first opportunity I have, I sneak back into Beth's room. There are no longer any traces of whatever it was she was hiding. My only hope is to find the real traitors but I'm getting no joy from the recruits and now I have nothing substantial on Beth, even though I try to keep her in my sights at all times. Besides, all the Families are involved in this, not just Montserrat, so I can hardly pin things on her and hope for the best. I have to find the root but I have no idea how. Tempting as it is to sneak up on Beth and force her to spill her guts, it doesn't seem particularly realistic. Torture is hardly my thing. I got lucky before in that O'Shea genuinely wanted to share his problems with me and gave in when I pressed him; somehow I don't get the same feeling about Beth. Besides, given my current situation, I'd probably have less than five minutes alone with her before Montserrat's goons descended. I'm certain I'm being watched constantly although I never catch anyone following me.

Ursus continues with his nightly themed PowerPoints. Fortunately, there are some breaks and we have the pleasure of other vampires as trainers. Alongside the best ways to drink blood directly from a human (which has the few of us who still haven't partaken of O negative squirming in our seats), there's some basic combat and fitness drilling. I imagine Lord Montserrat's face on a punch bag. When that stops working, I switch to the blond vampire who so callously killed Charity Weathers, and the dark-haired beast responsible for slaughtering everyone at Dire Straits. Imagining whipping their arses is, however, no substitute for the real thing.

My physical strength and vampiric abilities may be developing, but I'm feeling more and more strung out and less and less in control of my destiny. I don't like it at all and, by the end of the seventh night, one full week after I officially turned, I've just about had enough.

'Maybe you should drink,' Nell says. 'It'll make you feel better and help you to sleep more.'

'No.' Beth's answer is sharp.

'It's not as bad as you think,' Nell informs us. She'd succumbed the previous evening, ravenously downing three glasses of thick gloopy blood in a row.

'The longer you avoid drinking,' Beth says with a nasty look at

Nell, 'the more powerful you'll eventually become. It's about time the Montserrat Family had some powerful women to deal with.'

I perk up at her words. This is the kind of thing I've been waiting for. I'll have witnesses this time too.

'Yup,' agrees Nicky, stretching out her legs. She's still not used to being able to move her limbs. 'They are a bit testosterone heavy.'

'But some of that testosterone is so tasty,' Nell interjects with a wink.

I try to steer the conversation back to where I want it. 'It's a shame that only the Bancroft Family has a female Head.'

'Yeah, apparently she's a bitch, though.'

I sigh inwardly at Nell's words. You can't beat women for cattiness against their own sex.

'Imagine if it was the other way around,' I say casually. 'If it was four female Heads and only one man.'

'There'd be a lot of wine and chocolate,' grins Nicky.

'And episodes of *Sex and the City*.'

'It's not fair though, is it?' I push, looking at Beth as I speak. 'Out there, the fact that women hold fewer top jobs than men is explained away by them spending nine months out of the workplace pregnant and then staying at home to look after their kids. That's not the case here.' We'd already made much of the fact that we no longer had to worry about our periods. I'd wondered, albeit to myself, whether that would be the same if I made it to Sanguine. I wasn't sure whether it would upset me or please me.

'Women are weaker than men,' Nell asserts.

'Bullshit! No man could walk in these all smegging day long.' Beth points to the stilettos she continues to wear. I try to chuckle.

'When my family was attacked,' Nicky says softly, 'my mother tried to protect me while my father tried to fight back.' A dark shadow crosses her face. 'They broke in at exactly two o'clock in the morning and were there until almost five. I remember because I had a huge red digital clock on my bedside table. They went into my parents' room and I woke up and heard them so I followed them in. My father fought as hard as he could while my mother threw her body between them and me. That's the difference between men and women.'

I don't agree with her but I'm not in a position to say so. The others obviously feel the same and we lapse into an uncomfortable silence while Ria walks in with today's tray of blood offerings. Nell has been drinking all day and ignores her. Beth, Nicky and I look away.

'You know what we should do?' Nell says to no one in particular.

'What?'

Her eyes gleam with mischief. 'We should sneak out. Hit the town. Have a little fun.'

Nicky is shocked. 'Leave the house?'

Nell punches her arm. 'Live a little! We've been toeing the line up till now. We deserve a break.'

I try to assess whether she's serious or not. I'm surprised by how much I want to agree. Getting out of the stifling atmosphere of the Montserrat house might just be the tonic I need. Besides, by staying here all I'm doing is delaying the inevitable. Whether I'm executed first, or the Families all fall, the results for me personally will probably end up the same. I need to clear my name on the outside as well as here. This might be my chance to do both.

'We only have training until 2am,' I point out. 'Then we're free.'

'It's breaking the rules.'

'Not the real, serious, "we will execute you" rules.'

Nicky gives Nell a suspicious look. 'How do you know?' She doesn't make explicit reference to Nell's pre-turning comment about stealing but it hangs unspoken in the background.

'What were Ursus's exact words? Do not go out in the

sunshine. You must live in the Montserrat House. There's nothing to say that you must stay here trapped like a prisoner.'

'I like the idea,' I say, decisively. It's about time I took matters into my own hands again. And something to do will take my mind off the gnawing hunger leaching from my stomach into the marrow of my bones. I continue, 'It'll be pretty late by the time we can escape but I know just the place. The bouncers don't ask questions and we're unlikely to bump into any vampires.' We may bump into a lawyer of dubious intentions, though.

'No.' Beth shakes her head firmly. 'It's too dangerous.'

'How can a few dances and some tequila shots be dangerous? We're vampires now. It's not as if we need to be concerned with cirrhosis of the liver.'

'It's not drinking tequila that worries me,' Beth mutters.

She flicks me a worried glance, as if she thinks that I'll pounce on the nearest human and sink my as-yet non-existent fangs into their carotid artery. Why she has decided to pick on me instead of the younger and frailer Nicky, I have no idea. She should be more worried about me finding the evidence I need to prove her guilt – and my innocence.

'Don't come if you don't want to,' I tell her airily. I'm fairly confident she'll join in but for once I don't care. My gaze falls upon Peter, sitting morosely in the corner. He's the only other person apart from Nicky, Beth and me who's not yet partaken of the salty red stuff. Somehow I don't think it has anything to do with wanting to become a powerful vampire. 'In fact, safety in numbers. Let's ask Peter along.'

Nicky's face twists but Nell grins agreement. 'Brilliant!'

Less than two hours later, the five of us gather next to Montserrat's portrait. His dark eyes make me feel guilty so I turn away. Everyone has decided to come – even Nicky; it's just as well that she's with us as she appears to be the only one who kept her credit card when the rest of her things were taken. I have no idea where she normally hides it – perhaps under her own water jug – but I'm glad we'll have money to buy some drinks. There would be nothing more depressing than getting to the nightclub and realising we couldn't pay our own way.

'How exactly are we going to get out of here?' she enquires.

'Shhh,' I whisper, tentatively stepping down the path towards the towering perimeter wall.

The night is cloudy, although there's enough of a wind to reveal the crescent moon from time to time. Its gleam is heart-breakingly tiny. I'm torn between needing more time to do some proper investigating and wishing it was already the full moon so I could make my escape.

We skirt round the edge of some bushes and duck under the low hanging branches of an apple tree. There's a muttered curse from behind and, when I twist round to see who it is, I spot the lapel of Peter's jumpsuit caught in one of the twigs. His fingers scrabble at the offending branch but he only succeeds in getting more tangled. A scowling Beth traipses back to help with an exasperated sigh. She just succeeds in freeing him when a large shape flies overhead, cawing loudly and making us all leap in fright.

'What in hell was that?'

I scan the sky, squinting. 'A crow, I think.'

'There's a sodding reason why it's called a murder of crows,' Beth grumbles.

I watch her sullen expression, wondering what's making her so pissed off. It's possible she's annoyed that we're venturing into the outside world because it implies a lack of control over us on her part. Or is she worried that she'll slip up and give the game away? I can only hope.

We push forward, eventually reaching the wall. It's high and made of sturdy red brick. Someone, probably the gardener, clearly pays it almost as much attention as the plants, as it's moss free and well kept. This is unfortunate; a few crumbling spots would make it easier to find footholds. Beggars can't be choosers, though.

We edge along until we find a suitable tree to help us gain height. I reach up, pulling myself onto the nearest branch, then shimmy upwards, using the strongest part of the branches where they meet the trunk as safe places to hold my weight. Nell, irritatingly, just scampers up the wall in a flash and sits astride the top, grinning down at us all.

'You see? You lot should quit with all your posturing and take some blood. You're going to do it sooner or later. And once you do, climbing up something like this is a piece of cake.' She flexes her muscles while I mutter under my breath and push myself higher up the tree.

Once I'm as high as I can go, I look over at the wall. It's still three feet away. I sidestep towards it while the branch creaks menacingly under my weight. I'm not convinced it'll hold me. Nell casually extends an arm. 'Just jump, Bo,' she tells me. 'I'll catch you.'

I'm doubtful about this. I know from our training sessions that she's by far the strongest of us and I like to think that I keep myself in shape but still, it's a long way down. The others are catching up on me, however, and if I show signs of nervousness then neither Nicky nor Peter will jump. I need to get out of here and it'll look better for me if I'm not alone when I do it. I couldn't give a shit about Beth. A tiny part of me hopes that she falls. That's mean, but I can't help it.

I edge a little bit closer.

'Do it,' Nell urges.

I draw a deep breath, holding the air in my lungs, and then I leap. Initially, everything seems fine and I'm gaining height. It's barely a fraction of a second, however, before my body starts to fall. Nell's hand seems too far away and I'm certain I'm not going to make it. Panic sets in and I shut my eyes tightly, waiting for the inevitable pain. I misjudged Nell's reach though and, before it's too late, her cool hand grips my sweaty one and pulls me upwards.

She heaves me up until I'm lying on my stomach, my legs dangling down one side and my arms down the other. I force myself up, twist round to a sitting position and try not to gasp too obviously for air.

Nicky is now in position on the tree's branch. She looks pale. I bet when she first entered the Montserrat house, she never thought she'd soon be climbing trees. How strange it must be for her to have control over her legs after being in a wheelchair for so long. I shuffle along so that she has enough room and give her an encouraging smile.

'It's okay,' I whisper. 'Nell's got vampire strength.'

She shakes her head. 'I can't do this.'

'Of course you can. You're taller than I am and I did it,' I urge.

She bites her lip and pushes her hair away from her face. Then she jumps. This time, I watch Nell. She stretches herself out a few inches and grabs hold of Nicky, as if she were merely catching a frisbee. Even the muscles of her forearms don't appear tense as she yanks up Nicky's slight frame. Considering Nell has been fully vampired for less than five days, I'm terrified. How much stronger will the other vampires be that I'm up against? If I get caught in a fight with them, I've got no chance. Maybe I should just go ahead and drink some damned blood.

I scoot further along the wall with Nicky alongside me. Beth makes the jump irritatingly quickly. She has a lithe athleticism that's hidden by her façade of bottle-blonde hair and sharp red fingernails. I try not to scowl. Peter also leaps without seeming to worry about it. He seems almost disappointed when he makes it, as if he'd hoped to fall and break his neck.

'So, clever clogs,' Beth says, once we're all safely perched on the wall, 'how in smeg do we get down?'

She has a point. The Montserrat garden may be full of trees to aid the climbing process but the other side is a gaping chasm leading down to the grey cement of pavement.

Nell pushes herself off, landing squarely on her feet. 'I'll catch you.'

I look nervously at Nicky. This time our order is reversed, with Peter going first. He's the heaviest of all of us, and Nell staggers slightly. There's no problem though and, one by one, we make the jump down. When my feet are on solid ground, I take a deep breath. I'm strongly tempted to bend down and kiss the pavement in gratitude. I look back at the wall.

'It's going to be a lot harder to get back inside than it was to escape,' Beth says, echoing my thoughts.

'Let's worry about that when the time comes,' I say. I'm not sure I'm coming back. I don't have any doubts that Montserrat will find me in a heartbeat but hanging around until he decides to execute me isn't really much of an option.

'There's a cab!' Nicky calls suddenly. She leaps into the road and hails it.

The driver is unenthusiastic about having five passengers but Nell grins at him, displaying her growing fangs, and he hastily changes his mind. It's so late that the streets are quiet and we make it to the club quickly. Perhaps I can get used to this night-time living after all.

The bouncer at the door is the same one as last time. I have no idea whether he remembers me or not but fortunately he seems more taken by our matching midnight blue jumpsuits and Beth's killer heels than our faces. We trip inside and, while Peter and I wince automatically at the loud music, the others perk up.

I scan around, hoping that D'Argneau is here. Unfortunately the stools by the bar are empty and he doesn't strike me as the kind of person who's down for a boogie on the spangled dance floor. I'm disappointed My main purpose in coming here is to quiz him again; without his presence this is a wasted trip.

Nell, it seems, has an entirely different idea of wasted on her mind. She beckons the bartender, ordering a bottle of vodka and a range of mixers. Ever the one for detail, she even makes sure there's a bucket of ice. Nicky appears blasé about handing over her credit card to pay for our drinks. I'm not sure I'd allow Nell free reign – not at London prices – but once we're settled at a table and sipping at our glasses, I start to chill out. No, I shouldn't rely on alcohol to settle my nerves but damn, this is a drink I've been waiting for.

Unsurprisingly, Beth's lip curls. 'It's not the kind of establishment I normally frequent.'

The buzz of alcohol almost makes me throw caution to the wind and tell her exactly what I think, but Nicky interrupts before I do.

'I think it's cool. It's been a long time since I had a girls' night out.'

Nell's eyes gleam. 'This is what being a vampire is really about. Having fun and damning the consequences.' She takes a long swig of her drink. 'I wonder if vampires get hangovers.'

Nicky clinks her glass against Nell's. 'Only one way to find out.'

'We've only got about two hours until we head back,' Beth cautions. 'We can't risk getting caught when dawn breaks.'

I'm surprised that she sounds so schoolmarmish. 'I'd never have thought you were a stickler for the rules.'

'Those rules exist for a reason,' she snipes back.

'Yeah? And so are the rules about there being only five Families.' The words are out of my mouth before I've had time to think and they hang there while Beth frowns at me. If I didn't know better, I'd say she was confused.

'Rules shmules!' trills Nicky. 'Let's dance!' She pulls Nell up by one arm and a reluctant Beth by the other. Eyeing me with a mischief I've not seen in her before, she jerks her head towards the small dance floor. 'Come on, Bo.'

I glance at Peter. He's muttering to himself. 'I'll stay with the party animal here and keep him company.'

A flash of something I can't determine crosses Nicky's face, then she shrugs amiably and guides the other two off, immediately flinging herself into the beat of the song. This is a side of her I've not seen before. I guess she didn't have much opportunity to go out and dance when she was in a wheelchair. Bless her. Nell seems keen to match her energy although Beth, surprisingly, looks awkward. Her expression makes me think that she'd rather have her blood red fingernails pulled out one by one than dance.

The colour of Beth's nails brings me back to the topic that never seems to be far from my mind. I look at Peter, whose fingers are drumming fretfully on his collarbone.

'How are you doing with the whole blood avoidance thing?'

'Huh?'

'Not drinking. You, Beth, Nicky and I are the only ones who've yet to drink blood. The thought makes me feel queasy but I'm finding it harder and harder to not have some.'

'So why don't you?' Peter's voice is mild and lacking in curiosity but I still feel compelled to answer.

'I want to be a powerful vampire.' I force a hollow laugh.

He looks at me over the rim of his glass. 'Bullshit.'

I'm shocked. 'Peter, I've never heard you swear before.'

'Well, I've never been a vampire before.' He pours another a shot. 'I've been watching you, Bo. You don't want to be a vampire. There's a part of you that's disgusted by anyone who is.'

'That's not true!' I protest.

'Yes, it is,' he replies quietly. 'You told me your reason for being here. I can't help thinking it's bullshit. Are you sure you're not really here for revenge?'

I am, just not in the way that he thinks. I wonder how to talk myself out of this. He continues before I can think of anything smart to say. 'It's a powerful motivator, you know, but it won't make you feel any better. It's not a dish best served cold. If you're planning revenge, you're better off digging two graves, not one, because it'll kill you in the end.'

'I'm not doing this for revenge,' I tell him, trying to sound sincere. 'I suppose I don't really want to be a vampire after all.' I hope that the half truth is enough to appease him.

He sighs heavily. 'I feel the same. I can't help wondering if I've made one of the worst mistakes in my life.' He looks at me frankly. 'You're not telling me everything but, for whatever reason, you're trying to become Sanguine.'

I'm surprised that he's even heard of the term, let alone linked it to me. He laughs softly at my expression. 'I did my research before I signed up.'

'Then you know how hard it is to resist the urge.'

'I do.'

'Are you doing the same? Are you trying to become Sanguine?'

He laughs again but there's a cold, hard edge to it. 'No. Much as I wish I'd chosen a different path, I'm already damned, Bo. I deserve all this.'

I'm about to ask him what he means when I notice a new customer stroll in. My back stiffens immediately. Lo and behold, it's Harry D'Argneau.

'So he's why we're really here,' Peter comments.

I shoot him a look. 'Peter, I'm sorry...' Guilt blazes through me. Whatever Peter is going through, it's obviously hell. If things were different then I'd do whatever I could to draw him out. But I need to talk to D'Argneau and get my pound of flesh. My clock is ticking.

Peter pats my shoulder. 'It's okay. I understand.'

I don't think he really does. 'Look, I won't be long. I just need to talk to that guy for five minutes. It's really important.'

He doesn't appear hurt and gives me a gentle push. 'Go on. Do what you have to do.'

'You're not even curious, are you?'

All I receive in return is a half-hearted shrug. 'I'll be back,' I promise. 'This won't take long.'

I grab an empty glass and fill it with ice and vodka. A peace offering might help my cause. Then I walk up to D'Argneau and tap him on the shoulder. He turns and, as soon as he registers my face, his eyes widen and he steps away. I hold out the drink.

'Please, Harry.' I keep my voice soft. I'm pretty sure he's trying to decide whether to run away or not so I try to appear as small and unthreatening as possible. It must work because his muscles relax and he peers at me. 'You look different.'

'I've been recruited,' I tell him.

He freezes. 'Which Family?'

'Does it matter?'

He grabs my shoulders and grips them tightly. 'Which Family?' he repeats.

My eyes scan his face. 'Montserrat.'

His shoulders slump.

'What? What's the problem?'

He takes the drink and throws it back in one swift gulp. 'You're an idiot, Bo Blackman. That's the problem.'

21

RED SKY IN THE MORNING

D'Argneau guides me to a small table at the back where we're hidden from view. I'm glad; the last thing I want is bloody Beth interrupting. We're also further away from the speakers here so there's less need to bellow into each other's ear. There's always the possibility that when you do that you'll be caught out during the abrupt breaks between songs.

'Talk to me,' I tell him, once we're seated.

He raises his eyebrows. For the first time, I realise that they're tweezed into perfect arches. 'You're the one in the Montserrat heartland, Ms Blackman, you should know. Although if you've only just been recruited, isn't it a little odd that you're out and about?'

I ignore his question. 'What do you mean, I should know?'

He draws his hands together thoughtfully under his chin. 'So they're keeping their own members in the dark? Interesting.'

'We're not treated as full members until the lunar month is complete,' I say, irked by his implied criticism of Montserrat policy. 'What exactly are we being kept in the dark about?'

D'Argneau leans back, obviously pleased to be in possession

of information which I need. 'I've done a little digging since you contacted me. I don't appreciate being threatened, even if it's by short females in handcuffs.'

I bristle but hold my tongue. Right now, I need him much more than he needs me. 'The Families are being hit and being hit badly,' he says. 'Everyone has suffered losses. I'm sure you heard about Tommy Glass.'

I shake my head. I've no idea who he's talking about.

'Sequestered from the real world,' he half whispers to himself, as if making a mental note. 'Tommy Glass is – or rather was – a button-nosed, blond cherub of a toddler who was ripped apart four days ago while playing in his garden. His unfortunate mother was there but she was no match against a triber.'

I feel sick. 'You mean vampire.'

He nods.

'A Montserrat vampire?'

D'Argneau nods again. I rub my forehead. A toddler? Damn O'Shea and his stupid spell.

'As you can imagine,' he continues, 'there are many humans who are rather concerned by this turn of events.'

'No shit,' I murmur. Whoever is behind all this is clearly stepping up their campaign. Discrediting the Families and turning the humans against them is a smart move; it means the new 'super Family' can step in and take over. All they need to do is create a little spin about how they saved Britain from being terrorised by the five Families and no one will question them. Not until it's too late.

'The tabloids are all on board, of course, screaming for justice, demanding that human laws be put into force against the Families. I think your Lord Montserrat has done a lot to smooth things over but when you're faced with photos on the internet of tiny Tommy's mutilated limbs, and the grieving parents are on television every night... ' He shrugs. 'Well, he can't work miracles.'

I feel a rush of sympathy for Michael. No wonder he thinks I'm involved, he must be desperate to find someone to blame. Then I remember the cold look in his eyes the last time I saw him.

D'Argneau watches me, a self-satisfied smirk on his face. I realise he's not finished talking.

'What is it?' I ask him.

He runs his tongue over his lips. 'Tommy Glass is public knowledge.'

I wait. He's like an eager puppy straining at the leash and proud to show off what he knows. 'What's not public knowledge is something you may find more interesting.' His eyes dance. 'I didn't mention the last time we met that a Family hired me to go after O'Shea. That same Family is reported to have someone in custody who has information about the perpetrators of the recent attacks.'

I grip the arms of my chair. 'Who?'

'I don't know who they have in custody.'

'But you obviously know which Family,' I growl. If it's Montserrat, I'm going to be seriously pissed off. Like 'ripping someone's head from their shoulders' pissed off.

D'Argneau leans back. 'Naturally.'

My frustration is building. 'Who?' I snap again.

He cocks his head. 'Tell me, Ms Blackman, what do I gain by passing on this little titbit? I can see what's in it for you; you seem to be inextricably tied up in all this. But what's in it for me?'

I've had enough of this. 'You forget I'm a vampire now,' I snarl.

He lifts up his index finger. 'Actually, looking at you, I don't think you are. Not yet. You're different from before, certainly, but I don't sense vampire.' He smiles unpleasantly. 'You've not drunk yet, have you?'

I glare at him malevolently.

'And,' he carries on, 'that means you're still as weak as a

human. Probably weaker.' He lowers his voice. 'I've heard the cravings are enough to drive you insane.'

'You don't know enough about vampires to tell whether I've drunk yet or not.' I'm taking an educated guess here.

'Show me your fangs then.'

I scowl. The lawyer is more confident now. He grins. 'As I thought.'

'Harry. Please. Tell me which Family.' I abandon my attempts to threaten him.

He throws back his head and laughs. 'Or what? You'll screw me outside on the pavement?'

I wince. I knew I was going to regret that little episode.

'Look,' he says. 'You rub my back and I'll rub yours. *Quid pro quo.* You'll simply owe me a favour. It'll be of my choosing and I'll call it in when I see fit. I could benefit from a vampire on my side.'

I have a bad taste in my mouth. There's no telling what he could ask for. Initially I thought that he was a good guy; now I'm not so sure. Of course, Michael Montserrat currently wants my head. And even if he doesn't take it, whoever wants to supplant all five Families seems likely to achieve their goal. If that happens, it's unlikely I'll hang on to my life. If I'm dead, D'Argneau can't collect. I'm not completely stupid though.

'You realise I won't be able to go against the Montserrat Family, no matter what happens? As a full vampire, my loyalty to them will be absolute.' I neglect to mention the Sanguine part. I think Mr D'Argneau already knows more than is good for him.

'I understand that,' he says. 'And I'll be kind and include your own blood family in that.'

I think about all the other people he could make me hurt. 'I won't physically harm anyone. Not unless there's a very, very good reason.'

'Favours come in all shapes and sizes, Ms Blackman. I'm sure I can come up with something that will keep your conscience clear.'

I stare at him. He's trying to play hardball and there's a part of me that likes him for it. 'Fine. Tell me which Family.'

'Give me your word.'

'You have it.'

'Very well.' He leans forward, picks up his glass and drains it. He swirls the remaining ice cubes. 'Bancroft.'

'You're sure?' It would make sense if they were involved. Bancroft has the only female Head. She has a good reputation and she's immune to O'Shea's spell, regardless of what form it takes. Maybe she's had enough of playing in a male-dominated world. I can't help wondering whether Montserrat has thought of this; surely it's crossed his mind.

'Thanks.' I stand up. D'Argneau does the same, as if in some old-fashioned show of gallantry. It seems so unfitting for the occasion that I smile.

'What's going on here?' says Nicky, appearing at my shoulder.

Her presence is so unexpected that I jump. That's not as bad as D'Argneau, however, who drops his glass onto the floor where it shatters. He lets out a muffled curse and crouches down to pick up the larger shards.

I wink at Nicky. 'Just getting to know this gentleman a little better,' I murmur, before I bend down to help D'Argneau.

I've barely reached his level when I smell it. I don't need to see him sucking on his finger to know that he's cut himself; there's a cloud of iron-rich air circling round him. A deep animalistic rumble that I'm barely aware of begins in my throat and my eyes fix on the thin trail of blood rolling down his skin. It looks so good. Behind me, half-smothered by the music and the loud drumming of my own heartbeat, I hear Beth snarl. I don't care. D'Argneau has ceased to be a person; now he's just food.

He glances up at me, eyes widening as he registers my reaction. Immediately, the scent of his fear mingles with that of his blood. If anything, it makes it more alluring. He's prey and I am predator.

I leap forward, my mouth wide open like a cavernous killing machine. Nicky's presence annoys me. I want this flesh all to myself. I knock her out of the way as I fly, landing on D'Argneau's chest and making him fall backwards with a heavy thump. He tries to push me out of the way but his hands are weak, flailing. I slap them aside and curve my head down. I may not have fangs yet, but I can still taste.

Then something is pulling me off the lawyer's body. I howl in frustration and kick. Whatever is holding me tightens its grasp. I shove my elbows back and my captor gasps but still doesn't let go.

'Get him out of here,' a voice says.

Beth: the knowledge flickers in the recesses of my brain. I don't like Beth. I don't trust Beth. She's stopping me from getting what I want. I kick back harder.

'Bo.' She sounds calm. Bitch. 'Bo Blackman. Remember who you are and stop this now.'

I snarl. Nell picks up D'Argneau and drags him out of my line of vision. I lunge forward but I can't break Beth's hold.

'Bo,' she soothes, 'he's gone. You need to calm down and relax.'

I twist to my left and then my right. The bartender is staring at me with wide, frightened eyes. I jerk in his direction and he takes an involuntary step backwards. Then I sniff the air. The reek of blood remains but it's dissipating fast. My heart pounds painfully against my ribcage and I squeeze my eyes shut.

'He's gone, Bo,' Beth repeats, loosening her grip slightly and reaching up to smooth my hair. The part of my consciousness that is really me returns.

'Sure?' I croak.

'Sure.'

I start to tremble. 'I almost…'

'Shhh,' she says. 'It's okay.'

Wrenching myself from her hold, I turn to face her. 'No. Beth, it's not fucking okay. It's never going to be okay. I…' I can't finish the sentence.

A large figure comes and stands beside us. 'You need to leave.' The bouncer's expression is grim and his arms are folded across his chest. 'Tribers aren't welcome.'

Beth grabs my arm. 'We're going.' She searches my face. 'Are you good?'

I'm still shivery and shaking, but I know what she means. I nod and we walk out of the door. 'Is he definitely…?'

'He's gone.'

Nicky, Nell and Peter are outside, huddled across the street and watching us wide-eyed. We cross over and Peter impulsively draws me into a hug. 'You didn't do it, Bo. You didn't drink,' he whispers.

But only because of Beth. If it hadn't been for her, I'd have ripped out Harry D'Argneau's throat.

I look at the other three. 'Why was it just me?' My words are quiet but I can hear the heartfelt plea in them. 'Why was I the only one who went for him?'

'As soon as I smelled the blood, I got Peter out,' Nell tells me. 'When I came back in for the rest of you, Nicky seemed okay and Beth was wrestling you like it was a prize-winning fight.'

My eyes flick from Beth to Nicky and back again. Beth looks uncomfortable although Nicky seems unconcerned. I'm glad this hasn't upset her too much. All I can really focus on, however, is that I lost control and they didn't. My chances of lasting to the end of the month are slipping away in front of my eyes.

'Dawn's not far away,' Nell says, her eyes scanning the lightening sky. 'We need to get back.'

Peter releases me and we stand on the pavement in an awkward circle. The laughter and joy of the night have completely vanished and it's all my fault.

IT TAKES MUCH LONGER to find a taxi this time. I'm too numb after my attack on D'Argneau to worry about it but it keeps running through my mind. The scent of his fresh blood had been so overwhelming. The mammoth task of getting to the end of the month seems impossible. I knew it was going to be tough but I didn't understand it would probably be easier to strike a match on jelly.

Beth takes charge. She ushers us to a main road where we'll have a better chance of finding transport home. Faint streaks of purple are appearing in the sky and Nicky, in particular, is getting twitchy. I'd like to calm her down but selfishly all I can think about is myself. Everything is such a mess. I briefly consider whether to make a run for it and find shelter away from the Family and everyone else. The flat that Rogu3 found for me will now be out of commission, but as long as I find somewhere out of the sun, I'll be fine. But there is a part of me that thinks perhaps I'll be better off letting the dawn do its worst. There seems to be little point in struggling on when my own nature is my enemy.

By the time we flag down a taxi, I've been sucked into a vortex of misery. I huddle into a corner of the back seat. Beth is giving me worried glances but I can barely muster up the energy to care. The cab trundles past the grey buildings and the shortening shadows. When we arrive back at the Montserrat headquarters, it's obvious we won't have time to sneak back inside before dawn strikes. We're going to have walk in through the front door and hope no one notices. It's a stupid plan. I consider pointing this out to the others and then decide I don't care. Rushing inside to avoid something as simple and beautiful as the sun's first rays is bad enough.

Nicky pays the driver and we step out. I can already feel my skin starting to burn. Nell, Nicky and Peter sprint to the main door. I stay where I am, on the pavement, sniffing curiously at the slight smell of burnt hair from my bare arms.

Beth grabs me and shakes me. She gets right up into my face. 'Do you have a bloody death wish?' she hisses.

I shrug back helplessly. Maybe I do.

She mutters something then pulls me towards the entrance. The others have discovered that it's locked. Oops.

Nell pushes against the door with her shoulder. 'Why in the hell is it locked? Vampires are creatures of the night! This door should never be freaking locked.'

It's locked, I think, to keep us monsters in and the rightfully vengeful humans out. Because one of our so-called Family members slaughtered an innocent two-year-old child. One of our brothers.

Nicky swears loudly. She thumps on the door to get some-one's attention. 'We're going to burn out here!' she yells. Nell joins her, their fists creating a rhythmic drumming on the worn wood.

I turn away and gaze out at the location of the old Tyburn gallows. And I start to giggle. It begins as a hiccup in my guts, and then escapes through my nose and mouth. My shoulders shake as the giggle transforms into a laugh and I clutch my stomach, then sit down cross-legged, facing away from the door towards the trail of crimson red sky above Hyde Park.

'Red sky at night, shepherd's delight,' I half-sing to myself, 'red sky in morning, shepherd's warning.'

'Bo, will you get a fucking grip?'

I laugh harder.

There's a creaking sound from behind. The thunderous face of Michael Montserrat stares at us from the threshold. I raise my arms and cackle, then turn back to the sky, lifting up my face while my cheeks and forehead prickle, burn and blister.

Arms encircle me from behind and drag me upwards. I

protest but they merely tighten their grip. 'Lemme go,' I moan. 'I'm enjoying the sunrise.'

The arms scoop me up. Montserrat is holding me against his chest like a child. 'You should let me go,' I tell him matter-of-factly. 'This way you don't have to wait for proof to execute me. I'll just be dead.'

His expression is granite stern. He shifts my helpless weight and then stalks inside.

TRUTH

THE DREAMS THAT FOLLOW ARE DARK, TERRIBLE AND STEEPED IN blood. I have brief moments of lucidity, soon destroyed by bouts of dizziness and vomiting. I'm aware of people hovering over me, murmuring. I shut them all out and concentrate on the pain in my stomach and the ever-increasing desire for blood. At one point, someone changes my sheets because they're soaked in clammy sweat, and I allow myself to be moved to a chair like a doll. When I sleep again, I have disturbing nightmares of the one-eyed doll's head from Wiltshore Avenue. It talks to me in a little girl's voice but its words are so awful that I scream in agitation.

I hallucinate. O'Shea's body, bleeding out in that small grubby room. Me, down on all fours like an animal, lapping greedily at his blood. Then I'm in the office at Dire Straits, and the vampire who murdered Tam isn't the indistinct form of the dark-haired man. It's me, sinking my teeth into his neck and ripping out the soft, tasty flesh.

The images flit from one to another, as if I'm being forced to endure a never-ending reel of grotesque film. Someone tries to make me drink some water and I lash out, pushing them away until I'm left alone in the darkness. Arzo speaks to me, then

Michael Monserrat. Sometimes Peter is there, sometimes Beth and Nicky.

'Bo.' The voice penetrates through my thick, throbbing skull.

'Bo, I'm sorry. It took longer than I thought.'

Yet another glass is placed at my lips. I moan and shake my head. I already know it's not blood and it's blood that I desire above all things. I push it away.

'Bo. The guard will only be gone for a few moments. You need to drink this now.'

I can't make sense of the words. The glass tips and my lips are wet. I tentatively taste the liquid and start to choke. It's poison. Panic writhes through me like a twisting snake. They're feeding me O'Shea's spell and there's nothing I can do about it.

'Smegging hell, Bo! Stop it and bloody drink!'

Hands tip back my head. I close my mouth firmly to avoid more of the foul-tasting liquid but sharp fingers pinch my nose and I can't breathe. I try for as long as I can, but eventually I have no choice but to open my mouth and gasp for oxygen. As soon as I do, the liquid is poured in while I gag and splutter.

'Everything will be fine now,' the voice says, as the welcoming darkness returns yet again.

WHEN I WAKE UP, for a heart-pounding moment I think I've gone blind. It takes me a few seconds to realise that my eyes are glued together with such a build-up of gunk that I can't open them. I fumble with one hand, searching for the jug that's always on my right and scoop some water into my palm then rub it onto my eyes so I can pry open my eyelashes and finally see again.

I blink several times, clearing my vision. I'm still in my room and in my own bed. My arms and legs are covered in welts and scratches and I trace the marks with the tips of my fingers, wondering where they came from. I feel light-headed, but alive.

I'm not sure how long I've been out for; it has to be at least a day but my memories are so foggy, I can't be sure.

There's a soft knock at the door.

'Come in,' I call, except it's less of a call and more of a croaky whisper. My lips are cracked and sore.

The door opens a few inches and a familiar face peers in.

'Arzo,' I smile, then wince at the stabbing pain as my mouth moves into a position it's clearly not ready for.

He looks white but his relief is palpable. 'You're awake.'

I pull my knees up to my chest and give him a small smile. 'I guess so. What in hell happened to me?'

Arzo wheels himself inside, braking to a stop by the edge of my bed. It's an oddly uncomfortable situation. The relationship I had with him involved little more than me checking what Tam's schedule was. Now I'm in my standard issue vampire pyjamas while he gazes at me like a concerned parent.

'It's the bloodlust, Bo. It's what happens.'

I frown. 'You didn't tell me it would knock me out and make me hallucinate. It kind of makes investigating anything a bit difficult.'

He shifts in the wheelchair and looks away. 'We thought you'd have enough time,' he mumbles. 'Before this happened. And if you found nothing, well…' His voice trails off.

'Jesus, Arzo! That was the big plan? Hope I had enough time to find a traitor that the combined might of the five Families couldn't uncover before I collapsed into a coma?'

'It shouldn't have happened so quickly,' he protests, half-heartedly.

'But you were expecting it.' My voice is flat. No doubt the abrupt appearance of D'Argneau's blood speeded up the process. Lucky old me.

He nods his head. 'It always does. It's why so few ever make it to the final stages of the lunar month. The hallucinations and pain can be … difficult.' He frowns. 'Lord Montserrat was about to order your feeding. You were past the point of no return. I don't understand how you managed to recover.' He shakes his head. 'I've never seen that before.'

I think I understand how it happened. Or at least who was responsible. What I really don't know is why. It's a piece of information I'm going to keep to myself for now.

'What about the others?' I ask. 'Peter, Nicky and Beth?'

He looks surprised. 'They're fine. The man – Peter? He's a bit wan and frail but he's coping. The girls appear barely bothered.' His brow crinkles. 'They said that you got talking to a man who cut himself on some glass but they managed to get out before it affected them. It was fortunate you had someone with you who has already completed turning.'

I keep my lips buttoned. Until I know more about what's going on, my plan is to make sure my theories stay with me. It's becoming more and more obvious that I'm just a very small cog in the Montserrat machine. Apparently neither Arzo nor Michael Montserrat cares that much for my well-being. But I'm surprised I was to be given blood to help me survive the transition; surely it would be easier to simply let me slip away? I say as much to Arzo and he looks pained.

'I had words with Lord Montserrat about that one. He should never have thought that about you. He's under a lot of pressure, Bo.'

Like he's the only one. I snort. 'So that's it? Now he believes I'm not part of this gigantic conspiracy because you simply told him so?'

He won't quite meet my eyes. 'Well, that's not the only reason.'

'Go on.'

'Bancroft has uncovered one of the traitors. They admitted to throwing that woman under the train, as well as attacking the daemon.'

Bancroft again. It's high time I departed this Montserrat gig and went to find some answers there instead. I just need to work a way to manage it. 'Blond hair?' I ask. Arzo nods. 'What's going to happen to him?'

'It's already happened. He was executed four days ago.'

That doesn't make sense. How could I only be hearing about it now? Tentacles of dread snake through my veins. 'Arzo, how long have I been out for?'

'A little over a week.'

'A week?' I shriek. I can't believe I've lost so much time. In some ways it's a good thing – it means the full moon is closer. But it leaves less time to discover what is really going on.

'Is that it?' I ask, desperately. 'Did Bancroft find out who's really behind all this? Is it over now?'

Arzo moves himself over to the window and gazes out, avoiding my eyes. 'No. No. And no.'

'Nothing?'

'He was apparently being coerced. He could tell us what he'd done but not who was responsible for the planning.'

'O'Shea's spell.'

'We can only presume so. Bancroft tested him before he died. He was incredibly submissive and open to suggestion.'

'But also sexually aroused?'

Arzo looks embarrassed but nods.

'I don't suppose anyone has thought to speak to O'Shea to see if he can come up with a way to reverse the effects?'

'It's too late. Once the spell was transformed into physical form, it was beyond his control.'

I shake my head. What a mess. I swing my legs out of the bed and stand up. My head spins but I'm pretty sure I'll be okay. I wouldn't mind several pints of O negative to see me on my way but the bloodlust doesn't seem much worse than it did before my attack on D'Argneau. Despite Arzo's gloom, it's hard for me not to feel optimistic.

'Bo, what are you doing? You should rest.'

I give him my death-stare. For once it apparently works

because he blanches ever so slightly. I smile at his reaction. 'I'm going to save your sucky Montserrat arses, that's what.'

IT TAKES some time to persuade Arzo to leave but, as soon as he does, I move into high gear and head for the shower, almost colliding on my way out with the guard who is posted outside my room. After he calms down from his sudden-attack stance and carefully looks me over, he nods and leaves. I wonder whether he's been there to guard me from potential threats from the others, or whether he was my own personal prison guard in case *I* was a threat to *them*. Regardless, now that I'm conscious and walking, I must be free.

There's a layer of grime covering every inch of my skin and, despite a few lingering moments of light-headedness, the pleasure I take in scrubbing it away under the spray of hot of water is almost immeasurable. Once I'm done, and feeling much improved despite having to clamber into another silly jumpsuit, I stride over to the social area in search of Beth.

Almost everyone is there. I spot Peter, hunched in the corner. Arzo wasn't kidding when he said he was looking frail; I'm amazed he can still sit up. I'd like to check on him but the others spot me and rush over, and I'm inundated with smiles and messages of goodwill. I'm taken aback by the positive feeling about my recovery.

'So,' Nicky says, 'you've still not drunk then?'

I shake my head. 'I don't know how I managed it,' I tell her, 'but I've been to hell and come out the other side.'

'There are only eight days left, you know.'

'Yup. When are you planning to, you know, drink?' The word sounds so innocuous yet carries so much meaning.

She smiles weakly. 'Any day now. I'm feeling worse and worse.' She looks away. 'I dropped in on you. You were too far out of it to notice, of course, but there's no way I'm putting myself through that. You were screaming and…' Her voice trails off and she shudders.

'It was pretty nasty,' I agree. 'I'm not doing that again.' When I say the words, I realise that it's true. I don't want to be a vampire. Short of finding those responsible for screwing up my life and killing my friends, there's nothing I want more than to become Sanguine. Deep down, however, I know I can't go through that pain again. I'm desolate at the thought until I spot Beth hovering in the background. I catch her eye and focus on the matter in hand, looking meaningfully at the door. She nods.

I extricate myself from the others. As soon as I'm in the corridor, I open my mouth to speak but Beth puts her index finger to her lips. She starts to move away. I follow.

We end up in the now-familiar garden although we veer away from the path and towards a small section of shrubbery overlooking a fountain. Her stilettos make small indentations in the grass. I have to admit that I'm impressed she climbed a tree wearing them.

'The noise from the fountain will help cover us,' she tells me quietly, 'but you still need to keep your voice low.'

I raise my eyebrows.

'Guards,' she explains. 'Apparently, Lord Montserrat has the entire place on lockdown after our ill-advised escapade. And you know that vampires have highly attuned hearing.'

I murmur noncommittally. As much as I needed to talk to D'Argneau, I still feel guilty that it was my 'ill-advised escapade' and that I was almost responsible for his death. Beth seems to understand and places her hand on my shoulder.

'How are you?'

'I'm okay.' She's going to continue with the niceties so I press forward. 'You gave me that drink, right? When I was hallucinating and sick?'

She doesn't move or say anything but the answering flicker in her eyes confirms it.

'Let me guess,' I add drily, 'it was something that came in a little white envelope which you hid under your water jug.'

'Until you decided to get nosy. You've no idea how difficult it was for me to find another hiding place. You don't make life easy, Bo.'

'You could just have told me about it. What is it anyway? Some kind of bloodlust control thing? It's got to be why I recovered instead of having blood rammed down my throat.'

She shrugs. 'I'm not sure exactly what goes into it. But yes, it's meant to control the cravings. It won't remove them. Although you're better than you were, you are still on the edge. You need to be careful.'

'You've given it to Peter and Nicky too?'

'No.' Beth's confusion is clear. 'I have no idea why they're still doing so well. I've been taking it almost since the beginning.'

I absorb this information before asking my next question. I'm pretty sure I know the answer. 'Why did you give it to me?'

She plucks a leaf off a shrub and starts shredding it. 'I promised I would do whatever it took to keep you safe and stop you drinking.'

'Promised who, Beth?'

'I'm also not supposed to let you know I'm doing it.'

'I think that cat is out of the bag.'

'You have to understand that I owe him. A few years ago things were rough. He helped me out. I was on the streets, tangled up with a group of tribers who were definitely on the shadier side of the supernatural.'

I wait for her to go on but she obviously doesn't want to talk about it. I grit my teeth trying to control my anger. 'And this is how he's making you pay him back? By forcing you to become a freaking vampire?'

She looks surprised. 'Oh, I was already signed up. I want to do this. I specifically want to be part of the Montserrat Family. I did my research and I'd have waited another ten years to apply if that's what it took. But I promised your grandfather I wouldn't drink until either you did, or we made it to the end of the month. He gave me the powder to help.' She gives a short laugh. 'You've no idea how many smegging times I tried to sneak it into your water. Except I never got close enough to manage it without getting caught. There was one occasion when I managed to get into your room and then Nicky came in after me. I think she was looking for you. I came up with the most appalling excuse to explain why I was there.'

I rub my forehead. My bloody meddling grandfather. I should have known; he'd accepted my entry into the Montserrat Family far too easily. And the amount of energy I'd expended thinking that Beth was one of the traitors… I sigh. 'What a sodding mess.'

Beth gives me a sympathetic glance. 'He's only trying to help you.'

'He could have told me about the powder. He didn't need to be so underhanded.'

'He seemed to think you wouldn't accept his help.'

I think about that. I can be bloody minded at times and, yes, if I can avoid his assistance, I will. But I went to him for help with O'Shea. And when it comes down to the difference between ending up as Sanguine and ending up as a fully blown vampire – hell, I'd crawl on my knees through broken glass to ask for help with that.

'You're quite alike, you know,' she comments.

I snarl quietly. Beth merely grins.

'Do the vampires know about this powder?'

'I have no idea.'

I wrinkle my nose. I'd like to think that if Arzo and Michael Montserrat knew about it, they'd have given it to me but I can't be sure. Either way, it doesn't change my next move. 'You can consider yourself absolved of any further obligation,' I tell her.

'My agreement is with your grandfather, not you.'

I look at her sternly, underlining the fact that I'm not going to brook any argument on this. 'You've done what you needed to do. Besides, I owe you now because I thought you were one of the Montserrat traitors.'

'Traitors?' She looks shocked. Obviously she knew no more about my real motives than I knew about hers.

'I'll make sure he knows you've fulfilled your oath,' I promise. 'You're free to drink if you really want to.'

'Thank you.' Her voice is quiet. She digs into the pocket of her jumpsuit and pulls out the little envelope. 'You only need a couple of grains every day mixed with water. Mr Blackman – I mean, your grandfather – was very clear about not taking more.'

Considering the side effects of O'Shea's spell, goodness knows what might happen if you overdose on this stuff. Perhaps ignorance is bliss. I take the envelope then lean over the fountain, trailing my fingers in the water.

'Actually, Beth, there is one more thing I need you to do.'

'Name it.'

'I have to get out of here so I can go where I need to be.'

The expression in her eyes says it all. 'After last time?' she shrieks, then claps her hand over her mouth when she realises how loud she's been.

'It'll be okay,' I reassure her. 'I won't be near any human blood.'

'Why? Where are you planning to go?'

I smile humourlessly. 'It's time to pay the Bancroft Family a little visit.'

23

SPA TREATMENT

I'M NOT A COMPLETE FOOL. EVEN WITHOUT BETH'S COMMENT about the increased number of guards around the Montserrat complex, I know there is little chance of me sneaking out a second time. No doubt the Montserrat PR machine is still working at full throttle; they're not about to let any more thirsty new recruits onto the streets again. I imagine heads are still rolling because we managed it once. I suppose I'll have to seek out Lord Montserrat. I have to admit I'm surprised when he appears suddenly on the path as Beth and I head back inside. His figure is shrouded in shadow, but there's no mistaking his broad shoulders and aggressive stance.

'What are you doing?'

I smile disarmingly. 'Out for a little stroll, my Lord. It's such a wonderfully balmy evening, don't you think?'

Beth inhales sharply at my disrespectful tone. I have no idea how Michael Montserrat feels about it, as his face remains hidden by the darkness. Irksome.

'Beth, if you'd be so kind?'

She walks off so quickly that her stilettos spray up gravel in her wake. I raise my eyebrows. 'I'm impressed, my Lord. I didn't think Beth was scared of anyone. Congratulations.'

He takes a step towards me, moving into the moonlight so his dark scowl becomes visible. 'Tell me exactly what you thought you were doing,' he growls.

I blink, a picture of innocence. 'I told you. We came out for a walk.'

His hands ball up into fists although they remain by his sides. I've never before seen someone so genuinely intimidating. I'm going to stand my ground though, no matter what.

'Bo, you know what I'm referring to. Your little jaunt into town. You know, the one where you almost killed someone and destroyed yourself?'

I shrug and inspect my fingernails. 'Considering the last conversation we had involved you telling me my name was top on the list for execution, I hardly thought you'd care.'

'I had my reasons for that.'

'And I had my reasons for going out.'

He takes another step towards me. 'We have never, ever, had any recruits sneak out in the middle of the goddamn night before.' He's not shouting, but he doesn't need to. His voice is so dangerously quiet it's making me shiver.

'What you mean is that you never *caught* any recruits sneaking out before.' I'm dancing with death by taunting him but the perverse part of me that's still glad to alive – and human – can't help it.

'You almost killed someone.'

'Are you pissed off about that or that we pulled the wool over your eyes?'

'You assured me several times that you didn't want to be a vampire. How stupid can you be to think that you could go outside and not be tempted?'

'I had to do something!' I'm starting to lose my temper. 'This is my life on the line. You stopped talking to me, like we were bloody schoolgirls having a spat. How else was I supposed to continue investigating? You didn't tell me anything about Tommy Glass. I was out of the loop on freaking everything! I gave up my life for this, my Lord.' I enunciate the last two words as clearly as I can. I might understand his position but I also want him to appreciate the disdain I feel for him right now.

'Do you think this is all about you? There are five Families, Bo. That's two thousand five hundred lives to consider. Not to mention what will happen to all the humans if we are destroyed. The universe doesn't revolve around you.'

'You came to *me*,' I remind him. 'You begged *me* to help you.'

His dark eyes flash. 'Only because you had nothing left to lose. You were convenient.'

I feel a tug of something inexplicable as I glare into his eyes. For once I'm glad that I'm not taller because the tie that was created between us because of the way he turned me is affecting my baser instincts. I can smell his deep musky aftershave and my stomach flutters. I glare harder to dampen my traitorous emotions. It doesn't work. He, however, seems to sense my capitulation because he relaxes slightly.

'You had bloodfever. You were screaming for hours on end and we were about to force feed you. How did you recover, Bo?'

Because my sneaky grandfather blackmailed someone into giving me a secret powder that helped stop the urges. I can hardly tell him that; I have a feeling he won't take too kindly to Arbuthnot Blackman knowing how to curtail bloodlust when the Families don't.

'Just lucky, I guess,' I say softly.

He rolls his eyes disbelievingly. 'Luck appears to be a bankable commodity when you're around.'

'If it helps, I don't feel particularly fortunate right now.'

His fists uncurl and for a brief moment he appears almost vulnerable. 'I'm sorry.' He says it quietly.

'Excuse me?' My voice is much louder in return. 'I didn't quite catch that.'

The vulnerability vanishes. 'You heard me the first time.'

I stick a finger in my ear and wiggle it around. 'No, no, I'm not sure I did.'

He sighs. 'Fine.' He steps up to my ear and bends his head. 'I'm sorry,' he whispers into it. 'I should not have jumped to conclusions about you.'

'I'm sure you can do better than that,' I murmur.

'Don't push your luck.' It's a low growl. The fluttering in my stomach intensifies and I finally move away.

'Okay,' I shrug, aiming for insouciance. I'll fake it until it's true. 'Tell me what else I've missed.'

If he's surprised by my sudden *volte-face*, he doesn't show it. Instead he gets down to business. 'Arzo told you about the Bancroft vampire.'

I nod.

He pulls out a smartphone and flips through a few screens, then holds it up. I squint. It's a very bloody looking vampire with short blond hair and fear in his eyes.

'He doesn't look too happy,' I comment. 'You do realise that if he was given O'Shea's adapted spell, it might not be his fault?'

'A traitor is a traitor.'

I shake my head. 'The world is not black and white, my Lord.'

'Michael,' he tells me.

I give him a look. I'm not quite ready to go back there just yet.

'Do you recognise him?' he asks.

'He's the one from the train station.'

'That's what we thought.' He puts the phone away.

'You know, it might have been helpful if I could have spoken to him before Bancroft killed him.'

'It wasn't my decision to make.'

I eye him. No, it wasn't but I bet he could have encouraged the

Bancroft Head to hold off if he'd really wanted to. 'Did you talk to him?'

'It was a Bancroft matter.'

'So he was only dealt with in-house? Why wouldn't you or the other Heads question him too? You're all threatened by what's going on here.'

He scowls. 'It's not the way we do things.'

I let it go for now. 'Is there anything else I should know?'

'We can't find the Dire Straits attacker. No one in the Families can find evidence that anyone else is involved. But twelve more vampires from across all the Families have turned up dead.'

'And little Tommy Glass,' I point out.

He runs a hand through his hair. 'Unfortunately he's not the only human. He's just the only one we didn't manage to get to before the press.'

'How many others?' I ask quietly and for a long moment he doesn't answer. Then he sighs.

'Too many. Things are falling apart, Bo. I don't know how long we have left before everything collapses. Someone is behind this but we don't know who and we don't know what they're waiting for.'

I watch him carefully. Fatigue and frustration are etched into his features. I put a hand out as if to pat his shoulder, then think better of it. 'I wasn't getting out of here on a jolly. There was a lawyer…'

'D'Argneau.' At my look, he explains. 'We thought it might be worthwhile to know what was so important that you had to venture away from the safety of the Family.' His jaw tightens. 'He told me how you met.'

'Did you find anything else?' I ask awkwardly. 'It seemed too strange to be a coincidence that I bumped into him and he turned out to be the one who hired us to investigate O'Shea.'

'I had people check it out,' he says distantly. 'I agree the coincidence part appears unlikely but we could find nothing to suggest otherwise.'

I nibble a fingernail. D'Argneau has served his purpose and I'm desperate to change the subject. 'I need to speak to the Bancroft Head.'

He jerks in surprise. 'Tell me what you need to know and I'll talk to her.'

'No.' I'm adamant about this. 'I need to see her in person and I need to do it alone. If you're there, she'll react differently.'

'Bo,' he begins.

I reach out again with my hand and place it on his arm. 'Please, my Lord. Just trust me. I have to talk to her and it's better if I do it alone.'

'Absolutely not.'

'My Lord.' I try again. 'Michael. The spell only affects male vampires. It's better if you stay away.'

His eyes narrow. 'The rest of us aren't idiots, Bo. We checked her out. It's the first thing we did. You can't pin the blame on her just because she's not a man. Bancroft doesn't want to upset the status quo any more than the rest of us.'

No, I think. You just don't want to believe that Bancroft would do that. Plus, she's covered her tracks well. After all, I checked her out myself by telephoning that spa. What I didn't consider at the time is that she very cleverly set herself up with an alibi. Until D'Argneau's information that she was the one who'd set him onto O'Shea, that is. Add that to the fact that the blond prick who killed Charity Weathers was conveniently executed by her within a few days of his treachery being discovered – and before he could be questioned by anyone else. She was the obvious suspect from the beginning. Maybe that's why she's gotten away with it for so long; she was so obvious that it seemed ridiculous that it could be her. She sets up false rumours of a new Family to cover her tracks and, hey presto, everyone's running around going crazy while she laughs from the sidelines and puts her plans of vampire domination into action. I'm not going to say anything to Montserrat until I have absolute proof but I'm fairly certain I know how to get it. I haven't spent years being manipulated by my grandfather without learning a thing or two about the process.

'Well, if you're so sure it's not her, then you've got nothing to worry about, have you? Let me do this. It's going to be easier with your permission than without.'

He gives a short laugh, his dimple appearing momentarily. 'I'm clearly being punished for something I've done in a former life.'

I smile sweetly. I know I've won.

'Fine. I'll set it up,' he tells me.

'Thank you. But I need a car to get me there so I can avoid any untoward encounters with bleeding humans or ultraviolet rays along the way. I'll set up the meeting with her on my own. And some kind of recorder or listening device, if you have one.'

'She's a Family Head, Bo. She deserves your respect. As far as she's concerned you're nothing more than a human.'

I grin. 'Hey, as far as I'm concerned I'm nothing more than a human either.'

I skip happily along the corridor, looking for Beth. I feel slightly guilty about receiving more of her help, especially after being convinced she was betraying her new Family. Let's face it, I treated her no differently to how Lord Montserrat treated me – although I wouldn't have threatened to execute her, of course. However, I can think of no one who'll be able to pull off my plan with more aplomb than her. The worst thing is that it's still only Monday. Ms Bancroft won't be back sampling the joys of Spa De Loti for another two days. Even more troublesome is that she'll be there during the day and sunlight is definitely not my friend. Without Montserrat's help, I'll never get there.

I'm at the foot of the main staircase when I spot Peter shuffling along. I bounce up to him. 'Hey,' I say, slapping him on the back, 'how's things?'

He looks at me bleakly. 'You were half dead this time yesterday, Bo. Why are you so chipper suddenly?'

'Because I was half dead this time yesterday.' I beam at him. 'There's nothing like almost dying to make you feel good.' Not to mention solving the greatest vampire murder mystery of this century, I think breezily.

'Technically, if you'd drunk a bit of blood, you wouldn't be dead either,' he points out. 'Vampires aren't any more dead than humans.'

I pay him more attention. 'Then why are you still blood free? It's a damn long time to hold out.'

'They're taking bets on which one of us will last the longest,' he says glumly.

I frown. 'Who?'

'Everyone. They've never had four recruits hold out for this length of time.' His lip curls. 'My odds are long apparently.'

Frankly, I'm not surprised; he's starting to look more dead than alive. There's a faint sheen of sweat on his brow and an odd sour smell coming off his body. My heart goes out to him. 'You don't care about being powerful and you don't want to be Sanguine. Why don't you drink? You can't keep putting yourself through this, Peter. Believe me, I know how bad it gets.' I'd give him some of Beth's powdered stuff if I thought he'd want it. The trouble is, I'm not sure he knows what he wants.

'I deserve to suffer.'

My eyes widen in alarm. This kind of self-flagellation is not healthy. 'Peter, nobody deserves to suffer.'

'Yeah?' he scoffs. 'What about your boss? The one you were in love with? Don't the vampires who killed him deserve to suffer?'

I'd forgotten all about that little story I'd spun. 'Er...'

Nicky appears from behind me. 'Bo! You were in love with your boss and a vampire killed him? No way! That's so awful.'

For once, I'm irritated by her abrupt appearance as well as the line of questioning. Before D'Argneau's revelations, I'd have milked this conversation for all it's worth. After all, it was my plan to gain the others' confidence and encourage them to tell me if they'd been approached by any vampires looking to organise a mass-scale betrayal. Now I know that Bancroft is behind it all, I'm less interested in possible minions who might emerge from the woodwork. I don't need the followers when I can nab the leader and achieve my goal.

'I don't really want to talk about it.' I shift uncomfortably.

Peter moves past us. 'Now you know how I feel,' he mutters.

I watch him wander off then turn back to Nicky. Not for the first time, I register distaste in her eyes when she looks at him. 'You don't like him, do you?' I say. 'He's actually a nice guy if you give him a chance.'

She faces me, her eyes clear and guileless. 'It's not his fault,' she tells me frankly. 'He just reminds me of … you know.'

I suddenly feel like a shit. 'The people who attacked your family?' I ask gently.

She nods, her eyes welling up. I pull her into a hug. 'I'm so sorry, Nicky. It must be impossibly hard for you.' I feel her body tremble while she sniffs into my shoulder. 'Why does Peter remind you of them?'

She sobs harder and clutches at me. I hold her and wait until her racking cries subside. I smooth her hair, telling myself that she doesn't want my advice or guidance, she just needs a bit of comfort. I hope she gets over her feelings for Peter though, not just for his sake but for hers too. Irrational dislike is never healthy, even if it seems unavoidable.

Eventually she pulls away. 'Thank you, Bo. You're so kind and helpful. I don't know what I'd do without you.'

Warmth spreads through me and I feel oddly embarrassed. It's part of being British, I suppose, this inability to accept a genuine compliment. I smile awkwardly at her. 'I'm always here, Nicky. You know, if you ever want to talk about it.'

She sniffs tearfully. 'You're the best.' Then, before I can say anything else, she runs up the stairs, quickly disappearing from sight.

TWO DAYS LATER, dealing with Nicky's fragility and Peter's increasing weakness seem easy in comparison to what Beth and I are about to attempt. It is hard enough staying awake beyond dawn; every time I stifle a yawn, Beth does the same. The rhythmic sounds of fatigue from the pair of us add to the tension in the back of one of Montserrat's helpfully blacked-out cars.

'I can't believe I let you talk me into this,' she mutters.

I try to keep my tone light. 'Hey, at least we're doing this with the full consent of our Lord and Master this time.'

'Are you going to tell me what's really going on?'

'It wouldn't be fair. First of all, it's meant to be confidential information and, second, I don't want to worry you.'

'You realise that there is nothing more worrying than the phrase "I don't want to worry you", right?'

'"I think you should sit down"?' I suggest.

'Okay, yeah, that's never good to hear.'

'"This isn't going to hurt much"?'

'Fine.'

'"Our nuclear facility has run for a full seven days without an accident"?'

'Bo?'

'Yes?'

'Shut the smeg up.'

I grin. 'Chill out. All you need to do is keep them busy so I can get to Bancroft.'

Beth glances out of the heavily tinted window. 'Assuming we can actually get from here to there first.'

'It's just a bit of sunshine. And it's less than five metres to the door from here anyway.' I'm not sure whether I'm attempting to reassure her or myself. Thanks to my fabulously unnatural healing powers, the blisters I incurred in my mad suicide attempt to see the sun rise have already healed. I can still remember what it felt like – and smelled like – to frazzle in the sun's rays, though. And that was at dawn. Now we're barely an hour past midday and there's not a single cloud in the sky. 'Being a vampire isn't all it's cracked up to be,' I comment sardonically.

'It's only for a couple of years. Then we build up immunity to the ultraviolet light.'

'You could have completed the process, you know. I wouldn't have minded if you'd drunk.'

Beth shakes her head. 'Nah. This'll go easier if I'm still clean. By this evening, however…'

I smile at her, even though it doesn't quite reach my eyes. Despite my earlier misgivings about Beth, the thought of this bright, resourceful woman becoming a full vampire seems tragic. I can't help feeling that she's throwing away her future. Fortunately, if Beth knows what I'm thinking, she doesn't comment and we are distracted by a cough from the driver in front.

'Lord Montserrat told me to inform you that you may still change your mind,' he says. He's not referring to fully fledged vampirism, unfortunately.

I look at Beth. 'Last one out is a deep-fried semi-human.'

She winks at me and pulls up the protective hood until her face is covered. It's made of some kind of odd reflective material. Apparently, it's the perfect material to be wearing should one ever find oneself in the midst of a nuclear attack. I don't feel any better knowing that the sun now has the same effect on me that a thermo-nuclear device would have.

I do the same, then kick open the car door and rush out while

Beth follows at my heels. The heat is searing and, even though I'm covered from head to toe, it feels as if every layer of skin is being scorched from my body like a marshmallow in a campfire. Then we're inside and moving away from the large glass windows – more out of instinct than because of any residual rays that might be seeping through.

I yank down the hood and paste on a wide smile for the receptionist. She is staring at us with the sort of horror that she usually reserves for people who've left the house before blow-drying their hair. I'm glad that I'm with Beth and her bouffant hairdo.

Beth saunters forward. 'Angelique! Darling, how are you?' She reaches across the desk for a double air kiss.

Angelique, recovering her professionalism, purrs, 'It's so wonderful to see you again!' She's never seen Beth in her life before, of course.

'Well, darling, you can see the trauma.' Beth flips out a hand in my direction and I manage to look suitably contrite. 'I mean, those curls! So last season. We simply must do something about them immediately.'

The receptionist looks me over, nodding. 'Yes, indeed. Do you have an appointment?'

'Angelique, this is an emergency! There's no time for appointments. We must see a specialist right away.'

If I'd not been standing there, I'd have believed Beth was far too melodramatic to suit our purpose but it's clear from Angelique's expression that she agrees this is an ER situation. She frowns. 'I can fit you in tomorrow. Around 10am?'

'No,' Beth replies firmly. 'That will be far too late. Can't you do a little shifting here and there and work your magic so we can see someone now?'

Angelique shakes her head. 'We have a special client. She's booked out the entire facility.'

'Where is this client?' Beth asks, sounding surprised.

'In the massage treatment room. She…'

'Well, then! We won't go anywhere near there. I absolutely promise.'

'I'm sorry. This client is rather particular. We can't afford to…'

'Angelique. You know me. I would never upset the rhythm of your wonderful spa. We will stay far away from your client.'

'I don't think….'

'Angelique.' Beth leans towards her. I think some of the unawakened vampirism in her blood must be working its magic because the receptionist pulls away and there's a flicker of fear in her heavily mascaraed eyes.

She yields. 'You must understand I can't be responsible for what happens if the other client sees you.' What she really means is that she won't be responsible if Bancroft drains the pair of us of our blood for daring to venture close to her.

Beth tosses her head. 'Darling, that's absolutely understood. We'll just head straight on up. The hair specialist, what's his name again?'

'Lars.'

'Of course, Lars. I can never remember those foreign-sounding names. Well, we'll stay with Lars. No one will even know we're here.' She waves her fingers in the air. 'Toodle-do!'

And with that, we move quickly to the lift and get in before Angelique changes her mind. 'Nicely done,' I say, when the lift doors close.

Beth shrugs. 'All in a day's work. Besides, that was the easy part. Lady Bancroft is hardly going to be here unaccompanied. She could have a dozen guards with her.'

Actually, I'm betting on the reverse. It would be a show of weakness for one of the Family Heads to travel with a vast entourage. I'm banking on the fact that she'll be virtually alone. I hope.

The lift doors open and we step out. 'You'll need to keep this Lars occupied,' I tell Beth. 'Just in case Angelique gets curious.'

'No problem. But Bo?'

'Mmm?' I say, glancing down the corridor and inhaling the heady scent of lemongrass and jasmine.

'You need to be smegging careful. It's not just your life that's on the line if you mess up whatever it is you're about to do.'

'You can play innocent. Say that I placed you under a compulsion spell or something.'

'I'm not talking about the vampires. If you get killed doing this, your grandfather will have my head.'

I want to protest but I have to acknowledge the truth of her words: revenge is his strong suit. For this reason, I've already penned him a letter and given it to Montserrat to send if my little foray into the heart of the Bancroft action doesn't work out.

I squeeze Beth's arm, then set off to the right. I need to be bloody smart about this. Guards or no guards, Lady Bancroft isn't the head of one the five Families because of her charm.

I duck my head to avoid the CCTV camera at the end of the corridor and creep on until I hear the murmur of voices from behind one of the doors. I listen for a moment, but I can't make out the words. It's of little consequence. I don't need to know what they're saying about exfoliation, I just need to get past them without being seen. I take a few steps backwards and quietly open the door to the adjoining room. Peering cautiously inside, I make sure it's empty before I sneak in and shut the door behind me. I prop a chair underneath the handle to keep it closed. It won't hold a vampire back for more than a few seconds but it'll probably be good enough to prevent any of the spa staff from entering.

I search the room. I'd hoped for a connecting door but that would be far too bloody easy. However, examining the layout of this room will probably help me enter the one next door. Companies like this tend to follow the same floor plan and I'm fairly certain that all the rooms are the same size. That means Bancroft's spa room will probably be the same as this one.

There are several shelves with artfully arranged, scented candles next to wooden bowls filled with fresh jasmine petals. For no apparent reason, each bowl includes a perfectly aligned set of chopsticks as if, at any minute, patrons can wander along and partake of the flowers as a pre-therapy snack. A massage table sits to one side, covered by fluffy towels; on the other, there's a bath that looks big enough to swim in. I whistle softly and pad through an archway to another section of the room. A large plastic coffin-like structure sits in the centre. I glance at it warily. This must be the sensory deprivation tank. It looks more like a bizarre torture chamber.

I try to work out how to open it. After a few moments I find the mechanism and, when I lift the lid, it's heavier than I expected. I frown at the silky looking water inside. There are tiny lights embedded around the inner edge of the tank, together with what appears to be a speaker. That's good. If Bancroft enjoys listening to music while lying in the dark, I'll have a better chance of sneaking in. I imagine where her head will be when she's inside. There's no sign of a pillow so it's difficult to judge which end to aim for. I'll just have to take my chances.

Once I'm satisfied with my inspection, I walk to the window. Heavy curtains tied back with fake rustic ropes frame the glass. I finger the material thoughtfully. No doubt they'll be closed to create a sense of privacy in Bancroft's room. I turn my attention to the window. Unfortunately for me, it's been designed with health and safety in mind and it opens out only a scant five inches. I may be small but I have no chance of squeezing myself through that gap.

I need to get into the room next door without being detected. There is obviously at least one spa staff member inside – which means at least one human. Even with my daily dose of the blood-lust dampening powder, attacking them and inadvertently drawing blood will lead to my undoing. Besides which, I'm sure there will be a minimum of one Bancroft Family companion. I'm still a weak recruit; I've got no hope against a genuine vampire. I press my palms against my temples and try to think. My musings are interrupted by a dull thud from outside.

I freeze. My heart beat ratchets up a notch and I strain to hear more but the walls are well insulated. I tiptoe carefully towards the door, grabbing one of the candles as I go. It's encased in a tubular glass container so I scoop out the candle then press the container against the wood, with my ear at the other end. There are two voices although I only understand a few words, which seem to be something to do with the effect of natural papaya enzymes. I relax, realising they must be spa staff. With any luck, they've just left Bancroft alone in her plastic tub.

I take the glass away from the door and notice the peephole set into the middle of it. I curse myself for not noticing it before. It's a nice touch for a private spa that wants to reassure its guests – and particularly helpful for me. I rise back on tiptoe to peer out and confirm that the two people outside are human. Both of them are wearing white coats as if to suggest that they are serious medical practitioners. They wander off.

I sink back down and lean against the door. Perhaps this won't be so difficult to manage after all. I return the glass to the shelf and lift up one of the chopsticks. Despite its decorative purpose, it feels sturdy. It won't serve as a stake to slam through Bancroft's black heart but nevertheless it might do some effective damage.

I have only one shot at this and if there's more than one other Bancroft Family vampire in the room, my goose is well and truly cooked. But I feel a surge of confidence. I can do this. The adrenaline coursing through my veins will provide me with the momentum I need. I straighten my shoulders. I can do this, I tell myself again.

I open the door and poke out my head. The corridor is empty. The CCTV camera at the far end is blinking in my direction so I pull down some hair to cover my face and step out. My stomach churns, more as a result of excitement than nerves. It's been a damn long month in the life of Bo Blackman and it's finally about to end.

I look through the peephole in Bancroft's door. There's a gleam of light but I can't make out much else. I lean forward to listen but it all seems quiet, so I take a deep breath and knock twice. Then I wait, gripping the chopstick until my knuckles whiten.

It feels like an eternity – although it's probably less than ten seconds – before a shadow crosses in front of the peephole. I draw back my fist and slam the narrow point of the chopstick through it, shattering the glass and ramming it into something soft on the other side. As soon as I feel it connect, I kick open the door, knocking down the vampire inside. He's clutching at his face, scrabbling at the chopstick protruding from his red, bulging eyeball and screaming like a pig at a slaughterhouse. No one is leaping to his aid but, from deeper inside the room, I can hear the plastic lid of the tank being pushed up. I waste no time in pushing the massage table against the door as a temporary barricade and jumping over one-eyed Jack to get to Bancroft before she gets to me. Her lightning vampire speed serves her well, though; by the time I leap through the arch she's already standing there, dripping wet and with a mask of fury etched on her face.

NANCY DREW

I FEINT RIGHT, THEN LEAP BACKWARDS AND YANK THE CHOPSTICK out of the bodyguard's eye. It makes a soft sucking sound that turns my stomach. I don't have time to do anything other than wave it threateningly in Lady Bancroft's direction before she lunges at me and slams my body against the wall.

'Your little spell won't work on me,' she hisses.

I blink. Spell? She registers my confusion and her eyes narrow. 'Who are you?'

Her hand grips my throat so tightly that I can't breathe, let alone speak. Perhaps this wasn't the most well-thought-out plan after all. She releases her hold slightly and repeats, 'Who are you?'

'Bo,' I manage to croak. 'Bo Blackman.'

Surprised, she takes her hand away and frowns. 'The Montserrat recruit? You're the traitor after all?'

This isn't going as I expected. 'No. *You're* the traitor. I can't be the traitor, I'm only a recruit.'

The bodyguard moans and, without missing a beat, she glides over, bends down and snaps his neck, pulling his head away from his body at the same time to ensure there'll be no return for this particular triber. I stare, open-mouthed.

Lady Bancroft shrugs. 'If he's not much use as a bodyguard, he's not much use as anything.'

I'm horrified by her casual violence until I remember that I'm the one who rammed a chopstick into his bloody eye. I twist so that I'm facing away from his corpse.

'Now,' she continues, 'tell me why you think I'm the traitor and why, as a recruit, you can't be.'

'Er…' Her clear green eyes fix me with such vivid intensity that I find it hard to concentrate.

She flicks back her sopping wet hair. 'Sorry. Force of habit.' Then, as if a switch has been turned, her gaze softens and something inside me relaxes.

'You mean you were…'

'Controlling you?' she asks impatiently. 'Yes. Now answer my questions.'

I'm stunned by the power she can yield and more than a little terrified. I'm also starting to appreciate that I've made a terrible mistake. Not in coming here to confront her – although clearly that was an error when I don't have anything beyond a fragile eating utensil with which to subdue her – but because it's obvious she's not behind the plot to destroy the Families.

'Speak, girl!' she snaps.

Her imperious tone snaps me out of my daze. 'We're not in the nineteenth century. I'm not some bloody scullery maid you can order around.'

Lady Bancroft's lips twitch. 'Montserrat was right. You do have some fire about you.' I scowl. 'I suppose you imagined you could attack me and win.'

'I didn't need to beat you. I just needed you to confirm that you were the traitor.'

'How would that help if I tore your head off before you could pass the information to someone else?' Her tone is mild but the threat is still there. Especially with the fallen body of her bodyguard lying just a few feet away.

I look at her steadily. She cocks her head then smiles. Her hand swipes at me in one flashing movement, ripping my jumpsuit and revealing the tiny microphone and wire underneath. Her body stills when she sees it.

'So,' she hisses in a dangerous undertone, 'Montserrat thinks I'm the one.'

I find my voice. 'Actually no, he doesn't. This is broadcasting somewhere else.' In fact just down the hall to Beth: the transmitter is too weak to signal anywhere further. That's another reason why Beth had to come with me. She couldn't listen in but everything is being sent to a miniature black box recorder hidden in her clothes. In the event of my death or dismemberment, all she has to do is take it back to Montserrat who'll de-encrypt it to discover the truth.

'All very well,' she says with a sniff, 'but it suggests a rather careless disregard for your own well-being.'

'Whoever's behind this has already destroyed my life. Finding them and putting them down is my *raison d'être*.'

She laughs, a high musical sound. 'Really?'

I'm offended. 'Really.'

'We have our own investigators, you know. We did look into you.' She taps the corner of her mouth thoughtfully. 'Let me think, what was it? The bottom rung of a two-bit private detective firm? A one-bedroomed flat in a seedier part of London? A few friends, no love life, no family?'

'I've got family,' I tell her stiffly.

'Your mother is on the other side of the world and relations with your grandfather are stilted.'

'Perhaps my definition of a good life and yours are different.'

She laughs again. 'I doubt that. Besides, you have five hundred members of a brand new Family. Why would you want to throw all that away?'

'I don't want to be a damned vampire,' I say through gritted teeth.

She's surprised. 'Why ever not?'

'I have no desire to be beholden to blood or to live an unnaturally long life. Human suits me just fine.'

Her hand shoots out again, grabbing my throat. She pushes me into the air while my legs kick involuntarily and my fingers scrabble at her hand.

'Can a human do this?' she enquires.

My eyes bulge and she sighs and lets me go. I fall into a puddle at her feet.

'Humans can't be hit by a stupid daemon-created passivity spell,' I croak.

She bends down. 'No, but you know they'll be destroyed by its results in the end.'

I stand up unsteadily. 'So why is someone doing it?'

She shrugs. 'Power.'

I think back to my earliest musings about O'Shea's spell. Tam always believed in sex and money as motives, but the allure of power is equally strong. I acknowledge her words with a nod. 'Why not you?' My voice is soft and non-threatening.

'You mean, why am I not initiating this Family takeover? Why am I not the traitor? Because, darling, I've got it good. I might be a woman in a man's world but I know how to play those boys.'

I find it hard to think of Michael Montserrat as a boy, but wisely I stay mute.

'At least you have one thing correct,' she says. 'Whoever is behind all this has to be a woman.'

'Because the spell only affects males?'

'Indeed. There would be far too much danger of leakage or contamination for it to be wielded by a man. Although the silly girl who is pulling the strings has no idea that you don't need magic to make men dance to your tune.'

Something about her tone makes me shiver. 'One of the witnesses said it was a woman.'

'Charity Weathers.'

I nod then glance at her, askance. 'You said you thought a recruit could be the perpetrator.'

'No. What I *asked* is why *you* think a recruit can't be.'

'It doesn't make sense. A recruit or a human wouldn't have access to the Families to involve so many vampires in the first place. As far as I understand, this has been going on for a couple of months.'

'The first death was February 15th.'

'Well then,' I say. 'It couldn't be a recruit. It has to be a Family member.'

She's amused. 'We don't live cloistered away like monks and nuns. Plenty of vampires have regular access to humans. Anyone could have given them the solidified spell.'

'You expect me to believe that a bunch of vampires, who've lived longer than anyone else, are stupid enough to fall for a trap and take a dodgy spell from a dodgy human?'

'Humans are craftier than you give them credit for,' she snorts.

'Are vampires stupider than you give them credit for?'

'There's a vast difference between stupidity and naivety.' She sighs. 'Perhaps that's been our downfall. We've been lulled into a false sense of security after decades of peace and power.'

I watch her carefully. I can't sense any dissembling. She might be right. I may have spent weeks making silly assumptions – but I still can't understand why a human would want to take down the five Families in order to set up a new Family in their place. It would disrupt years of the delicate power balance. Look at what happened in France during the Revolution when there was only one Family around. No one would want to see a return to those times, and humans and vampires co-exist quite happily these days. There's no need to change that. If you want to become a vampire, then just apply.

'What about disgruntled applicants who've not been recruited?' I ask suddenly.

Lady Bancroft looks at me like I'm a particularly disgusting form of fungus. 'We've done that. We investigated them all.'

'But…'

'Look, Montserrat might admire you but if you think you've got all the answers and that we've not already exhausted these possibilities, then you're even more stupid than I realised.'

I bristle. 'Hey, I've made some mistakes…'

'Some? You've wasted time and energy coming after me. This spell has the potential to destroy us all and we have no idea when or where it's going to happen. Meanwhile, you've been running around like Nancy Drew, uncovering nothing of note.'

'Nancy Drew is a good detective,' I mumble, although I'm gallingly aware that she's right. Since I entered the Montserrat Family, I've achieved a big fat zero. *Nul points* to Bo Blackman. Between wasting my time over Beth as a potential minion and Bancroft as the potential evil lady, I've discovered squat. There are only five more days until the end of the lunar month when I'll either become Sanguine or be a bloodguzzler. Unless I – or someone with more wits – find out who wants to make a new super Family, my days are numbered. Not to mention everyone else's.

The lack of sympathy on Lady Bancroft's face isn't helping. 'Why did you kill the blond vampire?'

'Who?'

'The one who killed Charity Weathers. It wasn't his fault.'

She nudges her dead bodyguard with her toe. 'It wasn't his fault you barged in here and disturbed me. I don't see you crying over his corpse.'

I stay on topic. 'You didn't let anyone else speak to him.'

'He had nothing to say. He'd been stripped of who he was and become a suggestible, pliable moron.'

'He couldn't tell you where he got the spell from?'

'He had no idea. Even as a vampire he dabbled in drugs. We assume his heroin was switched for the spell.'

I try to imagine what a Class A drug does to a vampire and fail. Then I remember the syringe I found back at the house on Wiltshore Avenue. I should have followed that up earlier. Charity had clearly been involved in drugs too to force her involvement. If Tam had been around to offer some guidance, I would probably have done more to follow that particular line of enquiry. Instead all I've done is let his memory down. My shoulders sink in defeat.

'Dire Straits,' I say.

'Indeed,' agrees Lady Bancroft.

'No, Dire Straits. My firm. Why did you hire D'Argneau to look for O'Shea? You've got your own investigators. You don't need a bunch of humans. You hired D'Argneau who hired us.'

'The lawyer? We tried our own methods and failed. He came highly recommended.'

'By whom?'

'Lots of people. What does it matter? We inadvertently discovered the daemon was the spell's originator thanks to a Valentine's Day card he sent to one of our first victims. He'd written it in code but a child could have cracked it.' She sniffs. 'So we went after him with D'Argneau's help to serve a summons for something else to cover our tracks.'

I pinch the bridge of my nose. I wonder if their sudden action to find O'Shea precipitated his attempted murder – and my framing for it.

'You need to leave now,' Lady Bancroft says without further preamble. She walks back to the sensory tank.

'You're going back in?'

'Why wouldn't I? If our world is going to end any day now, then I want to enjoy myself before it does.'

I struggle to see how shutting yourself into a tiny space equals enjoyment.

'Look,' she says more kindly, 'you've bitten off more than you can chew. Montserrat placed too much faith in you and it wasn't fair. You're too inexperienced and too damn human. It's not your fault. If we manage to get past this, come and see me when you've finished turning. You might be Montserrat now but I can always use a plucky vampire whose heart is in the right place.' Her condescension, even if it is well meant, is overpowering.

'I'm not going to be a vampire,' I snap. 'I only have five more days then I'll be Sanguine.'

She laughs, lifts up the roof of the tank and climbs back in. 'Sure.'

I throw her a dirty look but she's already disappeared from view. I run my hands through my hair. She's right. I arrogantly assumed that I'd be able to solve what the might of the five Families couldn't. Super Bo to the rescue! To quote D'Argneau, I'm an idiot.

I FIND Beth in a room at the other end of the corridor. Her fingers are splayed while a youngish looking man – Lars, I imagine – delicately re-paints them pillar-box red. The pair of them are watching a computer screen and giggling. I feel slightly miffed that she's having such a good time while I've been facing the dragon, until I spot the tension in her neck and the relief in her eyes when she sees me.

'Bo! Is everything okay?'

'Fine,' I mutter. 'Can we go now?'

'Absolutely not!' interrupts Lars, looking alarmed. 'Your nails haven't dried. Besides, I've not shown you the video of the vampires fighting.'

Beth looks apologetic. I'm keen to get out of here before the bodyguard's body is discovered and all hell breaks loose, but I sit down stiffly by her side.

'Don't you have that quick drying stuff?' I ask.

Lars sniffs dismissively and turns back to Beth. He taps something into the computer and a video comes on. 'Here,' he says. 'This is some dude from Gully getting it on with another from Stuart. You can tell which Families they're from because of the colours they're wearing,' he adds helpfully.

'Thanks,' Beth murmurs. Clearly, Lars has not cottoned onto her recruit status yet.

I turn to the screen and watch what appears to be CCTV footage from some dive of a nightclub. A tall vampire bumps into another one, inadvertently spilling his drink. It takes less than three seconds before they descend into a spectacular fang-flashing, artery-spilling brawl.

'The day after this, the Gully and Stuart heads met in broad daylight. In Hyde Park! They must have taken it seriously because they frown at each other and have all these bodyguards surrounding them.' Lars leans in and whispers confidentially, 'But, they met in public so everyone would understand that they weren't allowing their Family members to go around and kill each other.'

He taps the keyboard again, while I shift in my chair. 'We need to go, Beth.'

She nods and rises. 'I'm sorry, Lars. We have another, um, appointment to keep.'

He looks disappointed. 'You can see them drinking blood! At least it looks like blood. There's a waiter bringing more over to them. The dude with the camera gets in his way and then they almost fight as well.'

'Bye Lars,' I say firmly, turning to the door.

'Another time,' Beth chirps out, far more enthusiastically.

I've just put one foot outside into the corridor when I hear a tinny voice shouting from the computer. I freeze then, ever so slowly, turn back. I know that voice.

'Lars, can you just rewind that for a moment?'

'I thought you had to go,' he says sullenly.

I shove him out of the way and start the video again. He

mutters something but I ignore him and focus on the screen. Sure enough, Lord Gully and Lord Stuart are seated at a linen-covered table in the midst of a clearing. They are some distance away but it's still possible to make out the red liquid in their glasses. I swallow hard and focus on the tuxedoed man carrying the tray. His back is turned to the camera. Then the cameraman helpfully moves forward into the waiter's path. They almost collide and, for a moment, all I can see is the black material of the tuxedo jacket as the camera gets caught up in it. Finally it points in the waiter's face while he snarls obscenities. I reach forward and pause the video, then stare, sickened.

'What is it, Bo?'

'I was going to watch this video weeks ago,' I murmur absently. 'Except I got distracted.'

'I don't understand.' Beth touches my sleeve, but I don't respond. I'm too focused on the face filling the computer screen.

'I know him.'

'The waiter?'

I nod. I want to punch and kick and scream. Because the waiter glaring out at us with twisted malevolence isn't a waiter at all. It's Boris.

25

PLAYING POSSUM

I RAIL AGAINST MYSELF THROUGHOUT THE JOURNEY BACK TO THE Montserrat headquarters. Beth is increasingly alarmed, but I can't reassure her. I'm simply too pissed off.

As soon as we cross the threshold of the mansion, I spot Montserrat in the foyer. He's standing smack bang in the centre, arms folded, his expression brooding and tense. When he sees me, he relaxes slightly and moves forward with swift grace. I meet him halfway and look up at his chiselled face. Before he can open his mouth, I demand access to a phone.

A muscle throbs in his cheek. 'Why, Bo?'

'I need to speak to Arzo.'

'Can't you at least tell me what happened with Bancroft first?'

'Nothing worth mentioning,' I mutter. Bancroft was a waste of time. The trip to the spa wasn't. Now I know who I really need to speak to.

'Bo, you are under my jurisdiction yet you insist on keeping me in the dark. Perhaps you're confused as to how the chain of vampire command works.'

I force myself to take a deep, calming breath. 'I've screwed up a lot since arriving here. I'm not about to make any more assumptions until I can confirm something with Arzo. Then I'll speak to you.'

His dark eyes rove over my face. For a moment I think he's going to refuse and I'll have to run back into the terrifying, sunlit street to find myself a sodding phone box – if any exist in this part of the world – but he jerks his head and leads me in the direction of his office. Even though I'm in a hurry to talk to Arzo and I move as quickly as I can, I find it hard to keep up with his long-legged stride.

'I'm glad you're okay,' he says conversationally.

'Mmm.'

'We have an unspoken rule in the Families that no one is allowed to touch each other's Family members without gaining permission first. But Lady Bancroft can be,' he pauses, 'volatile.'

I wonder what he'd think if he knew she thought she had him and all the other Family heads wrapped around her little finger.

'As you can see,' I say, 'I'm fine.'

'And as I said, I'm glad.'

'However,' I continue, 'didn't you tell me that she'd think of me as little more than a human? If I'm still a recruit and haven't drunk blood yet, does that make me a Montserrat Family member?'

He smiles. 'A distant cousin, perhaps. I made it clear to her that you weren't to be harmed.'

My eyes narrow. 'She knew I was coming?'

'No. We had already spoken of you, though.'

I glare at him suspiciously. I'd surmised as much from Lady Bancroft but that doesn't mean I'm happy about it. He gives me a grin which I don't bother returning.

Once we reach his office, he follows me in and closes the door. He points towards his desk where a shiny, old-fashioned, phone sits.

'Don't you have a mobile?'

'I prefer this.'

I look at him. 'Just how old are you?'

His eyes dance. 'It's rude to ask the age of your elders, Bo.'

I grunt. 'Are you going to leave?'

'It's my office.' He sits down in a leather-backed chair and leans back, propping up his feet on top of the desk.

I roll my eyes at him then pick up the phone. 'Do you have his number?'

He reels it off from memory. My surprise must have shown on my face, because he comments, 'I can chew gum and walk at the same time too.'

'Whatever.' I dial the number and wait.

Arzo answers almost immediately. 'My Lord.' Caller display, I figure.

'Er, no. It's Bo.'

'Bo! Are you alright? What happened with Lady Bancroft?'

'Not much. There's a hell of a lot of people suddenly concerned with my welfare though.' Montserrat grins at this but doesn't speak.

'Arzo, who knew about my assignment at Wiltshore Avenue?'

'Myself and Tam. Why?'

'Anyone else?'

He doesn't hesitate. 'No. We kept who was responsible for which assignment quiet, Bo. Loose lips sink ships. Besides, it caused less rivalry between you lot that way.'

'Tansy didn't know?'

'No.'

'What about Boris?'

'How would he have known?' He sounds baffled.

A wrench hammers into my heart. 'When I was in the ceiling, right before you were attacked, Boris came in to see Tam. He told him I was wanted for questioning because of what happened at Wiltshore Avenue. Some contact of his had been in touch. Or perhaps it was the police scanners he'd been listening to.' I'm irked that I can't remember this salient detail.

'Right. Boris spent a lot of time listening to the radio call-outs and cultivating police snitches.' He sniffs disdainfully. 'They rarely came up with the goods though.'

'Arzo, he knew the assignment was to do with a daemon. He said as much to Tam. Then he left, Tam called you in and the vampire attacked.'

I can feel Montserrat's eyes on me but I stare down at the desk. Arzo sucks in a breath. 'He couldn't have known. The only people who know O'Shea is a daemon were you, Tam and myself. Even the police wouldn't have worked it out that quickly. They'd have had to send his blood to their labs first.'

'The police would have known if whoever tipped them off told them.' My voice is quiet while I wait for Arzo to connect the dots.

'Boris wouldn't have known unless the tip-off told him too.'

'Or he was the tip-off.'

Arzo is silent.

'Tam called you in to the office because Boris couldn't have known that detail about O'Shea and me unless he was involved in some way that he shouldn't have been.'

I picture Arzo nodding to himself and stroking his chin. 'He was a canny man, our boss. He knew something was wrong.'

I close my eyes for a moment. I'd taken that overheard conversation as proof that Tam was involved in my set-up. It was actually the opposite. There's a loud noise from the other end of the line. 'I'm going to kill that bastard myself.'

I take a deep breath; it's about to get worse. I tell him about the YouTube video. Arzo is confused. 'I don't get it.'

'As a waiter, he'd be in a perfect position to drop a little something into their glasses.'

'But Gully and Stuart are fine. Some of their lower-level vampires have been involved, of course, but not the Heads.'

'He must be biding his time. Waiting for something. He's not the one in charge, Arzo. We know that's a woman. But he's got himself into a position where he can do what he needs to when he needs to. A trusted Family servant.'

Montserrat has pulled his feet off the desk and is no longer leaning back. His whole body is tense. He takes the phone from me. 'I need a photo of this Boris now. We need to circulate it to all the Families, especially Gully and Stuart.'

I look at him. 'You can't kill him, Michael. We need him alive.'

He nods sharply. Arzo says something else then hangs up. I look at Montserrat with anguished eyes.

'It's Boris. It's all Boris. He's the reason I was framed for O'Shea. He's the one who sent that crazy vampire after everyone at Dire Straits too. I can't believe I didn't think about him conveniently leaving before that vampire showed up. Or that I didn't talk to Arzo about what he'd said to Tam.' Tears spring unbidden. I've wasted all this time running round in circles chasing my tail when the answer was right in front of me all along.

'He's not the person in charge of all this, Bo,' Montserrat says quietly. 'Even if you'd worked out earlier that he was involved, it might not have changed anything.'

I look at him angrily. 'Stop trying to make me feel better! If only I'd…'

He holds my hands and forces me to be still. 'Bo. Every single one of the five Families, who are more powerful and far-reaching than you could ever imagine, have been trying to find out who is responsible for this. This isn't about you. It's about all of us.'

A single tear escapes and tracks a slow path down my cheek. Montserrat brushes it away with his thumb while I grit my teeth and nod. 'We need to find him and we need to find him now.'

He gives a small smile. 'We will, Bo. So help me God, we will.'

He bends down and kisses me chastely on the lips. I'm so surprised that I don't have time to react. Then he picks up the phone and galvanises the entire Montserrat Family into achieving one goal – finding Boris.

IT TAKES LESS than sixty minutes for teams from each of the Families to break into Boris's apartment and ransack the place. It's obvious that he's long gone. Apparently the food in the fridge, what little of it there is, is mouldy and rotten and it was difficult to open the door because of the pile of junk mail, bills and letters behind it. But there's no clue as to where Boris has run to.

Although he's not seen hide nor hair of the burly prick for almost a fortnight, Lord Gully confirms that Boris has worked for them on and off for the past two years. All of us are horrified at that. This operation has been planned for a very long time; no wonder we're constantly on the back foot and always playing catch up.

Montserrat gives me detailed files with photos taken from every angle of Boris's flat, as well as photocopies of everything they could scan. The results are chilling. There are notes on every one of the Families, including lists speculating which Family will be the most likely to start early recruitment. It brings me back to Lady Bancroft's words that a recruit or a human could be behind everything that's happened. The thought that one of my fellow wannabe bloodguzzlers could be the perpetrator makes my stomach churn. And that's nothing compared to the file on me. Boris knows everything: details about my grandfather and my parents; my vulnerabilities, including my apparent naivety; he even questions how I managed to rescue O'Shea when I lack the, in his words, 'gut instinct to sense when there's trouble'. I search desperately for a clue that might lead us to him or his mistress. Other than a constant tone of enmity and bitterness in every-thing he's written, there's nothing I can use. The Families' own investigators have come to the same conclusion. After the rush of adrenaline caused by having a suspect who might know some-thing worthwhile, the soul-sucking desperation at our inability to locate him casts a pall over everyone.

THIRTY-SIX HOURS LATER, there's still no sign of him. Whatever the vampire equivalent of an all-points bulletin is, it's certainly in force. But Boris has gone to ground and the frustration of being unable to find him is overwhelming. I hold Beth's hand while she finally – sadly – drinks three pints of gloopy blood and makes the eventual slide into full-blown vampirism. I try to look engaged during various training sessions with Ursus, Ria and a whole host of others, before giving up and going back to re-read the files on Boris for the umpteenth time. I pace up and down the corridors of the Montserrat mansion on more occasions than I care to mention.

Even with the mysterious powder which is keeping the worst of my bloodlust at bay, I feel the desperate cravings. With only two days to go until the end of the lunar month and the full moon, I'm sure I can make it. It's not easy, though. One moment I break into cold sweats, then hot flushes the next. More alarmingly, my hands have developed an almost permanent tremor which makes holding anything, even a glass of water, incredibly difficult. I've not slept for what seems like weeks. I have no idea whether that's down to guilt for not identifying Boris's role sooner, or whether it's a result of the cravings. Either way, I'm getting weaker by the day.

I've been to see Michael several times, both to check on the progress of the hunt for Boris and to plead with him to let me go outside to join it. He appears sympathetic but remains adamant that I need to be kept inside for my own good. One look at my shaking hands is enough to remind me of that. It occurs to me that by joining the ranks of the Montserrat Family I've become much more emasculated than I ever was under my grandfather's thumb or working for Tam.

The lack of progress becomes more terrifying when I go to visit Matt. After almost two weeks of slipping in and out of consciousness, he finally seems to be recovering. Recovering from his hanging, though not from the twisted version of O'Shea's spell. When I see him, he's sitting on an infirmary bed flicking through what appears to be a children's book.

'Hey, Matt,' I say softly.

He looks up and gives me a huge grin. 'Bo! It's so good to see you!'

I'm taken aback by his genuine happiness. 'You look … pleased,' I tell him cautiously.

'Lord Montserrat told me I should be less grumpy.' His grin stretches wider. 'So now I'm not grumpy at all.'

'What else did he tell you?'

Matt shrugs. 'Not much. He wanted to know why I'd said your name when I woke up.' His grin turns beatific. 'You were singing the Bee Gees and I wanted to hear more. I wanted you to come and sing more.'

I have an appalling singing voice. Sympathy for the large, muscled ex-soldier builds inside me. 'Matt?'

'Yes?'

'If I asked you to do twenty push-ups right now, what would you do?'

It is a rhetorical question but Matt doesn't treat it that way. He springs off the bed and drops to the floor to start pumping out push-ups. He's reached three before, horrified, I stop him.

'I can keep going, Bo. I'll do as many as you want.'

Sickened, I turn away. The tentacles of the passivity spell have wormed their way into his psyche. As much as I disliked him before, my pity for his condition now is overwhelming. He's acting like a brain-damaged child. I wonder if he'll ever recover.

Montserrat is kind when I bump into him a few minutes later as I high tail it away from Matt's room and back to my own quarters. It seems he's been looking for me, because he's not in the habit of wandering the recruits' corridors. It is hard to ignore the zing I feel in my heart at that thought. I immediately put it down to the annoying side effects from having been turned by him personally and move quickly towards him to express my anxiety at Matt's condition. Unfortunately I'm hit by a sudden wave of dizziness that makes me stagger and fall. He reaches out with lightning-fast reflexes, catching me before I hit the ground, then pulls me to his chest. The top of my head barely reaches his chin.

'Are you alright?'

I step back out of his embrace. He offers no resistance. 'I'm fine.' I'm embarrassed to appear so weak.

He stares down at me with a mixture of empathy and frustration, then opens his mouth to say something. Abruptly he closes it again, leaving me wondering. 'Good.' Without saying any more, he turns and leaves.

I remain where I am, gazing after him, thoroughly confused. He obviously wanted something and thought better of it. The frustrating thing is that I have no idea what he was after.

I find myself wandering through the crooked paths of the Montserrat garden a couple of hours later. I'm looking up at the pregnant moon, as if I can will it to reach full status, when I'm interrupted by Ursus and Ria. I wait for them to come close then paste on a smile.

'The professor and the PA,' I say, in an attempt to be charming.

Ursus's expression doesn't flicker although Ria raises a single eyebrow. 'The recruit with a well of hidden secrets.'

'Well, they wouldn't be secrets if they weren't hidden,' I murmur. She doesn't look impressed.

'We want to know what's going on,' Ursus says, ignoring the byplay between Ria and me.

I shrug. 'Ask Lord Montserrat.'

'He's been closeted in a meeting all day with the other Heads. This is our Family. You're not even a proper vampire and yet you have access to information that we need to keep our Family safe.'

Ursus takes a threatening step towards me. 'You're going to tell us what you know.'

'And if I don't?' I inquire mildly.

A twisted snarl crosses Ria's face. I can empathise with them. Despite their relatively youthful exteriors, they've probably been trusted members of the Montserrat inner circle for decades. Now vampires are going missing from all the Families, and they're being kept out of the loop. But doubtful as it seems, there is still the danger that one or both of them is involved in the treachery. It's certainly not my place to tell them what's going on. But it must be frustrating for them to see me, a complete nonentity, with their Lord's ear. I'd like to tell them it's simply my bad luck that has put me in this position but by the look on their faces, I don't think they'll accept that.

'You're going to begin by telling us how you escaped the bloodlust.'

I was wondering when that little matter would come up again. I'm surprised more hasn't been made of it before now. 'You're the experts,' I say. 'I was pretty much out of it. I don't know what happened.'

'Nobody's ever come out of the bloodlust. In fact, within hours of it starting, we normally give the sufferers blood to bring them out. Lord Montserrat wouldn't let us give you any.' Ursus's eyes are hard. 'Why?'

I feel a rush of warmth towards Michael at that little titbit. He must have known it would be almost impossible for me to survive the cravings once I fell unconscious. And yet he hung on, avoiding forcing me to drink blood because he knew I didn't want to become a real vampire.

'Not just that,' Ria adds, 'but there's not been an intake since the eighteenth century where there were still three recruits who'd not drunk less than forty-eight hours before the full moon.'

'Nicky and Peter are nothing to do with me,' I say, although I ponder her words carefully. It *is* strange that they remain in the odd twilight world of half human and half vampire. I've got my magic powder to help me: what do they have?

'We've been through your stuff. Are you Christian? Is that it?'

I frown. They've nosed through my belongings? 'What do you mean, you've been through my stuff?'

'You don't think we just throw away the things you enter with, do you?' Ursus leans forward until I can feel his hot breath on my face. 'Why do you have a crucifix?'

Oh. I suddenly remember that I scooped up Peter's after he left it behind during that first meeting with the Family. 'It's not mine,' I tell them.

'You're just keeping it for a friend?' Ria is sarcastic.

'Actually, yes. And what in the hell are you doing going through my things?'

'You're one of us now. What's yours is ours.'

'Somehow I don't think that works in reverse,' I mutter.

'Where's the daemon?'

I honestly have no idea. I've not seen or heard anything of O'Shea since my recruitment. He's probably still holed up in Michael's palatial penthouse.

'Who's this Boris fellow?'

Ursus grabs my arm. 'Has he been killing our friends?'

I pull back. Enough is enough. 'You're asking a hundred questions that I can't answer. Like I said, if you want to know what's going on, ask Lord Montserrat.'

'We're asking you.'

Something in Ria's eyes snaps. I recognise her loss of control just in time and flip right to avoid her attack. 'We're Family members now,' I say, keeping out of her reach. 'Are you supposed to attack your sister?'

'You're no sister of mine. You've not drunk yet, remember? That makes you fair game.'

Fear runs down my spine. Ria's words may be melodramatic

but I can sense the anger in them. And people – or vampires – who are hurt and angry don't think straight. And I'm no match physically for them .

Realising that I'm not going to be able to talk my way out, I opt for flight. Both Ursus and Ria can outrun me, but they won't dare make a move in the presence of others. I need to get back inside to the relative safety of the mansion where other people might be wandering the corridors. I open my mouth as if to speak, then bolt, scarpering past them towards the door. Instead of a direct line, I zigzag in order to throw them off.

It takes less than a couple of heartbeats for the pair to react. I don't turn round but I hear Ria's hiss of frustration. I run as fast as my legs will carry me but with all the symptoms of the blood-lust coursing through my body, I don't make it very far before one of them grabs hold of my jumpsuit collar and yanks me backwards. I know instinctively that neither of them genuinely want to hurt me. Indeed, if they were thinking more rationally they wouldn't be trying this on in the first place. Out of options, I let my body go limp. If defensive thanatosis – playing possum – works in the animal world, I'm going to make it work for me too. I roll my eyes into the back of my head and slow down my breathing. Then I hope for the best.

To begin with, I don't think it works. With my vision obscured, one of them – I can't tell which – body-slams me. It takes every ounce of self-control not to cry out at the pain. I just about manage it, hopeful that they might leave me alone, when I hear a grunt of dissatisfaction.

'She's out cold,' Ursus says, in a deep and unhappy rumble. 'This was a stupid idea. He'll be pissed off if he realises we confronted her.'

'He shouldn't have compromised himself by sleeping with a fucking recruit.'

I have to concentrate to keep my body still at those words. They must think I'm winning myself favours by sleeping my way to the top. I should be flattered, I suppose, that both Ria and Ursus believe my feminine wiles are so alluring. Instead I'm rather annoyed that they think the only way I can be in Lord Montserrat's confidence is by shagging him.

'What should we do with her?'

'Leave her. She'll wake up sooner or later. With any luck, she won't go blabbing about this.' I hear some of the tension leave Ria's voice and relief trickles through me.

'That's not going to happen. This was a stupid idea, Ria.'

'What choice did we have?'

I feel their frustration. I'm certainly not going to snitch on them. Quite frankly, I think the entire Montserrat Family has bigger problems than dealing with a few irate bloodguzzlers who are trying to take matters into their own hands.

They give up and leave, their feet crunching away on the gravelled path. I stay where I am for several long moments, counting slowly to two hundred in my head. Then I sit up carefully, trying to look as if I've just come round in case they are watching from a distance. It's not hard. If I felt shaky before my encounter with them, I'm now like an alcoholic before her first drink of the day. Even my legs are trembling.

It takes me some time to stagger to my feet. I hit my head pretty hard when I went down and cut it on something. When I put my hand up, it comes away wet and bloody. I sniff curiously. Apparently my own blood does nothing for me. Just in case, however, I wipe the blood off on my thighs rather than licking it off. I can't be too careful. With a sigh, I limp slowly back inside.

I'm almost back at the staircase when I spot the familiar shape of Peter coming towards me. He's shuffling along, bouncing off the walls as if drunk. I give a humourless smirk. We must look like a right pair.

'Hey Pete,' I call out.

He barely registers it. Painfully, I drag myself over to him and peer up into his face. 'Hey, Pete,' I say again.

He jerks his head, his eyes focusing on me as if he's surprised to find me standing there. 'Oh, it's you.'

'There's no need to be so effusive,' I comment with a half grin.

He looks puzzled. This is not the same man who I sat beside three weeks ago; physically, he's a pale shadow of himself. He's really starting to worry me. 'You don't look good,' I tell him.

He chokes out a laugh. 'Neither do you.'

He probably has a point. Right now, I'm finding it difficult to stand up straight. I pull my shoulders back in an attempt to look more alive. Peter doesn't even try.

'There are only two days to go,' I say softly. 'You can change your mind about all this. It's not too late.'

He reaches up to his neck, as if searching for something that isn't there. His hand drops down to his side when he doesn't find it. 'You're holding out for some thunderclap that will happen when you make it to the end of the month and you're still human. That's because you've got reason to care. You want to live.'

I wonder how someone in Peter's mental state managed to get onto the final list of recruits. It'd be easy to put down his current state of mind to the bloodlust but he wasn't much happier when I first met him. He must have some mad skills that the Montserrat Family is after.

'Why are you here? You're obviously not after longevity. You said you deserved to suffer and you're definitely doing that, but…'

He turns away. 'I've already made it clear I don't want to talk about it.'

I curse myself for prying. I'm trying to make him feel better, not alienate him. Really, I should know better by now.

'I have to go,' he says, shuffling off.

I watch him go, wishing there was something I could do to help him. My thoughts are foggy and it's hard to grasp anything clearly but, eventually, I realise what his hand was unconsciously seeking around his neck. The same thing that Ria and Ursus mistakenly thought was mine: his crucifix. He abandoned it when he entered the Montserrat mansion. Perhaps by returning it to him, I can make him feel a bit more connected to reality. Until now I'd forgotten all about it; I suppose I have Ria and Ursus's attack to thank for reminding me. Even if Peter doesn't want it back, tracking it down will give me something to focus on. Not blood. Not crazy-ass vampires. Not Boris and his very personal betrayal. Just a little golden cross. I nod decisively and head back down the corridor to find where our belongings are being kept.

26

THE CLOCK FACE

I'VE BEEN COOPED UP IN THE MONTSERRAT MANSION FOR LONG enough to know where our belongings definitely are not. I've respected the caveat about not entering any doors with ribbons tied around them but I'm pretty sure I know what most of them contain. From what I've seen of the comings and goings, the higher levels are bedrooms and dormitories, with a few social areas. Not many of the Montserrat vampires stay here, but I guess it helps to have spare accommodation should it be required for those unhappy souls like Ria and Ursus who are expected to stick around to advance the recruits. The middle floors include various laboratories and offices, while the main meeting areas and Michael's office are on the ground floor. It makes sense that the storage areas will either be very high up in the loft space, or very low down in the basement. The thought of climbing several sets of stairs on my shaky legs puts the fear of God into me, so I search for steps leading downwards instead.

Using my scant knowledge of old buildings, I figure that any staircase leading to a dim basement area would have originally been used by servants. That means it is probably in the kitchen area towards the back of house. Thankfully, that's not far away so

I lurch over with little difficulty. Matters deteriorate when I enter the large kitchen, however. Vampires eat solid food from time to time, but it's more out of pleasure in the taste and habit rather than physical necessity. As a result, the kitchen is neat, tidy and very empty. I open and close at least half a dozen cupboards and doors before I find one that leads to a set of spiral steps.

I peer down into the gloom. There must be a light switch somewhere but I can't see it. I sigh and brace my arms against the walls then slowly feel my way downwards. At one point, my foot slips and I almost crash down. Fortunately, I manage to right myself by grabbing the banister and clinging on for dear life. Once I regain my equilibrium, I continue with my descent. If this turns out to be a waste of time, I'm going to be very pissed off.

When my tentative edging forward tells me that there are no more steps, I loosen my grip on the banister and fumble around the walls. I find a light switch fairly quickly, managing to illuminate the room in weak electric light from an old fluorescent strip. As well as the light, however, it also immediately starts a low and continuous buzz, as if I've managed to get an annoying flying insect stuck in my ear. At least it seems that I've found the right place. There are rows and rows of neatly stacked shelves containing boxes labelled with names.

I walk down one aisle, expecting to find everything in alphabetical order. It doesn't take long to realise that's not the case. Judging by the boxes in the first aisle – worn, faded and very dusty – each shelf is organised by the date of recruitment. I must be wandering amongst those belonging to the oldest vampires. I keep a curious eye out for Michael Montserrat's box. It's not that I particularly want to snoop through his things but after his evasion about his real age, I'm interested in finding it out. Feeling even slight traces of lust for someone who by rights should be little more than dust in a box buried six feet under doesn't sit well with me. My attempt is half-hearted, however. I don't have the energy to scour the whole place so, when I don't see his name immediately, I shuffle back to find the more recent additions.

The basement area is quite large and it takes me a while to find the row containing my group's boxes. I trail my fingers along the edge of the shelves, brushing them against the different names. Nell Mickleson. Matthew Baldwick. Peter Allen. Nicola Temerlaine. Finally, I reach my own name and stand for a moment, staring at the pitiful container of my human life. I remind myself that I'll be Sanguine – and more human than vampire – in a couple of days, then pull off the lid.

My clothes have been laundered and neatly folded. I glance down at my regulation jumpsuit then back at my trusty leather jacket. It takes me half a second to decide to pull it out and shrug it on. The familiar touch of it against my body, along with the unmistakeable smell, instantly makes me feel better. I'm not leaving this inside any damn cardboard box. If Beth can get away with her stilettos, then I can wear my own sodding jacket.

I dig inside the pocket, hoping that Ria and Ursus put Peter's little cross back in the same place where they found it. The last thing I want is to confront them to find out what they've done with it. As soon as my fingers connect with the chain, I exhale in relief.

I pull it out and hold it up to the flickering, buzzing light. It's a fragile thing. I hope that it helps Peter and provides some kind of physical sustenance for him. I drop the cross carefully back into my pocket and turn round to leave. As I do, I catch the faintest edge of familiar scent. I sniff more deeply then swallow hard while my stomach flips. The sweet, fragrant smell of rosewater may be weak but it's definitely there. And I could swear it's the same smell that I identified back in the Wiltshore Avenue house.

I shuffle to my left, bending down and inhaling deeply. I'm barely more than a foot along when it's no longer detectable so I move back to my right, past my own box and beyond. By the time I reach Matt's section, it's starting to disappear again. I stay completely still and swivel my eyes back to the left. Matthew. Peter. Nicky. Me. I look at Peter's box, then Nicky's box. In Beth's words, smegging hell.

My gut tightens and I hear the rush of blood in my ears. I unfreeze my muscles and carefully removing the lid of Peter's box. I duck down and smell. There's aftershave and male musk clinging to the clothes and the other belongings inside but there's nothing to suggest roses.

I return the lid to its original position and move to Nicky's box. I take a deep breath and flip it open. Immediately the strong smell assails my nostrils and I pull back, clasping my hand over my mouth and staring in horror. I know I've made a lot of wrong assumptions since I arrived in the Montserrat fold. And it's only a smell. I'm sure lots of people use rosewater as a scent. Am I leaping to more ridiculous conclusions? My mind whirls through what I know of her. She was in a wheelchair as a result of a brutal attack that killed her parents. She's young and seemingly fragile. She doesn't appear to be the kind of person who would fit the profile of a genocidal maniac. And yet ... I think about the way she reacted around Peter. She explained her distaste of him by claiming he reminded her of someone who attacked her. Maybe it's simpler than that: maybe she doesn't like him because he's male and not under the effects of a passivity spell. She appears to have been unaffected by bloodlust too. I can't see how she'd be linked to someone like Boris though. Regardless, I need to talk to her and I need to talk her now.

I'd like to be able to say that I immediately spring into action. Unfortunately, it's more of a slow walk. I don't bother turning off the basement light. Yes, I'm aware it's not good for the environment but the potential to fall flat on my face if I climb back up in pitch darkness is too great. I heave myself upwards, eventually making it back into the silent kitchen. I force my trembling limbs to keep moving. With any luck, I'll find Nicky in one of the ground-floor meeting rooms so I won't need to clamber up any more stairs.

Unfortunately Lady Luck remains elusive. Nicky's not there. When I peer into one room, I catch sight of Ria whose eyes narrow in my direction. I can't worry about her right now; Nicky is my priority. Slowly, painfully, I make it to the main staircase just in time to see Beth tripping down.

'Hey! How're things?' Considering she has now turned into a full vampire by drinking blood, she has a remarkably healthy demeanour. I can't help feeling irritated, even though I'm relieved to bump into her.

'I need to find Nicky.'

Beth looks at me seriously. 'Is this something to do with all this traitor business?'

'Please, Beth. I don't have much energy and it's imperative that I speak to her now. Could you find her for me? Quickly?'

'These shoes aren't really designed for rushing around in,' she comments, although she gives me a reassuring grin and heads back upstairs.

I sit on the bottom stair and rest my head against the banister. I can't shake the dizziness. I must have dozed off because, within what feels like the blink of an eye, Beth is back by my side. 'I can't find her.'

I pull myself together, trying to ignore a trickle of alarm. 'Her room?'

'It's empty. She's not in the social area or the bathroom. No one has seen her for a couple of hours.'

'She's got to be somewhere.'

Beth shrugs. 'I have no idea where.'

I try to think. 'How about the garden?'

'It's pretty much the only place left.'

I straighten up. I waver slightly and Beth grabs my arm, alarmed. 'You stay here,' she says. 'I'll check outside.'

'I'll come with you.'

'Bo, you can barely smegging walk.'

'I said,' I repeat through gritted teeth, 'I will come with you.'

Beth chews her lip. 'Fine.' She hooks her arm through mine. 'Just don't collapse on me, alright?'

I force a smile. 'Alright.'

It's already close to midnight and, after my encounter with Ursus and Ria, there's now a sinister edge to the garden that I'd not felt before. At least with Beth by my side, that pair will think twice before confronting me. The air feels heavy and oppressive, as if a storm is brewing. The clear skies are now obscured with cloud. Even the bright moon is barely visible.

Beth opens her mouth to call out for Nicky but I hush her. 'Just in case,' I mutter.

She raises her eyebrows as if to ask in case of what but, probably aware that I won't give her a satisfactory answer, helps me onto the grass next to the path instead.

'Gravel can be noisy.'

I smile, pleased she's taking me seriously. We make our way around the entire area. It appears that the garden is empty.

'She's not here,' Beth comments.

I shake my head. Something's not right. 'Let's go round one more time.'

We start again. The trees and bushes cast lengthy shadows and there's the occasional skitter from an urban-dwelling animal. Everything else seems quiet. I pause when we reach the section of the garden where we clawed our way through to make our escape to the nightclub. 'Are those guards still around?'

'Of course. I don't think Lord Montserrat has recovered from our little trip beyond the walls.'

I frown. If there are guards on duty to prevent recruits from misbehaving, then why wouldn't they have intervened when Ria and Ursus attacked me? None of us were quiet and vampires are supposed to have exceptional hearing: they couldn't have missed that altercation. Beth's eyes reflect my thoughts: if there are guards posted in the garden then where in the hell are they?

I tug Beth over to the gap in the bushes leading to the spot where, days earlier, we climbed the tree to escape. It's more difficult getting through the bushy flora this time around. She hisses from behind me, 'You better not be thinking about getting over that wall again.'

That's the last thing I'm thinking about when I look up at the familiar tree. Beth moves up beside me and draws in a swift breath when she sees what I'm looking at. 'Smeg.'

There are two of them. Their faces, despite the bulging pallor of death, are recognisable: they are presumably the poor guards who were on duty. No wonder they didn't intervene when Ria and Ursus attacked me. Their bodies are slumped against the tree trunk, each one with frozen fingers clutched around a stake. Except the stakes they are holding have been violently thrust into the other's body, not their own.

Beth recoils. 'It's as if they simultaneously murdered each other,' she whispers. 'It doesn't make any sense.'

I stare at them. It does make sense if you're so passive that you'll take any suggestion given to you. I crouch down and examine them carefully. Their bodies are cold and stiff; they've clearly already been here for a couple of hours.

'How does someone break into the Montserrat stronghold and kill two vampires without anyone noticing?' Beth breathes.

'Because she wasn't breaking in,' I tell her. 'She was breaking out.'

THE DISCOVERY of the corpses has given me an adrenaline boost. I drag my body back out of the undergrowth and break into a run back to the mansion. Beth stays with me, even though I'm aware she could far outstrip my efforts.

Inside, I head straight for the meeting room. Ria's still there and I stride up to her. 'Where's Lord Montserrat?' I yell.

She snarls, 'What's it to you, recruit?'

Others begin to rise, alarmed at our aggression. I ignore them and lean towards her. 'Where. The. Fuck. Is. He?'

Before Ria can say anything, Beth interjects. 'There are two dead vampires in the garden.'

The mood in the room changes abruptly. I keep my gaze fixed on Ria. 'You need to tell me where he is. You said he was meeting the other Family Heads.'

Her face is pale and she nods. 'You don't think…'

'I do think. Unless someone has seen Nicky in the past few hours, then I goddamn well do think.'

I'm met with astonishment.

'The crippled recruit?'

'She's not in a wheelchair any more,' I say grimly. The time for obfuscation is over. Lord Montserrat can be pissed off with me later. 'Besides, when you have a spell that makes the users impotent in every sense of the word, as well as open to any suggestion, then who needs to worry about physical strength?'

'A spell?'

'The daemon.' Ursus comes up quietly. 'That's what all this is about.'

I meet his gaze. Recognition of what happened in the garden passes between us, along with a silent agreement to put it behind us. 'Yes. Females aren't affected but, as far as I can tell, the effects are irreversible on male vampires.'

'Matt.' Beth's voice is soft.

'I think that Nicky is behind it. And I also think that she's gone to wherever the Heads are to make sure they take it and do whatever she wants.'

Ria is sickened. 'Because *we* will do whatever the Heads want.'

'Indeed.' I turn to Ursus. 'You said they're all closeted

together. We need to get there now and warn them. Can you call?'

He shakes his head. 'It's a closed session. No phones or computers allowed.'

I avoid rolling my eyes. They really should know better. What if there was some kind of emergency? Like, say, a crazed girl on her way to subjugate them to her every whim? 'Then you need to call all the other Families. Every female vampire within a fifty-mile radius needs to get to where they are. We have to stop her.'

'Lady Bancroft is there. She won't be affected by it. Does that mean that she…?'

'I'm pretty sure she's not involved.' I have no idea how Nicky is planning to bring her down though. 'Where are they, Ursus?'

'Big Ben.'

I blink, not quite sure I heard him properly. 'Uh?'

'It's a large tower with a clock at the top,' Beth says, regaining some of her composure. Her sarcasm alleviates the tension a little.

'Funny.' I take a moment to look round. 'We need to prevent Nicky from getting anywhere near them.'

'You can't just send girls.'

I understand Ursus's annoyance at being sidelined but it doesn't mean I have to agree with him. 'It's too dangerous otherwise. If she gets to you, she can turn you against us.' I give him a brief flicker of my death stare, just enough to prove that I'm serious. 'Irreversible,' I remind him.

A muscle throbs in his cheek and his big shoulders bunch in anger but I know he'll stay away.

'You need to remain here and hold the fort. If things don't work out, then batten down the hatches and don't let anyone in. No matter who they are.'

He nods. 'Can you drive a motorbike?'

I'm reminded briefly of Zupper and I smile. It's enough for Ursus because he throws me a set of keys. 'It's parked out front.'

'Thank you.'

'Look after my pride and joy,' he growls. I know he doesn't just mean his bike.

Thirty seconds later, the room is empty.

As soon as I step back into the cool night air, I spot Ursus's bike. I whistle in admiration. It's a lean, gleaming beast and obviously his prized possession. There's no sign of a helmet and I don't waste time looking for one. Instead I straddle the seat and turn the key, revving the engine. Behind me, Ria, Beth, Nell and the other female vampires in the Montserrat mansion are running out to a motley selection of other vehicles. I don't give them a backward glance, I'm already whizzing down the street.

Wind whips past me as I career round the first corner. The bike builds up speed and the dark buildings and closed shop fronts become a blur. I turn right sharply and into a tight alleyway. I narrowly avoid hitting a fox nosing at a trio of overflowing garbage bins as I skid back out on to the street ahead. Tower Bridge isn't far away.

I'm tempted to take the most direct route but I know it's also the one most likely to be monitored by the police. I can't afford to have them slow me down or turn on their sirens to chase me and alert Nicky – and whoever else is with her. I skid right again to avoid some of the bigger streets but maintain my speed for as long as possible. I ignore the traffic lights blinking red, forcing myself to forget how similar their colour is to arterial blood, then squeeze out just a little more horsepower from the bike. Less than three minutes later, the Houses of Parliament are in view while Big Ben towers ominously above them. I realise I have no freaking idea how to get inside.

I park as close as I dare then clamber off the bike and run towards the building, keeping low. Every so often the shapes in front of me start swimming as I lose my vision then, abruptly, the dizziness clears when I shake my head. I'm so focused on finding a way in that I miss an uneven paving slab. My foot catches the edge of it and I'm sent flying onto the hard cold pavement. It's just as well, however, because when I look up from my prone position, a broad-shouldered man comes into sight. That's when I know for sure that this time I've not made a mistake. Boris, it appears, is on bodyguard duty. Ten yards behind him, Nicky's slender shape is also visible.

I close my eyes for a second. As relieved as I am to finally identify the traitor, there's still part of me that can't believe it's innocent little Nicky. I count my blessings that they've waited until now; this might have been over and done with already. But when Big Ben chimes to signal two o'clock in the morning, I understand why. Nicky's not in this for sex or money. It's not even about power, although that might be a welcome bonus. No, her motives are much more pure. What Nicky is after is revenge. She told me the attack on her parents that also forced her into a wheelchair had started at two in the morning, although she'd never said who the attackers were. She must think that vampires were responsible; it's the only thing that makes sense.

The pair of them disappear through the gate. They must have disarmed the security system. Ideally, I'd wait for the others to arrive; I'm on my last legs and I need a bit of vampire girl-power beside me. But I'm too worried that I only have a short time to get inside before the alarms are re-set. The element of surprise is going to be more useful than anything else and, while setting off the security system would alert the Heads, it would also alert Nicky and Boris. They've been planning this for a long time and I'm sure they'll have back-up. Just about the only thing they won't have factored in is me.

I pick myself up from the ground, run across the street and clamber over the gate after them. My heart is thudding and my lungs feel tight. Tam's face flashes in front of my eyes and I grit my teeth. I need to keep it together; if nothing else, I owe his memory that.

I jog along a cobbled path, with the high walls of Portcullis

House looming over me. This time I take care to watch my step; it's imperative that I stay quiet and undetected. But I need to be fast and catch Nicky before she gets to the Family Heads. Up ahead I hear a door bang and I realise they have already entered Elizabeth Tower – the real name for Big Ben. With the path ahead clear, I can afford to speed up.

When I reach the door, I freeze and listen. Everything seems still and quiet so, moving carefully, I turn the knob and go in after them. The base of the tower is both smaller and more modern than I expected. The walls are smooth beige and there are a few olde-worlde benches around the edges. I head for the stairs.

I move up one step at a time. Although the situation reminds me hauntingly of attempting to sneak up on O'Shea at Wiltshore Avenue, at least these stairs are made of sterner stuff and won't creak and give me away. I can move quickly. I have to catch up with Nicky and Boris now; I can't risk them unleashing O'Shea's spell.

My increased speed is why I round the next bend without paying enough attention. I barely reach the top step when a fist connects sharply with the side of my head. I go flying, fortunately into the room rather than back down the stairs but, nevertheless, I'm a flailing mass of limbs when the kick comes. I curl into a foetal position to protect myself from the next one. When it doesn't come and the pain starts to subside, I open my eyes. Boris is standing above me with a twisted smirk on his face. I look for an exit but he's blocking the staircase. There's a tiny window behind me but, even if it were big enough to leap through, a heavy rusting metal object sits in front, effectively blocking it.

My stomach sinks. Still, I aim for light-heartedness. 'Hey, buddy. What gives?'

He laughs sharply. 'Oh, so now you're playing nice?'

I clamber to my feet, trying not to hug my aching belly too

obviously. I clearly don't do a very good job, because glee crosses his face.

'Beautiful, inept Bo,' he says. 'Do you have any idea how much trouble you've caused me?'

'You mean because I didn't allow myself to be framed for O'Shea's murder?'

He licks his lips; it's not a pleasant sight. 'Indeed. Things would have gone so much smoother if you'd let yourself be banged up. I was doing you a favour, you know.'

'Because if I was in prison I'd have avoided the massacre at Dire Straits.' I say it flatly, but really I want his confirmation that he was responsible. Besides which, I know now that it was sheer luck that I was assigned to O'Shea.

'We were trying to wipe out any connection to the daemon.' Boris shrugs. 'It didn't work out so well.'

I snarl, 'It didn't work out too damn well for Tam and everyone else either.'

'The best laid plans of mice and men gang aft agly.'

'I never took you for a literary man.'

'I was forced to do some reading at school.'

'Imagine that,' I murmur. I gaze at him speculatively. It takes every ounce of self-control not to spit in his face. 'Why, Boris? Why have you done all this? Is it the spell? Does Nicky have you under her thumb?'

'I don't need a spell to be loyal to someone who's going to rid the world of vampires.' He says the last word with such venom, that I start to get an inkling of his real motives.

'You don't like them?'

'Goddamn freaks and criminals. Fucking tribers think they own the place. They've got every human kowtowing to them. They don't belong here.'

'So why are you trying to create more? Nicky's becoming a vampire.'

'*Nicola* is doing what's necessary to beat them at their own game. Anyway, she's not going to be a vampire. By the end of tomorrow night, she'll be Sanguine. Not vampire. Sanguine is when…'

'I know what it means to be sodding Sanguine. How has she avoided the cravings?'

'How have you?' he retorts.

I stare at him. Eventually he grins. 'I suppose we all have a few tricks up our sleeves.'

I guess they have some of my grandfather's magic powder or something like it. If I get out of this I'll have to tell Montserrat about it. It's clearly more widely available than I'd assumed. And I don't share Boris's confidence that Nicky wants to be Sanguine. I reckon the thought of supplanting the five Families with her own Family is too tempting.

Boris bares his teeth. 'Well, time is ticking away and I don't want to miss the fireworks upstairs. I can't wait to see those jumped-up bloodguzzlers crawling on their hands and knees and doing our bidding.'

'It won't be your bidding,' I point out. 'It'll be Nicky's.'

He opens his mouth to speak but is prevented by the sudden high-pitched peal of an alarm, signalling the others' arrival. Without missing a beat, I reach behind into the window alcove and grasp the chunk of metal that sits there. It's heavier than I expected but I manage to lift it and fling it at Boris. I aim for his head but either it's too heavy or I'm too weak and it ends up landing against his shins. The element of surprise helps me, though, as he screams and falls backwards, hitting his head on the floor. I grab his hair, pulling up his head then slamming it back down. His body jerks and stills: he's out cold. I scoop up the card which has fallen from the alcove and read: 'Original Bell Hammer'.

'Well, I might be weaker than a kitten,' I tell his inert form, 'but it looks like I still beat you hammer and tongs.'

I waste no more time. The others will soon be here to take

care of Boris. The alarm will no doubt have spurred Nicky into action, however. I need to get to her. I make for the steps. The spurt of adrenaline that allowed me to dispatch Boris is dissipating fast and the pain in my stomach is returning. I have to cling to the banister to heave myself upwards. I'm terrified that my legs will give way at any moment.

On the next level there's nothing more than the elaborate clock mechanism that keeps Big Ben working. It's huge and intricate – but it's not what I'm looking for. I lurch past it and up the next set of stairs. This time I have to keep pausing to catch my breath and stop myself toppling over. The steps seem endless. I have no idea what I'll see when I finally come across Nicky and the Family Heads. I can only hope she's not yet had the chance to unleash that fucking spell and turn them into mindless robots. Blood is pounding in my ears and my senses are dimming. That's why I don't hear the voices until I'm almost upon them.

'You know I could have brought a whole host of bloodguzzling followers to help me.'

I close my eyes for half a second as I register Nicky's familiar voice.

'So why didn't you?' Dulcet tones encase the steel of Lady Bancroft's response.

'Because I don't need them to destroy you.'

'I'm female. Your mumbo-jumbo won't work on me any more than it'll affect you.'

'Just like your mind mumbo-jumbo won't work on me,' Nicky snarls.

I yank out every last molecule of energy I have inside me. Pure rage is driving me now. With one final spurt, I run up the remaining steps and round the corner. Lady Bancroft and Nicky stand in front of the giant illuminated face of Big Ben. I glance around desperately for signs of the other Family Heads but I can't see them anywhere.

Nicky turns in my direction and Lady Bancroft takes advantage of her distraction to leap forward and grab her. Her face is a vicious frozen mask of anger. I lunge forward to join her.

'Bo,' Nicky croaks, from underneath Bancroft's tightening fingers. Then she smirks with a confidence that freezes my bones. From nowhere she pulls out a sharply honed stake. Before I can react, she twists away from me and slams it into Lady Bancroft's heart.

The vampire doesn't have time to make a noise. Her eyes widen for a split second then she crumples to the ground. As I watch, her skin turns grey then black as her body decomposes with sickening speed. Nicky steps away and dusts off her palms.

'That was even easier than I thought,' she comments. Without warning, she snaps forward and grabs my throat. Her face swims up against mine and she strokes my cheek with one finger. 'So gullible, Bo. So keen to believe that a little girl like me wouldn't be the one you were looking for.'

I choke and writhe.

'Oh, yes,' she laughs. 'I knew exactly who you were and what you were after. I've been one step ahead of you the entire time. You thought I was weak because I was a cripple. All I had to do to get your trust was to simper and giggle. It never occurred to you that I'm the one who's going to save us from the vampires, did it?'

I watch her, aghast. She's right. I forgot everything I've ever been taught and judged her on her appearance. But the clues were there, if I'd thought to look for them.

Nicky's laugh is a harsh, grating sound, far removed from her usual giggle. 'I wouldn't feel too bad about it. You're hardly the only one I fooled. Even before I became a recruit, getting close to vampires was ridiculously easy. They took one look at my wheel-chair and dismissed me. Well, I showed them!' She laughs again.

My chest feels tight and it's getting harder to breathe. Nicky's fingers are claws around my throat. She brings her face up close to mine.

'Even though you weren't smart enough to work out the

truth,' she says, 'you still managed to get in my way. If you'd not rescued that daemon, all this would have been so much easier. No one would have realised I was turning the Family members into mindless drones until it was too late.'

'Why?' I gasp.

'Why did I do it, you mean? Because they ruined my life. They put me in a wheelchair and messed with my mind, just like she tried to.' Nicky kicks Bancroft's desiccated remains. 'They thought they could make me believe I was the one responsible for all that.'

I try to speak again but nothing comes out other than a choking sound. Nicky loosens her grip enough to give me enough air to speak. 'You killed your parents?'

She kicks me, hard. 'You're not listening. *They* killed my parents. The vampires. They destroyed my life. They made me think I'd gone mad and done it myself, but I found out the truth and now I'm going to destroy them. They're bloodguzzling bastards who think they should control the world and take whatever they want, whenever they want it. Well, they can't fool me any longer. I've been planning this for fucking years.'

'Vampires wouldn't have attacked your family and killed them, Nicky.'

'You wanna bet? There's a lot more to getting recruited to the Families than you realise. Just a couple of weeks ago they killed a toddler. A sweet two-year-old boy.'

I cough weakly, struggling to breathe. 'Because you made them!'

'Innocents suffer in every war. Deaths like his were necessary to wake everyone up to what the vampires really are. Besides, they made me believe I was responsible for slaughtering my own parents. I won't be made a fool of, Bo. I'm going to take my revenge and no one is going to get in my way. I'm smarter than the whole lot of you. I'll make my own Family and together we'll help people. We won't fuck with them, like the Five Families do.

You may not live to see it but I'm going to make the world a better place.' Her face contorts. 'For once, however, I find myself on the back foot. Where are the others?'

I have no idea what she means. She shakes me and my body spasms in pain. 'Gully. Stuart. Medici. Montserrat. Where the fuck are they?'

'Here.'

There are four figures crowding into the space. I recognise them all but it's the glittering rage visible on Montserrat's face that makes me weak with relief. He's alright.

'You knew I was coming,' she snarls.

He nods. 'We did. We didn't know it was you but we knew the traitor would come.' His eyes flick to me then back again to Nicky. 'Let her go.'

She reaches into her pocket. I know she's about to pull out whatever physical form of O'Shea's spell she's created and I moan in warning. I struggle against the vice-like grip of her hand.

'It wasn't us who hurt your family,' Montserrat says quietly.

'I was there,' she snarls.

'You were a little girl. Your memory is twisted and you remember things that didn't happen. You did it. You killed them. We took you in to help you, Nicky. You need help. You don't want to do this.'

She laughs again. It's a cold hard sound.

'Kill her.' It's Medici. His eyes, a light almost transparent aquamarine colour, are emotionless.

I move my left hand into my pocket, finding the little canister of pepper spray. It's useless against vampires but it'll work against Nicky.

Her hand feints forward and Medici flinches. Nicky giggles. 'You can try. But as soon as you do, I'll unleash my little wonder drug and before you can so much as say fuck, you'll be mine to do with as I please. You fucked with my life, now I'm going to fuck with yours.'

'Let Bo go, Nicky, then we can talk.'

'But I don't want to talk, Lord Montserrat. I want to destroy you.'

Without warning she lets me go, one hand curving out towards the group of Family Heads and the other pulling out a gleaming blade which flashes in my direction. I have no more time. I pull out the pepper spray and hold it up, pressing down on the nozzle at the same time as I feel the steel sink into my flesh. Both Nicky and I scream. I'm dimly aware of figures leaping forward and someone grabbing me again, although this time it's with gentle hands rather than a force wanting to kill. I push outwards, trying to stop Nicky getting what she wants and throwing the spell in the Heads' direction. Instead my hand meets air and I'm sinking. Blackness forms around the edges of my vision, and the light of the clock face disappears into a tiny pinprick. Then there's nothing.

2 7

EPILOGUE

'So you're Sanguine then?' The voice above me is familiar but I can't quite place it. 'You know it's quite a feat. There are only three Sanguines in the world.'

Someone murmurs a reply. I struggle to open my eyes. When I do, I see Peter and Nell. They grin at me then abruptly disappear through the open door. A minute later, Montserrat appears. For once he's dressed casually, in a tight black v-necked t-shirt. The edges of his winged tattoo are just visible from beneath his sleeves.

'You're awake.' He looks worried, although I can't think why. He places a cool hand on my forehead and brushes away a few errant curls. 'You almost didn't make it.'

'What happened?' I croak.

'Your timely intervention with that spray gave us enough leeway to get her.'

'Is she…?'

'Dead?' he shakes his head. 'Actually, no. She's being held at one of our facilities. She's a troubled young woman.'

I almost laugh. 'Troubled' doesn't even begin to cover it. 'She wanted revenge.'

Montserrat nods. 'When she was ten years old, she killed her parents and then tried to kill herself by leaping out of a window. She convinced herself that vampires were to blame. She created an entire set of false memories to fuel her vendetta. It was easier for her to find someone else to blame rather than to remember the truth.'

'The recruitment process is supposed to be stringent.' I want to yell, but I don't have the energy to manage more than a whisper.

'We knew what she'd done. She was a child when it happened, Bo, a screwed-up kid who suffered years of abuse at her father's hands while her mother stood idly by. Something in her simply snapped. Under those circumstances, can you really say it was her fault?'

I stare at him mutely, thinking about the real effects of O'Shea's spell. It would offer a way to ensure you were never a victim again.

He continues. 'After the attack, she spent ten years in a mental institution before she was released. She fooled everyone into thinking she was alright.'

'You recruited a murderer.'

'We're vampires, Bo. We already walk on the dark side. We recruited her to help her.'

'You're not supposed to be evil.'

'We're not. We offer respite to many who end up on the wrong path. We give them a way out. Your friend Beth was a prostitute who had a sideline as a gang member and who was definitely living on borrowed time. Nell was a thief. We've got drug addicts and murderers. Not everyone is a criminal but for those who are, we provide an alternative. We help those whose lives are on a trajectory to hell. It's what we were trying to do for Nicky but we didn't realise the extent of her false beliefs about that night.'

He gazes at me for a moment, as if willing me to understand. I think about the other recruits in my group – the ex-politician with the shady past, Peter's mysterious comments about deserving to suffer, Ria and Ursus's violent attack, my grandfather's admonition that I couldn't trust the vampires … it had been staring me in the face in the entire time. Is every single vampire someone who should be behind bars instead of roaming around freely?

'Arzo's not a criminal,' I say weakly.

'Not everyone is. Not everyone's darkness involves breaking the law.'

Arzo's only fault had been falling in love with the wrong person. I wonder what Michael's darkness involves. I am finding it hard to get my head around it all. The fact that vampires are above human law now feels like an affront to humanity. I admit that the shroud of secrecy around the vampires' recruitment policies is starting to make a lot more sense. By taking in criminals, they keep the rest of the world safe. But they give those criminals unlimited power when they reap the benefits from drinking blood. They should be punished, not rewarded.

Michael seems to know what I'm thinking. 'It's amazing what a little structure and loyalty can do, Bo. Our Families keep everyone in check. Think of us as a military boarding school but more permanent. We keep everyone's darker natures at bay because of what they become when they drink. But after they turn, they also toe the line and make amends for their previous lives. We see to it that they do. If there's the slightest hint of criminal activity, they're executed. Quite frankly, until Nicky we've never had a problem. And why would we suspect her above anyone else? Your friend Peter is another one, you know. Many people find that they can achieve redemption through joining us.'

My mouth twists. 'Drinking blood absolves you of your sins? It seems to me it just creates more.'

'The humans who offer themselves to us do so freely,' he says, gently chiding me.

I scowl. 'So you say. Forget the humans. Your vampires should be in jail.'

'What's the purpose of prison? Is it to rehabilitate or to punish? We make people on the fringes of society into useful contributors to the world.'

'Nicky was not a useful contributor to anything.'

His expression shutters. 'With her we made an error.'

'You bet you fucking did.'

I realise that Montserrat felt the same way about Nicky that I did. Pity for her situation moved him to help her by allowing her recruitment, in the same way that pity for her led me into believing she was an innocent. She pulled the wool over all our eyes. But it doesn't change the fact that Tam and Charity and everyone else would still be alive if it wasn't for the way the Families do things.

I struggle into a sitting position. I feel a bit sore but otherwise alright. It's a miracle considering how it felt when Nicky plunged that cold steel into me.

I think about the fact that Montserrat didn't show up at Big Ben until it was almost over. 'Lady Bancroft. Is she dead?'

His muscles tense and he jerks out a nod. 'She knew the risks.'

'It was a trap. You knew that if you told everyone you were going to meet, you'd lure the perpetrator to you.'

'It was too good an opportunity to miss. We had it all planned. Until you showed up.'

'You didn't damn well tell me your plan, did you? If you had, I'd have left you to it.'

A ghost of a smile races across his lips. 'No, you wouldn't. I've got to know you quite well over the last weeks. You'd never let the action slip by.'

'You could have told me,' I say stubbornly.

He sighs and pushes back his hair. 'I was going to. I was even going to invite you to wait with Bancroft.' He throws me a remorseful glance. 'We thought that with her ability to control others with her mind, the traitors wouldn't have a chance. But Nicky's mind was already so warped that anything Lady Bancroft tried couldn't work. Maybe if you'd been there things would have been different, but you were too weak, Bo. You could barely stand up.'

'I could stand up well enough to climb to the freaking top of Big Ben.'

'And apparently knock someone out along the way.'

I'd forgotten about Boris. 'Is he…?'

'The police have him. He should be grateful. Medici would have quite happily tortured him for the rest of his natural life.'

I mull over all that has happened. Lack of communication was my downfall, not just with the final showdown with Nicky but all along the way. I think about the laptop I was given. I had the information about Nicky at my fingertips but I dismissed her out of hand because she was a recruit like me. Lady Bancroft knew instantly that the mastermind could be a recruit but I didn't talk to her until it was too late. I can blame Michael Montserrat all I want but I've made a shitload of mistakes too. There were so many points when communicating more clearly and with more honesty would have made life easier. I resolve never to let that happen again.

My stomach grumbles and I realise I'm absolutely starving. I need to get something to eat. 'What day is it?'

'Monday.'

My heart sings. 'It's over. And the lunar month is over.'

Montserrat looks away. Doubt trickles through me. 'What?' I reach out and grip his broad forearm. 'What is it?'

'Your injuries were very severe, Bo.'

'But I'm fine,' I tell him. 'I feel fine.'

He turns his gaze back on me. There's some unfathomable emotion in his dark eyes. I shake my head. 'No.'

'Bo, there wasn't a choice. You either took strength from human blood or you died.'

'No, no, no, no, no, no.'

'Bo,' he begins.

'I heard someone say I was Sanguine!' I burst out. 'Two minutes ago! Right after I woke up!'

Montserrat stands up and begins to pace. 'If there had been another way, I'd have done anything I could.'

'I heard…'

'Peter,' he says. 'Peter Allen is Sanguine. I don't think his heart was ever in vampirism, despite the relief it would have offered him.'

My mouth is dry. I try to speak but the words won't come out. He's got to be lying. This is some kind of sick vampire joke. Montserrat sighs and hands me a small mirror. I swallow and stare down. The truth stares me in the face. Inside both my pupils there's the telltale red dot.

'It's not so bad, you know. You might grow to like it.'

I bring the mirror closer to my face. I'm a fucking vampire. Not only that but I'm a fucking vampire surrounded by criminals. All I feel is despair.

Montserrat clears his throat and hands me a glass. I take it morosely. It's filled with blood and my stomach grumbles again as I swirl the viscous red liquid. I can feel tears springing to my eyes. I squeeze them shut, lift the glass to my lips and drink.

ABOUT THE AUTHOR

After teaching English literature in the UK, Japan and Malaysia, Helen Harper left behind the world of education following the worldwide success of her Blood Destiny series of books. She thanks her lucky stars every day that she's able to do so.

Helen has always been a book lover, devouring science fiction and fantasy tales when she was a child growing up in Scotland.

She currently lives in Edinburgh with far too many cats – not to mention the dragons, fairies, demons, wizards and vampires that seem to keep appearing from nowhere.

A Charade of Magic complete series

The best way to live in the Mage ruled city of Glasgow is to keep your head down and your mouth closed.

That's not usually a problem for Mairi Wallace. By day she works at a small shop selling tartan and by night she studies to become an apothecary. She knows her place and her limitations. All that changes, however, when her old childhood friend sends her a desperate message seeking her help - and the Mages themselves cross Mairi's path. Suddenly, remaining unnoticed is no longer an option.

There's more to Mairi than she realises but, if she wants to fulfil her full potential, she's going to have to fight to stay alive - and only time will tell if she can beat the Mages at their own game.

From twisted wynds and tartan shops to a dangerous daemon and the magic infused City Chambers, the future of a nation might lie with one solitary woman.

Book One – Hummingbird

Book Two – Nightingale

Book Three – Red Hawk

The complete *Blood Destiny* series

"A spectacular and addictive series."

Mackenzie Smith has always known that she was different. Growing up as the only human in a pack of rural shapeshifters will do that to you, but then couple it with some mean fighting skills and a fiery temper and you end up with a woman that few will dare to cross. However, when the only father figure in her life is brutally murdered, and the dangerous Brethren with their predatory Lord Alpha come to investigate, Mack has to not only ensure the physical safety of her adopted family by hiding her apparent humanity, she also has to seek the blood-soaked vengeance that she craves.

Book One - Bloodfire

Book Two - Bloodmagic

Book Three - Bloodrage

Book Four - Blood Politics

Book Five - Bloodlust

Also

Corrigan Fire

Corrigan Magic

Corrigan Rage

Corrigan Politics

Corrigan Lust

The complete *Bo Blackman* series

A half-dead daemon, a massacre at her London based PI firm and evidence that suggests she's the main suspect for both ... Bo Blackman is having a very bad week.

She might be naive and inexperienced but she's determined to get to the bottom of the crimes, even if it means involving herself with one of London's most powerful vampire Families and their enigmatic leader.

It's pretty much going to be impossible for Bo to ever escape unscathed.

Book One - Dire Straits

Book Two - New Order

Book Three - High Stakes

Book Four - Red Angel

Book Five - Vigilante Vampire

Book Six - Dark Tomorrow

The complete _Highland Magic_ series

Integrity Taylor walked away from the Sidhe when she was a child.
Orphaned and bullied, she simply had no reason to stay, especially not
when the sins of her father were going to remain on her shoulders. She
found a new family - a group of thieves who proved that blood was less
important than loyalty and love.

But the Sidhe aren't going to let Integrity stay away forever. They need
her more than anyone realises - besides, there are prophecies to be
fulfilled, people to be saved and hearts to be won over. If anyone can do
it, Integrity can.

Book One - Gifted Thief

Book Two - Honour Bound

Book Three - Veiled Threat

Book Four - Last Wish

The complete _Dreamweaver_ series

"I have special coping mechanisms for the times I need to open the front
door. They're even often successful..."

Zoe Lydon knows there's often nothing logical or rational about fear. It
doesn't change the fact that she's too terrified to step outside her own
house, however.

What Zoe doesn't realise is that she's also a dreamweaver - able to access other people's subconscious minds. When she finds herself in the Dreamlands and up against its sinister Mayor, she'll need to use all of her wits - and overcome all of her fears - if she's ever going to come out alive.

Book One - Night Shade

Book Two - Night Terrors

Book Three - Night Lights

Stand alone novels

Eros

William Shakespeare once wrote that, "Cupid is a knavish lad, thus to make poor females mad." The trouble is that Cupid himself would probably agree…

As probably the last person in the world who'd appreciate hearts, flowers and romance, Coop is convinced that true love doesn't exist – which is rather unfortunate considering he's also known as Cupid, the God of Love. He'd rather spend his days drinking, womanising and generally having as much fun as he possible can. As far as he's concerned, shooting people with bolts of pure love is a waste of his time…but then his path crosses with that of shy and retiring Skye Sawyer and nothing will ever be quite the same again.

Wraith

Magic. Shadows. Adventure. Romance.

Saiya Buchanan is a wraith, able to detach her shadow from her body and send it off to do her bidding. But, unlike most of her kin, Saiya doesn't deal in death. Instead, she trades secrets - and in the goblin besieged city of Stirling in Scotland, they're a highly prized commodity. It might just be, however, that the goblins have been hiding the greatest secret of them all. When Gabriel de Florinville, a Dark Elf, is sent as royal envoy into Stirling and takes her prisoner, Saiya is not only going to uncover the sinister truth. She's also going to realise that sometimes the deepest secrets are the ones locked within your own heart.

<u>The complete *Lazy Girl's Guide To Magic* series</u>

Hard Work Will Pay Off Later. Laziness Pays Off Now.

Let's get one thing straight - Ivy Wilde is not a heroine. In fact, she's probably the last witch in the world who you'd call if you needed a magical helping hand. If it were down to Ivy, she'd spend all day every day on her sofa where she could watch TV, munch junk food and talk to her feline familiar to her heart's content.

However, when a bureaucratic disaster ends up with Ivy as the victim of a case of mistaken identity, she's yanked very unwillingly into Arcane Branch, the investigative department of the Hallowed Order of Magical Enlightenment. Her problems are quadrupled when a valuable object is stolen right from under the Order's noses.

It doesn't exactly help that she's been magically bound to Adeptus Exemptus Raphael Winter. He might have piercing sapphire eyes and a body which a cover model would be proud of but, as far as Ivy's concerned, he's a walking advertisement for the joyless perils of too much witch-work.

And if he makes her go to the gym again, she's definitely going to turn him into a frog.

Book One - Slouch Witch

Book Two - Star Witch

Book Three - Spirit Witch

Sparkle Witch (Christmas novella)

The complete *Fractured Faery* series

One corpse. Several bizarre looking attackers. Some very strange magical powers. And a severe bout of amnesia.

It's one thing to wake up outside in the middle of the night with a decapitated man for company. It's another to have no memory of how you got there - or who you are.

She might not know her own name but she knows that several people are out to get her. It could be because she has strange magical powers seemingly at her fingertips and is some kind of fabulous hero. But then why does she appear to inspire fear in so many? And who on earth is the sexy, green-eyed barman who apparently despises her? So many questions ... and so few answers.

At least one thing is for sure - the streets of Manchester have never met someone quite as mad as Madrona…

Book One - Box of Frogs

SHORTLISTED FOR THE KINDLE STORYTELLER AWARD 2018

Book Two - Quiver of Cobras

Book Three - Skulk of Foxes

The complete *City Of Magic* series

Charley is a cleaner by day and a professional gambler by night. She might be haunted by her tragic past but she's never thought of herself as anything or anyone special. Until, that is, things start to go terribly wrong all across the city of Manchester. Between plagues of rats, firestorms and the gleaming blue eyes of a sexy Scottish werewolf, she might just have landed herself in the middle of a magical apocalypse. She might also be the only person who has the ability to bring order to an utterly chaotic new world.

Book One - Shrill Dusk

Book Two - Brittle Midnight

Book Three - Furtive Dawn